# *on* COLLIS AVENUE

## A MYSTERY BY

### ELIZABETH T. MILLER

On Collis Avenue
Copyright © 2018 by Elizabeth T. Miller

Book Cover Design and Interior Typesetting by Melissa Williams Design
Cover flower shape © lunokot, Shutterstock

ISBN: 9781723912894

*For my children and my friends.*

*You put the icing on my cake.*

# PART I

## ROGER MILLS

*O*n the night of January 15, 1939, Roger Mills did not go home. He was alone—shoeless and cold—in the basement of his drugstore, just two blocks from his house on Collis Avenue.

Outside, a lake-effect winter storm was busy burying Allenburg, Ohio, with a record-setting snowfall. Big white flakes began floating, like feathers, from the low-hanging clouds early the previous afternoon. The air was soon filled with smaller and more densely packed flakes. By six o'clock it was snowing in earnest. All outdoor items became indistinguishable mounds of snow. Dog houses became igloos. Parked cars assumed the shape of humpback whales. By midnight, the snowstorm had turned its initial onslaught into a determined march. The temperature hovered around zero. Every flake stayed where it fell, waiting to be buried by the next.

Late into that snowy night, Roger's wife, Anna, sat in her favorite chair, her feet curled under her like a cat, staring at the glowing embers of the dying fire. She laid the book she had been reading on the table beside her chair and walked to the living-room window. She watched the snowflakes swirl around the streetlight, like moths—only thicker. The clock on the mantle chimed twice.

Shuddering with a mixture of worry and disgust, she muttered to herself, *Why, Roger? Why do you do this to us? I'm sick and tired of you and all your drugs. I'm not going to put up with this anymore. I've made up my mind—I'm leaving you for good!*

Anna gave a determined sigh through her clenched teeth as she pulled her sweater closer and began climbing the stairs to Charlene's bedroom. Shaking her eighteen-year-old daughter by the shoulder, she said, "Wake up, Charlene. We have to go to the drugstore. Your father didn't come home again. We have to go and get him. The snow is getting worse, and it'll take both of us to bring him home if he's in his usual condition."

She watched her daughter burrow deeper into the blankets, her voice barely audible through the layers. "Not again! It's cold, and it's snowing. I'm sick of this! Let him sleep it off. He's nothing but a drug . . . ist!"

"That's not funny, Charlene. Now, please get up and get dressed."

Charlene was too sleepy to argue. She begrudgingly sat up in bed, swiveled to the edge of the mattress, and lowered her bare feet to the cold floor. Her warm toes reacted with a jerk, jolting her out of her stupor. Now fully awake, Charlene was ready to argue.

"How long can this go on? Papa is nothing but a junky. He's his own best customer. If he's not taking paregoric, he's doping on codeine or laudanum, or all three. Why should I have to go out in the middle of the night to help drag him home? I need my sleep. Don't forget, I have class tomorrow. Besides, it's snowing. I won't go."

Anna stood by the window in Charlene's room, staring down at the streetlight below. Its glowing oval shape looked like a disembodied head wearing a dunce cap of snow. The snowflakes swirled toward it in a frenzied dance, filling her with eerie fascination and a sense of foreboding.

Turning to face her daughter, she said, "I know this is hard for you. Well, it's hard for me, too, but I promise both of us that this will be the last time. This is 1939—a new year—and putting an end to this situation is my New Year's resolution."

"Okay, Mom, that's my resolution, too. I'm moving to Chicago and staying with Aunt Grace. I can go to college there just as well as here."

Mother and daughter stared at each other without blinking. Charlene's words echoed Anna's own thoughts. "If you want to go to Chicago, fine. We'll go together, and the sooner the better."

"Good. You need to get away from here. You deserve a normal life."

Charlene pulled a heavy sweater and a long woolen skirt over her flannel pajamas. She put on two pairs of socks, calf-high rubber boots, her winter coat, rabbit-fur mittens, and her knitted cap. She wrapped a bright red hand-knit scarf around her neck and over her nose and mouth. Only her eyes peeked out.

Shrugging into her own heavy coat and tying a silk scarf around her head, Anna looked at her daughter's overdressed, snowman-shaped bulk and said, "You're not in Chicago yet."

They both laughed.

Anna took the spare drugstore key from its place beside the clock on the mantelpiece and put it in her pocket. She retrieved two flashlights from the drawer of the small table beside the front door and handed one to Charlene. They stepped out into the night. It was cold. It was dark, and it was deadly quiet. Each lost in her own thoughts, they trudged the two blocks to the drugstore, through the steadily falling snow. The only sound was the crunching of the snow beneath their boots. Anna knew, beyond a doubt, that this snowy January night would be forever remembered as their last trip to the drugstore. No matter what this evening brought, she and her daughter would begin planning their move tomorrow.

The drugstore was located around the corner and across Boyd Boulevard, which ran parallel to Collis Avenue. When they arrived, the store was dark, and the door was locked. Ignoring the "Closed" sign hanging in the window, Anna took the spare key from her pocket and carefully unlocked the door. She eased the door open, reached inside and pressed the light-switch button. Obediently, the lights came on.

"Roger? Roger, are you in here?" Anna called. No answer. The drugstore was deserted. "Charlene, you look in the pharmacy and look behind the lunch counter, too. I'll check the basement."

Near the front of the store, next to the marble-topped lunch counter, an area had been set aside for four round tables. Each table had four chairs. The tables and chairs had legs made of thick, black wire, twisted around and around and ending in a loop-foot where the leg met the floor. Anna had always marveled that those spindly legs could support the weight of the more well-padded customers. She gave the tables-and-chairs area a quick glance as she walked down the center aisle between the rows of neatly displayed sundries. Nothing looked out of place.

Standing at the back of the store, Anna looked around again. Roger was nowhere to be seen. Turning to face the closed basement door, she warily opened it, expecting darkness. An overhead bulb, hanging from its cord at the bottom of the basement stairs, glowed eerily like a lone star above a dark and placid lake of silence.

"Roger? Roger, are you down there?" Anna called nervously. No answer. She called again, but still no answer.

From across the store, she heard her daughter's voice. "He's not in the pharmacy, and he's not behind the lunch counter. Let's go home."

"Your papa left the basement light burning. I'll go down and turn it off. Shine your flashlight on the stairs, so I can see to come back up."

Anna moved cautiously as she went down the wooden stairs, one step at a time. Irritated, she grumbled aloud, "Oh, Roger, why won't you put up a handrail? One of these days you'll break your neck!"

At the bottom of the stairs, just before reaching for the cord to turn off the overhead light, she glanced around the familiar storeroom. Three walls were lined with shelves holding well-ordered boxes. The contents of each box and its date of arrival were clearly labeled in Roger's own precise lettering. Against the fourth wall stood a work table but no chair.

On the floor, in the center of the room, was a pair of men's shoes, neatly placed, and an overturned straight-backed chair. Directly above the chair was a pair of argyle socks dangling in midair. Inside the socks was a pair of feet. Attached to the feet was Roger Mills, hanging by his neck from a ceiling joist.

Anna screamed, "Oh no! Roger! Roger! Oh my god! Roger! Charlene, come here. Hurry! Help me. I need your help now!"

Charlene stood at the top of the stairs, looking down at her mother, who was frozen in place with one hand holding the light bulb's cord and the other hand holding her flashlight, which pointed to the pair of suspended socks. She ran down the stairs to join her mother. In shocked disbelief they stared at the argyle socks. Neither moved nor spoke. Then Charlene began to cry. She buried her head in her mother's shoulder and burst into sobs. Anna wrapped her arms around her daughter's shaking body and stroked her hair in an effort to comfort her. She, herself, was trembling uncontrollably.

Between sobs, Charlene choked, "Papa, Papa . . . Papa's dead! What are we going to do?"

Anna struggled to gain some amount of composure. She swallowed her initial shock and fought against the screams caught in her throat. She wiped at the tears running down her cheeks as she collapsed on the bottom step. Charlene, still shaking with a mixture of grief and horror, sat down beside her.

"Oh, Mom, what are we going to do?"

Anna felt a physical pain of anguish and heartache as she held her sobbing daughter closer. Struggling to remain calm, she said, "It's going to be all right, Charlene. I'll take care of you. Now, don't panic. Together we'll do what needs to be done. Your papa is gone. He has taken his own life, and we can't help him now. His neck is broken. We need to do what makes the most sense. Papa wouldn't want people to know he took his own life. He never wanted people to think he was weak. The drugs made him weak. He tried so hard to give them up, but they wouldn't let him go.

"He was afraid we would get into Hitler's war and that in wartime he wouldn't be able to get the drugs he craved.

7

He was afraid he couldn't face life without his drugs. He was afraid people would find out about the drugs. He was afraid the drugs would kill him. Papa was afraid we'd leave him and move back to Chicago. He was afraid we wouldn't have enough money to get by. Your poor papa was afraid of everything."

"What are we going to do?"

Struggling to suppress her own feelings of shame and guilt, Anna gently lifted her daughter's face and looked into Charlene's tear-filled eyes. In a quiet voice she said, "Once, I loved your papa. Now he's gone. As weak as he was, he took care of us the best he could. Now, we must do what's best for him. We owe him a proper funeral. We can never tell anyone how we found your papa. Promise me that, Charlene. We'll let people think he fell down the basement stairs and broke his neck."

"But people will find out."

"Not if you help me. Go upstairs and look in the display cabinet with the Swiss Army knives, and bring me the biggest one. We'll cut the rope and get him down."

Charlene stood on the straight-backed chair and cut the rope from the ceiling joist while her mother held poor dead Roger by the knees. They watched in horror as he fell to the basement floor with the heavy thud of a wet sandbag. With great effort, Charlene forced her father's shoes back onto his argyle-sock-clad feet while her mother removed the rope from his neck. Anna undid the noose, rolled the rope into a neat coil, and handed it to Charlene.

"We'll burn this in the fireplace at home."

Anna returned the straight-backed chair to its usual place beside the work table. Together mother and daughter dragged Roger's lifeless body across the basement floor to the bottom of the stairs. There, they began their terrible trip to the top of the staircase—one step at a time—with the corpse between them. It was hard work because Roger was not a small man. They pulled him up the first step, rested, got a tighter grip, and pulled him up another step. Their progress was slow but steady. Roger's body bumped and thumped from step to step. Finally, all three made it to the top. Anna and Charlene rested for a few minutes, wiping the sweat from their brows, which ran down their faces and merged with their tears. Then together, mother and daughter gave Roger a great push and watched as he somersaulted down the basement stairs, landing with a resounding thump on the concrete floor, breaking his neck, again.

Roger's wife and daughter stood next to his crumpled form, holding hands, and said their last goodbyes. They retrieved the rope and turned off the basement light. Using their flashlights, they climbed the stairs one last time. They closed the basement door and walked to the front of the store. Before turning off the remaining lights, Anna said, "Did you put the knife back?"

"No, it's in my pocket."

"Well, put it back in the display cabinet in the exact place where you found it. While you're over there, bring me a towel from under the lunch counter. The snow we tracked in has melted into puddles.

9

Charlene did as she was asked and waited by the door while her mother mopped their way out. "I want to leave this awful drugstore and run out into the snow—I want to run and run—I want to run all the way to Chicago," Charlene sobbed.

* * *

They turned off the lights, locked the door, and began the slow trek back to their house on Collis Avenue. The snow continued its steady assault. The falling snowflakes seemed to say, "There are lots more of us yet to come." Charlene was carrying the rope, and Anna was carrying the towel.

"What are you going to do with the towel?" asked Charlene.

"When we get home, I'll put it in the dirty clothes basket like always."

"What about the rope? If we try to burn it, the smoke will smell up the house. Why don't we just put it in the garage with all the other ropes that Papa doesn't need but insists on keeping?"

"That's a good idea. We'll hide it in plain sight where no one will ever notice it."

Plodding home they listened to the snow crunching under their boots and to a dog barking half-heartedly in the distance. The falling snow was steady and quiet as it covered their tracks. None of the houses showed lights from their windows.

They climbed the snow-covered steps to their house on Collis Avenue and went inside. Charlene took off her heavy coat, hat, scarf, mittens and boots. Anna put the extra key to the pharmacy back in its place on the mantel.

Turning to face her daughter, Anna said, "Charlene, I'm sorry you had to find your papa like that. It's awful, but we can get through this. We did the right thing. Promise me again that you'll never tell anyone about tonight."

"I promise. I'll never tell. I couldn't bear to tell anyone ever. I feel so ashamed about what Papa did and what we did, too."

"You mustn't feel guilty. None of this is your fault. You are a good girl. Now, you'd better go to bed and try to get a few hours of sleep. I love you so much."

"I love you, too, Mom."

They embraced in one final good-night hug. With tears in her eyes, Charlene turned and began to climb the stairs.

She watched her daughter through her own tears. *How lucky I am to have a daughter like Charlene!*

Anna went outside again, by way of the kitchen door, and crossed the backyard to the garage carrying the rope. Inside the garage, she placed it among similar ropes that were suspended from hooks on the wall near the window. Anna was pleased to see that the hanging rope blended in with the others. She left the garage and retraced her steps to the house. After removing her winter gear, she went upstairs to get some rest.

\* \* \*

At seven o'clock, Anna got up and put on her plain blue housedress with the big white buttons and her sensible shoes. She rolled her dark brown hair around the hair rats she had fashioned from strands of her own hair, which she had saved in the china hair receiver on the dresser. She put on her navy blue cardigan with the patch pockets. From Roger's top drawer, she took a white linen handkerchief-in-waiting and placed it in one of the sweater's pockets. Then she telephoned the police.

"This is Mrs. Roger Mills on Collis Avenue, and my husband didn't come home from the drugstore last night. I'm frantic with worry. The snow is really deep, and I'm afraid that something has happened to him. I tried calling the store, but he doesn't answer the telephone. Can you go by the drugstore and check on him?"

"Sure. We'll check," the police officer answered. "Don't worry. I'm sure everything will be fine."

Anna hung up the telephone and went into the kitchen to make a pot of tea. Then she sat down to wait. She needed to think. Her emotions were a combination of sadness and relief, a feeling of finality and of a new beginning. Her guilt was overcome by her will to survive. How could she explain her feelings to her sister, Grace, when they got to Chicago?

*Roger and I were married for twenty years. The early years, when Charlene was a baby, were good years. Then he hurt his back and was in pain for a long time. That's when he started taking pain killers. After his back was better, he continued with the drugs. He didn't need a doctor's prescription. He just helped himself to the drugstore's inventory. I hated the irresponsible way he acted when he was on drugs. The last five years have been a nightmare. It hurt Charlene, too. I should have taken her and left Roger long ago. How ironic—I was planning to tell him we were leaving the very day of his accident.*

Anna knew her instincts had been right. Her husband's death needed to look like an accident. Roger's reputation had always been important to him, and he didn't deserve the legacy of a death by suicide. He would want to be buried in consecrated ground.

Charlene didn't deserve the humiliation of a parent's suicide either. Neither she nor Charlene needed to be involved in the discovery of Roger's death. Then there was the life insurance.

* * *

Two hours later, Anna heard a knock at the front door. Answering the knock, she saw two policemen standing on the porch. They were holding their hats in their hands and looking very serious.

"Did you find my husband? Is he all right?"

"May we come in, Mrs. Mills?" the first policeman asked.

The policemen stood in the middle of the living room, still looking very serious. The first one said, "Please sit down, Mrs. Mills. We have some bad news. We found Mr. Mills in the drugstore. Apparently, he fell down the basement stairs and broke his neck. He didn't survive the fall. We wanted to help, but we were too late. He was already deceased when we found him. We're so sorry."

Anna covered her face with her hands and half screamed, "Oh no. No. No . . . not Roger!"

She started to moan and sob, all the while rocking back and forth on the edge of the couch.

The sound of voices downstairs woke Charlene. She came into the living room still dressed in her flannel pajamas and wearing two pairs of wool socks. She ran to her mother.

"What's happened? Where's Papa?" Charlene cried.

"Your papa is dead!" sobbed Anna. "He fell down the basement stairs at the drugstore and broke his neck. Oh, Charlene, Papa's gone . . ."

Charlene gasped and broke into tears. Then she, too, started sobbing. The two women held each other and cried and rocked, as though they were learning of the accident for the first time.

The policemen just stood there. Finally one said, "Let us call someone to be with you. Maybe a neighbor?"

Anna nodded.

* * *

The neighbors came. Some brought sympathy. Some brought casseroles or congealed salads. Some brought curiosity.

"What will you do?" they asked.

"We'll move to Chicago to be near my sister, Grace. This house is too sad. We can't stay here anymore. Charlene can go to college in Chicago."

A funeral mass was celebrated at the Catholic Church on Boyd Boulevard. Roger was buried in consecrated ground in the little cemetery behind the church. The drugstore inventory was sold to Roger's cousin, also a pharmacist, who was next in line to run the family business. The life insurance company, from whom Roger had purchased a substantial policy on the day Charlene was born, sent a sympathy card and a check made payable to Anna Mills.

Anna explained to Charlene that she wasn't going to sell the house on Collis Avenue. "We'll keep the house in case things don't work out in Chicago."

Anna and Charlene put their furniture in storage, packed their personal items, and took the train to Chicago. Later that week, a "For Rent" sign went up before the little house on Collis Avenue—just as it began to snow.

# PART II

## CHAPTER 1

*T*he "For Rent" sign had stood in the middle of the small front yard of the house on Collis Avenue since February. Now it was June—June 1939.

The day was unusually hot. Hot and humid. The three occupants of the green Terraplane automobile sweated and sighed as the great Hudson Motor Car Company vehicle glided, in slow motion, down Collis Avenue. Harry and Louise Hoag, along with their small daughter, Frances, were looking for a particular address. One of Harry's coworkers had told him about a house on this street that had been available for rent since February when the owner and her daughter had moved to Chicago.

The coworker had said, "You won't not have to worry about a nosy landlord. The owner lives far away. She's a widow.

Her late husband was killed in a freak accident. You won't hear from her. Besides, the rent is only forty dollars a month."

That sounded good to Harry and Louise. Forty dollars was just about what they could manage on Harry's income.

The Hoags were poor. In 1939, everyone was either poor or hard-up. It was still the Depression, after all. The senior Hoags didn't think of themselves as poor. They were proud of their college educations, their professional occupations, and their solid middle-class American upbringing.

"We aren't really poor," they explained to their four- (almost five-) year-old precocious daughter. "We're just temporarily going through a tough time."

Frances didn't believe her parents. She had overheard Aunt Rose tell her mother that the fox-fur skins she wore around her neck had cost eighty dollars. Frances loved those foxes. Their fur was soft. Each fox's mouth was like a clothespin. One fox would open his mouth and bite the other fox's tail if his chin and the upper part of his nose were squeezed just right. Sometimes, her aunt let the foxes nip at the ends of Frances's fingers. The foxes had green glass eyes that stared at nothing. Frances didn't know much about money, but she did know that those foxes cost a lot more than the monthly rent for the house on Collis Avenue. Eighty dollars was a lot to pay for blind foxes.

The other piece of evidence proving Frances's we-are-poor theory was that she wanted a bicycle more than anything. Every time she asked, her parents told her they couldn't afford one. *If we can't afford a bicycle, then we're really poor,* Frances reasoned.

17

The Terraplane came to a stop at the curb in front of a two-story red-brick house with a "For Rent" sign in the front yard. A rental agent was standing in the shade of the porch. He was a slightly overweight man, wearing a seersucker suit, brown-and-white spectator shoes, and a broad smile. The Hoags got out of the car and walked toward him. Frances liked the looks of the house, but she wasn't as sure about the man on the porch.

"Hi there. Hot enough for you? You must be the Hoags. I'm Ben Cole. We talked on the telephone." Extending his hand, he continued, "I'm really excited about showing you this house. You'll love it! And guess what, little lady, you can have your own bedroom."

Frances liked him better after that.

While her parents toured the house, Frances inspected the yard. The front yard was small. It had a row of uninteresting bushes along one side and more bushes next to the front porch. A sidewalk ran parallel to the street. Between the sidewalk and the street were two large silver maple trees. Five concrete steps led to the front porch, which stretched the width of the house. Frances was not impressed. She walked around the house toward the backyard.

The backyard was fenced, but it had a gate. Frances opened the gate and entered a fairy-land of flowers. The backyard was huge. It was the largest backyard she had ever seen. On one side, there was a garage. The other sides were banked with flower beds. There was a cherry tree and two apple trees. A big white rosebush, taller than Frances, stood between the garage and the house. Across the back fence was a row of hollyhocks, standing at attention, behind a planting of daylilies. Larkspurs and daisies bloomed everywhere. The flower beds on the sunny side of the yard were edged with nasturtiums in full bloom. Their endless array of every red, orange, and yellow possible excited Frances. She loved bright colors, and she clapped her hands in approval. It wasn't just a backyard. It was a garden, and Frances loved it. It was almost, but not quite, as good as a bicycle.

A few minutes later, her parents appeared on the back stoop. Harry called, "Frances, this is where we're going to live, and this backyard is where you're going to play. Come and see your room."

"Come and see all of the flowers," Frances called back.

She heard her parents exclaim with enthusiasm as they fell in love with the backyard and its beautiful plantings. They were excited about the fruit trees and charmed by the flower beds.

Looking at the flower beds, Louise wondered aloud, "Who planted those nasturtiums? All the other flowers are perennials, but the nasturtiums had to have been planted this year."

"I'm not sure," replied the rental agent. "Ronald Lay, our part-time maintenance man, keeps the grass mowed and the bushes trimmed. Occasionally, he'll pull weeds, but I don't see him planting seeds."

"That's odd," said Louise.

Mr. Cole looked at his watch. "I need to get back to the office," he said, shaking Harry's hand. He waved to Frances. Then he got into his car, cranked the engine, and drove away.

Three days later, the Hoags moved into the Collis Avenue house. Frances had her own bedroom for the first time in her life. From her bedroom window, she could look down into the backyard and see the flowers. Her mother had always loved flowers and enjoyed gardening. Her father had always wanted to grow vegetables. This yard had an ideal space for a vegetable garden between the driveway and the fence. Frances decided that the perfect location for a sandbox was under the cherry tree. The Hoags couldn't wait to put their hands in the dirt.

With all the unpacking, getting settled, and yard work, there was so much to do.

* * *

Frances's birthday was just one month away. She hoped her mother would want to make this, her fifth birthday, a happy one. "Mom, can I have a party?"

"You know parties make me nervous. Besides, I don't know whom to invite. I don't have any friends in this neighborhood."

"We can always invite some people from my office," her father offered.

"That won't do. We need children. Five-year-old girls need five-year-old friends, and I don't know any five-year-olds, except you," Louise said, frowning at her small daughter. "Frances, you'll have to make your own friends in this neighborhood."

The following morning Frances walked down the sidewalk looking for children with whom she could make friends and turn into party guests. Three houses away she saw two boys and a girl about her age playing tag. She stood on the sidewalk watching them for a while. They ignored her.

"You need another girl," said Frances. "If you let me play, I'll invite you to my party."

"Are you the new girl who lives in the haunted house?" one boy asked. "Mr. Mills died in that house."

"Did not! He died in his drugstore," the other boy said.

Frances interrupted, "I know the real true story. I'll tell you what happened if you come to my party."

"What kind of party is it?" asked the girl.

"It's going to be a ghost-story-telling birthday party, and we'll have ice cream."

"Can I bring my little sister? I like to watch her get scared," asked Bobby, the tallest boy.

"Okay. But everyone has to bring a present."

"Okay. We'll come to your party, and you can play tag with us, but you have to be *it*."

At lunch Frances described her new friends to her mother. "There's Bobby, and he has a little sister. There's Dickey, and he lives right next door. Carol is a year older than everyone else and has two grandmothers living in her house. She has a mother and a father and two brothers who are really old. They go to high school. Her house is very full of people, and she said they yell at each other all the time. I heard them yelling."

Louise, who hadn't really been listening to her daughter, said, "That's wonderful, Frances. I wish I made friends as easily as you do."

21

"All my new friends are coming to my party, and they're all bringing presents."

"What games would you like to play at your party? How about Pin the Tail on the Donkey?"

"No. I promised that you would tell us some ghost stories."

"Frances, this is going to be a birthday party—not a Halloween party!"

"But I promised! If you won't tell us some ghost stories, I'll tell the one about Aunt Rose's boss grabbing her and her not even screaming when he bumped his head and how she had to kiss the bump to make it all better and got lipstick all over his face and how his wife said she was going to kill both of them. That's pretty scary."

"Oh, Frances, Frances, Frances," her mother groaned. "You're not supposed to eavesdrop on adult conversations. You keep quiet about Aunt Rose."

\* \* \*

The day of the birthday party arrived—clear and sunny and not too hot. It was decided that the party would be held in the beautiful backyard. Chairs were arranged, and a card table was set up to hold the birthday cake. The guests began arriving.

Bobby came bringing his little sister and his mother. Dickey brought Zina, the Stevens's housekeeper. Dickey's mother couldn't come because she was too sick. She had the kind of sickness that no one ever talked about. Carol arrived with an impressive entourage. She brought her mother and both of her grandmothers.

All the new friends brought birthday presents. There weren't enough chairs, so the children sat in the grass. Everyone sang "Happy Birthday," and Frances began opening her gifts.

Bobby and his little sister gave Frances a box of crayons and a coloring book. Carol's gift was a small wooden paddle with a ball attached by a thin rubber band. Frances liked Dickey's present the best of all. It was a shallow bowl containing a small amount of water and a rock. Near the rock was a turtle about the size of a silver dollar. It crawled all around, but it couldn't scale the slippery sides of the bowl. The children clamored to see Frances's new pet.

"Zina got this turtle at the dime store," Dickey boasted. "It likes to eat bugs."

While the children searched the grass for bugs to feed the turtle, Louise brought out the birthday cake and the ice cream. There was a big slice of cake for everyone, but there wasn't enough ice cream to go around since there were more adult guests than had been expected. The adults said, "Let the children have the ice cream."

Carol's Grandmother Mercer took exception to that idea. "Children should respect their elders. I'll have ice cream," she said, filling her ice cream bowl to the very top.

Carol's other grandmother glared at her through thick glasses and said, "*Schwein*! (Pig!)"

The grandmothers proceeded to have a loud argument. Only Carol's mother understood what they were saying because they were arguing in German. Carol's mother ignored both grandmothers and turned to talk to Bobby's mother.

23

When the refreshment dishes were cleared away, Louise asked the children what games they would like to play. Bobby answered, "Frances promised that you would tell us a ghost story."

Everyone turned to look at Louise. "I don't know about a ghost story. I do know a story about a scary wolf. Once upon a time there was a little girl who had a bright red cloak with a hood. Everyone called her Little Red Riding Hood."

"Mom, that's not scary," interrupted Frances. "Tell us a real ghost story like the one Aunt Rose tells about Raw Head and Bloody Bones who live in the attic. Or how Aunt Rose's boss's wife is going to kill her just because she kissed his hurt place and messed up his collar with her lipstick."

"Now, that's a story I would like to hear!" said Grandmother Mercer, scraping her bowl for the last spoonful of ice cream.

"That boss's wife is going to kill both of them," Frances elaborated.

"Frances, be quiet!" her mother ordered. She wasn't sure whether to apologize for Frances or for Rose or for both. Instead, she burst into tears and ran into the house.

The party was over. Bobby, his little sister, and his mother went home. Dickey and Zina went next door. Carol's grandmothers walked up Collis Avenue, still arguing. Frances overheard Grandmother Mercer say, "That Rose is such a hussy!"

The other grandmother said, "It's all that boss's fault. *Sein Gehirn schlüpft in seine Hose!* (His brains have slipped into his pants!)" Frances wondered what they were talking about.

The grandmothers agreed they would like to hear more of the Rose-and-Boss story. It was one of the few things they had agreed upon in over twenty years. They decided that Frances's birthday party had been the most interesting social event they could remember attending on Collis Avenue.

* * *

Louise locked herself in her upstairs bedroom. She lay across the bed, shaking with sobs. She couldn't stop crying. She felt as though the world was going to end, or worse yet, that the world was moving on and leaving her behind. She had never expected to be a mother. She was trained as a teacher, and she had planned to teach other people's children until she retired, not deal with her own. Then along came Frances when Louise was thirty-five. Harry was delighted. Louise was devastated. She didn't care for babies and small children. She felt children should be docile and should sit obediently in classrooms.

Frances was a shock. Louise had serious doubts about her own parenting skills and was sure Frances would come to a bad end. Raising a child was more of a challenge than she felt she could handle. Actually, she was afraid of the responsibility her daughter represented.

Many things frightened Louise. She now had one more thing to add to her ever-growing list of fears. The birthday party had been a disaster, in her opinion, and the idea of ever hosting another party made her cringe in trepidation.

This child she was supposed to be raising didn't seem to be afraid of anything. Frances was consumed with curiosity and always wanted to try something new. Harry and his sister, Rose, were brave, too. They didn't believe in superstitions like she did. They weren't afraid of thunder and lightning, or the dark, or loud noises, or strangers. Both enjoyed sampling new foods and visiting new places. They weren't afraid to drive cars or ride bicycles.

Louise refused to learn to drive. She had recurring nightmares about being in a car wreck, and her fear of falling kept her from trying to balance on a two-wheeler. Now, her own daughter wanted a bicycle. The idea of Frances peddling into oncoming traffic terrified Louise.

As her sobs subsided, Louise felt a headache coming on, one of the really bad headaches, the kind that made her see bright lights and feel as though her head were about to split open. These headaches always made her vomit. For that reason, she called them sick headaches. There was nothing to do except to pull down the shades and lie still, waiting for sleep to come.

*If I live until tomorrow*, she promised herself, *I'm going to take Frances and go home to my family for a while. Living in this house makes me nervous.* With that thought in mind, Louise drifted off to sleep.

* * *

Frances knew all about her mother's sick headaches. They happened way too often. Frances pretty much ignored them. She took her new coloring book and crayons out on the front porch, where she climbed onto the glider and waited for her father to come home. While she waited, she colored in the new book, being careful to stay within the lines only when it suited her. One page showed a girl playing with a kitten. Frances gave the girl a yellow-green sweater and a red-violet skirt. She was startled to see how pretty those colors looked together. It made her happy to look at them. She colored the kitten blue, just for fun.

The Terraplane could be heard coming down Collis Avenue long before its protruding headlights could be seen. *Here comes my daddy, home from work!*

Harry always drove past the house before turning into the alley and pulling the car into the back driveway, in front of the garage doors. Frances ran to the backyard to greet him.

"Happy birthday, Miss Five Years Old," Harry said to his daughter as he got out of the car. "How was your birthday party?"

"It was good. I got a real turtle, and Carol's grandmother ate most of the ice cream, and then both her grandmothers yelled in German. Mom started crying and went inside, and then everyone went home."

"Where's your mother now?"

"Upstairs having a sick headache."

Harry had learned from years of experience that things would not go well if he disturbed his wife when she was having one of her sick headaches. Turning to Frances, he said, "Let's go inside. I'll make you some supper."

Frances followed her father to the kitchen, but she wasn't hungry. "I already ate."

"Too much birthday cake, I expect. I'll make myself a sandwich. You can have one later if you want."

Harry got a beer out of the ice box to go with his sandwich. He sat on the back steps eating his sandwich and drinking his beer while Frances played in the backyard. When the beer was gone, Harry got another and then another. He was beginning to feel a little foggy when he heard the *honk* of a familiar horn as a car stopped in front of the house. It was his sister, Rose, come for a visit.

"What are you doing back here?" Rose asked as she rounded the house on her high-heeled, sling-back pumps. "Got another beer?"

"Sure, Rose. Help yourself, and while you're at it, bring me another," slurred Harry.

Rose went inside and soon returned to the back steps carrying two beers. "Harry, you're already two sheets in the wind, but I don't need you to talk. I need you to listen."

Since it was starting to get dark, Harry and Rose moved to the front porch. Frances followed them, curling up on the soft glider cushions, where she could listen. Her father sat on the front steps. Her aunt sat in the rocking chair and began telling another really scary story about her boss. Harry was ten years Rose's senior, and he was used to acting as a fatherly sounding board for her stories. Rarely did he comment on her escapades. As Rose continued talking, Frances wondered how a man, who was a boss, could be *all hands. Where was the rest of him?*

Frances's head began to nod. Just before she dozed off, she overheard her aunt say, "I wouldn't be surprised if his wife really does kill him this time."

# CHAPTER 2

*L*ouise woke early the next morning. Her headache was almost gone. Just a dull, distant ache remained, along with total exhaustion. She was wrung out and depressed. Gingerly, she got out of bed and put on her housecoat and bedroom slippers. After a bathroom visit, she walked across the hall to the guest room door, which was closed. She opened the door and saw Harry, still wearing his shirt and pants, stretched out on the top of the bed. The coat and tie he had worn to work the previous day were thrown across a chair. His shoes were near the chair, where he had dropped them. His mouth was hanging open, and he was snoring loudly. Louise didn't disturb her husband. She didn't have the energy to deal with him this morning, neither sober nor hungover.

Looking into the bedroom at the end of the hall, Louise found Frances in her bed sound asleep. She had kicked the covers off during the night and lay on her bed wearing only her underpants.

Louise thought about eating something, but she wasn't hungry. *I need a cup of tea*, she said to herself as she put on the teapot. Turning from the gas stove, she was surprised to see several packages and a note from Rose sitting on the kitchen table.

*Good morning! I hope everyone is feeling better today. I stopped by the bakery on my way to work and got you a box of doughnuts. The gift is for Frances. Sorry, I'm a day late on the birthday.*

*Love to All, Rose*

While the tea was steeping, Louise inspected the box of doughnuts. They were the cake type covered with powdered sugar—Harry's favorite. The idea of eating anything, especially a doughnut with powdered sugar, repulsed Louise. She covered the doughnut box with a dish towel so she wouldn't have to look at it. She took her tea and went out into the garden.

Louise sat in one of the high-backed, wooden Adirondack chairs and put her feet on a matching footstool. While sipping the hot, sweet tea, she heard the back door close as Harry, carrying his small brown suitcase, began crossing the garden on his way to the garage.

"Are you feeling better this morning?" he asked.

Louise didn't answer. She closed her eyes and leaned her head back on the chair's headrest.

"I have to go out of town for the rest of the week. I tried to tell you about my trip last night, but you were too sick. I guess

I wasn't in the best shape myself. Anyway, if you don't have a headache when I get back, we can go to the cafeteria for dinner one night," he said as a peace offering.

Louise ignored him. She wouldn't even look in his direction. This didn't surprise Harry. It was typical Louise. She never spoke to him on mornings when he had enjoyed a few beers too many the previous evening. Harry waved to Louise, walked to the garage, and stored his suitcase in the trunk of the Terraplane. He got into the driver's seat, put the big car in reverse, and backed down the driveway and out into the alley, where he turned and drove away from the house on Collis Avenue.

Frances stuck her head out the back door and announced, "I'm hungry."

Louise refused to acknowledge Frances's existence. After all, it was Frances who had caused all the trouble at the birthday party by bringing up the subject of Rose and her errant boss. Louise decided to punish Frances by not speaking to her all that day.

"Are you still sick?" Frances asked.

When her mother didn't answer, Frances was no more surprised than her father had been. She went back into the house and soon discovered the box of doughnuts her aunt had left on the kitchen table. She proceeded to enjoy as many doughnuts as she liked. Then she went outside, by way of the front door, in search of playmates.

Louise realized she was all alone. Salty tears began to ooze down her cheeks and drip off her chin. One tear splashed into her lukewarm tea. *Everyone has left me. No one cares about me and my feelings.*

As she sat rolling around in her own misery, something caught her attention. It, or rather they, were bobbing their bright red, yellow, and orange nasturtium heads at her and acting downright happy. They began to pull Louise out of her puddle of self-pity.

"Those nasturtiums have no right to be so cheerful," she said out loud.

"Yes, they do," answered a voice from across the fence. "Dickey and I planted those seeds back in the spring so Miss Jean could see them from her window. You know, Miss Jean is really sick and she's not going to get better."

It was Zina, the Stevens's housekeeper, talking to Louise. Without waiting for an invitation, Zina opened the gate and walked right into the Hoags' backyard. She continued her one-sided conversation with Louise as she sat in the other Adirondack chair.

"Sometimes, if Miss Jean is having a good day, I help her into a chair near her bedroom window where she can see the flowers. She's the one who needs cheering up."

"Where did you get the nasturtium seed?"

"Mrs. Mills, who lived here before you, gave them to me and Dickey. She always planted those flowers and saved the seed from year to year. Last winter, she knew that come summer she would be gone, and she wanted to leave something pretty for Miss Jean to see."

"How long have you worked for the Stevens family?"

"Just about one year. I'm not from around here. I come from down in the country, but I don't see spending my life there. That kind of life is way too hard. So I thought I'd come to Allenburg. This is a college town and I mean to meet a college man. You might say, 'I come to be went with, but I ain't yet.'"

Louise bit her bottom lip to keep from smiling. She liked Zina. Since moving to Collis Avenue, Louise had made no friends. She wondered if Zina would be her friend.

"Tell me about the Mills family," Louise said. "Mrs. Mills must be a very nice person to think about planting flowers for Mrs. Stevens to enjoy."

"Mrs. Mills and Miss Jean were good friends before Miss Jean took so sick. Mrs. Mills was nice enough on the outside, but I don't know that I would say she was so nice on the inside. There has been talk about her and Mr. Mills. He was a real strange one—always acted like he was drunk, staggering around and falling over things, but he never took a drink. Strange. Mrs. Mills and that daughter of theirs, Charlene was her name, were always talking about moving to Chicago. Then after Mr. Mills died, they did."

"How did Mr. Mills die?"

"The word is that he fell down the basement stairs in his drugstore and broke his neck. But something else was going on that night, I tell you. I saw it myself."

"What else was going on?" asked Louise excitedly, pushing her gloom from center stage to the outer wings of her mind.

"Well, that night it was snowing like all get out. It was January fifteenth—the biggest snow we ever had around here.

Miss Jean was having a bad time, and I was helping her as best I could. I gave her a big dose of painkillers. Then I sat by the window watching the snow swirl around the streetlight while I waited for sleep to come for her. About two thirty, I saw Mrs. Mills and Charlene, all bundled up, come out of their house and walk toward the drugstore. About two hours later, I saw them walking back. The next morning two policemen banged on our door. At first I didn't know what to think. Then they said that I should go over and be with Mrs. Mills because Mr. Mills was dead."

"Did you go over to be with the Mills?"

"Nope. I had to stay with Miss Jean and Dickey. I told the policemen that I would telephone some other neighbors who could go. I called Grandmother Mercer because I knew she could get away and that nothing scares *her*."

"Did you tell the policemen what you had seen that night?"

"Course not. I'm not one to go looking for trouble, and you're not to tell this. You're the only one I've ever told about that night. I thought you ought to know since you live in that house."

Just then Louise and Zina were interrupted by squabbles coming from the kitchen as Frances and Dickey divided up the remaining doughnuts.

"I'd better get back to Miss Jean. Remember, some things is better not told."

"Tell Mrs. Stevens hello for me and that I hope she has a good day," Louise called as Zina slipped through the gate between their houses.

Louise's Depression, as was its wont, gave up its place to Fear. *What if Zina is right and something was going on that night?* A cold chill ran through her mind and trickled down her back between her shoulder blades. Louise shuddered. *What if this house on Collis Avenue is haunted? What did happen to Roger Mills? Why will no one talk about it? What's the matter with Jean Stevens, anyway? Everyone says that she's dying, but of what? No one will talk about that either.*

Deciding that it was too much to think about, Louise went back inside to get another cup of tea. The tea in the pot was cold, and that made her feel sad. Even her teapot disliked her. She turned from the stove and saw the now-empty box of disgusting doughnuts staring at her. With vengeance, Louise picked up the empty box, mashed it flat, and stuffed it in the trash can under the sink. She reached over to retrieve the dish towel from the kitchen table but stopped abruptly. Her mind whirled. *There is something under that dish towel. The doughnut box was the only thing on the table just a few minutes ago.*

Remembering the birthday gift Rose had left for Frances, Louise lifted the dish towel guardedly and looked at a flat, thin package wrapped in the colorful comics section of the Sunday newspaper. The package had no bow. It was held together with plain kitchen twine.

"Oh, that Rose!" she admonished the package. "Why can't she use regular wrapping paper like everyone else?"

Unopened packages filled Louise with both dread and hope. She was accustomed to her personal balancing act between Depression and Fear. Hope and Fear did not play so well together. Forgetting about giving her daughter the silent treatment, she decided to let Frances open the package.

Frances and Dickey were on the front porch taking turns with the paddle and ball, Carol's birthday gift. Frances's hands were covered with a red sticky substance.

"What's wrong with your hands, Frances? Have you hurt yourself?" Louise asked anxiously.

"It's jelly from the jelly doughnut that she wouldn't share and it's getting all over the ball and paddle," Dickey said.

"Jelly doughnuts are my very favorite, and Aunt Rose always puts one in the box, just for me, and I don't have to share them with you," Frances informed Dickey.

"Rose left you a birthday gift, Frances. You can open it now," Louise said, handing Frances the comic-section-wrapped gift.

Frances sat on the glider and tore the wrappings away, revealing a book. It was a very unusual picture book. The illustrations were unlike any Frances had ever seen. The book had words as well as pictures, but Frances couldn't read them. Frances couldn't read anything.

"Mom, will you read us this book?"

"Well, let's see," said Louise as she sat down beside Frances on the glider. Dickey sat on her other side so he could see, too.

"The name of this book is *Madeline*. It is a new book by a man named Ludwig Bemelmans. I read a review of this book in last Sunday's paper. It is about a little French girl who goes to a private school along with eleven other little girls. All the little girls are good and do what they are told, except Madeline, who sometimes gets into trouble. She's like you, Frances."

"Read it to us," Frances said.

"Okay. The book is a poem, and the lines rhyme," said Louise. Then she began reading aloud.

When her mother had finished reading the book Frances said, "Read it again."

Dickey said, "Let's go find Bobby."

Before Louise could begin reading the book for the second time, the children galloped down the front steps, headed for Bobby's house. She was left sitting alone, holding the open book.

*Even children don't want to be with me*, she thought sadly.

Louise stared at the book. The house in the book looked like a haunted house. It looked exactly like the little house on Collis Avenue. Then she took a second look. The house in the book looked nothing like the house on Collis Avenue. However, a scary thought had entered her mind, and it would not be dislodged.

# CHAPTER 3

*L* ouise's growing fear of the imagined Ghost of Mr. Mills and her looming dread that the house on Collis Avenue might be haunted were soon replaced by even greater fears.

In the summer of 1939, Hitler's boots were marching, marching, marching all across Europe. Poland had fallen. England and France declared war on Germany while Hitler made plans to invade Norway and Denmark. Japan and China were already at war. In the face of all this turmoil, the United States continued to maintain its position of neutrality and isolation, all the while building its military force and its stash of weapons. It was a very scary time for all the world.

During that awful summer, an even more frightening curse was marching across the heartland of the United States. It was a *Plague*. It was an *Epidemic*. Its name was *Infantile Paralysis* and its favorite victims were children. There was no escape. No one was safe. Even President Roosevelt could not stop that awful disease, with no known cause and no known cure. All the way from Batavia, New York, to Allenburg, Ohio, and beyond, the evil that was polio marched, marched, marched, searching for the next warm body to own, not rent. The country was scared. Louise Hoag was in a state of panic.

The early morning banging at the front door startled Louise, causing her to spill tea down the front of her housecoat. "Who can that be? It is too early for anything except bad news."

Louise peaked around the curtain at the front window and saw Grandmother Mercer, who was yelling in German, as she hammered on the door with her fist. Her face was white with fear. When Louise opened the door, she could see that Grandmother Mercer had been crying.

In broken English, her German neighbor stammered, "Kurt has the polio. *Unser Haus ist verboten* (Our house is forbidden). Frances cannot play with Carol." Turning, she hurried down the front steps and headed toward the next house in the block.

Louise stood in horror in the open doorway. *Kurt Mercer? Carol's older brother has polio? How can that be?*

Louise slammed the front door and turned the lock. *What am I thinking? You can't lock polio out. I have to get away. I have to get away right now.*

Her worst fears had come true. Polio knew where they lived. Polio knew where *she* lived. She had to take Frances and leave the little house on Collis Avenue. They would go to her sister Helen's house. Louise could think of no other alternative. She picked up the telephone and asked the operator to ring Roanoke, Virginia.

"Hello," said a sleepy voice on the other end of the line.

"Helen, this is Louise. A terrible thing is going on here. This town is overcome with polio and I have to get away. I can't stay here any longer."

"Well, good morning to you, too, sister. Now, settle down, Louise. The entire country is in the midst of a polio epidemic. Allenburg is no worse than Roanoke. We're all worried about polio. Other than that, how are you and Frances doing? How's Harry?"

"I can't stay here any longer," repeated Louise, ignoring Helen's inquiries concerning Frances and Harry.

"What does Harry say about this? Have you talked to him about getting away for a while?"

"No, I haven't talked to Harry, but he'll want us to be safe."

"I'll be glad to have you and Frances come for a visit until you can get a handle on this. You need to calm down and make some plans. First, you need to talk to Harry, and then you need to decide when you'll leave and what you'll need to pack. Train tickets need to be purchased and arrangements made. Who'll water your flowers while you are away?"

Louise realized that Helen was trying to alleviate the worst of her fears by giving her a list of specific things to do. They had danced this dance before. She hated being manipulated by her older sister. Busy work could fill the gap that hysteria was trying to claim, but not for long.

When Harry came home from work that afternoon, Louise had already packed the big tin suitcase with clothes for herself and Frances. She had asked Zina to water her flowers while she was away. She had telephoned the railway station and checked on train schedules going to Roanoke. Louise had also written a list of questions for Harry. Did he want the milk delivery stopped? What about the newspaper? If he had an out-of-town trip, would he remember to ask Ronald Lay to mow the grass? And on and on . . . She had been a very busy lady that day. The only thing she had forgotten to do was to fix dinner.

"I'm hungry," said Frances.

"Me, too," replied Harry. "Come on in the kitchen and I'll fix us something."

Frances had a bowl of Wheaties, and Harry had a sandwich and a beer, then another.

* * *

Louise was up early the next morning. She sat at the kitchen table drinking tea while Harry made himself some scrambled eggs and toast.

Harry begged his wife to reconsider leaving. "Things won't be any better in Roanoke. They have polio down there, too. If you want to visit your sister, that's one thing. If you think you can escape an epidemic, you're wrong."

Louise didn't answer him.

"Okay. You've obviously made up your mind. I'll pay for the train tickets. You and Frances can visit Helen for two weeks. After that, you are to come home. I know Helen is always glad to see you, but you shouldn't wear out your welcome. Helen's house is small. I don't even know where she'll find room for you and Frances to sleep."

Harry counted out traveling money, and a little extra, for Louise. She grasped the bills tightly in her fist without thanking him or looking in his direction. He came over to his wife's side of the kitchen table and tried to give her a goodbye kiss. She turned away.

Louise let her daughter sleep late. At nine o'clock, she woke Frances. After scrubbing her in the big bathtub, she dressed the five-year-old in her darkest-colored dress and her brown lace-up Buster Brown shoes. While Frances ate the generous breakfast laid out for her, Louise put on her navy blue traveling suit and her matching navy blue hat with the veil. Navy blue was Louise's favorite color. The railway station would be dirty and the train seats would have been used by strangers. Louise believed that dark colors could help ward off the worst of the offending germs. *No need to advertise your presence to lurking germs.*

"Eat all you can, Frances, because you won't be getting any lunch. I'll pack something for you to eat later at dinner time."

"When will we get to Aunt Helen's house?" asked Frances, smearing another piece of toast with butter and strawberry jam.

"Not until after dark. You'll like the train ride."

"Will you like the train ride?"

"No. Trains make me nervous, but we have to do this."

Frances gave her mother a quizzical look.

At eleven o'clock, a taxi cab stopped in front of the house on Collis Avenue. The driver put the big tin suitcase in the trunk and slammed the lid with a loud thump. Louise and Frances sat in the back seat. When they arrived at the station, the driver took the suitcase inside. Louise paid him, and he was gone.

"You sit on the suitcase while I get our tickets," Louise instructed.

While she waited in the ticket line, Louise became aware of a decaying stench. A disgusting odor seeped from the wooden floors, held together by years of wax and dirt. It mingled with the smell of coal and grease and human sweat. Strange people wandered around asking questions and looking at the posted departure-and-arrival schedules. A giant clock with two faces, one on each side, was bolted to the wall near the ceiling. She had the odd feeling that the clock was watching her, from two directions at once. Porters in red caps hurried about carrying other people's luggage. *Were they stealing suitcases? Could they be trusted?* Her mind whirled.

Louise looked at Frances, who was still perched on the big tin suitcase. Suddenly, she remembered a long forgotten adage, *He travels fastest who travels alone.* Shaking the temptation from her mind, she signaled a porter. She glanced up at the departure board on the wall and said, "Please take the tin suitcase with the little girl sitting on it to Track Four." She handed him a quarter.

"A quarter is a lot of money," Frances commented.

"And he had better appreciate it," was her mother's tight-lipped reply.

Frances and Louise sat on a hard wooden bench and waited for their train. Since Frances's feet didn't reach the floor, she stuck them straight out. Frances looked at the people. Louise looked at the clock as her nervousness rolled itself into a hard ball and settled in the bottom of her stomach.

In the distance, a whistle blew. People started gathering their possessions. "What's that noise?" asked Frances.

Louise couldn't hear what her daughter was saying because of the piercing whistle and the loud rumbling sound that shook the air and rattled the entire station. The train grumbled loudly as its iron wheels ground against the tracks, making its brakes scream. A huge blast of steam, with a terrible hiss, rose from the train as it slid beside the platform. Frances was excited. Louise was terrified.

A man in a uniform was standing in the middle of the station waiting room. In a loud voice, he announced, "Track Four. Arriving from . . ." and he rattled off a long list of towns. "Track Four. Departing for . . ." and another long list of towns. Then he repeated the entire announcement again.

They went out onto the platform. There was the train. *Their* train. It was huge. The platform was filled with people, all pushing and shoving for a place at the front of the crowd. Men in striped overalls were crawling between the cars with big oil cans. Other men were unloading suitcases, boxes, and trunks from the baggage car. Still others were putting boxes onto the dining car. All at once, the train's doors opened, and a stream of people poured onto the platform. They surged through the waiting crowd, calling, "Red Cap. Red Cap."

A few minutes later another man wearing a different uniform stood in the open doorway of one of the train's many cars. He was looking at his pocket watch, which was attached to a heavy chain coming out of his vest pocket. He descended the steps to the platform, put his watch away, and shouted, "All aboard. All aboard."

"Who's that?" asked Frances.

"He's the conductor," answered her mother.

Louise grabbed Frances by the hand and hurried her up the steps and onto the train. Entering the first car on the left, Louise looked for a pair of empty seats. She could see only one option. At the end of the car was a double section, comprised of four seats. One pair was facing forward, and the other pair was facing backward. Louise didn't like this arrangement. She didn't want to share the space. She didn't want strangers looking at her. And, for sure, she wasn't going to ride backward. They made their way to the end of the car and settled into the forward-facing seats. Frances sat next to the window and watched as the baggage handlers loaded the big tin suitcase into the baggage car. Louise began to worry about whom their seatmates would be.

Soon another mother, accompanied by a little girl about Frances's age, entered the car looking for a place to sit. The only vacant seats were those in the section with Louise and Frances. The new mother was fat and looked friendly. The girl was skinny and had a head covered with at least a dozen small braids, each with a red bow. Frances smiled. Both the new girl and her mother were the color of hot chocolate. The new mother said, "Hello." Louise did not respond. She was busy looking out of the window. Frances answered, "Hello. I'm Frances."

The new mother and her daughter smiled at Frances and took their places in the backward-facing seats. The whistle blew one long blast as a stream of steam erupted from the smokestack. The engine gave the train a few jerks and then lurched into motion. They were underway. The train gained speed while Louise continued to look out of the window, and the other mother began reading a tattered paperback book.

"Where are you going?" asked the new girl, whose name was Sue.

"Roanoke to see my Aunt Helen," answered Frances.

"Well, we are going to Norfolk to see my daddy. He works for the navy."

Frances and Sue played Cow Polka as they rumbled through the countryside. Neither girl was good at counting above ten, so they just called out when they spotted a cow grazing in a pasture.

Soon the conductor entered the car and walked down the aisle saying, "Tickets. Tickets." All the adults fumbled around looking for their train tickets. When the conductor stopped at the end of the car, Louise handed him their tickets. He punched holes in them, then returned the tickets to Louise.

They crossed a big river on a high metal bridge that held only train tracks, no cars. Louise announced, "That is the Ohio River."

The new mother said, "We are still in Ohio and will be until we get to the other side."

The river was filled with barges carrying coal. Sue and Frances tried to count the barges. Their counting skills had not improved since they had tried counting cows. There were fewer steam ships than barges on the river, so they counted those.

They were in West Virginia. The train tracks followed the rivers as they wound through the mountains. The tall skeletons of the coal tipples looked like ghouls to Louise. The piles of slag heaped on the hillsides looked like the dead ashes of crematory remains.

"What are they doing down there?" Frances asked.

"Loading coal from the mines," answered her mother.

"Men dig a deep hole in the mountain and carry the coal out," explained Sue's mother. "That's where coal comes from."

"What are those other buildings?" asked Frances. "They all look alike."

"Well, there is an office, and there are houses where the miners live, and there is a school for the children. Of course, there is the company store, too," explained Sue's mother.

"What's a company store?" asked Sue.

"It's a special store where the miners have to shop because they don't have any real money. They get paid in company script, which is good only at the company store," Sue's mother said.

This idea frightened Louise. *What if all the money we had was in company script?* she thought in horror. Turning to Sue's mother, she asked, "How do you know so much about coal-mining towns?"

"I grew up in one." Sue's mother turned and looked out of the window. The conversation was over.

As the train chugged deeper into the mountains, it passed through many tunnels. Frances and Sue tried to count them, but there were too many. Both mothers helped the girls keep track of the number.

The door at the other end of the car opened and the conductor walked down the aisle again. This time he said,

"Dining car now open. Dining car now open." Louise hated the fact that he always said everything twice.

Sue's mother stood up. "We had better eat now before we get into Virginia."

Louise and Frances stayed in their seats. They bought sodas to go with their homemade sandwiches from a porter who was pushing a little cart down the aisle. When Sue and her mother returned from the dining car, Sue told Frances that she had a ham sandwich and a bowl of Jell-O topped with whipped cream in the dining car. This was exactly what Frances had eaten except for the Jell-O. Frances had two cookies. She gave one to Sue.

It began to get dark outside. The girls played I Spy. Then the conductor came through again. This time he didn't look very happy. In a monotone voice he said, "Mason-Dixon Line. Jim Crow car in the rear. Mason-Dixon Line. Jim Crow car in the rear."

Sue and her mother gathered their things and left the car. They would not be coming back again this trip. Frances and Louise said, "Goodbye." Neither Sue nor her mother answered.

"Why are they leaving? Where are they going?" asked Frances.

"We are in Virginia now and they have to go to a special car in the rear of the train."

"Why?"

"It's the law," answered Louise, turning to look beyond the window into the blackness of the night. She felt a shiver run through her body as worry clouds filled her mind. *What will happen to me if they make women and children go to a special car, too?*

# CHAPTER 4

$\mathcal{H}$elen and her seventeen-year-old son, Richard, were
waiting on the platform when Louise and Frances's train
pulled into the Roanoke station. Helen gave her sister and niece
big hugs. Richard said, "Hi." He then dedicated himself to
ignoring his cousin and aunt for the duration of their stay.

"Richard, please help Louise with her luggage," Helen said,
nodding in his direction.

Richard rolled his eyes before retrieving the big tin suitcase
from the platform and stowing it in the trunk of his mother's
new car. When everyone was settled, Richard drove them to
the small two-bedroom duplex that he and his mother shared
with their cat, Tomas. Richard had his own bedroom. Helen
occupied the other bedroom. All of the rooms belonged to
Tomas.

Helen's husband, Richard's father, had once lived with
them. One day he went to work and didn't come home. One of
his coworkers, an attractive younger woman, disappeared the
same day. Neither was ever heard from again. Richard was only

seven at the time. From that day on, Helen had supported herself and her son on her meager teacher's salary. The four-room apartment they called home was the best she could afford. She prayed that her new car would outlive its monthly payment schedule.

Louise glanced around the modest living room and asked, "Where am *I* supposed to sleep?"

"You and Frances will be sharing the sofa bed here in the living room."

"Does your cat wander around in the night? You know I don't like cats."

"Don't worry. Our cat hates that couch. He won't bother you."

"Where did you get that cat anyway?"

"He was a gift from a student. His name is Tomas."

"I hate the way cats look at me and the sneaky way they slink around," Louise said, remembering a story from her childhood about a neighbor's newborn baby dying of suffocation when a cat jumped into his bassinet and took a nap curled up on his head.

\* \* \*

When Louise woke the following morning, her joints were sore. As Helen had predicted, Tomas had avoided the couch. That was a good thing because Louise didn't just dislike cats. She was *afraid* of cats—all cats.

At the breakfast table, Louise complained, "That sofa bed is an implement of torture. It's as hard as a sidewalk. It'll take some getting used to." Before her sister could reply, she asked, "Has the polio epidemic spread to Roanoke?"

"Yes, it sure has. We have not been spared. The schools have delayed their fall opening. The public library and many churches are closed. Movie theaters and swimming pools are off limits. People are being told to avoid crowds."

Because of the epidemic, Frances wasn't allowed to play with any of the children who lived in Aunt Helen's neighborhood. Tomas was her only companion. When Frances had first met Tomas, it was true love, at least on her part. Tomas considered Frances a curiosity until Richard gave her a sardine, straight out of the can, and told her to carry it in her pocket. After that Tomas followed Frances everywhere. Louise was shocked and disgusted.

Since school was closed, Helen had plenty of time to listen to Louise, who talked on and on. Louise repeated herself over and over. Louise talked. Helen listened. Louise told her older sister all about the house on Collis Avenue and about the previous owner, who died in a terrible freak accident. She described her neighbors and shared her feelings of unease. She told Helen that Harry drank too much and that his sister, Rose, was of doubtful character. She went on to describe her terrible sick headaches and her recurring bouts of what she called "the blues."

Helen's patience was stretched to its limit. She had known Louise her entire life, and nothing had changed. Louise repeated her stories and complaints over and over. For the first time, Helen prayed that school would open soon and she could escape her sister's ongoing sagas.

Two weeks later, the Roanoke schools did open. Helen and Richard were very happy to be back in school and away from Louise's constant monologue. Helen told Louise that it was time for her and Frances to go home. Louise did not agree. She had gotten used to the routine at Helen's house. Plus, she hadn't had one single headache the whole time she had been in Roanoke. When Helen was around, Louise wasn't so fearful. With her sister as an audience, she consigned her depression to backstage and savored the spotlight.

"When are we going home?" Frances asked.

"Not right away," her mother replied. "We need to stay here for a little while longer."

That night Harry telephoned. "I sure do miss you, Louise. Are you and Frances ready to come home? It's been lonely here without you. The polio situation is calming down. There have been fewer and fewer new cases each week. You can be safe here."

"We aren't ready to come home yet. We'll stay for another few weeks."

"But we agreed that you'd be gone only two weeks, and it's been three weeks now. Just a few more days, and then I want you to come on home."

"We'll see," said Louise, and she hung up the telephone.

* * *

Helen and Richard were gone all day, and Louise had no one to listen to her tales of woe. There was nothing to do at Helen's house, so she and Frances walked to the nearby public library, where they spent a delightful morning browsing through books—novels for Louise, picture books for Frances. Louise took the books they wanted to borrow to the checkout desk.

"May I see your library card?" asked the librarian.

"I don't have a Roanoke library card, but I'm sure my sister has a card. She teaches at the high school."

"Everyone must have her own card. It's the rule."

"Well, how do I get a card?"

"Just fill out this application," replied the librarian, handing Louise a piece of paper.

Louise filled out the form with her name and her Collis Avenue address and handed it back across the desk.

"Oh dear! This will not do. We can issue library cards only to Virginia residents, and it appears you have an out-of-state address. I'm sorry."

Louise was dumbfounded. *How can this be? I'm an educated woman. I was a teacher.* She left the books on the counter, grabbed Frances by the hand, and marched out of the library. When they got back to Helen's house, Louise broke into tears. Frances went to look for Tomas.

The next day Louise received a letter from Harry urging her to come home. She threw his letter in the trash. The following week she received another letter from her husband, insisting that she end her visit. She tossed that letter in the trash, too. On Saturday Harry telephoned. This time he demanded that she and Frances come home immediately. Louise hung up on him.

Helen, who had overheard her sister's half of the telephone conversation, said, "Louise, I agree with Harry. It's time for you and Frances to go home."

"I'm not ready to go home," Louise snapped.

"Well, you had better get ready. You can't stay here permanently. I'll give you two days to pack your things. Then you must leave."

"Are you throwing *me* out?"

"Yes, I am!"

"Very well. I'll get a job teaching school, and I'll get my own apartment."

"Louise, you don't even have a Virginia teaching certificate. Who would take care of Frances?"

*Frances, Frances, Frances . . . always Frances. She is such a burden,* fumed Louise.

"Then I'll get a job working in a department store. I can sell things."

"There are no extra jobs just sitting around looking for workers to fill them. In case you haven't noticed, we're still in a depression. I'll give you two days to pack and leave. You need to go back to Harry while he'll still have you."

Louise stormed out of the kitchen. She would have gone to her bedroom, but she didn't have a bedroom. There was only a couch, and that she had to share with a five-year-old. Slamming the door behind her, she went outside and sat on the front steps. Never had she felt so awful. She was trembling so hard that she couldn't even cry. *What will happen to me? Where will I go, and what will I do?* Her thoughts were muddled—her mind petrified with fear.

Then from the side of the house came Tomas. He bounded to the step where Louise was sitting and rubbed against her. She screamed. Jumping up, she ran down the sidewalk as fast as she could. She ran and ran until a pain stabbed her side and her breath came in gasping pants. Slowing her pace, she began walking aimlessly, turning up one block and down another, until she was totally lost.

Louise realized she couldn't find her way back to Helen's house. She had to do something. Across the street, she saw a drugstore and decided to go there for directions. The first person Louise saw, as she entered the store, was a young woman straightening items on one of the shelves.

"I'm visiting here and don't know my way around. Can you tell me how to find Washington Avenue, near the library?"

"I'm new here myself. I'll ask the pharmacist. He's downstairs."

Louise watched in horror as a dark-haired man wearing a white coat emerged from the stairwell and walked toward her. Terror flooded her mind, as she heard the clerk call, "Roger, a customer needs your help with directions."

*Oh my god! It's Roger Mills,* was Louise's last conscious thought before she fainted.

# CHAPTER 5

*L*ouise lay crumpled on the drugstore floor. The first person to come to her aid was not Roger Mills, but Roger Johnson, the pharmacist. He held an ammonia-saturated cotton swab under her nose and helped her to a chair. She looked up at the white coat hovering above her and realized that she had made a terrible error. The name tag clearly said, "Roger Johnson." It was a case of mistaken identity. Louise sat motionless. For once, she couldn't think of anything to say.

Mr. Johnson said what everyone always says when someone falls down. "Are you all right?"

Louise didn't answer.

Another voice asked, "Are you all right, Aunt Louise?" It was Richard, standing there, Coca-Cola in hand.

She didn't answer him either.

Using the drugstore's telephone, Richard called his mother, who came immediately, bringing Frances with her. Working together, they helped Louise into the back seat of the car and drove to the duplex. Once they were inside, Helen tried to talk to her sister, but Louise refused to respond.

"Why don't you lie down on my bed and rest for a while?" Helen suggested.

That night Frances shared the lumpy couch with her aunt while her mother slept soundly in the other room. The next morning Louise was up early and acting as though nothing unusual had happened the previous day.

"Helen, you're almost out of tea," she called from the kitchen.

Helen stood up, shrugged her cramped shoulders, and rotated her stiff neck. Sleepy-eyed and with tousled hair, she shuffled to the kitchen and asked, "What are you doing up so early, Louise?"

"It's time to get up. There are lots of things that need to be done around here. I'll help you clean this place. You can dust and vacuum and do the laundry while Richard washes the windows and mows the grass. I'll polish the silverware."

"Louise, what are you thinking? This is *not* your house. It's mine, and I'll clean it on my own schedule, not on yours."

"Don't forget. I live here, too, and I'll be staying here until I can find a nicer place—a bigger and *cleaner* place."

"Louise, I told you yesterday, you *cannot* live here. You have to leave—no later than tomorrow!"

"Now see here, Helen, just because you're my older sister doesn't mean . . ."

A loud knock interrupted their argument. Frances ran to open the door and squealed with delight when she saw her father standing on the stoop. She jumped into his outstretched arms and giggled as he hugged and kissed her.

"Oh, Frances, honey. I'm so glad to see you. I've missed you so much."

"Daddy, Daddy. I want to go home."

"Harry, what are you doing here?" Louise demanded in a shrill voice.

"I've come to take you and Frances home."

"Well, you can forget that. I live here now, and I won't leave."

"Louise, please don't be hardheaded. You don't live here. You belong at home with us. Now get your things. We're leaving."

"I'll help you pack," Helen offered.

"No! No! No! I'm staying here!"

"Louise, I'm tired of this. You and Frances have been here for too long, and it's time for you to come home. If you won't come with us, Frances and I will leave without you."

"Why would you take Frances and leave *me*?" Louise shouted angrily.

\* \* \*

Richard helped Harry load the big tin suitcase into the trunk of the waiting car. Frances sat beside her father in the front seat, waving to Tomas, the cat. Without saying goodbye to either her sister or her nephew, Louise climbed into the back seat alone. Harry thanked Helen, shook Richard's hand, and turned the car toward the highway, headed north.

Louise cried silently, refusing to speak, for most of the trip. She was buried in her own thoughts, revisiting the memory of her stay at her sister's house. *It was a good visit. Not once did I have a headache. There were only two bad things. Helen's cat scared me, but that was to be expected. Anyone can see that awful cat is evil. And the incident of mistaken identity at the drugstore was distressing, but those things happen all the time.*

However, one question really puzzled Louise. *Why have my headaches stopped?* This mystery continued to gnaw at her mind as they sped along, mile after mile. Then the answer came to her like a jack-in-the-box exploding from its container. It was obvious.

"Sleeping with you causes my headaches!" she announced in a loud voice.

"Louise, what are you talking about?" asked Harry over the sound of the Terraplane's engine, straining against the steep grade of the mountain road.

She didn't answer her husband, but she did stop crying and spoke quietly to herself. *Well, there's a cure for that. I'll move into the guest room.* Her whole face broke into a smile, embracing this wonderful new idea. She was relieved and almost happy to have solved the mystery of her headaches. Then she remembered how sad she had felt living on Collis Avenue with no friends.

*As soon as I get unpacked and settled, I'll start making friends. I'll join a book club or maybe a sewing circle or some other club that meets in the daytime. Maybe I'll join a nearby church. Churches are good places to meet people and make friends.*

\* \* \*

After their long trip, the Hoags were tired but glad to be back on Collis Avenue. At least Harry and his daughter were happy to be home. Louise felt like an empty pitcher. She was mentally and emotionally exhausted, despite her new insight and her new resolution.

"I'm really glad to have my girls back. I've missed you both so much," Harry said.

"What's going on with the polio epidemic?" Louise responded.

She listened as Harry explained that things were beginning to get back to normal. Schools were open. People were no longer afraid of crowds. No new cases of polio had been reported in almost a month, and the mayor had lifted all quarantines. Those who had been initially stricken were beginning their long journey to recovery. Kurt Mercer had lost the use of his legs permanently. He now had leg braces and was learning to walk with crutches.

"Marvin Hall's wife will spend the rest of her life in a wheelchair," Harry said.

"Who's Marvin Hall?" Frances asked.

"The Halls live at the other end of Collis Avenue in the big house on the corner. They have a little girl about your age," her father answered. "Her name is Mary Lynn, and she will probably be in your class when you go to first grade next year."

"Can I play with her?"

"No, not now. There are two busy streets, with lots of traffic, between our house and theirs. Neither of you is old enough to cross those streets yet," Louise said.

Frances went to bed that night without protest. She was happy to be back in her own bed, in her own room. Harry and Louise retired early, too. Harry was happy to have his wife back in their bed. He put his arms around Louise and held her close. They made love. At least, Harry made love. Louise just lay there hoping she wouldn't get another headache. She still felt like an empty pitcher.

* * *

The Hoags slept late the following morning. It was Sunday, and they needed a day of rest. While Harry drank coffee and read the newspaper, Louise stood looking out of the living-room window.

"There goes Evelyn Fisher from next door, walking to church. Every time there's a crack in the church door, Evelyn slips inside. It's probably her only social life. She has no friends. That ugly red birthmark on the side of her face is enough to scare anyone away. Plus, Evelyn has no personality."

"Evelyn can't help having a birthmark," Harry said. "I think it's called a port-wine stain. As to personality, maybe she's just shy."

"We should go to church. It would be a good place to make some friends," Louise said.

"Church should be about more than just finding friends to improve your social life."

"Oh, here comes Zina, and she's carrying some dishes," Louise announced, forgetting all about going to church. "She probably wants to welcome *me* home."

Harry put down his paper and hurried to open the front door. "Come in, Zina. I smell something good. Can I help you with those dishes?"

Zina winked at Harry, then turned to Louise. "Hi, Louise. Glad to have you back. I brought you a casserole and a pie, still warm from the oven."

After lunch Harry went back to his newspaper, and Zina helped Louise put away the luncheon leftovers while she relayed the recent gossip. The grown-up talk bored Frances, and she went outside.

She walked up the sidewalk to Carol's house. She knew the Mercers would be home. Sunday wasn't a day of worship for them. Most of Carol's family went to synagogue the day before Sunday, but Frances couldn't remember the name of that day. Jack Mercer didn't attend on a regular basis because he said it was bad for business. Frances wasn't interested in the Mercers' church habits. She wanted to see Kurt's crutches.

Grandmother Mercer saw Frances coming up their walk and invited her inside. All the Mercers were in the living room watching Kurt walk, if what he was doing could be called walking. Kurt had heavy metal braces on each leg. He needed crutches to pull himself along. The crutches were made of metal, too. Frances had never seen crutches like these. They had wide leather straps that fit around Kurt's arms, just below his elbows. Jack Mercer helped his son stand up and get his balance. Kurt planted the crutches, one at a time, in front of where he was standing, being careful to line them up just so. He swung his body forward to catch up with the crutches, dragging his braced legs behind. He took two steps, then down he went. His father hoisted him to his feet again.

"*Nochmal! Nochmal! Du musst für das judische Volk laufen.* (Again! Again! You must walk for the Jewish people)," said Grandmother Mercer.

Kurt continued to try. He tried and fell. He tried and fell. He didn't stop trying. Both Kurt and his mother had tears running silently down their faces. His father was both firm and gentle each time he lifted Kurt from the floor to his feet. Grandmother Mercer continued to give orders. The other grandmother was nowhere to be seen.

"Kurt will walk again," Carol said.

Frances was not so sure.

# CHAPTER 6

As soon as Harry left for work the next day, Louise began implementing her new plan. She gave the guest room a good cleaning, put fresh linens on the bed, and began relocating her things from the master bedroom. She hung her dresses, sweaters, and traveling suit in the guest-room closet. The big tin suitcase was unpacked. Her hose, gloves, scarves, and underwear found a new home in the chest of drawers, which stood against the wall across from the bed. In one corner of the guest bedroom, Louise put up a card table and placed one of the dining-room chairs beside it. *This will be my desk,* she told herself.

That evening after the dinner dishes were cleared away and Frances was in bed, Louise announced, "Harry, I've moved my things into the guest room. It'll be my room from now on. I can no longer share a bedroom with you. Your constant snoring is what's been causing my headaches. I can't live with those headaches."

"Snoring doesn't cause headaches," Harry protested.

"Well, your snoring keeps me awake, and not getting enough sleep makes my head hurt. It'll be better this way."

Harry didn't respond. Louise couldn't feel the lump in his throat. He closed his eyes. She couldn't see the reflection of the hurt in his heart caused by her rejection.

Louise went into her new room and closed the door. Harry went to what used to be *their* room, but was now *his* room. He closed the door, opened the small brown suitcase, and took out a bottle. He sat on the bed drinking and thinking. *I care so much about Louise. If I can make her happy, maybe she'll care about me, too. I need to try harder.*

\* \* \*

Halloween came and went. Thanksgiving came and went. In two weeks it would be Christmas. Louise thought Christmas generated an undue amount of work. She would be glad when it was over. Frances hoped that she would get a bicycle. Harry loved his family, and he wanted to make their Christmas special.

"It's time to put up a Christmas tree," Harry announced. "Let's get a big one this year."

"When can we get it? When can we get it?" Frances asked excitedly.

"How about Saturday?"

"Can I help decorate it?" Frances begged.

At first Louise resisted the idea. Then it occurred to her that tree decorating could be a way for her to get to know the neighborhood ladies better. She replied, "Yes, Frances, you can help decorate the tree. We'll make a party of it and invite your friends to help, too."

When the appointed time for the tree-trimming party came, Frances's friends were there. Zina had to stay with Dickey's mother. Bobby's little sister had a bad cold, and his mother stayed at home with her. Carol came alone. Her mother wanted to stay with Kurt, and her grandmothers didn't participate in Christmas activities.

"The Germans invented Christmas trees," Grandmother Mercer told everyone who would listen. "That doesn't mean *we* celebrate Christmas."

The children decorated the tree, hanging the ornaments as high as they could reach. Louise stayed in the kitchen making hot chocolate and serving cookies. She felt very sad. *Why don't the other mothers want to be with me?*

* * *

Early Christmas morning Frances ran down the stairs, hoping to see a bicycle near the tree. There was no bicycle in sight. She was disappointed, but not surprised. Her Christmas stocking was hanging from the mantelpiece, filled with an orange, five individually wrapped Tootsie Rolls, some new socks, and a long knit stocking cap with a tassel. The cap had yellow and brown stripes and reminded Frances of a bumblebee. Under the tree was a pile of brightly wrapped presents.

"Don't open the gifts yet," her mother said. "We want to wait until Aunt Rose gets here."

Rose came in like a whirlwind. She burst into the living room, on a current of perfume, shouting, "Ho! Ho! Ho! Merry Christmas to all!"

She was wearing her fanciest dress and highest heels. Her arms were filled with presents for everyone.

"Merry Christmas to you, too," said Louise. "But why are you so dressed up, Rose? We're just family."

"The day isn't over yet," replied Rose as she handed out her presents.

Rose's gift to Harry was a flask disguised as a flashlight. He opened the flask and held it upside down. Nothing came out, but he seemed very pleased anyway. Louise frowned.

Rose gave Louise a purple silk scarf with big red roses on it. Louise frowned inwardly, even though she thanked her sister-in-law politely. Frances liked the scarf and asked to hold it. It felt soft to her touch, and its flowers were bright and cheerful. Finally, Aunt Rose handed Frances a gaily wrapped present with a big bow. Frances opened it carefully because she didn't want to mess up the bow. Inside the package was a small beaded purse. It was beautiful. A rainbow of color radiated from the opulence of the beads. The purse had a zipper closure, but the zipper was broken. Frances didn't mind too much about the broken zipper.

"You can close it with a safety pin or maybe a clothespin," Rose said.

"I need to check on our dinner in the oven," said Louise as she left for the kitchen.

"Where did you get that purse?" Harry asked his sister.

"It was a gift from you-know-who, and you-know-whose wife will kill everyone in sight if she ever finds out. It can be Frances's *secret* purse," said Rose.

"What do you put in a *secret* purse?" asked Frances.

"Secrets, of course," said Rose.

"But, Aunt Rose, I don't have any secrets."

"Honey, you will someday, if you're lucky," promised Rose.

Returning from the kitchen, Louise asked, "What are you talking about?"

"It's a secret," said Frances.

After Christmas dinner was over, it was time for Harry to bring out his gift. "Everyone stay right here in the dining room, close your eyes, and I'll get my present."

He went to the closet under the stairs and retrieved a very large box, which he carried into the dining room. It was a tall, brown cardboard box with a red bow on top.

"Okay. You can open your eyes now."

"What is it?" asked Frances.

"It's something special for my very special family," her father said.

Rose held the box steady while her brother opened it and wriggled out a brand new wooden Philco radio. It was a floor model and was almost as tall as Frances. Rose squealed with delight. Even Louise smiled and clapped her hands. Frances didn't know what to think, but she was glad everyone was happy.

"What is it?" she asked again.

"It's a radio for all of us. We can listen to the news and to music and baseball games and all kinds of great radio programs. You'll love this radio, Frances."

"Where will you put it?" asked Rose.

"Right here in the dining room," Louise said. "There're plenty of chairs in here. I'll be able to listen from both the kitchen and the living room."

Everyone agreed that the radio should live in the corner of the dining room between the window and the fireplace.

"Can I have the box?" asked Frances.

"Sure," said Harry. "It'll make a fine indoor playhouse."

"This has been great, but I've got to run," said Rose, pushing back her chair. She whirled around the room, giving everyone a hug and Frances a kiss. "Happy Christmas to all," she called as she skipped out the door.

The Hoags spent the rest of Christmas Day listening to their new radio.

Later that evening, as they were going up for bed, Louise told Harry that he could come to her room for a visit.

*It's the least I can do,* thought Louise. *After all, he did buy us a radio.*

\* \* \*

The next day was Boxing Day, and Louise decided that she and Frances should go next door to visit with Miss Jean and Zina. They found Zina in the kitchen ironing. Dickey was sitting at the kitchen table playing with his toy soldiers. He was still in his pajamas and bedroom slippers. His mop-like blond hair had not yet been combed.

Louise greeted her neighbors with a hearty, "Good morning and Merry Christmas."

"It's not so merry around here," Zina said. "Miss Jean is worse yet."

"We didn't even get to have a Christmas tree this year," complained Dickey.

"Oh, Dickey, your house looks very much like Christmas. There are bright red flowers everywhere," Louise said, glancing at the potted poinsettias that adorned the kitchen counter and stood on every table in sight. Two of the potted plants sat on the floor, flanking the front door.

"Poinsettias are one of Miss Jean's favorites. She loves the color red. Mr. Stevens bought two of the poinsettias, and I guess that sort of got the idea going. All their relatives sent poinsettias and so did most of their church friends and some neighbors. We look like a flower shop, and I'm supposed to keep all of them watered," Zina said with a grimace of resignation.

Zina sent Dickey upstairs to get dressed and to comb his hair, cautioning him not to wake his mother. She put away the iron and ironing board, poured herself another cup of coffee, and put the tea kettle on to boil.

"Do you think I could say hello to Mrs. Stevens and wish her a Merry Christmas?" asked Louise.

"She wouldn't even hear you. She's so doped up that she's not in this world. She doesn't even know that we have all those poinsettias. Those flowers can't help her, but they do help the people who sent them. Makes them feel better."

Suddenly, Louise felt very sad. *Why didn't it occur to me to get Jean Stevens a poinsettia? Why didn't the other neighbors mention the poinsettia idea to me? It's Frances's fault. She is in and out of the Stevens's house almost every day, and I'm sure she saw the flowers. Frances deliberately didn't tell me. I'll make that child stay in her room when we get home.*

Soon Dickey, fully dressed and with combed hair, returned to the kitchen. Zina poured Louise a cup of tea and offered the children some juice.

"We have presents for you," Louise announced as she laid two wrapped gifts on the table.

One package contained a yo-yo for Dickey. The other gift was for Zina. It was a purple silk scarf with big red roses on it. Frances recognized the scarf immediately. It was the one Aunt Rose had given her mother only yesterday. Frances didn't want Zina to feel bad, so she kept quiet.

While the children took turns with the yo-yo, which neither knew how to work, Louise and Zina visited over their hot drinks until it was time for Louise and Frances to leave.

* * *

"Let's listen to the new radio," suggested Louise, forgetting all about sending Frances to her room.

They listened to Christmas music until lunchtime, as Louise dusted the living and dining room furniture and Frances played in her radio box, which had now gone to live under the dining room table, out of the way. After lunch, Louise listened to *Our Gal Sunday, Ma Perkins,* and *Stella Dallas.* Later in the afternoon, Frances listened to *Terry and the Pirates, Jack Armstrong, the All-American Boy,* and *Sky King.*

After dinner that evening, Harry turned on the radio, and they listened to two news broadcasts. Both Walter Winchell and H.V. Kaltenborn read grave reports of the war in Europe. Things were not going well on that front. America continued to send shiploads of supplies and arms to England, while officially remaining neutral. Registration for the draft would begin the following fall—October 1940. When the news was over, The Hoags listened to *The Great Gildersleeve* and to *Fibber McGee and Molly.* The comedy shows were a welcome relief after the depressing war news. They agreed it was good to laugh.

The following day Harry came home from work carrying several packages. The bulkiest one contained a large cork bulletin board, which he hung on the wall near the radio. In another package was a rolled-up map of Europe, which he attached to the bulletin board. He also had a box of colored thumbtacks to mark spots on the map. For the next two years, the Hoags would listen to the war news on their radio and move the thumbtacks around Europe. In December of 1941, the map of Europe would be superseded by a world map.

\* \* \*

Jean Stevens died two weeks after Christmas. No one was surprised. She went to sleep one evening and didn't wake up.

Thanks to Zina's medicinal care, she had been beyond the reaches of pain for well over a month. The funeral was small and simple. A few of the neighbors attended, but Louise didn't go. She was sick herself, with another of her headaches. Grandmother Mercer represented the Mercer household and stood next to Bobby's mother at the grave site. When Jean Stevens was, at last, lowered into the ground, Grandmother Mercer stepped forward and said, "*Shalom.*"

It began snowing the day after Jean Steven's funeral and snowed for three days. Then there was a thaw and then another freeze. Huge icicles hung from the eaves of the garage behind the little house on Collis Avenue. The icicles were almost as tall as Frances. Bobby and Dickey broke the icicles away from the garage and pretended that they were swords.

*Edgar Bergan and Charlie McCarthy* had become one of the Hoags' favorite radio programs. The ventriloquist's dummy, Charlie McCarthy, was smart. The other dummy, Mortimer Snerd, was not smart at all. Frances liked Mortimer Snerd best. He made her laugh. When she looked at the icicles hanging from the garage, she thought of Mortimer Snerd. She called the icicles Mortimer Snerd's teeth. Her mother thought this was a silly way to look at icicles.

# CHAPTER 7

On January 15, 1940, Louise woke, headache free. Harry was out of town, and Frances was playing outside in what remained of the recent snow. Louise looked at the calendar and gave an involuntary start. It was the one-year anniversary of Roger Mills's death. Suddenly, Louise was seized by fright, which quickly turned to sadness for a man she had never met—a man who had once lived, loved, and laughed in this very house. *Someone should do something to remember poor Roger Mills.*

"I'll bake a cake for him. A pound cake!" she said out loud.

Immediately, she felt better and began assembling the ingredients. As she worked, Louise thought about Roger Mills. Her curiosity took over. She wanted to find out more about him. Whom could she ask? The neighbors never spoke of him, and his family had moved to Chicago. Who then?

*Oh, I know. I'll ask Ben Cole, the rental agent. He certainly had the opportunity to know quite a bit about poor Mr. Mills.*

Once the pound cake was safely in the oven, she telephoned Ben.

"Hello, Mr. Cole. This is Louise Hoag on Collis Avenue. There is something wrong with our hot water heater," she lied. "It makes a funny sound, and the water coming out of the faucets isn't as hot as it should be. Can you stop by and take a look at it? I would ask my husband to take a look, but he's out of town."

Normally, Ben would have sent the agency's handyman, Ronald Lay, to check on a routine maintenance problem. However, Ben was not too busy that day, and besides, he liked Mrs. Hoag's looks. She was an attractive woman. He smiled at the idea of getting to know her better. Plus, her husband was out of town . . .

"Sure. I'll be glad to take a look. I'll be there within the hour."

The pound cake was done. Louise took it out of the oven and placed it on the kitchen table just as Ben Cole knocked on the front door. After taking off his coat, he asked to see the ailing water heater. He knew nothing about water heaters, but he put on a good act. He thumped on its side and shone his flashlight underneath its tank. Louise didn't pay any attention to these maneuvers. She was waiting for an opportunity to quiz him about Roger Mills.

After his superficial examination of the perfectly performing water heater, Ben said, "I need to check the hot water faucets both in the kitchen and in the bathroom to see if you're getting hot water now."

As Ben expected and Louise knew, there was plenty of hot water. While they were upstairs checking the hot water supply in the bathroom, Ben Cole noticed that the each of the Hoags had their own bedroom. He smiled.

Back in the kitchen, Louise offered Ben a cup of coffee and a slice of the still-warm pound cake. They sat at the kitchen table and discussed hot water heaters in general. Then they discussed the weather in particular. They agreed that it snowed too much in Allenburg. Ben finished his cake and gratefully accepted a second slice.

Louise changed the subject. "I never met the previous occupants. What was their name?"

"The Mills family lived here before you," Ben answered. "Roger Mills died suddenly, and his wife and daughter moved to Chicago not long after the funeral."

"How did he die?"

"He fell down the basement stairs in his drugstore one night and broke his neck, or so the story goes. There are rumors that maybe he had some help falling down those stairs. For sure, there are rumors that he was on drugs. There was more to Roger Mills than most people knew."

"What do you mean?" asked Louise. Her eyes grew big as she felt a reflexive shudder.

"Roger Mills was quite a gambler. The whispers have it that he owed a lot of money to someone. But I don't know anything about that."

"Could he have killed himself because of gambling debts?"

Ben shot Louise a shocked look. "I haven't heard that! I doubt it was a suicide, probably just a plain accident like the police said. People do have accidents all the time."

As Ben prepared to leave, he thanked Louise for the delicious pound cake and told her to be sure to call him if she had any more trouble with the hot water heater. Without knowing it, Ben had reinforced Louise's fears and doubts concerning the circumstances of Roger's death. These doubts were now firmly fixed in her mind. They had found a home and had set up housekeeping. Drugs? Gambling? Louise had a lot of thinking to do.

A week later, Ben telephoned Louise under the pretext of inquiring about the health of the water heater. During the conversation, he suggested that they have lunch together so that he could tell her more about the maintenance of the Collis Avenue house. Louise politely thanked him for the offer but told him it wouldn't be convenient because she had to stay with Frances. Her only interest in Ben was his knowledge of Roger Mills, and that she had already gotten.

The more Louise thought about Roger Mills, the more she became convinced that something wasn't right concerning the story of his sudden death. *Was he really on drugs as Ben Cole said? Zina mentioned that Mr. Mills sometimes acted drunk, but he didn't drink. Is this more evidence of his drug usage? How can I find out? Was there an autopsy? If Roger was taking drugs the night he died, could that have caused his fall down the stairs? What about the gambling?* Louise knew nothing about gambling and didn't know how or where to begin exploring the subject. That would have to wait. She needed to start at the beginning, and the beginning was the drugstore.

* * *

The following morning, after clearing away the breakfast dishes, Louise decided to take a serious look at the scene of the accident. She and Frances would walk to the drugstore for lunch. The day had dawned clear and cold. A bright sun was shining on the light snow that had fallen overnight, turning the backyard into a carpet of sparkling white brocade. From the warmth of her kitchen, Louise imagined she could hear the crunch of snow beneath her bedroom slippers.

At lunchtime, she found her daughter lying on her stomach, half in and half out of her cardboard box under the dining room table. With her legs and feet inside and her head and arms outside, Frances looked more like a turtle than a little girl. She was busy coloring in a new coloring book. All the pictures were of birds, and she was intent on giving each the most colorful feathers possible. Louise stared at Frances, wondering how anyone could be so absorbed in something so trivial.

"Frances, put your coloring book and crayons away. We're going out to lunch. We'll go to the drugstore and get grilled cheese sandwiches. You may have a soda. This will be a treat for both of us."

Frances promised the birds in the coloring book that she would return soon to finish their feathers. She put on her stocking cap with the bumblebee stripes and wiggled into her coat.

At the drugstore, Frances wanted to sit at the lunch counter. Louise wanted to sit at a table. They both got their way. Frances sat at the counter, and her mother sat at a nearby table, where she could get a full view of the drugstore. Louise didn't really care if they ate together or not. As far as she was concerned, Frances was a distraction.

After ordering her sandwich and a cup of tea, Louise surveyed the layout of the store. She made mental notes about the location of the pharmacy, the way the merchandise was arranged, and where the windows and doors were situated. When her sandwich arrived, she asked the waitress, "Where does that unmarked door near the rear of the store go?"

"Oh, that's the basement door."

"Do you have a ladies room?"

"Sure. The restroom's at the far back. Just walk past the basement door, and you'll see it straight ahead."

"I need to wash my hands," Louise said as she got up and walked toward the pharmacy.

Standing behind the counter was a young man with red hair. He was wearing a white coat and was counting pills into a small glass bottle. Louise looked at him carefully. Hanging on the wall behind his head were several framed items. One appeared to be a college diploma. Another was a pharmaceutical certificate. Two of the framed items were portraits of different men, both wearing white coats. Louise stared at the portraits.

"Who are those men?" she asked.

The young man looked up from his task, smiled at Louise, and glanced over his shoulder at the pictures on the wall. "The one on the left is my uncle, Walter Mills. He started this store back in the 1920s, right before the crash. The Depression just about wiped him out, and he didn't live long enough to see the store succeed. The man on the right is his son, my older cousin, Roger Mills. He died in an accident last year. All three of us went to pharmacy school. I'm George Mills, and I'm running the family business now. How can I help you?"

"Where is your ladies room?"

"It's in the far back. We don't have a separate ladies room, just one restroom for everybody. So you'll want to latch the door."

George Mills stared after Louise as she turned and walked toward the back of the store. She could feel his eyes following her. *He is a strange man. I don't trust him,* she told herself. She stopped before the closed basement door and looked over her shoulder. George was busy with another customer. She reached out and touched the doorknob. *I'll just open it a crack and take a tiny peek inside.* The knob was cold, hard, and unyielding. A tremble ran through her hand and up her arm as she imagined a vibration coming from the door.

*I can open this door.*

*No, you can't,* she heard a voice inside her head say.

Louise dropped her hand. The Voice was right. She couldn't open the door. Frightened, she hurried to the door marked "Restroom." She rushed inside and latched the door. A mirror hung on one wall with a sink beneath. No one else was in the room. Louise glanced at the mirror. Looking back at her was a middle-aged, rather attractive woman with a look of panic on her face. At first, she didn't recognize her own reflection. She gasped. She felt her mind running away, leaving her body behind. Then an unexpected sound startled her back to reality. It was the sound of a toilet flushing. She bent down and looked under the stall door. No feet and no legs were visible.

"Who's there?" she asked in an alarmed voice.

"Just me," said Frances, bouncing out of the toilet stall.

"You scared me. I've been looking everywhere for you. I even looked under the stall door, and I couldn't see your feet."

"I had to stand on the toilet seat to reach the chain for the tank."

Louise narrowed her eyes and stared at her daughter. She wished Frances was someone else's child. *Frances is the one who always upsets me. She does it on purpose. She is ruining my life.* Louise knew full well that those thoughts were not reasonable, but she couldn't make them stop.

"Come on. We're going home," she said.

They left the drugstore without Louise eating her lunch or paying for their meals. The waitress told the pharmacist that the customer who didn't pay was Harry Hoag's wife.

"Oh, I know Harry Hoag," the pharmacist said. "He's a good guy. I'll put the lunch on his tab."

Frances and her mother stood at the curb beside Boyd Boulevard, waiting to cross the street. Suddenly, Louise was hot all over. She felt light headed and no longer in control of her own body. Her breath came in quick, shallow pants. She pounded the sharp pain in her chest and tried to run, but her legs refused to move. Louise was frozen in panic. She couldn't step off the curb even when there was a break in the traffic. *They're all going too fast. If I step into the street, I'll be killed.* She wrapped her arms around herself and shook. Her knees threatened to fold.

Frances glanced at her mother and then back at the street. She looked up and down, left, then right, then left again. No cars. She pulled on her mother's coat sleeve and guided her across the boulevard. Once safely on the other side, Louise was able to walk home. Frances didn't know it then, but she had just become the mother.

"I don't feel well," Louise said when they were back in their house. "I'm going up to my room and lie down for a while."

Frances settled into her box where she could finish coloring bird feathers and to listen to the radio.

* * *

Shortly after midnight, Louise woke to the shattering pain of someone or something hitting one side of her head with a hammer. This pain was all too familiar. Another sick headache had come to torment her. It had come with no warning and wouldn't stop. It was the worst headache she had ever experienced. Her head was in a cruel vise that refused to let go. Louise divided her time between stumbling to the bathroom to vomit and lying on her bed moaning. For three days her migraine continued. She survived on saltine crackers and hot tea. Her stomach would tolerate nothing else. On the third day, Harry found his wife lying on the bathroom floor, unable to speak. He picked her up, carried her to her bed, and telephoned the doctor. He described his wife's symptoms and asked what he should do.

"Try to get her to drink some water. I'll stop by and take a look at her on my way to the hospital. She might appreciate a damp, cool cloth on her forehead, too."

An hour later, the doctor was standing on the front porch with his black leather bag in hand. "Come in. Come in. Thanks for coming," Harry said, as he opened the front door and led the doctor upstairs to Louise's bedroom.

"I understand you have a problem," the doctor said to Louise. "Can you tell me about it?"

Louise closed her eyes and didn't answer.

The doctor took out his stethoscope and listened to her heart and lungs. He took her blood pressure and temperature. He looked down her throat, into her ears and nose, and shone a bright light into her eyes. Louise was too exhausted to protest.

"Everything looks normal. I suspect that you're suffering from a severe migraine headache and that you're most likely dehydrated and weak from the lack of solid food." Turning to Harry, he asked, "Has she had these headache episodes in the past?"

"Not for over a month. I was hoping that she had gotten over them. How can I help her?"

"The best thing you can do is get some fluids in her— plenty of water, and try to get her to eat something. Start with soft foods at first—chicken broth, Jell-O, applesauce. When she can keep the soft foods down, encourage her to eat small portions of a regular diet."

"I can do that," Harry said.

"I'll order some medication to help with the pain. You can get this filled at the drugstore," the doctor said as he pulled out his prescription pad and began writing. "This is for codeine. Be careful not to exceed the recommended dosage, and keep the pills out of the reach of young children."

The doctor stowed his pad, pen, and, instruments in his black leather bag and got up to leave. He turned to Louise, smiled, and said, "I hope you feel better soon. I want to see you in my office one week from now."

After closing the door behind the doctor, Harry went back upstairs. He checked on Frances, who was still sound asleep. Then he went to Louise's room. "I'm going to the drugstore to get your medication. I'll be back as soon as I can."

Louise turned away from him without answering.

When Harry returned, he found Frances in the kitchen eating a bowl of dry cereal. She was wearing her flannel pajamas—the ones with kittens printed on them. Her cereal made a crunchy sound when she chewed.

"Why didn't you put milk on your cereal?" her father asked.

"I can't reach the milk bottle."

"I can fix that," Harry said as he reached to the back of the top shelf in the refrigerator and handed Frances the bottle of milk. "I'll put the milk on a lower shelf where you can reach it. Okay? I have to go to work after I give your mother some medicine. She'll probably stay in bed again today. So you can be in charge."

"What do you want me to do?"

"You should stay inside and play quietly. Try not to disturb your mother. See if you can get her to drink lots of water, or maybe some juice. You need to fix your own lunch. I'm going to open a jar of applesauce and put it where you can reach it. Your mother can eat applesauce for lunch. Most important— take care of my special little girl."

Giving Frances a hug, Harry headed upstairs carrying a glass of water and the bottle containing the codeine pills.

"Louise, I have your medicine. You need to take one of these pills now."

Louise forced herself into a sitting position. Weakly, she took a pill from Harry's outstretched hand and put it in her mouth. Before swallowing it, she coughed and covered her mouth with her free hand, secretly spitting the pill into her fist.

"Oh, I dropped the pill," she mumbled.

"Don't worry. Here's another one," Harry said.

Louise swallowed the second pill and washed it down with a big gulp of water. She watched as Harry put the pill bottle in his pocket. After he left the room, she swallowed the first pill, too.

# CHAPTER 8

$\mathcal{L}$ ouise slept through most of the day, except for the lunchtime adventure.

Frances knew when it was time to make lunch because the *News at Noon* program was coming from the radio. She went to the kitchen and looked in the refrigerator. There was leftover ham, a dish of macaroni and cheese, the jar of applesauce, and milk—all items within her reach. Since she wasn't allowed to turn on the stove or use sharp knives, her options were limited. She decided on peanut butter and crackers and chocolate milk for herself. She ate a little of the applesauce, too. There were a few saltine crackers left in the box. Knowing that her mother liked saltines, Frances crumbled the crackers into a cereal bowl and poured on some milk. Then she stirred the mixture until the crackers melted. She tasted the results. Not so good, she decided. She topped the mixture with some applesauce and stirred again. The applesauce helped, but more help was needed. She poured on some chocolate sauce. That was better!

She stuck a spoon into the concoction and carried it to her mother's room.

"Time for lunch," Frances said.

Louise was half sitting up, having just returned from the bathroom. She was still so sleepy. "What is that?"

"Your lunch."

Louise tried to eat, but she couldn't manage the spoon. So Frances took the spoon and fed her mother. Louise actually ate most of Frances's invention. Then she drank some water and went back to sleep. She woke again at three o'clock. She didn't open her eyes, but she knew someone was watching her. Slowly, she opened one eye. There was Frances, standing beside her bed, holding a glass of water. She opened both eyes and looked at her daughter.

"I don't want any more water. I want some tea—nice hot tea."

"But I can't make tea. I'm not supposed to turn on the stove," Francis objected.

"You can go next door and tell Zina that I'm sick and need some tea. Ask her to help you make tea."

Frances crossed the backyards to the Stevens's house. Inside she found Zina and Dickey busily working at the kitchen table. Spread out in front of them were Dickey's crayons and a tablet of white paper.

"What are you doing?" asked Frances.

Dickey covered the paper he was working on with his hands so Frances couldn't see. We're making Valentine cards. I'm making one for my dad and one for you, too. You can't see because it's supposed to be a surprise."

"You can see the Valentine I'm making," said Zina.

Frances explained her errand, and Zina said she would be glad to help out with the tea making. Dickey gathered his Valentines, crayons, and tablet of paper, and they all crossed the backyards to the Hoags' house. Zina filled the tea kettle with water and set it on the stove to boil. Frances got out her own crayons, and the children spread the Valentine-making supplies on the kitchen table. When the tea was ready, Zina poured a cup and took it to Louise.

"How are you feeling?" she asked.

Louise took the tea from Zina and said, "Fine. Thank you."

Zina returned to the kitchen and looked around. The children were busy at work with the crayons and paper. Neither child could write, so they drew pictures. Since Frances could draw better than Dickey, she drew the pictures they wanted, and Dickey colored them. They were totally happy and content. Dickey finished the Valentine he was making for his dad and the one for Frances. He let Frances see both. Frances made cards for her father, Aunt Rose, Dickey, and Zina. She knew she was expected to make a Valentine for her mother, but she saved it for last. For her father, she drew a stick-figure man with a big smile standing beside a big green car. She drew a heart on Zina's card. She drew lots of hearts on Aunt Rose's card. For Dickey, she drew a rainbow. On her mother's Valentine, Frances drew a single flower standing alone in the center of the white paper.

"This place is a mess," said Zina. "I'll do some straightening up and wash those dishes."

\* \* \*

While the children and Zina worked, Harry Hoag was getting some good news—very good news, indeed. The vice president in charge of sales called Harry to his office and congratulated him on getting a promotion. Harry would now be in charge of sales for the surrounding states, not just Ohio, and he would be getting a big raise to go with his new responsibilities. Harry knew he deserved the promotion and that he could do the job, but he was surprised at how soon the position had been offered to him. He was astonished to learn how much a regional sales manager made in salary. He was even more amazed to learn that he would be getting a percentage of the commissions earned by the salesmen he would be supervising. Harry's grin was wide as he thanked the vice president and shook his hand.

"Harry, we're happy to have you on the team. I look forward to working with you."

Both Harry and the vice president knew that Harry's promotion was a wise move for the company. Harry was a good salesman and a great people person. Plus, he was thirty-six years old—too old for the draft that was bound to come and young enough for a life on the road. The vice president remembered when he had been a regional sales manager and how the job had kept him away from his family most of the time. He didn't mention the downside of travel. Harry would find out soon enough.

On the way home, Harry remembered it was Valentine's Day. He stopped at the drugstore and picked out Valentine cards for his daughter and his sister, Rose—the people who loved him. Next, he chose one for his wife. *Sometimes you need to get a card for someone just because it may be the only one they'll get.* He continued looking through the cards, hoping to find one for Zina. The more sentimental ones appealed to him when he thought of his neighbor. Instead, he selected a funny Valentine for Zina. He took his cards to the cash register, tended by George Mills.

"Hi, George, how much sun is shining on you today? And how much do I owe you?" Harry asked.

"Good to see you again, Harry. I haven't seen you since early this morning. So I guess the sun has been shining all day," George joked. "The cards are twenty-five cents each. That's one dollar, and you owe me another dollar-twenty-five for your wife and daughter's lunch earlier in the week. Grand total of two dollars and twenty-five cents."

"Seems about right," said Harry, pretending to be serious. "What about the medication I picked up this morning?"

"Medication goes on a separate account. I tally it up at the end of the month because I have to turn in a prescription-drug report to the county coroner's office. Makes no sense to me, but you know city hall."

Harry counted out the correct amount and handed the money to George.

"How about joining us at Jack Mercer's poker game next Wednesday?" George asked as Harry turned to leave.

"We'll see," said Harry, waving a cheery goodbye.

\* \* \*

Frances and Dickey had finished making their Valentines and were listening to *Jack Armstrong, the All-American Boy* on the radio. Zina was looking through the kitchen cabinets in the hopes of finding the ingredients for making a dinner for Harry and Frances and for Louise, if she would eat. Suddenly, there was a loud bang and a rush of cold air. Rose burst through the front door. She was dressed all in red, from her shoes to the sassy bow in her short-cropped black hair.

"Where's everyone?" Rose called.

"Here we are," said Frances, running to welcome her aunt.

After giving her niece a big hug, Rose went straight to the kitchen, greeted Zina, and opened the refrigerator, looking for a beer. Another whoosh of air flooded in through the back door as Harry pushed it open. Now everyone, except Louise, was in the kitchen exchanging Valentines and hugs. Rose reached in her purse and brought out a bag of Hershey's Kisses.

"These are for after dinner," she said, holding up the bag of candy. "Harry, how are you? Why do you look so happy? Is it because your little sister is here?"

"You look happy, too. What's going on with you?"

"Tell you later."

Soon everyone settled down. It was decided that Zina and Dickey would stay for diner. Rose was invited to join them, but she said she would have to take a rain check since she had a previous offer.

Zina said, "Okay, it's time to get cooking. No, I don't want any help. Not a one of you knows the way around a kitchen. I'll make a salad, mash some potatoes, and open a can of Spam."

The children went back to their radio program. Rose and Harry carried their beers to the living room. Zina began peeling potatoes. Harry told Rose about his promotion and raise. Rose told Harry about her Valentine's date with her boss, who was taking her to a new, fancy restaurant downtown.

"That place is so popular. How did you guys manage to get a reservation on Valentine's Day?"

"Harry, dear, I'm not the best secretary in the world for nothing. I, myself, made the reservation months ago and in my own name."

"That was brave. What if your boss had decided not to go along?"

"He isn't the only one who'd like to dine with me," Rose laughed.

Harry and Rose toasted each other with their beer bottles held aloft. Then they broke into the song they used to sing together on such occasions when they were children.

"For *we* are jolly good fellows, which *we* will never deny . . ."

Soon Zina and the children joined in the singing.

Upstairs Louise was listening and pouting. She buried her head in her pillow and sobbed. *No one cares about me. I'm the sick one. They should be thinking of me.*

As Rose was putting on her coat to leave, Frances came into the living room. Rose leaned over and whispered, "Can you keep a secret?"

Frances nodded, and her aunt slipped a Hershey's kiss into her niece's outstretched hand. Frances put the chocolate in her pocket. Later, she would hide the foil-covered treat in her secret purse.

# CHAPTER 9

*L*ouise stayed in bed for another two days, recovering from her headache. The pain was gone, but she was weak from lack of food. Frances kept a steady stream of water and applesauce flowing in her mother's direction. It was definitely more applesauce than anyone should be expected to eat. Finally, on the third day, Louise got out of bed, dressed, and went downstairs on shaky legs. She crossed the kitchen and opened the refrigerator, looking for something more substantial to eat. All she saw was milk, some spoiled items, and jars and jars of applesauce. Apparently, Frances and Harry had been living on sandwiches for a week. From the looks of the trash, Harry had been bringing home some take-out food, too. Louise opened the pantry door and surveyed the shelves. That was better. She took out a can of chicken noodle soup and poured it into a pan. As soon as it was warm, she ate the entire can of soup. Then she ate two slices of bread and butter. Returning to the refrigerator, Louise removed all the jars of applesauce and lined them up on the kitchen table. If a jar was unopened, she hid it in the very back of the pantry. If it had been opened, she threw it in the garbage.

Exhausted by this flurry of activity, she went into the living room and stretched out on the couch. She closed her eyes and let her mind go where it would. *Why had Harry and Frances been giving her so much applesauce? Was it possible to kill someone by feeding them too much applesauce?* Louise promised herself that she would never eat another bite of that horrid, mushy stuff again—as long as she lived. She dozed fitfully on the couch, struggling through nightmarish scenes of people drowning in applesauce. All the people in her dreams looked like her.

* * *

Harry broke into a happy smile when he saw his wife, up and dressed, wide awake and sitting on the couch. He put the take-out boxes he was carrying on the kitchen table and hurried over to give Louise a kiss on the cheek. He squeezed her shoulder. She didn't react.

"Oh, Louise, I'm glad to see you're up. You must be feeling better."

"I am better, despite all the applesauce you and Frances made me eat. What do you have in those boxes?"

"I picked up some German food from Jack's Deli on the way home. We've got hot German potato salad, sauerkraut, pumpernickel bread, and an assortment of cold cuts. I even got a cheesecake."

"Why did you get those awful sour pickles?" Louise asked, inspecting the contents of the boxes. "No one, except you and Rose, likes dill pickles. Frances and I hate them."

"Rose may stop by for a short visit when she gets off work."

"There's nothing here I can eat. Well, maybe the cheesecake," conceded Louise, sitting down at the kitchen table, fork in hand, with the cheesecake in front of her.

Harry sat across from Louise, sucking on a dill pickle. "Remember, when the doctor was here, he said he wanted to see you in his office in a week. I made an appointment for you to see him next Tuesday. My new boss said I could take a day of personal leave. I'll drive you to the appointment and stay with you while you talk to the doctor."

"I have no intention of going to the doctor. I'm perfectly well now," Louise said firmly between bites of cheesecake.

"The doctor and I want you to stay well. You need to have a checkup in case there is a physical problem causing your headaches."

"Of course there is a physical problem causing my headaches. I'm not imagining them," Louise snapped.

"You know this doctor is the best. He's the one who prescribed the codeine pills that helped with your headache. After your exam, he may recommend something that will work even better. He might be able to prescribe something you can take on a continuing basis as a preventive measure."

Louise stared at Harry for a full minute before saying, "Okay." She put down her fork and started up the stairs to her room. At the top of the stairs, she stopped and eavesdropped as Harry telephoned Zina.

"Hello, Zina. This is Harry. I hope you're doing okay . . . Louise is much better, thank you. . . . The reason I'm calling is to ask a big favor of you. I'm taking Louise to see the doctor for a follow-up visit next Tuesday, and we need you to watch Frances. Would that be okay? . . . Zina, you're an angel. We owe you. . . . No need to feel sorry for us. We'll do fine. I'm sure the doctor can help Louise. . . . Thanks, Zina. Bye."

On Tuesday, Harry and Louise put on their *hopeful hats* and headed for the doctor's office. Zina watched them drive away. Out loud, she said to herself, "I'll be a-hoping for them. But we don't always get our hopes."

\* \* \*

While the doctor examined Louise, Harry waited in the reception room, thumbing through an issue of *Field & Stream*, the hunting and fishing magazine. Neither pastime was of interest to him, but the pictures were nice. After a few minutes, he asked the receptionist for some paper and a pen and began making a list of questions he wanted to ask the doctor. Harry was worried about Louise. He was aware that something, other than physical, was wrong with his wife.

For over a year, Rose had urged him to get help for Louise. "She isn't right. All she ever thinks about is herself, and even I know that's not how a mother should think. Most of the time she ignores Frances. That sweet child is raising herself."

"I know. I know. I'm spending too much time either pacifying Louise or staying out of her way. I've got to find help, not only for her sake, but for Frances's sake, as well. Who'll be there for Frances if I have to be on the road traveling for weeks at a time?"

* * *

After a thorough examination, during which he found Louise to be in excellent health, the doctor asked her to get dressed and meet him in his office. He began by asking Louise what her biggest complaint was, aside from her recurring migraines.

"I have no complaints," she said.

"Well, what would you change about your life if you could wave a magic wand?"

"Probably Harry. He causes my headaches."

"What does he do to cause your headaches?"

"He snores and keeps me awake. I've had to move into my own room to get away from him. I'm sure sleeping with him isn't good for me."

"Is it the snoring? Or the sleeping with Harry? Or is it marital relations?"

Louise was shocked. "All of those things," she said, blushing hotly.

"I can assure you that none of those things cause migraine headaches. It must be something else. Your health is excellent. Your vital signs are good. Your heart and lungs are strong. I see no physical cause for your problems. You can afford to gain a few pounds, but other than that, I can find nothing wrong."

"This has been a complete waste of time for both of us," Louise proclaimed, rising from her chair.

"It's never a waste of time to keep tabs on your health, Louise. Please sit down. There are several options I can offer. First, I have not ruled out the possibility that your headaches may be a sign of an early menopause."

Louise's temper flared. She was very sensitive about her age. On her next birthday, she would be forty years old—four years older than Harry. She didn't like to share that information with others. She never discussed her age nor her birthday, which she refused to celebrate.

"I'm not *that* old."

"Of course you're not old. Some women go through menopause at a very *early* age," the doctor said.

Louise glared at the doctor.

"I can prescribe some medication you can take on a continuing basis. It may help. We can give it a try."

"You already prescribed codeine, and that helped some."

"The codeine works after the headache has begun. The medication I'm recommending is to be taken daily, even when you feel well. It's a preventive measure."

"Okay. I'm willing to try that. Are you sure my problems aren't husband- related?"

"I'm positive," the doctor assured her. "One more thing, I'd like for you to talk to a specialist whose expertise is in the area of your problems. I can recommend a very good doctor at the Cleveland Clinic. In fact, I can make an appointment for you."

Louise jumped from her chair, took two steps, spun around, and yelled at the doctor. "I know you. You want to send me to a psychiatrist. You think I'm crazy. I won't go! Now give me that prescription."

She snatched the paper from the doctor's hand and stormed out of his office. Motioning for Harry to follow her, she marched through the waiting room to the outer door. When they were in the car, Harry asked her what the doctor had said.

"He said I should take this new medication," Louise said, shaking the written prescription under her husband's nose.

Since Louise obviously wasn't going to elaborate, Harry talked about the weather as he drove to the pharmacy. Louise ignored him. He parked in front of the store and went around to open the car door for his wife. She refused to get out of the car. He sighed, turned, and walked alone toward the drugstore. Inside, Harry saw his friend, George Mills, working behind the pharmacy counter. He smiled broadly as he handed George the prescription.

"Hi, George. Can you fill this right away? Louise is waiting in the car."

George took the prescription from Harry and read it quickly. He was a little surprised, but his expression didn't change. The prescription was for a placebo.

"Are there any side effects with this medicine?" Harry asked.

"None at all."

*Except maybe your wife will be a little sweeter,* the druggist thought.

While Harry looked for flashlight batteries, George filled a large glass bottle with small white tablets. The druggist wondered what would happen to the drug companies that manufactured sugar pills if sugar were to be rationed, as was predicted. His thoughts then shifted from feeling sorry for drug companies to feeling sorry for Harry Hoag.

*How can he put up with that nutty wife?* George wondered.

Harry returned to the counter, batteries in hand.

"Your medicine is ready. Is Louise still taking codeine for her headaches? You know not to leave the codeine where your daughter could get it by mistake, right?"

"I'm very careful with the codeine. I keep it locked up. Louise only takes it when she has a really bad headache. What about this new medicine? Is it dangerous?"

"No, it's perfectly safe, and it has no side effects. By the way, Harry, I want to invite you to the poker game next week. We meet at eight o'clock in the room above Jack's Deli. We usually break up around eleven. It's not a high-stakes game, just friends getting together. Hope you'll join us."

"Sounds good," said Harry. "I'll be in town next week. Tell Jack I'll see him on Wednesday. Thanks."

* * *

After dinner the following Wednesday, Harry drove the Terraplane to Boyd Boulevard. Frances was in bed. Louise had settled in for the evening with a novel from the library. There had been no more headaches. The new job was going well. Rose was still her happy self. *Life is good*, Harry decided as he parked the car in front of the drugstore, next door to Jack's Deli.

The poker players, Jack Mercer, George Mills, Ben Cole, and Marvin Hall, were assembled. Harry knew everyone. Greetings, handshakes, and beers were passed around. Harry was glad he had decided to join this friendly group. Jack Mercer dealt, bets were placed, and the game was on. Harry wasn't a very good poker player, and he knew it. He hoped the others wouldn't notice. They did. He lost consistently for the first two hours. Then his luck began to change. His cards were no better, and his skills had not improved. But, to his surprise, he began winning.

A few beers later, Marvin Hall stood up and announced, "I've lost twenty dollars and that's my limit. I'll see you next week." And he was gone.

"What's going on with Marv?" asked Harry.

"He always leaves as soon as he loses twenty dollars, no matter what time it is. If he's winning, he'll stay until exactly eleven o'clock. You can count on it. Guess his wife won't let him lose more than twenty dollars of *her* money," Jack said, as everyone else laughed, nodded and helped themselves to another beer.

"What do you mean, *her* money?" Harry asked.

"Don't you know? Marvin Hall came from nothing, and he has nothing. It all belongs to his wife, including both hardware stores. She inherited everything her old man had, and he had plenty. She may be in a wheelchair, but she keeps a tight hold on the family purse strings," said Ben Cole.

Harry continued to win. Hand after hand, the others folded, leaving Harry and Jack to go it alone. Jack was obviously a better poker player than Harry, but he did stupid things. When it was time to call the evening to a close, Jack owed Harry forty-five dollars. Harry was surprised. He had enjoyed the company more than the cards, and being the winner didn't seem right.

"Harry, you'll have to come back next week and give me a chance to get even," Jack said.

Thanking Jack for a good evening, Harry promised he would join them the following Wednesday. He buttoned his overcoat and started down to the first level. The stairs seemed more wobbly than before. *What's wrong with these steps? They're shaky.* Harry gripped the handrail more tightly. Once out on the sidewalk, he saw the Terraplane was still in front of the drugstore, waiting to take him home. He reached for the car's door handle and stopped. He had no business driving. He had drunk too many beers. So Harry decided to walk home. After all, it was only two blocks to Collis Avenue.

On the way home, he began to realize that Jack had let him win. *Why? Was Jack hustling him?* Harry might not know much about poker, but he knew people. He resolved to be careful around Jack Mercer. *Did Marvin Hall's early departure have more to do with Jack than with his wife's money?*

Louise was waiting when he stumbled through the back door. "Harry, you've been drinking. I thought you were going to play cards, not get drunk."

He reached into his pocket, extracted a wad of bills, amounting to forty-five dollars, and handed it to Louise. "Not too drunk to win for you."

Louise was angry, but not so angry that she refused to take the money. "We'll talk tomorrow."

# CHAPTER 10

*T*he next morning it was Harry who woke with a headache. He felt awful. At least he knew the cause of his affliction, and he knew it would be temporary. He just needed some black coffee, a couple of aspirin, and some fresh air to clear his head.

*Just how much did I drink at that poker game, anyway?* He showered, shaved, and dressed while the coffee perked. He ate a piece of bread and drank three cups of black coffee before swallowing two aspirins.

On his way to the garage, he remembered the Terraplane was parked in front of the drugstore. *The walk will serve me right for last night's behavior. Besides, some outdoor exercise will do me good.* The walk gave Harry time to think. He resolved to slow down, if not totally quit, his drinking.

At the office, Harry checked his calendar book and saw it showed a heavy travel schedule. He had arranged visits with each salesman, who now reported to him, and with some of the company's more important customers in his region. That amount of travel would take several weeks, but it needed to be done. To help with his large, new responsibilities, a private secretary was assigned to Harry, and he was given access to a company car. The secretary could keep up with his schedule, and the Terraplane could stay home and rest.

*Can I leave Frances alone with her mother for several weeks at a time? What if Frances gets sick during the night? Will Louise take care of her?* Harry struggled with these questions the rest of the day as he went about his routine tasks.

Driving home that evening, Harry had an idea. He could ask Rose to help out. Maybe she would be willing to spend nights at their house while he was away. Frances would be thrilled to have her aunt staying with her, and Louise would see Rose's presence as an opportunity to unload some of the responsibility for looking out for Frances. Now, if only Rose would agree.

\* \* \*

Louise had been doing some thinking that day, too. In her mind, she replayed all the doctor had said about Harry's snoring not causing her headaches. *Could that be true?* The doctor had stressed that sleeping with Harry didn't cause the headaches, either. There must be another cause. Louise decided to get a second opinion. She would ask the pharmacist.

Later that day, at the drugstore, Louise marched straight up to the pharmacy counter and told George Mills that she had a question for him. "My husband, Harry, snores very, very loudly, and his snoring keeps me awake. I think that's what causes my headaches, but the doctor said snoring doesn't cause headaches. What do you think?"

George let out a sigh of relief. Louise Hoag's concern wasn't about the prescription he had recently filled. She hadn't discovered the sugar-pill hoax. He had been ready to deflect any blame thrown at him to her doctor.

"Oh, I can help with that. I was afraid the new medication wasn't agreeing with you." The pharmacist put on his serious face and continued, "If you couldn't hear your husband snore, then his snoring wouldn't cause problems. I suggest that you try wearing earplugs at night and see if that helps."

"Good. I'll take your advice," Louise said.

Walking home with the new earplugs in her purse, Louise continued to struggle for the root cause of her headaches. Earplugs might help, but she knew they weren't the answer. Then it hit her! Neither the snoring nor the sleeping with Harry was the culprit. It must be the odor of alcohol that clung to Harry's clothes when he had been drinking. He would have to stop his beer habit. After dinner, she would tell him he had to give up all alcohol—now and in the future.

Louise was so preoccupied with her thoughts that she walked right past her house on Collis Avenue. She stopped. She was standing in front of the Mercers' house, from which came a cacophony of loud voices. Several people were shouting at once, all in German. Louise felt very uneasy. The angry voices frightened her. She hurried home without looking back.

After dinner, Louise washed the dishes, and Harry dried them. Frances went to bed early. Louise and Harry turned to each other and said, at the same time, "I've made a decision."

"You go first," Louise said.

"I've decided to give up drinking for good," Harry announced. "My drinking isn't helping anyone. Not you. Not Frances. Not my job."

"I agree. Your drinking is the cause of my headaches. You stop drinking, and I'll wear earplugs. Maybe we can sleep together more often."

"Oh, Louise, that is good news. I'm so happy we agree on this. You can count on me to do my part." Harry beamed. "Does this mean you'll move back into *our* bedroom?"

"No. Not at all. It means exactly what I said: *You'll stop drinking and I'll wear earplugs.* I still need my own room."

That was not the answer Harry had wanted, but he understood about the art of compromise. "Is tonight a night I can sleep over?"

"I guess so," Louise said begrudgingly as she headed up the stairs to her bedroom.

Harry followed. He didn't want to press his luck by bringing up the idea of Rose's helping out while he was away. That discussion could wait until after he had talked to his sister.

\* \* \*

The next day Harry and Rose met for lunch. After they ordered, he began to explain his concerns about leaving Frances in the sole care of her mother while he was traveling.

"Rose, you know I'm having to spend more and more time on the road because of my job. Frankly, I don't feel comfortable leaving Frances alone with Louise when I am out of town. You know how she gets sometimes. She can be totally irresponsible when it comes to looking after that child. If Frances needs help at night, her mother ignores her. Louise has no idea where Frances is or what she is doing much of time. Thankfully, Frances turns to Zina during the day, but Zina is not there at night. I need your help. Frances needs your help. Could you possibly sleep over at our house when I'm away?"

"Oh, Harry, you know I want to help, but I don't want to move out of my apartment for days at a time whenever you're on the road. Of course I'll be there in an emergency, and I can check in occasionally, but not every single night, especially if Louise doesn't want me there. Talk to Louise and see what we can work out."

That evening Harry broached the subject with his wife. "Louise, I worry about you and Frances every time I go on a business trip. I can't be in two places at once. What do you think about having Rose stop by to help out or even sleep over occasionally when I'm away?"

"Rose could be a lot of help, I suppose. I'm not opposed to her staying over occasionally, but I don't want her here every time you're out of town."

A workable compromise was reached. Rose would not be spending nights on Collis Avenue, except in an emergency, but she would stop by on her way home from work each day. Louise agreed to telephone Rose anytime she needed extra help. For once, everyone was satisfied.

# CHAPTER 11

$\mathcal{T}$he days of March, with their winds and unpredictable weather, blew through the calendar without disturbing the Hoags. April came to northern Ohio, bringing crocuses and early daffodils. Grandmother Mercer announced, "Old Man Winter's back is broken."

Then came May and spring at last. The days were warm, even though some nights were still chilly. Flowers were popping up all over the Hoags' backyard. Louise was eager to plant summer annuals outside. She had already started some seedlings on the kitchen window sill, and she was determined to continue the tradition of planting nasturtium seed. Harry bought a hand-push plow from Marvin Hall's hardware store and prepared his first vegetable garden, ready for planting. Everyone was waiting for the final frost of the season.

Memorial Day arrived. It was beautiful, like a watercolor cut from a greeting card. The blue of the cloudless sky was the perfect canopy for the apple trees, which were in full blossom. The plain bushes that served as shrubbery across the front of the house revealed their secret. They were a mixture of flowering spirea and forsythia. After the long, cold winter, Louise was delighted to see the flowers. Her favorite was the huge white rosebush, covered from top to bottom with lovely old-fashioned pure white roses. She could not get enough of it. It was the finest rosebush she'd ever seen. It seemed to welcome her, and its flowers beckoned her with their sweet, exotic fragrance. When she stood near the white rosebush, she could feel her troubles vanish, and she felt whole again.

The Hoags had big plans for Memorial Day. Rose would come by at exactly ten o'clock, and they would drive to the little cemetery beside the Episcopal Church where they would tidy up the graves of Harry and Rose's parents. In preparation for this family tradition, Harry loaded the trunk of the Terraplane with gardening tools. Louise put in a pair of gardening gloves for herself. When they returned from the cemetery, they planned to begin their first efforts at gardening in their beautiful backyard.

Rose was right on time, as usual. One thing about Rose— she was prompt. Louise thought that might be her sister-in-law's best feature. After giving everyone a hug, Rose asked, "Louise, do you have some flowers we can take to the cemetery?"

"I'm sure we can find some," replied Louise, leading the way to the backyard, clippers in hand.

"Oh, I never knew how beautiful this garden was in the spring," Rose exclaimed. "So many gorgeous flowers! Frances, Louise, please help me choose."

Louise began picking a mixed bouquet. Rose looked at the big white rosebush and said, "We must have a few of those. Mama would love them."

Louise didn't want to pick her beautiful white roses for people she had never known. Seeing Harry's imploring look, she relented and picked exactly six white roses. She went into the house and returned with an empty peanut butter jar.

"We can bury this in the ground, fill it with water, and the flowers will stay fresh for at least a few days."

"That's thoughtful of you, Louise," Harry said, beaming at his wife with gratitude.

* * *

At the cemetery, it took them a little while to find the family plot. Most grave markers were hidden beneath a tangle of weeds. When they did locate his parents' graves, Harry began to clear a year's overgrowth with the pruning shears. Frances and Rose got down on their knees and pulled weeds. Louise stood beside a tree and looked around. Wherever she looked, there were graves. Graves and more graves. She began to shake. She knew that she couldn't stay there.

"I'll wait for you in the car," Louise called to the others as she turned and hurried toward the Terraplane.

Harry dug a hole for the peanut butter jar while Frances filled it with water from a nearby spigot. Rose arranged the flowers in the jar. Then she stood and reached for Harry's hand. Brother and sister, holding hands, stood near the graves of their parents, each saying a silent prayer. At the spigot, they cleaned their hands and rinsed away the dirt clinging to the garden tools. Walking toward the car, all three held hands, with Frances in the middle. Louise was sitting in the back seat of the car, all alone. The others snuggled together in the front seat as they drove back to the house on Collis Avenue.

Rose couldn't stay for the lunch Louise had prepared ahead of time. She was off and away. The others ate quickly, then hurried to the backyard, eager to begin their long awaited spring planting. Louise could feel her spirits lift as she worked among the flowers. She transplanted the seedlings she had started earlier. She let Frances help plant the nasturtium seed.

Frances liked planting the large seeds. They didn't get lost if she dropped one. Every time she pushed a big, fat, wrinkled beige seed into the earth, she asked, "What color will this one be? Red? Yellow? Orange?"

Following Marvin Hall's advice, Harry planted two rows of half-runner green beans, one row of sweet corn, a package of yellow goose-neck squash seed, and six tomato plants. This was his first attempt at vegetable gardening, and he didn't know what else to plant. He supposed more plants could always be added later. Harry tamped the earth gently over the seed and watered everything thoroughly. He was done with gardening for the day. There was plenty of time remaining to work on a project he had been planning for weeks. It would be a special surprise for Frances.

"Hey, Frances, come and help me," he called as he headed for the garage.

"Help with what, Daddy?"

"How would you like to have a swing in one of the apple trees?"

"A swing? A real swing with a seat and ropes? Yes, I want that," Frances said, jumping up and down. "Can I help make it?"

"Sure. First, we'll need a board just the right size for a seat, and we'll need a really long rope. You can help me pick out the perfect board, and you can choose the rope, too."

Harry and Frances looked through the pile of lumber stacked in the corner of the garage until they found a board the right width, but it was too long. Harry marked off the desired length and began to saw. It wasn't easy to cut through the thick board with a hand saw. Meanwhile, Frances looked for a proper rope. There were lots of ropes hanging from hooks on the garage wall. She thought one, in particular, looked about right and showed it to her father.

"How about this one?" she asked.

"It's too short. We need a much longer rope."

Harry kept sawing and Frances kept looking for a long rope. Finally, the seat was the right length. It was time to bore the holes. Frances helped hold the seat steady as best she could while her father turned the hand drill. Her attention span was growing thin. She decided that working with wood took too long.

"I really like this rope even if it's too short for a swing," Frances said, holding up the first rope she had taken down.

"It's not only too short, it's too coiled on the ends, but I guess we can make the coils go away if we soak the rope in water for a few minutes."

"I want a jump rope," Frances said.

"It's just about the right length for a jump rope," her father agreed.

They put the short rope in a bucket of water to soak while they chose a nice long rope for the swing. Harry sanded the swing seat with some rough sandpaper, threaded the long rope through the holes, and pronounced the swing ready to hang.

He took the short rope out of the water, straightened its coils, and tied a knot in each end. "Here's your jump rope, sweetie," he said, handing Roger Mills's hanging rope to Frances.

She ran to show her mother her new jump rope.

Louise took one look at the rope and, without knowing why, froze in utter horror. She couldn't speak. She couldn't move. Her mind raced frantically around the backyard looking for an escape. When the big white rosebush came into view, her fear exploded. There was a tall man standing beside the rosebush, and he was smiling directly at her. She recognized him immediately. He looked exactly like his picture, which hung behind the pharmacy counter at the drugstore. He was supposed to stay in the drugstore, but somehow, she knew he belonged here in this backyard.

Then Louise's mind did the strangest thing. It jumped out of her body and ran away, leaving her sitting on the ground near the flower bed she had been weeding, mouth hanging open, staring at the specter of Roger Mills, standing beside the big white rosebush.

\* \* \*

Louise didn't notice Frances running through the gate in search of friends to whom she could show her new toy, nor did she notice that Harry was hauling a ladder out of the garage in preparation for installing the new swing. She sat alone on the ground. Her whole body was shaking with fear. The entire elapsed time, between Louise's shock at seeing her daughter's new jump rope and the terror she felt at seeing the strange man, was less than two minutes. It seemed like so much longer. Reluctantly, her mind moved back into her body and began to settle down. The man, who had so recently and so visibly been standing beside the rosebush, was gone.

As her mind cleared, Louise began to realize that she had just suffered a fit of panic. Such spells were all too familiar to her. She had been having them off and on since she was in high school. They were infrequent and never lasted long. Her initial thought was that it must have been years since her last episode. Then she remembered the terror she felt trying to cross Boyd Boulevard, when she and Frances were leaving the drugstore. *What about the time I fainted from mistaken identity at the drugstore in Roanoke? What about the fear that gripped me this morning at the cemetery?* She hadn't told anyone about those episodes, and she wasn't going to tell anyone about what had just happened here in the backyard. *What about the man standing beside the rosebush looking at me? Was he real or was he a hallucination?*

She could remember having only one other hallucination. That had occurred when she was a child attending her mother's funeral. She couldn't remember the details, but it did have something to do with white roses.

*This is different,* Louise thought. *There really was a man standing over there a few minutes ago, and he was wearing argyle socks.*

Slowly, Louise's physical strength returned. She got up and sat in one of the Adirondack chairs until she felt steady enough to go inside. Once inside, she looked at her dirt-speckled hands and arms. The bathroom mirror told her that there was dirt on her face, too. *Have I been crying and rubbing my eyes?*

Dropping her dirty clothes on the bathroom floor, Louise stepped into the shower. She let the hot water beat down between her shoulder blades. It felt so good. She rubbed the soapy washcloth over her entire body and shampooed her hair. Shower over, she toweled off, dressed herself in her best bathrobe, and went downstairs. She was just settling onto the living room couch, with the newspaper and a cup of tea, when she heard Harry shouting.

"Help! Help! I need help!"

*If I can hear Harry's shouts, others can hear him, too. Besides, I'm not properly dressed to go outside.*

Zina did hear Harry's shouts and hurried over to the Hoags' backyard to see what was wrong. "Where are you, Harry? I can't see you. Where are you?"

"Up here. I'm up in the apple tree, and I can't get down. The ladder fell over. Please help me."

Curiosity, not concern, got Louise's attention. She stood at the open dining-room window, looking out at Harry in the tree, the ladder on the ground, and Zina shaking her head in amusement. She watched as Zina leaned the ladder against the tree and steadied it while Harry climbed gingerly down. The rope lay on the ground.

"What were you trying to do?" asked Zina.

"I was trying to put up a swing for Frances. The first thing I did when I got up on the limb was drop the rope. Then the ladder fell over, and I couldn't get down."

"Okay. I'll show you a better way to put up a swing. Watch what I do, and do what I say. You are about to learn the oldest trick known by every country boy and girl in Ohio. First, go find us a rock about the size of a baseball."

When Harry returned carrying the rock, Zina expertly tied one end of the rope around it. She instructed him to throw the rock over the apple tree limb, as she held the other end of the rope. Over the limb went the rock, pulling the rope behind it.

"Put a slipknot in the end of the rope without the rock. You do know what a slipknot is, right? Untie the rock and stick that end through the slipknot. Now pull away, Harry, as hard as you want."

As Harry pulled, the knotted end began to rise up into the air, as if by magic, until it reached the limb, stopped, and locked itself in place. The loose end of the rope dangled free. Harry was amazed. He gave the rope another tug, but he could not pull the apple tree over.

"Now, get out your pocketknife and cut the rope off about one foot above the ground. Do the same trick all over again with the other section of rope," Zina said.

Harry looked at the two ropes hanging loosely before him. "What about the seat?"

Zina showed him how to thread the ends of the rope through the drilled holes in the swing's seat and secure them with knots on the reverse side.

"Zina, you're a genius," Harry said, giving her a hug.

"No, I'm just a country girl with five older brothers," she replied, hugging him back.

"Well, I'm grateful for your rescue and for your teaching me how to hang a swing. Thank you. Thank you. I don't know how I'll ever repay you."

Zina winked at Harry and grinned, "I'll think of something." As she turned to leave, she said, "By the way, you could've used a hangman's noose instead of a slipknot."

Louise backed away from the open window. The whole exercise had been interesting, but why did Zina have to say something so scary?

# CHAPTER 12

Memorial Day marked the end of the spring term. School was out for the summer. Frances was excited. She was looking forward to having Carol available as a playmate every day. Dickey was not much fun anymore. Bobby always had to drag his little sister, Molly, along, and she was no fun at all. Molly was three years old, and she couldn't even talk. She cried a lot. Her mother said she was just shy. Louise and Zina said something was wrong with Molly.

On the last day of school, Carol brought home her final report card, a few leftover school supplies, and a six-year-old body filled with the chicken-pox virus, ready to explode into running sores. The other members of the Mercer family were immune. They had all had chicken pox long ago. Carol shared her malady with her friends. Frances, Dickey, Bobby, and little Molly all came down with chicken pox at the same time. After the first three days, the children were up and about, feeling fine, covered with oozing poxes, and spreading their contagion everywhere they went. Harry, Louise, and Rose were also immune since they had the disease as children. The only two adults who didn't escape the current chicken-pox outbreak were the Hoags' next door neighbor, Evelyn Fisher, and Rose's boss.

Poor Evelyn. She was so sensitive about her birthmark. Now, she had chicken pox. "Life isn't fair. At least it's not fair to me," Evelyn protested aloud to her image in the mirror.

She had a fever, and she ached all over, plus, she was covered with those awful sores. She covered her bathroom mirror with a towel so that she wouldn't have to look at herself. Actually, Evelyn was lucky—she had quite a light case and recovered quickly. Not so, Rose's boss.

He was really sick. His temperature remained elevated for over a week. He couldn't get out of bed, and he had to close his office for the duration of his illness. When his pox erupted, they plunged him into an ocean of pain and itch. He didn't seem to be getting better. He was only getting worse. His wife telephoned the doctor.

"This is one disease that will just have to run its course," the doctor said. "I can prescribe some lotion to ease the itching, and he can take some aspirin, but that's about all. My biggest concern is that often a man his age may be left sterile after one of these childhood diseases."

That was the best news that either the boss or his wife had heard lately. They already had five children and were not looking for more. In fact, they had named their youngest child Hope, hoping she would be the last. It was the family joke. Hope didn't think it was funny at all. The boss accused the children of giving him the chicken pox, but they had all had the disease two years earlier.

"Where on Earth did you get chicken pox? You didn't catch it from the kids when they had it. Why now?" his wife asked.

"I have no idea. I just want to get well," he groaned.

He hated having chicken pox for many reasons. One, he felt miserable. Two, he looked awful. Three, he was afraid the guys would make fun of him. Four, he missed spending time with Rose. And, five, he missed his trysts with Evelyn Fisher.

* * *

Rose's boss was a lawyer, but not a very successful lawyer. He had his own practice and one employee, Rose. He wanted to expand the practice and take in a partner, but there were not enough clients. His practice consisted almost entirely of drawing up wills, doing title searches, and facilitating real estate closings. Occasionally, a client would show up wanting to sue someone. However, the boss was a good negotiator, and he usually persuaded the opposing parties to settle out of court.

"One half of all lawyers finish law school in the bottom half of their graduating class. I'm in that group," he liked to say.

Everyone laughed at this joke. Rose wasn't so sure it was a joke.

She liked her job. She was well paid and didn't have to work too hard. She could get time off whenever she wanted to do a personal errand. Plus, she was learning a lot about the law. Since her boss didn't like spending time at the Registrar of

Deeds office, researching deeds and property transfers, he regularly assigned that task to Rose. It was interesting work. She did all the typing for the practice. She especially liked typing up wills. Who owned what property, when they had bought it, how much they had paid, and who was named in their wills gave Rose access to a storehouse of information.

Rose enjoyed having a good time, and her boss could be fun if he could get away from the office and away from his wife. Rose loved to go dancing, and her boss was a good dancer. On evenings when he told his wife he had to work in the Registrar of Deeds office, he and Rose often went out for a nice meal and then dancing. Their personal relationship was an ongoing arrangement. Rose just wanted to have fun. She didn't take their affair seriously. He wanted a break from worrying about how to house, feed, and clothe five growing children. A harmless fling with his secretary was a welcome distraction.

The boss had other extracurricular interests, as well. In addition to Rose, there was Evelyn Fisher, who lived with her widowed mother on Collis Avenue, next door to Rose's brother and his family. Sometimes, the lawyer liked to spend time with Evelyn. She thought he was brilliant. She listened with awe as he embellished his imaginary legal accomplishments. She was not attractive, but she was grateful for his romantic attentions.

\* \* \*

Rose's boss sat in his small office looking through the plate-glass window at the sidewalk crowd scurrying by on errands or to lunch. "I just saw your brother go into the post office," he said to Rose, who was typing away in the next room. "And there goes Jack Mercer. He seems to be in a hurry."

The boss continued to watch Jack Mercer's progress down the street. Jack walked briskly to the corner and sat on a bench at the bus stop. Soon, two men approached Jack and sat down on the bench beside him. There were no formal greetings. All three looked dead serious. Jack did most of the talking. The other men nodded. Shortly, Jack stood up and handed one of the men an envelope. They shook hands. Jack walked back in the direction he had come. The two men walked away in the opposite direction.

Rose came into her boss's office, adjusting her perky new hat. "I am going to lunch now."

"Doesn't your brother play poker with Jack Mercer?"

"On Wednesday nights, if he is in town."

"Well, tell him to watch his back around Jack Mercer," the boss warned.

When Rose returned from lunch, her boss was ready to leave for the day. "I have to go home and take care of the two youngest while my wife takes the three oldest to get new shoes. I don't know which is the hardest—babysitting the kids or paying for their shoes," he said in resignation.

"Fine. I'll finish up the typing and get the letters in the afternoon mail. Then maybe I can leave a little early, too."

"Sure. That'll be fine."

While Rose finished the paperwork, she thought about her boss's warning. She decided to stop by Harry's house, on the way home, and talk to him about Jack Mercer.

The afternoon turned out to be busier than Rose had expected. One client stopped by to pick up some papers, and two prospective clients called to set up times to go over their wills. There was even a call from the boss's dentist, reminding him of an appointment. Rose had to rush to the post office before it closed for the day. She didn't get away early after all.

\* \* \*

Harry was already home from work when Rose arrived. He was sitting on the front porch idly watching Frances and Carol jumping rope on the sidewalk in front of the house. He seemed deep in thought.

"I need a beer," Rose announced, climbing the steps to the porch.

"We don't have any beer. I've stopped drinking altogether. The beer was starting to interfere with my real life, so I gave it up. It's been over a month since I've had a drink," Harry said.

"What do you have?" asked Rose as Louise opened the screen door and came out onto the porch carrying two glasses of iced tea—one for Harry and one for herself.

"Tea," said Harry. "That's it. Tea."

"Well, tea will have to do," said Rose, taking the glass of tea Louise had intended for herself. "Thanks, Louise."

Louise went back inside to begin dinner and sulk. Harry and Rose sat on the porch, sipping iced tea and watching the girls jump rope as they chanted, "Old Mr. Leary, lives in the cemetery, he looks so scary . . ."

"Looks like Frances is enjoying her new toy," said Rose.

123

"I made that jump rope for her. I hung up a swing for her, too," Harry bragged.

"Hanging a swing must be hard."

"Not really, if you know how. Sometime I will teach you proper swing-hanging techniques," Harry said in his big-brother voice as his thoughts centered not on the swing, but on how warm and welcoming Zina's hug had felt. He smiled to himself.

"I don't need to know how to hang a swing," Rose retorted. "I'm not interested in hanging anything. I just stopped by to give you a message from my boss."

"What message?"

"He said you should watch your back around Jack Mercer. I don't know why, but that is what he said."

"Tell him thanks for the advice, but I already figured that one out for myself."

Rose had complete confidence in her brother. "Good. I know you can take care of yourself. When I got here, you were off in a world of thought. So, what had you looking so serious?"

"This new job of mine has both rewards and challenges. I am traveling more, working harder, and making more money than I had expected. I can handle the travel and the responsibility, but I'm not sure how to handle the money coming in without changing our lifestyle. Louise wants us to move to a new and larger house. I think the timing is wrong for that. A war is coming. We don't need to assume a big mortgage if there is another bust—like in 1929. If we're not going to move, Louise says we should get some new furniture. New furniture is fine with me. However, I want to make some long-range financial plans. We grew up in a depression, and I don't want to spend my old age worrying about money. There are investment opportunities everywhere, but I just don't feel right taking a big risk. We have to think about Frances's future. I'm determined to save enough to send her to a good college."

Rose gave her brother a surprised look. "I didn't know you were making so much money that you're worried about how to spend it all. What a problem to have! Not knowing how to spend money will never be a problem for me. Have you talked to any of your friends about investments? How are they saving for the future?"

"Most of my friends are just getting by from month to month. George Mills is still making payments for the drugstore inventory he bought from his cousin's estate. Ben Cole just rocks along—not rich, not poor. Marvin Hall has no assets of his own. Everything they have belongs to his wife, and it's all tied up in property her father left to her or in trust funds for her and the children. Jack Mercer is the only one who has anything extra. For the life of me, I cannot see how he supports himself, a wife, three children, his mother, and his mother-in-law from what he makes in that deli of his. The Mercers seem to have anything they want. Jack is always flush."

"My boss struggles along, too, trying to make ends meet from the law practice's meager profits. All those new shoes, an enormous grocery bill, rent, utilities, and fees for five children in parochial school! No wonder the poor man needs a little fun in his life. Where do you think Jack Mercer gets all his money, if not from the deli?"

"I don't want to know."

"Why don't you buy some of those bonds that the government is selling? I hear they are safe and will mature in ten years—just a couple of years before Frances will be going to college. My boss always reads the financial news, and he says the government is trying to decide whether to raise taxes or to sell bonds to finance the war. He is betting the bond idea will win out."

Harry was dumbstruck. Why hadn't he thought of that? His little sister, Rose, was the smart one. She didn't know how smart she was. Harry jumped from his chair and ran over to where Rose was sitting. He gave her a big hug and planted a kiss on top of her head. He didn't even notice that she was wearing a hat.

"Harry, you are a nut, but I love you," Rose said as she put down her iced tea glass and prepared to leave.

"Thanks for stopping by, and tell your boss I'll take his advice and watch my back."

Later at the dinner table, Harry announced, "On Saturday we'll go shopping for the furniture you want, Louise. I think we should get a new refrigerator, too."

"I'd like for us to get a new couch, but I don't know about a refrigerator. They're so expensive."

"Think of a new refrigerator as an investment. When we get into the war, we may not be able to buy appliances made of steel, at any price. All of the steel is already headed for the war effort. Sugar has been rationed for over a month now, and other consumer goods won't be far behind."

# CHAPTER 13

When Harry arrived at his office the following morning, he went directly to the personnel office, where he made arrangements to have a sizable amount deducted from his paycheck each month for the purchase of government bonds. He made sure the amount withheld could be increased or decreased at his discretion. The bonds were to be issued in his name, with Frances as the beneficiary. He decided that Louise didn't need to know about the bonds. They were for Frances's education. Not by accident, Harry confided his investment scheme to his boss. He watched as the vice president's high opinion of him rose even higher.

"Harry, you're not only a great salesman and a good manager, you're the most patriotic person I know," said the vice president, congratulating himself for having chosen Harry as his protégé. "This will make all of us look good."

\* \* \*

Louise, too, was busy that morning. She hurried through her breakfast—no time for a second cup of tea. She was eager to get started. If they were getting new furniture, she needed to do some cleaning and to discard some unwanted items. She began in the dining room since it was the room that got the most usage. It was where they ate and where they listened to the radio. Its windows gave the best light and had the best view of the backyard. She began by decluttering the room—gathering things *she* didn't want to put in the trash bin. Out went a stack of outdated magazines and Frances's old coloring books. In a drawer, she found the flask/flashlight Rose had given Harry the previous Christmas. It had to go. She was almost done. The last piece of disposable junk was the cardboard radio box Frances kept under the dining room table—the one she was always crawling into and doing who knew what. Louise pulled the box from under the table and mashed it as flat as she could. Then she hauled it to the trash.

As she ran the carpet sweeper over the rug in the center of the room, Louise wished she owned an electric vacuum cleaner. Maybe they could buy one on Saturday. The morning was gone. It was lunchtime, and here came Frances, hungry as usual, carrying that terrible jump rope.

"Put that jump rope away. Lunch is ready," Louise snapped at her daughter.

Frances went into the dining room, intending to store the jump rope in her radio box. "Where's my box? It's gone!"

"I threw it out while I was cleaning. I mashed it flat and put it in the trash."

"I want my box back," shouted Frances as she started to cry. Her tears turned to sobs.

"Young lady, don't you ever shout at your mother. That old box was just a piece of trash."

Frances stared at her uncaring mother and muttered, "I'm not going to speak to you for the rest of the day."

She jumped up from the lunch table and ran to the trash bin behind the garage. She wanted to rescue her box. Maybe she could fix it. Frances had to stand on an overturned wheelbarrow to peer inside the trash bin. The box was, as her mother had said, just trash. Frances looked at the remains of her cardboard playhouse and cried quietly to herself. As she was getting down from the wheelbarrow, she saw something shiny lying in the grass. It was her father's flashlight/flask. Frances lifted the flask from the grass and examined it. It didn't appear to be damaged. She hugged it close to her chest and stroked it. If she couldn't save her box, she would save the flashlight/flask. A worrying thought ran through her mind. *Mom* gave *the Christmas scarf from Aunt Rose to Zina. She threw Daddy's gift away and ruined my box. Did she do something bad to my beaded purse?*

Frances stuffed the flask down the front of her dress and raced back to the house. She hurried through the living room, right past her mother. She ran up the stairs and into her room. Her most prized possessions were kept in the bottom drawer of her dresser. Her secret beaded purse should be there. Frances opened the drawer and looked inside. There was the secret purse, all safe and sound. She took the purse out of the drawer and held it tight. It was a good purse, and she would not leave it alone again. Frances put the flashlight/flask in the very back of the drawer and hung the purse's handle around her wrist.

Still unhappy about the fate of her box, she went to the backyard and played on her swing until Dickey came over. They took turns pushing each other in the swing, the secret purse still dangling from her wrist.

After finishing her lunch, Louise began cleaning the living room. It was a nice room with a brick fireplace at one end. Two windows flanked the fireplace, one on either side. A third, and larger window, looked out onto the front porch. The front door opened directly unto the porch. Beside it stood an antique washstand that had belonged to Harry's grandmother. The stairs going to the bedroom level were at the opposite end of the room from the fireplace, near the front door. Under the stairs was a coat closet. An unattractive couch stood against the remaining wall, facing the front door. Two equally unattractive chairs flanked the fireplace. Beside the couch, a pair of French doors led into the dining room.

"This room needs all the help Harry can afford," Louise told the fireplace as she dusted its mantelpiece.

* * *

Saturday came, and the Hoags set off on their furniture-shopping expedition. Harry dropped his wife and daughter in front of the store while he looked for a parking place. Without waiting for Harry to join them, Louise went inside the furniture store. She immediately spotted a pair of elegant wingback chairs across the showroom floor. She was sitting in one, talking to a salesman, when Harry joined them.

"I want these chairs," she said.

"I thought you wanted a couch," Harry countered.

"I do. These chairs will go beautifully with any couch I pick out."

"I think we should check out the refrigerators first," Harry said, hoping to divert Louise's attention from the expensive-looking chairs.

The smiling salesman shook Harry's hand and introduced himself. He said, "We can do both. Why don't you and this beautiful little girl go to the back left corner, where we keep the appliances, and let my brother show you our newest refrigerators? I'll help your wife decide on living-room furniture. It has been my experience that the men know more about electrical items and the ladies are better at decorating."

*He is slick,* Harry thought to himself. *He understands the separate-and-sell technique very well.*

Harry took a long time looking at the refrigerators. He wanted to know about the special features of each. Frances liked looking at the refrigerators, too. They were so big, and the salesman's brother said they could keep all the ice cream they wanted in the freezer section. Harry decided that the Amana model best suited their needs.

"I think this one will work for us," he told the salesman. "But my wife should look at it first. She's the one who'll be using it the most."

"Good idea," said the salesman. "She'll love the adjustable shelves and the nice, large freezer compartment. As a special favor to her, we can promise delivery this afternoon."

"Will it come in a big box?" asked Frances.

"It sure will. After your new refrigerator is installed in your kitchen, we'll take the old refrigerator away and dispose of the box."

"No. I want the box. Daddy, you promised . . . " Frances said, tugging at her father's sleeve.

"Of course you can have the box," Harry assured his daughter.

"You stay here and admire *your* new refrigerator, and I'll go over to see if your wife is ready to be impressed with your choice," the salesman said, deliberately leaving Harry facing a row of new kitchen stoves.

Harry glanced across the store in Louise's direction. *What is taking her so long? Is she looking at more things than just the chairs? She'll have to choose between the chairs and a couch. We can't get both and a refrigerator, too. As it is, I'll need to have a little less bond money deducted from my paycheck this month.*

"Harry, I've found the most wonderful couch. It goes perfectly with the wingback chairs. Come and see," Louise said, hurrying excitedly to the appliance sales area.

"Louise, what do you think about this refrigerator?" Harry asked.

"Oh, it's fine," she said, giving the refrigerator a cursory glance. "Now, come and see the couch I chose."

Harry looked at the couch. It was both beautiful and elegant—a perfect companion for the chairs. It was a Duncan

Phyfe style with a gracefully carved piece of wood across its back and lovely curved legs that ended with brass lion-claw feet, complete with individual toes. It was the most expensive item in the entire store. Harry gasped when he looked at the price tag.

"Louise, this couch is way too expensive. It costs more than I make in a month. You'll have to decide between the chairs and the couch. We can't afford both."

"I want both."

"Choose one."

"Okay. Then I'll take the chairs," Louise snapped with irritation.

On the drive back to Collis Avenue, Louise was quiet. Harry could tell that she was more than just a little annoyed at not getting her way. He hoped the new chairs and the new refrigerator would brighten her disposition.

The furniture store's delivery truck arrived midafternoon. Louise directed the movers to place one wingback chair on either side of the living-room fireplace. They looked great. By comparison, the old couch looked even more tired than usual. The new refrigerator was installed in the kitchen, and the old one loaded onto the truck for disposal. The refrigerator's box was left behind. Harry helped Frances move it into the dining room and slide it under the table.

Frances looked up at her father with a happy smile. "This new box is better than the old one. It's almost as good as a bicycle."

\* \* \*

The following afternoon, Harry packed his suitcase in preparation for the two-week business trip he was scheduled to begin on Monday. He would be driving the assigned company car for the first time. He was both excited and nervous about this trip. He had never left Louise and Frances alone for this length of time. He prayed that all would go well on the home front. He telephoned Rose to tell her about his trip. She assured him that she would be available to help out if Louise needed her.

Monday morning Harry kissed Louise and Frances goodbye and headed for the first stop on his itinerary—Williamsport, Pennsylvania.

Louise left Frances with Zina and Dickey that same afternoon while she went shopping. She took the city bus downtown and got off at the corner nearest Farris's Furniture Store, where the new refrigerator and the wingback chairs had once lived. The salesman who had helped her on Saturday was waiting just inside the door. His face was one big smile of recognition and anticipation.

"Hello, again. How can I help you? Are you back to take another look at *your* couch?" he asked.

"Oh yes. I have been thinking about that couch and some other things, too."

*This woman is too good to be true,* the salesman thought as he resisted the urge to pat himself on the back. *Luck is with me today, and to make the candy even sweeter, her husband isn't with her.*

To Louise he said, "Great. I knew your good taste in decorating would not let you stay away long. I have my pad and pencil right here. What other items are you interested in seeing today?"

*The couch sale is locked up. So get her to buy some other things first,* he reminded himself.

"What about a nice pair of end tables to go beside *your* lovely couch? You'll want some new lamps to go on *your* end tables, too, and you really need a coffee table to complete the look. Coffee tables are all the style now."

"Okay. Let me see your end tables."

One hour and fifteen minutes later, as the salesman was tallying the items on his sales slip, Louise said, "I've been thinking about a mantelpiece clock, too. What do you have in clocks?"

A handsome Seth Thomas steeple clock was added to the list. It had Roman numerals, and it proclaimed the hours and half hours with melodious chimes. It was the finest clock Louise had ever seen—the perfect accessory to complete *her* newly refurbished living room. She beamed with pride, imagining how envious the neighbors would be.

"If you pack the clock in a box, I'll take it with me now. When can you deliver the other things?" Louise asked.

"We can deliver everything to your house around noon tomorrow, if that's okay. How would you like to pay for these things?"

"Put everything on my husband's account, and send him a bill. He'll take care of it."

The salesman held the door for Louise as she left the store carrying a shopping bag with handles, in which sat the carefully boxed clock. Before he could pat himself on the back, his brother gave him a playful punch on the shoulder. Each slapped the other heartily on the back and said in unison, "Gee, I love that woman."

When Louise returned home, she carried the shopping bag containing the new clock to her bedroom and hid it in the closet before going next door to retrieve Frances. She didn't want Frances to see the clock.

As promised, the furniture was delivered the following day. Indeed, the new couch did look wonderful in the Hoags' living room. Its accompanying end tables, with their matching lamps, and the new coffee table further enhanced the look. The new wingback chairs welcomed their furniture-store friends. The old couch was hauled away by the delivery men, but not before Frances appropriated its crocheted afghan for her new refrigerator box.

\* \* \*

Two weeks later, Harry returned from his business trip, tired but satisfied. The trip had been a success. He now knew enough about his salesmen and many of their customers to begin some long-range planning. But first, he wanted to see his family. He parked the company car in front of the house and entered through the front door. Harry did not recognize his own living room. Everything was different. *Where did all this new furniture come from? Is this someone else's house?* Harry stared in amazement. Then he remembered the new couch from the furniture store.

"Louise, what have you done?" he called out.

"Hi, Harry. I just thought we should go ahead and get some of the things we need to go with the new chairs," said Louise breezily as she came into the living room from the kitchen.

"We agreed, Louise, that the chairs and the refrigerator would be our only purchases. We cannot afford all these other things. They'll have to go back to the store."

"Harry, before you say anything else, just sit on the new couch and see how comfortable it is. Then if you don't like it, we'll talk more."

Harry, still in shock, sat down. He admitted to himself that the couch was indeed comfortable. However, if they kept all this new furniture, there would be no government bond buying for at least three months. What was he to do? He didn't want to lie to his wife. They could afford the furniture, but he didn't want to tell her about his bond-buying scheme. Harry was in a quandary. He looked up at Louise and said nothing.

"Harry, this couch will take the look of poverty off your face. It will outlast you," Louise said, ending the discussion.

# CHAPTER 14

*I*f *the look of poverty* had ever been on Louise's face, it was gone now. She made sure everyone within earshot knew about *her* new furniture. She bragged to all the neighbors, all the casual acquaintances at the bus stop and in the grocery store, the mailman, and all tradespeople who came her way. Louise beamed when her listeners nodded their heads at her lavish description of her new furniture. Before long, it was obvious that her bragging had outstayed its welcome in others' ears. People began to avoid Louise, even more than they usually did.

One morning, after listening to another of Louise's monologues about her furniture, Zina said, "Louise, you're furniture-proud, and that's not a good thing."

The bragging stopped.

*Maybe Zina's right. Telling the neighbors about my beautiful living-room furniture might not be the best idea. Maybe they should see it for themselves. Next week is Frances's birthday, and I could invite them over for birthday cake. While they're here, they can see just how lovely my living room is.*

Then Louise remembered Frances's last birthday party. What a disaster! Frances had embarrassed her and caused her to come down with a sick headache. *I won't make that mistake again! Besides, the neighbors could spill food on my new couch.*

Over the dinner table, Louise announced, "Friday is Frances's sixth birthday. We'll celebrate."

"Can I have a birthday party and invite my friends?" asked Frances.

"No," her mother replied. "We tried that last year, and it didn't work out for *me*. This year I'll make a cake and invite Rose to dinner. It will be a family celebration."

"Can I have a chocolate cake?"

"No, I'll make a pound cake and fried chicken. After we finish eating, you can open your presents."

Frances went to sleep that night with her fingers crossed, hoping she would get a bicycle for her birthday. She was glad her aunt was coming for dinner. Aunt Rose was fun.

\* \* \*

Louise was up early on Thursday morning—the day before the birthday dinner. She needed to go to the store to buy butter and eggs for the pound cake and a frying chicken. Frances went along, pulling her little red wagon to carry the groceries.

Walking home, Louise said, "I think I'll make the cake today. It's Thursday and that'll be fine. If I make the cake tomorrow, it won't turn out well."

"Why not?" asked Frances.

"Because tomorrow is Friday, and no one should start a new project on a Friday. Never plant a garden, cut out a dress, or bake a cake on a Friday. Fridays are bad luck."

"Is my birthday bad luck?" Frances asked. Her mother didn't answer.

While the cake was baking, Louise went into the backyard to admire the flower beds with their late summer blooms. The zinnias, marigolds, petunias, and nasturtiums waved to her in a blaze of color. On the opposite side of the yard, the big white rosebush towered above and outshone them all. It seemed to beckon to Louise. *What a wonderful rosebush. It's the Queen of the Garden*, Louise thought, as she walked toward it with admiration.

As Louise neared the rosebush, she felt a sudden, cold chill. She stopped. She felt as though she were being watched. She stood still and looked all around. She remembered seeing a man standing beside the rosebush several months ago, but today he wasn't there. Louise couldn't see him, but she could feel him. *He has an aura about him, and it's not a good one. I won't tell anyone about this. Whoever it is wants to talk to me, not them.*

\* \* \*

At exactly six o'clock the next evening, Louise watched as Frances ran down the porch steps to greet her beloved Aunt Rose, who was getting out of her small Ford coupe, carrying several items—a box from the bakery, the strings of two helium-filled balloons, and a flat package, wrapped in comic strip paper.

Frances ran to her aunt and hugged her around the waist. Since Rose had no free arms for hugs, she leaned over and kissed the top of Frances's head. Then Rose began singing, "Happy Birthday to you . . ." at the top of her voice. Frances clapped her hands in delight. Louise frowned. *No one ever sings "Happy Birthday" to me.*

Inside, Rose went straight to the dining room. "Hi, Harry," she said as she placed the bakery box and the flat package at the far end of the table.

"Hi to you, too. Glad you could come for the birthday," he said, tying the balloons to the back of Frances's chair.

Louise brought in the fried chicken and the side dishes. Everyone wished Frances a happy birthday, and they began to eat.

During dinner, the adult conversation turned to news of the war in Europe. Norway, Denmark, Poland, Belgium, and the Netherlands had all fallen to the Nazis, and in such a short time. Sweden remained officially neutral, but everyone knew they were Nazi sympathizers, either by inclination or by the need for self-preservation. Harry thought Sweden's stance was due to geography. Russia had decided to get into the war, as well, and had attacked Finland, which quickly surrendered. The Finns, like the Swedes, were pragmatists. With the relaxation of the arms embargo, the United States was selling fighter planes and weapons of all kinds to England and France.

The Secretary of Treasury, Henry Morgenthau, had finally convinced President Roosevelt to approve the program of bond purchases to finance the war effort, rather than to increase taxes. The National Defense Savings Program was set up to oversee the marketing and sale of the defense bonds. Bond-buying drives, radio commercials, and propaganda posters were everywhere. A defense bond sold for $18.75 and could be redeemed after ten years for $25.00. Ten-cent savings stamps were also available.

Louise asked, "How do people go about buying defense bonds?" Harry and Rose glanced at each other, then looked away.

Harry changed the subject. "Time for birthday cake."

Louise brought her pound cake from the kitchen, just as Rose was removing a chocolate cake from the bakery box.

Frances squealed with delight. "I want chocolate!"

Louise glowered. Rose looked embarrassed. Harry rolled his eyes. Frances dug into her piece of chocolate cake with enthusiasm. Louise helped herself to a generous piece of pound cake and turned to Harry, smiling. "Which would you like, Harry?"

Ever the diplomat, Harry said, "I'll have a little of each."

"What about you, Rose?"

"Oh, you know me, always watching my figure. I'll just enjoy watching everyone else enjoy.

"Time for presents!" announced Rose. "Frances, this is from me," she said, handing the flat package to Frances.

Inside the flat package was a thin cardboard box containing seven handkerchiefs, one for each day of the week. "What do those words say?" asked Frances, pointing to the embroidered lettering.

"Those are the names of the days of the week. This one says, 'Sunday'. This one says, 'Monday,' and on like that," Rose said. "Frances, do you know the days of the week?"

"I know the names of some days, but I don't know which day comes first. I know that Carol's Daddy has to go to work on Saturday, but my daddy can stay home."

"I'll help you learn all the days of the week when I get back from New York," Rose said.

"New York?" Harry and Louise exclaimed in unison. "You're going to New York City?"

"Yes," answered Rose. "My boss is going there on a business trip next week. He is going to a tax conference being held for lawyers. He's decided to expand his practice by doing tax returns, and he needs to brush up on the latest income-tax laws. He's asked me to go with him."

"Rose, are you going to be doing tax returns?" asked Louise.

"Of course not. I am just going along for the ride. We'll take the train," Rose said, and she turned to Frances, making loud *choo-choo* sounds and laughing.

"Rose, you be careful," Harry said.

"Louise, would you like to give Frances your present next?" asked Harry, before his wife could interrogate his sister further.

"No, you go next. I have something special for Frances, and I want to save it until last."

"My gift is out in the garage. I'll go and get it now," said Harry.

Frances closed her eyes and held her breath, daring to hope for a bicycle.

"Okay. Frances, here's your birthday present from me. Happy Birthday," Harry said as he returned pushing a bright blue scooter with a large red bow tied to the handlebars.

Frances's eyes widened. She had hoped for a bicycle, but here was a scooter, and that might be almost as good. She had never even thought about wanting a scooter. She had ridden Carol's hand-me-down scooter many times, and it was pretty good. She liked the idea of having her own scooter—a new blue one.

"Can I ride it now?" asked Frances.

"No, you have one more present to open," her mother said.

Louise went into the living room and returned carrying a shopping bag by the handles. It looked heavy. "I'll open it for you," she said, reaching into the shopping bag with both hands and lifting out the Seth Thomas clock. "It'll go on the mantelpiece in the living room. School will be starting in a few weeks, and this clock will help you get there on time."

"I can't tell time," said Frances, staring at the clock.

"I'll teach you how to tell time," her mother responded.

Harry and Rose looked at the clock with interest. Both noticed that the clock had Roman numerals. Neither mentioned this fact.

"It's lovely," said Rose.

"Yes, it'll look lovely in my living room," said Louise.

Harry looked at his wife and asked, "How much do I owe that furniture store anyway?"

"No more than you can afford," she answered.

"Well, I can't afford to stay any longer. I need to get home," Rose said, getting up and giving Frances one last birthday hug before skipping down the front steps to her waiting car.

# CHAPTER 15

The next morning after breakfast, Louise began teaching Frances to tell time. First, she decided, her daughter needed to learn how to read and write Roman numerals. Frances could count to twenty, but she couldn't write any numbers, much less Roman numerals. If her mother said a four was written as IV, Frances believed her. Of all the numbers, she liked the number ten best. Ten was easy to write—X. Frances was a quick learner, and before the morning was over, she mastered the writing of Roman numerals I through XII.

"I'll teach you about the minutes and hours tomorrow. After that, you can learn about the big and little hands on the clock," her mother said.

Lesson over, Frances was ready to play outside. Riding her father's birthday gift, she scootered all the way to Carol's house with her secret purse hanging from the handlebars. All the Mercers, who were at home, gave the new ride-on toy a nod of approval. Carol got out her scooter, and the two friends spent a happy hour sailing down the hill with the wind in their hair.

"There's *Oma*," Carol said. "Let's see if she'll give us some cookies."

Frances was always ready for cookies, and she was glad when Grandmother Mercer did, indeed, have a fresh batch ready and waiting for the hungry girls.

"Where did you get that nice beaded purse, Frances?" asked Grandmother Mercer.

"My Aunt Rose gave it to me, but the zipper is broken."

"How is your Aunt Rose? I haven't seen her lately."

"She's fine. She gave me some handkerchiefs and a chocolate cake for my birthday, and next week she's going to New York City with her boss," sputtered Frances through her cookie filled mouth.

"New York? That's interesting. Tell me more about your aunt's New York plans," Carol's grandmother urged.

Ignoring the subject of New York, Frances said, "Aunt Rose said she was sorry the zipper on my secret purse is broken. Can you fix it?"

Grandmother Mercer examined the purse carefully. "I can't fix the zipper, but I can sew a big snap at the top so you can open and close your purse whenever you wish. Now, tell me why you call it a secret purse."

"Where are your snaps?" asked Frances.

"Everything has its price," muttered Grandmother Mercer, opening her sewing basket.

Carol's grandmother continued to question Frances about her aunt while she sewed the snap in place. Frances told Carol that she had learned to write her numbers all the way to twelve. No mention was made of Roman numerals.

"They're going on the train," said Frances.

"Who's going on the train?" asked Carol.

"Aunt Rose and her boss when they go to New York City."

"Where will they stay in New York?" asked Grandmother Mercer.

"I can count out loud all the way to twenty," announced Frances, examining the new snap.

"I can teach you a better way to count. *Eins, zwei, drei, fier* . . ." said Grandmother Mercer, hoping to prolong Frances's visit long enough to learn more details about the *Rose-and-Boss* trip.

\* \* \*

While the little girls played at Carol's house, Harry was upstairs working on his region's monthly expense report. Zina had Saturday afternoons off and was probably shopping. Bobby's mother was busy with her family. Louise sat alone at the kitchen table feeling abandoned, sad, and irritable.

"Everyone has something to do—everyone except *me*," she said aloud to no one in particular. "I'll go out and check on the big white rosebush."

The rosebush was waiting for her in its usual place—in front of the garage, which was the perfect backdrop for the last of its summer blossoms. It stood at a distance, aloof from the other flowers. Louise sensed that it wanted to communicate with her. It seemed to have an intelligence beyond that which was expected of vegetation, but when she approached it, nothing happened. The rosebush stood quietly, looking as sad as she felt. *Have I done something to offend it? Does it want some fertilizer?* Louise was convinced that something wasn't right about the big white rosebush. *What does it want? Where did it come from? Who planted it? What is its connection to the house on Collis Avenue?* She decided to talk to Ronald Lay about it next week when he came to mow the grass.

Louise's rosebush ramblings were interrupted by the sound of Frances scootering toward the garage, bringing with her the snap-closed secret purse and the satisfaction that she could now count to twenty in English and to ten in German and that she could write numbers up to twelve.

Turning her attention from the rosebush to her daughter, Louise demanded, "Where have you been?"

"Playing at Carol's house. Her grandmother sewed a snap on my secret purse, and now I can close it. Why does Grandmother Mercer ask so many questions?"

"Some people are just too nosy."

\* \* \*

Grandmother Mercer wasn't the only one who asked too many questions. Louise had her own list of queries the following Tuesday as she sat on the back steps watching Ronald Lay mowing the grass. *Ronald is about my age. He lives alone. Why has he never married? His clothes always look too big for him. He probably doesn't eat right. What does he know about Roger Mills?*

The day was hot, humid, and overcast. The sky was dark and restless. Threatening rain hung over the Collis Avenue neighborhood. Louise looked at the looming clouds and wished them away. "Ronald, thank you so much for taking care of the grass today. You always do such a nice job," she called in a flattering voice as he put the lawnmower away.

"Always glad to please," said Ronald. "Looks like rain. I'd better head home."

"I need to ask you something before you leave. I'm concerned about the big white rosebush. It doesn't seem to be doing well. Should we give it some fertilizer?"

"Can't hurt."

"What about pruning it?"

"Not me. I was told not to touch that rosebush. When Mr. Mills planted it, he told me he would take care of it himself and for me to leave it alone."

"He's gone now, and someone else will have to care for it."

"Not me," repeated Ronald, walking toward his work-worn pickup truck.

"Please stay for just a minute. I made something special just for you," Louise said as she ducked into the kitchen and returned carrying a pitcher of lemonade and two glasses.

"Okay. I'm pretty thirsty," Ronald admitted.

"How well did you know Mr. Mills?"

"I helped him with yard work sometimes and cleaned the gutters twice a year. We were in the same parish, but we weren't close friends."

"Oh, so you knew him from church? Which church was that?"

"St. Joseph's. I'd see him there if I went to late mass on Sundays. He went to mass more often than I did. He was sort of *religious*. Father Mike, I mean Father Michael, seemed to worry about Mr. Mills. Every time he gave a homily about resisting temptation, he looked straight at Mr. Mills. Once, I was passing by the church just as Mr. Mills was coming out of confession, and Father was standing in the doorway shaking his head."

"Were you surprised that Mr. Mills died by falling down the stairs of his drugstore?"

"Not really. Mr. Mills fell down more than anyone I ever knew. Some say he took drugs and was dopey. I don't know about that, but he did have his problems."

"What problems?"

"I have to go now. Thanks for the lemonade," Ronald said, getting into his truck and cranking the engine.

As Louise watched the handyman drive away, she could feel a shroud of disappointment creep over her entire body. She had looked forward to, in fact she had counted on, learning something new and worthwhile concerning Roger's death. All she had gotten from Ronald Lay was an opinion that Roger might have been on drugs and that he might have had other problems. At least she now knew who had planted the big white rosebush, and she had gotten another name—Father Michael, pastor of St. Joseph's Catholic Church.

Louise looked at the threatening sky. It was roiling like an angry ocean. The dense clouds were getting darker. She could see them thicken. They were churning toward her in relentless dark blue waves, marbled with foamy white wisps.

*There's wind in those clouds,* Louise thought. *What if a tornado is coming to hurt me? Why do the clouds hate me?*

The wind—a hot wind—began to blow. The leaves of the maple trees rolled over to show their underbellies of flashing silver. A big drop of rain splattered in front of Louise. Then another and another went splat, splat, splat. Louise ran for the backdoor. Inside, seated at the kitchen table, she started to shake. The wind increased in intensity and threw heavy sheets of rain against the kitchen window, which rattled in response. It was impossible to see beyond the window. There was a bright flash of lightning and a clap of thunder so close they could have been seated on the other side of the kitchen table. Then all the lights went out. It was daytime, and it was dark.

Louise panicked. She ran to the kitchen door and locked it. Then she hurried to the front door and locked it. Frances, who was in her box under the dining room table, peeked out and watched her mother scurry from room to room.

"How can locking the door keep the storm out when it could just blow the door down?" asked Frances.

Her mother didn't answer. She dashed up the stairs and into her bedroom. She closed the door and pushed a chair under the doorknob. She flung herself onto the bed and put a pillow over her head. She was shaking all over. The shaking wouldn't stop.

* * *

Frances knew that her mother was afraid of storms, but she thought they were exciting. When she was sure her mother was safely hidden away in her bedroom, Frances unlocked the front door and went out onto the porch, where she sat on the glider and watched the storm. Next door, Dickey was sitting on his front porch watching the storm, too. Zina sat beside him with her arm around his thin shoulders. The lightening ripped the sky, and the thunder clapped in approval. The wind blew the rain in diagonal sheets across Collis Avenue. The tree limbs bowed to the majesty of the storm. Frances thrilled with excitement.

The thunderstorm rolled on as quickly as it had come. Sun replaced the clouds. The storm sewers couldn't handle the amount of rain that had fallen in such a short time span, and a miniature flash flood rushed down Collis Avenue. All the neighborhood children were in the street wading, dancing, and stomping in the rain river. The boys splashed water on the girls, and the girls splashed water on the boys. Everyone was laughing.

"I wish I was a kid again," Zina said aloud.

* * *

By the next morning, Louise's anxiety had turned into, as she called it, *the Blues*. She felt sad and overwhelmed by the hopelessness of her life. Her previous day's conversation with Ronald Lay had been a big disappointment. The thunderstorm had frightened her. She felt as deflated as an undercooked soufflé fallen flat. *No one really cares about me.* She couldn't remember ever feeling more depressed.

She stood by the dining-room window, staring out at the backyard, unable to summon the energy to move. Without warning, an unexpected sound startled her. It was the clock on the living-room mantelpiece chiming the hour. Everything began to slide into focus. Louise looked at the clock. Already, it was midmorning, and she had an appointment that afternoon. Actually, it was Frances who had the appointment. Louise had scheduled a pre-school checkup with their doctor for her daughter.

"Frances is healthy enough, but she needs a smallpox vaccination before she can go to school," Louise had told Harry that very morning. It didn't occur to her to mention the appointment to Frances.

# CHAPTER 16

The array of medical instruments at the doctor's office fascinated Frances. The doctor played games with her— getting her to open her mouth and say, "Aaaah," getting her to sit still and breathe in and out, and asking her to turn her head this way and that. He even had a little hammer to hit her knees and make them jump.

"I want to be a doctor when I grow up," Frances said. "I can do all these things, and I'd like to wear a white coat."

"First, you'll need to get good grades in school. Then we'll see how your life turns out," the doctor replied. "I'm going to go to my office now and talk to your mother. My nurse will help you with your vaccination."

Frances had no idea what a vaccination was, but she soon found out. She set up a loud howl and started to cry when she saw the nurse approaching with a long sharp needle. The vaccination was not fun. It hurt. She had been hurt, and she had been tricked. She wanted to go home.

She was still crying when her mother left the doctor's office carrying the vaccination certificate. On the way home, Frances didn't want to sit next to her mother on the bus, but she had no choice. At home Louise went to her room to lie down and Frances crawled into her box, nursing her sore arm.

* * *

Louise's case of *the Blues* continued for another week. Then a thought occurred to her. *I need to get out more. I need to spend more time with other people.* As this thought was settling in, there was a knock on the front door. There on the front porch stood Evelyn Fisher, their neighbor. Louise was too surprised to say anything.

"Hi, I just stopped by to invite you to go to a circle meeting at my church tomorrow afternoon. Bobby's mother is going, too," said Evelyn.

"Well, yes, I'd love to go," Louise stammered. "But I'll have to make arrangements for Frances."

"That's all been taken care of. Zina has agreed to keep Frances, Bobby, and Bobby's little sister while we're at the circle meeting."

Louise thanked her, and stood staring at Evelyn's back as she turned and walked down the front steps. She felt a sudden rush of embarrassment. *I didn't even invite Evelyn to come inside. Where are my manners? I've lived on Collis Avenue for over a year, and this is the first time anyone has invited me to do anything or to go anywhere. And now, of all people, Evelyn Fisher. I hardly know her, except to speak to her in the yard.*

Evelyn and Rose had been in the same class in high school, but they had never been close friends. Rose said she felt sorry for Evelyn during high school because she'd had no friends and pretty much stayed to herself.

"No one actually made fun of Evelyn, at least not directly, but everyone avoided being with her, especially the boys. It was that angry red birthmark on the side of her face. It looked like someone had slapped her with a bloody hand. Back then, we thought being pretty was everything, and Evelyn wasn't pretty. Her hair was too long, and she wore it in a strange way. She parted it on one side and combed it over the other side of her face to hide her birthmark. She plastered on a pound of pancake makeup, too. Her cardigan sweaters were always too tight and had the sleeves pushed up. She wore them backward with the buttons going up the back. Nobody else did that."

Louise thought about Evelyn's appearance. Not much had changed. She still combed her hair over half of her face and wore too much makeup, and she still wore tight fitting sweaters.

*Hide the face and flaunt the body* was probably the best option for Evelyn, Louise decided.

Louise, Evelyn, and Bobby's mother walked up the hill to the Presbyterian Church the next afternoon, leaving the children in Zina's care. Louise wore a hat. The others did not.

* * *

Frances's arm no longer hurt, but she did have a scab and would soon have a scar to serve as a membership pass to the

Been-Vaccinated Society. In spite of her unhappy adventure at the doctor's office, Frances was still interested in the various instruments she had seen.

"Let's play doctor," she suggested to her friends.

"Okay," Bobby said. "I get to be the doctor."

"No, I want to be the doctor."

"Girls can't be doctors. You can be the nurse."

"No, I don't want to be a nurse. I want to be the doctor."

"What about me?" Dickey asked. "I want to be the doctor, too."

The argument continued until Zina intervened. "Dickey, you can be the assistant doctor, and Frances, you can be the head nurse. Bobby can be the doctor if he'll let Molly be the patient. Now, you kids go over and play on the Hoags' front porch so I can read my magazine in peace."

Everyone was satisfied with his/her new title except poor little Molly. She began to cry.

"How sick she is? We have to help her get better. Put her on the glider and put this pillow under her head," instructed Doctor Bobby.

Head Nurse Frances said, "Come with me, Assistant Doctor Dickey. We need to get some things from inside."

Soon Frances and Dickey returned to the porch lugging a tin dishpan containing some cotton swabs, a Popsicle stick, a roll of ACE bandaging, a wooden spoon, a flashlight, and a bottle of pills. The pills had been borrowed from Louise's bedside table. They were the little white pills last prescribed by the doctor, not the codeine pills, which Harry kept in his briefcase. Molly was still crying, but Bobby was doing a good job of holding her down on the glider. Frances went back inside and returned carrying a glass of water and the crocheted afghan from her box. Now they could begin treating their patient.

Molly stopped crying and looked at the children with her big eyes. She didn't say anything. Head Nurse Frances covered Patient Molly with the afghan and handed Doctor Bobby the flashlight. With Assistant Doctor Dickey's help, he looked in the patient's ears, nose, and eyes. When he told Molly to open her mouth and say, "Aaaah," she began to cry again. Assistant Doctor Dickey hit Molly on the knee with the wooden spoon, but he got no reaction since she was lying down. By now, Molly was crying really hard. From next door, Zina heard the crying, but she thought nothing of it since Molly cried all the time.

"Give her a pill," Doctor Bobby said to Head Nurse Frances.

Head Nurse Frances found it was easy to give a pill to a patient whose mouth was already wide open, yelling. As soon as the pill went in, Molly clamped her mouth closed and chewed the pill. The patient quit crying and opened her mouth again. Head Nurse Frances popped in another pill and then another. Doctor Bobby and Assistant Doctor Dickey continued their examination while Head Nurse Frances fed little white pills to Molly. At one point, Frances dropped a few pills, but she picked them up and put them in her pocket. When Head Nurse Frances had run out of pills, Molly did the strangest thing.

She sat up and said, "More pills."

159

Those were Molly's first words. It was the first time in her three-year-old life that she had ever spoken. Doctor Bobby said, "She's cured."

Just then Zina appeared. "What are you children doing? How did you get Molly to talk?"

"We gave her some pills," said Head Nurse Frances.

"Where did you get pills? How many did you give her? Let me see that bottle," Zina said, grabbing the empty bottle from Frances's hand.

Zina looked at the pill bottle. It had a prescription number, date, the doctor's name, Louise's name, and directions for taking *one pill each morning*. There was no indication of the medicine's name.

"Okay. Bobby, you and Dickey walk Molly back and forth across the porch so she won't go to sleep while I call the pharmacist to find out more about these pills. Frances, you get Molly another glass of water," Zina ordered.

Everyone was a little scared except Molly, who seemed pleased to be the center of attention. She willingly walked back and forth with Bobby and Dickey, saying, over and over, "More pills. More pills."

Zina went inside and phoned the drug store. "Hello, this is Zina Atkins. I live next door to the Hoags on Collis Avenue. I need to know what to do about a bottle of pills you filled for Mrs. Louise Hoag. The children here ate them all. What should I do?" she asked George.

"What's the prescription number on the bottle? I'll look it up," he said.

When Zina read out the number, George gave a sigh of relief. He could tell from the number that the bottle had contained the sugar pills prescribed by Louise's doctor. He and the doctor had a strong difference of opinion concerning placebos. George believed that prescribing them was unethical, and he had told the doctor so more than once. The doctor continued to prescribe sugar pills. Of course, both knew that placebos work only if the patient is unaware of the fraud. George considered this lying. The doctor said he would gladly lie to help a patient, as long as no one else got hurt.

George could no longer hold his opinion to himself. Without thinking, he blurted out, "Those are only sugar pills. The children will be fine."

"Sugar pills?" Zina exclaimed with surprise. "What do you mean sugar pills?"

"Exactly what I said. This is totally confidential. You must not tell anyone that we had this conversation. Do not repeat what I just told you. Do not tell either Mrs. Hoag or Mr. Hoag. This is just between us. Do you understand?"

"I don't tell what shouldn't be told," Zina answered. "But Mrs. Hoag will see that her pills have gone missing."

"I'll refill the prescription and have our delivery boy bring it over right away. Now, remember you're to keep quiet about this."

Zina returned to the porch and gathered the children around her. "You children did a bad thing, a very bad thing. You should not give someone pills that aren't theirs. If you tell your parents about this, you will get in *big* trouble. If you stay quiet, I'll stay quiet."

The children understood. Frances, who had been standing in the dining-room doorway during Zina's telephone conversation, said softly under her breath, "Sugar pills?"

When no one was looking, she took the few remaining pills from her dress pocket, put them in her secret purse, and snapped it closed.

# CHAPTER 17

*R*ose returned from New York on schedule. Harry and Louise were both eager to hear all about her trip to the big city, and they were disappointed when she didn't telephone or stop by their house the following weekend.

On Sunday afternoon, Harry said, "I'm going to call Rose to make sure everything is okay."

"Welcome back, Rose. How was the trip?" he asked when his sister answered the phone.

"It was fine. I don't want to talk about my trip right now. I'll see you in a few days. Love you. Bye," and she was gone.

"How's Rose?" Louise asked.

"I'm not sure. I have a feeling she didn't enjoy her trip. She says she doesn't want to talk about it right now. I guess we'll find out about it soon enough."

"When Rose has had time to unwind from her trip, I'm going to have a dinner party. I'll invite Rose and Evelyn Fisher to come," Louise said. "She can tell us all about her trip then."

"Why Evelyn?"

"Evelyn has been very nice to me. Remember, she invited me to go to a circle meeting at her church last week. She and Rose knew each other back in high school. In fact, I got the impression that Evelyn is quite interested in knowing how Rose has been doing since they graduated. When we were walking home, she asked a lot of questions about how Rose liked her job and things like that. I think they would enjoy a reunion."

"You had better check with Rose before you invite Evelyn."

Harry rolled his eyes and looked at the ceiling. *Could it be that Louise and Rose are the only people in town who don't know that Rose's boss is a friend of both potential dinner guests?*

A few days later, Louise telephoned her sister-in-law and invited her to the dinner party.

"It's nice of you to think of me, Louise, but I need a rain check for now. Maybe in another few weeks. In the meantime, I'll stop by one afternoon on my way home, and we can chat then."

Louise hung up the telephone, crossed the room, and sagged into one of the new living-room chairs. She was sad. She had counted on having a dinner party. Now, that wasn't going to happen. She blamed herself. She should have known that no one, not even Rose, wanted to spend time with her. *What's wrong with me?* Her only answer was a sob.

\* \* \*

Rose telephoned on Friday afternoon. "Hi, Louise. If you and Harry are going to be home tonight, I'll stop by after work for a visit. No need to cook. I'll pick up some cold cuts at Jack's Deli on the way. Maybe a cheesecake, too."

"That'll be fine, Rose. We'll be here. Get some Cole slaw, potato salad, and a loaf of rye bread, too, please. Harry will pay for everything."

"Will do. See you at six."

Rose breezed through the front door with her take-out packages just as the mantelpiece clock was chiming six. "Ta-da, I'm here!"

Louise, Harry, and Frances stared at Rose. The person standing before them didn't look like the Rose they knew. This stranger was wearing a long-sleeve, kelly-green silk blouse and beige linen slacks. Their Rose had short black hair. This person sported a headful of tight blond ringlets. The trademark high-heeled sling backs had been traded for open-toed platform wedgies. Bright red toenails protruded from the open-toed shoes. No stockings.

"Rose, where did you get those clothes? What have you done to your hair?" Louise exclaimed.

Putting down her packages, Rose said, "In New York slacks are all the rage. Everyone says that we are going to war. Then women will be working men's jobs, and we had better get ready to wear the pants."

"Only men should wear pants," Louise said, frowning at Frances.

"Men and movie stars and the women who'll be in charge when all the men go to war," Rose said. "How do you like my hair?"

"You may be right about the pants," Harry said. "In time, your hair will grow. I remember when you really were blond."

"You mean that black isn't your natural hair color?" asked Louise in surprise.

Before his sister could reply, Harry said, "Let's eat. I'm hungry. Who wants a sandwich?"

Between bites of her sandwich, Frances announced, "I want some pants, too."

"Did you wear those clothes to work?" asked Louise. "What did your boss say about your wearing pants to the office?"

"Not much he could say. After all, he paid for them."

"Pass the potato salad," Harry said.

"If I'm not a doctor, I might be a movie star. Then can I have some pants?" asked Frances.

"If you're a movie star, you can have all the pants you want," her aunt assured her.

"I'll come to all your movies," added her father.

Dinner over, the Hoags were eager to hear about Rose's trip. "Tell us about your trip," Louise said. "Where did you go, and what did you see and do?"

"Frances, when I gave you the handkerchiefs for your birthday, I promised to teach you the days of the week. Well, now is a good time to do that. Get the handkerchiefs, and we can talk about the days of the week while I tell you about my trip."

Spreading the handkerchiefs on the table and pointing to the first one, Rose began. "This one's for Sunday. On Sunday, we rode the train to New York. We stayed in a hotel right across from Pennsylvania Station. This is Monday's handkerchief. On Monday, my boss had to go to the conference, and I went shopping at Macy's. They have an escalator, which is really just moving stairs. You would like it, Frances.

"On Tuesday, I took a four-hour bus tour that went all around Manhattan. The bus went from Wall Street to Central Park, with a one-hour stop at the Metropolitan Museum. Look at Wednesday. It has the most letters of all the days.

"On Wednesday, I went to the Empire State Building. It's really tall.

"On Thursday, I walked down Park Avenue and looked in all the shop windows. Tiffany's had the most wonderful ring in the window. It was a yellow diamond surrounded by white diamonds. It was displayed, sitting in a bird's nest, which rested in the fork of a bare branch growing from a pot of yellow tulips. I went inside and told a salesman I was interested in the ring. Guess what? He let me try it on. It was even more beautiful on my finger than in the window. When he told me it was a bargain at thirty-eight thousand dollars, I almost fainted. I told him I would have to think about it. He was such a nice man. He didn't laugh at me. He just smiled and said, 'It was a pleasure to serve you, madam. Please come again.' I'll spend the rest of my life thinking about that ring."

"Friday's handkerchief starts with an *F*, just like your name, Frances. On Friday, I went to a matinee performance at Radio City Music Hall and had fun watching the dancers. Boy, can they kick up their heels!"

"That's not very ladylike," Louise said, scowling at her daughter. "Ladies do not show their legs in public."

"I might be a dancer when I grow up if I'm not a doctor or a movie star," said Frances. "If I had pants, I could kick up my legs really high."

"Honey, you already kick," said Rose, laughing. Harry laughed, too.

Louise felt kicked—kicked out of the inner circle.

"This last handkerchief is for Saturday—the last day of the week. I wanted my boss to go sightseeing with me or maybe to a Broadway musical, but he said he was too tired. We went to the Stage Door Deli for lunch and had a sandwich so big we had to split it. We ordered a slice of cheesecake, but that really was too much. We each took a couple of bites. Then I wrapped the rest in a paper napkin and put it in my purse for later. Our hotel had a revolving door, and both of us got into the same section. We had to take little baby steps as we went round and round and laughed so hard that the cheesecake got squished, right in my purse."

"What about in the evenings? Did you go to any fancy restaurants or plays?" Louise asked.

"My boss didn't want to spend much money on food or entertainment. His idea of a dinner treat was Chock full o'Nuts. We had carryout Chinese twice. He liked to sit around in the hotel lobby and watch the people. He wasn't much fun."

"I think you learned a lot," Harry said.

"You'd better believe it," said Rose. She tossed her bouncy blond curls and left.

* * *

The following Wednesday evening, Harry decided to join the others at Jack Mercer's poker game. He was the first to arrive. Jack was busy setting up, getting out the cards and chips, and making sure there was plenty of beer. Harry offered to help.

"How have you been doing, Harry?" Jack asked.

"Pretty well. And you? Expecting a full house tonight?"

"Only in my cards," laughed Jack. "Ben Cole can't make it, but the others will be here."

As the game progressed, Harry said little and pretended to concentrate on his cards. Actually, he was concentrating on Jack Mercer's movements. Jack took a clean handkerchief from his pocket and wrapped it around his beer bottle. He said he didn't want his cards to get wet. The handkerchief absorbed the moisture from the bottle, and at the same time, it prevented others from seeing the level of beer left in his bottle. Jack took small sips and nursed one beer for two hours. During those two hours, Jack encouraged the other players to *drink up*. George Mills and Marvin Hall each drank four beers to Jack's one. Harry stuck with coffee. Another thing Harry noticed was that Jack never folded, no matter how bad his cards were. There was no way to tell if he held a good hand or not.

"I'm out," said Marvin Hall. "I've lost my limit."

"It's only ten o'clock," Jack said. "Too early to call it a night yet."

The talk turned to sports. It had been a lean summer for sports in Europe that year. The British Golf Open, the Tour de France, Wimbledon, and the French Open tennis tournament had all be cancelled because of the war. The summer Olympics had not taken place. In America, sports continued as usual. Bryon Nelson won the PGA championship, and it looked as though the Cincinnati Reds and the Detroit Tigers were headed for the World Series.

"We need to get up a baseball pool," Jack said. "Who's for the Reds?"

"Giving any odds?" asked George.

"I hope they're better odds than you gave on that Derby winner," said Marvin. "Who knew that horse could run?"

Before he knew what was happening, Harry had given Jack five dollars to put on Cincinnati in the World Series. With a start, he realized he had just placed his first bet with a professional bookie. All those deli customers going in and out of Jack's store had more on their minds than pastrami-on-rye sandwiches. There were bets to place and debts to pay.

Out on the sidewalk, as they were leaving, Harry turned to Marvin and said, "I've been told to watch my back around Jack Mercer."

"Good advice," said Marvin.

# CHAPTER 18

School was scheduled to open on the Tuesday after Labor Day. Louise had planned to spend the weekend organizing Frances's school supplies. However, on Saturday she didn't feel up to doing anything. She had no enthusiasm for her daughter's first day of school. She had been looking forward to having Frances at school every day. Now that the time was almost here, she felt depressed. Her only child was abandoning her. She was overcome with a sense of betrayal and fear. For two days, functioning was not an option. She sat in a chair staring straight ahead, not eating and not talking.

On Sunday afternoon, Harry telephoned his sister. "Rose, I hate to bother you, but Louise is sick. Can you come over?"

"Sure. I'm no doctor, but I'll do what I can. Little Sister to the rescue. Be there in an hour."

Rose took one look at Louise and said, "Harry, we have to do something. Did Louise take her pills? Louise, did you take your pills? Frances, go get your mother's pill bottle."

Louise turned her head, looked at the others, and said, "No, I didn't take my pills. I forgot."

Frances returned carrying the bottle of little white pills and a glass of water. She told her mother to "Open up." Louise obeyed. Frances popped a pill into her mother's mouth. Louise swallowed. Within minutes she began pulling herself from her self-inflicted quagmire and reclaiming the normal ground.

Frances stared at her mother. *She's like Bobby's little sister.* Giving Molly pills was a secret that she would never tell.

Louise leaned forward in her chair and said, "Rose, I'm glad to see your hair is back to its old style. What happened to the blond curls?"

"Oh, Louise, that was a wig. I was just wearing it for fun. Sure fooled you guys. I laughed all the way home."

"Rose, you are going to make my hair turn gray," Harry said. "I'll walk you to your car."

Rose slid into the driver's seat. Harry sat beside her on the passenger side. Both were wearing their serious faces.

"What are you going to do about Louise?" Rose asked. "She can't take care of herself, much less Frances when she gets like this. You have to do something. Right now, while we are sitting here in the front seat of my car, Frances is in the kitchen fixing her mother's supper. It should be the other way around. It's not right."

"Rose, I promise I'll figure something out if you'll just help me this week. I have to go out of town on Tuesday, and that's Frances's first day of school. Could you spend tomorrow night with us and take Frances to school on your way to work on Tuesday?" Harry pleaded.

"Okay. I'll do it this time. But, Harry, I can't be Frances's mother. She needs a full-time, live-in mother. I love you and I love my niece, and I worry about both of you. I'm willing to help out once in a while, when you're in a jam, but I may not always be around."

"Thank you, Rose. I owe you. And what do you mean by saying you might not always be around?"

"This is confidential so don't mention it to anyone, and that includes Louise," Rose said. "I don't want my boss to suspect, but I've started looking for another job. A new job could mean a move to another city or state. The situation with my boss is a *going-nowhere road.*"

"Rose, you can't move to another city. You're just a kid," Harry exclaimed.

"Harry, I'm twenty-six years old, and I'm not a kid anymore. I'm not old, and I'm not young, and I've got a little mileage behind the wheel. It's time I move on down the highway."

"What kind of job are you looking for, another secretarial position? You're a good secretary."

"Last week I filled out the government paperwork, and next week I'll sit for the Civil Service exam. What with the war coming, they will probably do a big-time background check on me. If they ask you, tell them that I'm the most patriotic sister you have. Don't mention that we know the Mercers. They are German. From now on, I never met a German," Rose said.

Harry was in shock. Rose moving away! Louise incompetent! Frances starting school, and he had to go out of town.

"I'll do whatever has to be done. Rose, promise that you'll keep me posted on the job situation. If you take another job and it doesn't work out, don't forget I'm still your big brother, and I'm still here."

"Love you, Harry. See you tomorrow evening. I'll look forward to taking Frances to her first day of school," Rose said, blowing Harry a kiss as she drove away.

Inside, Louise was sitting at the kitchen table eating a bowl of Jell-O and a pimento-cheese sandwich, thanks to Frances, who was stirring chocolate sauce into an overfilled glass of milk, some of which had sloshed onto the countertop. Louise was oblivious to Frances and the growing rivulet of milk beginning to trickle to the floor.

"Has Rose gone?" Louise asked. "I don't know what has gotten into her about that hair. It never looks right."

"Rose will be spending the night with us tomorrow. She's volunteered to drive Frances to school on Tuesday morning. Frances, you'll be the only kid in first grade with your own personal chauffeur," Harry said.

Frances clapped her hands with joy. Her face was one big grin. Tuesday was going to be wonderful—first grade and Aunt Rose in the same day!

"Good," said Louise. "Rose should drive Frances to school. She should help out, as many meals as she eats here."

Harry started to say something in Rose's defense, but stopped himself. What good would it do to argue with Louise? He would take out his frustration on the lawn by mowing the grass.

* * *

While helping Frances get ready for bed on Monday night, Rose asked, "What are you going to wear for your first day of school? It's a good idea to lay out the next day's clothes the night before so you won't have to rush around in the morning. Did your mother get you a new dress to wear?"

"Yes, but I hate it. It's ugly," Frances said, pointing to a plain navy blue dress with long sleeves hanging in her closet.

Rose took the new dress out of the closet and held it up for inspection. "You're right. This dress is all wrong for the first day of school. You can save it for funerals. Let's see what else is hanging in here," Rose said, looking through Frances's small wardrobe. "I have an idea. You choose. On the first day of school, a girl should wear whatever makes her happy."

"I know. I know," Frances said, pointing to a red-and-white checkered dress with a big white collar and a red sash. "It's the one you gave me last year, and I didn't get to wear it because Mom said it was too big."

"It looks about the right size now," Rose said.

The next morning, Rose and Frances joined the crowd of children and parents entering the old two-story brick school building, which served grades one through six. Rose signed the necessary papers and was given a list of books and supplies that Frances would need. Frances was directed to the classroom where she would spend her first-grade life. The teacher, Mrs. Dorothy Adams, pinned a name tag on Frances's dress and showed her to her desk.

Frances looked around. There were children everywhere. The only one she recognized was Dickey. She waved to him, but he didn't see her. He was looking down and clinging to Zina's hand.

"I'll be back to pick you up when school is over," said Rose. "I'm taking the afternoon off so we can go shopping for your supplies."

When all the parents had gone, Mrs. Adams stood in front of the class. She clapped her hands and said, "Good morning, everyone. My name is Mrs. Adams, and I want to learn your names, too. That's why each of you has a name tag. I can tell you are very smart. You already know your name. Don't worry. I'll learn all of your names before the day is over. Today you'll sit at a temporary desk. Tomorrow you'll get your permanent desk assignment. Now, let's begin by having some fun."

The children were instructed to sit on the top of their desks and repeat, in unison, the nursery rhyme *Humpty Dumpty*. When they got to the part where Humpty Dumpty had a great fall, they were to jump down on the floor. This exercise was repeated several times. On about the third jump, it suddenly occurred to Frances that she had not known Humpty Dumpty was an egg.

\* \* \*

The house on Collis Avenue was quiet. Louise stood in Frances's bedroom, looking out of the window into the garden. She stared at the big white rosebush. She couldn't see the man who sometimes stood there, but she knew he was nearby. She could feel his aura. Today his presence didn't frighten her. She was glad to have his company. He could help with the project she had in mind.

"It's been almost a year since I put the card table in the corner of my room, and I haven't really used it as I thought I would. Today is a good day to get my writing supplies organized and to set up a proper desk. I may need to buy a few more items, but we can start a list of things I'll need. Making lists is just one way I plan to use my desk," Louise said to the invisible rosebush man.

She went from room to room gathering the supplies she wanted. From the kitchen, she took two pencils, a pencil sharpener, and a ruler. From Harry's room, she took an ink blotter, several pens, and some stamps. Frances's room was a treasure trove. From there, Louise took a tablet of lined notebook paper, another pencil, an eraser, some crayons, and some colored construction paper. She added her own box of stationery to the mix and spread it all out on the card table. Realizing that the card table had no drawers, she emptied a drawer in the nearby dresser. It would have to do until she got a file cabinet, or at least a file box.

"You'll have to help me get an extra chair from the dining room. We have six dining room chairs, and we never need more than four," Louise said in the direction where the man seemed to be standing. "I'll need a trashcan, too."

With the extra chair and trashcan in place and the supplies stored in the dresser drawer, Louise was ready to begin work. On a piece of notebook paper, she wrote, "Supplies needed," and then listed the first item—file cabinet. She added a second item—large index cards. The list continued to grow: rubber bands, paper clips, file folders, stapler, staples, and on and on. As Louise continued to write, she became more and more excited. This was fun. This is what she had longed for—the house all to herself, with no Harry and no Frances, and with someone who was interested in her and who cared about her.

"I'll write a letter to Helen," Louise said aloud. "I sent her a small gift at Christmas last year and a birthday card, but I haven't written her a letter in months. She'll want to know how I'm doing."

Helen was very much aware of how Louise was doing. She and Harry talked on the phone weekly. She also wrote Louise a letter weekly, knowing full well that Louise never read her letters. But she loved her sister, and she didn't give up.

Harry appreciated Helen's concern, support, and encouragement. Earlier in the year, he had written Helen a letter telling her about the defense bonds he was buying, on which Frances was named as the beneficiary, and where they were located in case something happened to him. He asked Helen if she would make a home for Frances if he were not there to do so. Helen had agreed. Rose, too, had agreed that this was the best idea. Louise knew nothing of this arrangement.

"Dear Helen," Louise began. She then proceeded to describe all the unpleasant things going on in her life. She complained about Harry, Frances, Rose, and everything else in her world. She went into detail about how the thunderstorm had frightened her and how all the neighbors disliked her. The description of her own poor health took several pages. It was a gloomy letter, indeed. Louise signed her letter, "Your loving and misunderstood sister, Louise."

She reread the letter, wadded it up, and threw it in the trashcan. She began again, "My Dearest Helen . . ." The second letter was all sweetness and light, interspersed with a generous helping of bragging. Louise described her life in glowing terms and assured her sister that she was well, happy, and satisfied. She put the second letter in the mailbox, where it would be collected by the mailman when he made his rounds.

# CHAPTER 19

*T*uesday night Rose made other sleeping arrangements. On Wednesday morning, she stopped by the house on Collis Avenue early enough to help Frances get ready for her second day of school.

"You need help carrying your books and supplies to school. So I'll drive you," Rose told Frances. "I can't pick you up after school. You'll have to walk home with Dickey and Zina."

"Okay. Can I wear the same dress I wore yesterday?"

"Why not?" said Rose. "This weekend I'll help you organize your closet into school clothes and play clothes. That'll make it easier to choose what to wear."

Rose stopped her little Ford coupe behind a big black Cadillac parked at the curb in front of the school. Frances got down from the passenger side. Rose handed her the school items they had purchased the previous afternoon. A man wearing a black jacket and a funny black hat slid from behind the wheel of the car in front of them. He opened the rear door of the Cadillac, and a girl got out, her arms filled with the same books and supplies as Frances. Two things about the girl caught Frances's attention—her hair and her shoes.

The girl was about the same size as Frances, but that's where the similarity ended. On the girl's head was the biggest bush of yellow hair Frances had ever seen. Her hair was long and thick. It looked matted. When she walked, the girl's hair preceded her. It stuck out in all directions, like a large blond tumbleweed. Frances stared at the girl. She wondered how anyone could get a comb through that impenetrable, tangled mass.

"Look at that girl's hair," she whispered. "It's like a giant bird's nest. How can she comb it?"

"Maybe she doesn't. At least she won't have to worry about wearing a warm hat in winter. I've got to go, sweetie. Hope you have a happy day, and don't forget to walk home with Dickey and Zina," said Rose.

Frances turned her gaze to the girl's shoes. They were nothing like the brown lace-up Buster Brown shoes she and the other children wore. They were shiny black patent-leather slippers with little black straps to hold them in place. The heels of the shoes made *click-click* sounds as the girl walked. The girl's socks were white with lace edging, unlike Frances's plain brown socks.

In the classroom, Mrs. Adams was making sure that each child found his/her own assigned desk. She began each new school year by seating her pupils in alphabetical order. It helped her to learn their names, as did the seating chart she kept in her top desk drawer. There were five rows of desks with five seats in each row. Each wooden seat had a wooden desk top attached to its back. Mary Lynn Hall, of the bushy hair, was assigned to the second seat in the third row, directly in front of Frances Hoag.

"My name is Mary Lynn, and I saw you get out of your car," said the girl with the exploding hair, turning around and looking at Frances.

"I'm Frances, and I saw you get out of your car, too."

"Why is your chauffeur a lady?" Mary Lynn asked.

"That's my Aunt Rose. She's only a chauffeur sometimes. Mostly she works for her boss in his office. Why do you sit in the back seat of your car?"

"That's where you are supposed to sit when the chauffeur is driving."

"My Aunt Rose's car doesn't have a back seat. It has a rumble seat."

"I never rode in a rumble seat. Is it fun?"

Before Frances could answer, Mrs. Adams clapped her hands bringing everyone to attention. "Now that we all have our desks, we'll divide into reading circles," she said, pointing to a circle of five small chairs in the front of the room near her desk. "If you can read, raise your hand."

Three hands went up. Mary Lynn's was among them. Since Mary Lynn's hand was up, Frances decided to raise her hand, too. She did know how to read her *Madeline* book. While the others colored, the four readers were summoned to the reading circle. The teacher handed the first boy a book and asked him to read aloud. He did. The second boy could read the book, too, but he stumbled over some words. Then it was Mary Lynn's turn. Mrs. Adams handed Mary Lynn a different book. Mary Lynn opened the book and started reading very fast. She didn't miss a single word.

"Now, Frances, let's hear you read," said Mrs. Adams. "Which book would you like to read, the first book or the one Mary Lynn read?"

"I want to read my *Madeline* book," said Frances.

"I know that book," said the teacher. "It's an easy one to memorize. Can you read any other books, Frances?"

"Not really," said Frances.

The reading circles were decided. Mary Lynn was in the first circle. Frances was in the last. It was all boys, except for Frances. She wasn't happy.

"I want to be in the circle with Mary Lynn," Frances told the teacher.

"When you learn to read as well as Mary Lynn, you can be in her circle."

Walking home from school that afternoon, Frances told Dickey and Zina that she was going to learn to read as well as Mary Lynn and be in her circle.

"It's good to try," said Zina. "But all the time you're learning, she'll be learning more. You're not likely to catch up to her."

"Why not?" asked Frances.

"Hoags don't catch Halls. That's just the way it is."

\* \* \*

Over the weekend, Harry called his sister to thank her for helping out with Frances. "Rose, you are a blessing. I don't deserve you."

"I was glad to help out. Everything went well. I asked Zina to let Frances walk with her and Dickey to school and back every day and to let Frances go over to their house in the afternoons if Louise wasn't feeling well. I think you should offer to pay Zina a little something for doing this. And, Harry, you're right. You don't deserve me."

"I'll talk to Zina today. Thanks again. What can I do for you, Rose?"

"You can wish me luck with the Civil Service exam. I take it on Friday, and I'm a little nervous," Rose said before hanging up.

* * *

While Rose was taking the Civil Service exam, Mrs. Adams was evaluating the math skills of her students. "If you can count out loud to twenty, raise your hand."

Almost all hands shot up, including Frances's. "All right, Frances, please stand and count for us," the teacher said.

Frances was pleased to be the first one chosen to count. Maybe she could be in the first counting circle, if there was one. She stood beside her desk and began, "Ein, zwei, drei, fier . . ."

"No, no, Frances. In this class we will count in English," said Mrs. Adams, crossly.

Frances had to sit down and endure listening to everyone else count in English. She thought, *I know English, too. This isn't fair.*

"If you can write your numbers, raise your hand," the teacher said.

Five or six hands went up. Frances's was among them. Mrs. Adams recognized Frances's hand and said, "Okay, Frances, go to the front of the room, get a piece of chalk, and write the numbers on the blackboard."

Frances walked to the blackboard, picked up the chalk, looked at the class, and began writing, I, II, III, IV . . .

All the children, including Mary Lynn, looked puzzled. Mrs. Adams laughed in surprise. "Frances, this is going to be an interesting year," she said and announced that it was time for recess.

As the children were leaving at the end of the school day, Mrs. Adams beckoned Frances to her desk. "Frances, I didn't know that you could speak German. My father came from Germany, and I can speak German, too, but this isn't a good time to advertise our German heritage. Some people don't like Germans."

Frances was confused. She wasn't sure what *advertise* meant, and she didn't know the word *heritage*. She looked at Mrs. Adams and said, "I'm not German, and I don't speak German, but I like Germans, except Fred Mercer. He teases me and Carol sometimes."

"Then that'll be our little secret. I won't tell anyone you like Germans, and you won't tell anyone I speak German."

Frances nodded. "I know all about secrets. I keep secrets in my secret purse."

*What a strange child—a little German girl who writes in Roman numerals and who keeps secrets,* Mrs. Adams thought as she watched Frances leave the classroom. *What else does she know?*

* * *

It was a beautiful autumn. The nights were cool, and the days were warm. The mornings were crisp. It was a joy to be in the Collis Avenue part of the world. Every day was a rainbow to Frances. She loved the colored leaves. She and Dickey caught fat grasshoppers in the weeds of the vacant lots as they walked home from school. Sometimes, if she wasn't in a hurry, Zina stopped and let them pick up ripe beechnuts from under the big beechnut tree beside the Presbyterian Church. Even Louise was content, for once.

Then the cold wind blew. In October of 1940, the United States Congress voted to reinstate the military draft even though America was not officially at war. All men between the ages of eighteen and thirty-six were required to register for the draft. It was the first peacetime draft in the country's history. Harry had turned thirty-six on his last birthday and wasn't required to register.

Louise was back in the habit of reading her mail. She opened a letter from her sister, Helen, and learned that Helen's son, Richard, had joined the air force, rather than wait to be drafted by the army.

"Richard wasn't sure what he wanted to do after he finished high school," Helen wrote. "He said he didn't want to go to college, but I think he just said that because he knew we couldn't afford it. Once he comes back from the military, the government will pay for his college education."

*If he comes back*, thought Louise.

Louise answered Helen's letter in her usual style—one depressing letter for the trashcan and one optimistic letter for the mailman. She reread the letter she planned to mail and decided it sounded much too cheerful. She added a worrying sentence or two about how the much-talked-about rationing-to-come might affect *her*.

The shadow of war brought other changes to the Hoags, as well. Rose passed the Civil Service exam and was offered a job selling United States Defense Bonds. She telephoned her brother with the news and asked if they could meet for lunch. Harry was still her only confidant concerning her desire to change careers.

"Harry, I need to decide what to do about that job offer. I want to have a job with a real career path. What do you think?"

"I think you should take the job with the defense bond office," Harry said. "How does the new offer compare to your current salary? What about benefits?"

"The salary is about the same to start. After six months' probation, I should get a raise. The benefits are much better, especially if you count not having to deal with Mr. Gropey Hands. This job could lead to something even better."

"Mr. Gropey Hands has brothers everywhere. I'm glad you were offered the job. If you take it, you'll be staying in Allenburg, and I'm happy about that."

"Okay. First, I'll officially accept the job offer, then I'll tell my boss that I'm resigning. He won't be happy, but he can find someone else. He needs to find a new *friend*, too. Our extracurricular activities are over."

* * *

Rose was right about her boss. He wasn't at all happy about her resignation.

"Now who's going to do all the research at the Registrar of Deeds office? Who's going to do the typing and the filing? Who's going to run the office if I'm away or busy?" he groused.

*My wife won't be so suspicious, and I'll have more time to spend with Evelyn Fisher,* he thought, looking for the sunshine on a cloudy day. Deep down, he knew he would miss Rose. She was his bit of sunshine.

"Rose, you can't be replaced, but I'm going to have to get someone in here to do your job. Can you stay long enough to train the new secretary, please?"

"I can stay until the last of November. No longer. Yes, I'll help train the new secretary. Do you have someone in mind, or do you want me to write a Help Wanted ad for the local newspaper?"

Applicants for the job paraded in and out of the legal office the following week. The boss found fault with each. Finally, Rose said, "Time's up. You have to make a choice. Pick someone, or you'll be sitting here all alone, getting ready to spend the afternoon doing title searches."

A stout gray-haired matron was hired to become the new secretary. She was efficient and pleasant, but she was not Rose.

# CHAPTER 20

October was almost over. The Cincinnati Reds defeated the Detroit Tigers, winning the baseball World Series. Harry collected his winnings from Jack Mercer, who had placed bets on both teams, knowing his wins would cover his losses. Jack didn't care which team won or lost as long as his customers gambled on the final score, the number of home runs, the number of strikeouts, and a long list of other possible ways to lose their money.

Louise looked at the kitchen calendar. It was Halloween—the most hated day in Louise's year. Not only was it a scary time, it was also her birthday, and she never celebrated her birthday. She didn't like to be reminded of her school days when the other children had teased her and called her a witch because of her Halloween birthday. No one called her a witch now, but she knew that sometimes they wanted to call her a witch. Her birthday always reminded Louise that she was four years older than Harry. She didn't like to broadcast that fact. It made her feel old.

"Oh my god, I am old," Louise said aloud. "I am forty years old."

"I want to go trick-or-treating tonight," Frances interrupted, digging into her breakfast cereal. "I want to be a witch."

"You have to stay here and help give out the candy to the other children."

"But I want to get my own candy, and besides, Aunt Rose gave me a witch's hat to wear."

"No, I want you to stay here with me and give out the candy," her mother insisted.

* * *

At recess, Mary Lynn asked, "Are you going trick-or-treating? What are you going to be?"

"I'm going to be a witch," Frances said, neglecting to add that she would be sitting on her own front steps giving out candy while her mother would be upstairs cowering in fear of the costume-clad neighborhood children. "I don't think trick-or-treaters are very scary."

"I'll tell you who is scary," said Mary Lynn. "Stanley, the janitor, is scary. Did you ever see how he stares at us? He's always sneaking around with that stupid broom, pretending to sweep. I don't like him."

"Zina doesn't like him either. She told Dickey to stay away from him."

The bell rang, and the girls went back to their classroom. Frances decided she would stay away from Stanley, too. *He is pretty creepy.*

After dinner, Frances poured the bag of individually wrapped Tootsie Rolls into a wicker basket. Wearing her coat and her witch's hat, she sat on the front steps. When the trick-or-treaters, wearing their homemade costumes, came up the walk to the house on Collis Avenue, Frances gave each a Tootsie Roll. She gave Bobby's little sister two candies. Molly was dressed as a ghost, wearing a pillowcase with cut-out holes for her big eyes. This costume suited Molly. She had been as silent as a ghost since the sugar-pill episode. Frances slipped a few Tootsie Rolls into her own coat pocket. She would transfer them to her secret purse later.

Louise stayed upstairs until the trick-or-treaters were gone and Frances was in bed. It was only nine o'clock, and she didn't want to listen to the radio. Instead, she took the novel she was reading to the dining room and sat near the window, sipping hot tea while she read. The time and the pages flew by. The clock on the living room mantle chimed eleven. Louise looked up from her book. *How can it be so late? Why did the clock make that scratchy sound?*

She sat motionless—her senses focused on the unfamiliar noise. The scratchy sound wasn't coming from the clock. It was something else. *A mouse? Is there a mouse in the kitchen?* Louise started to get up to investigate. Just then, she saw something moving outside the dining-room window. At first it was just a shadow—a shadow that looked like the bony finger of a skeleton. The finger was scratching on the window pane.

Pure fear swept over Louise, sending her into a state of panic. She started shaking. She couldn't move her arms or legs. She couldn't even scream. The finger moved slowly, scratching back and forth, back and forth. Then it was gone. Louise sat, riveted to her chair, staring at the window and the darkness beyond for almost thirty minutes. She was still trembling when she called the police.

"Someone is in my backyard, trying to climb through my dining-room window," Louise said in a frightened voice. "Help me. Please help me."

"What is your name and where are you located?" asked the police dispatcher.

"Louise Hoag and I'm at my house on Collis Avenue. 1403 Collis Avenue."

"We'll dispatch a patrol car immediately to check on the situation. In the meantime, you should move away from the window and make sure all the doors are locked. Do not open the door to anyone. We'll be there soon."

Relief washed over Louise as she watched two uniformed officers get out of the patrol car parked in front of her house. There was a rotating blue light on top of the car. *That stupid light will frighten the intruder,* thought Louise. *He'll get away.* She didn't understand how she knew it was a *he* and that there was only one, but she knew he wanted to hurt her.

The patrolmen were standing on the porch, knocking on the front door. "Ma'am, this is the police. Are you all right?"

Without opening the door, Louise called out, "Yes, I'm all right in here. The person trying to break into my house is in the backyard."

"Okay. We'll check the backyard. You stay inside," said the older of the two policemen.

The officers approached the backyard from opposite sides of the house. They met under the dining-room window. Each shone his flashlight across the back of the house and over the back garden. They went to the garage and checked it thoroughly. It was empty except for a child's scooter, an assortment of tools, and the Terraplane, sitting in its usual place. They looked inside the car. Nothing. They checked the alley that ran behind the property and investigated the backyards on either side of the Hoags'. Nothing in the alley. Nothing in the Stevens's yard. Nothing in the Fishers' yard.

"Whoever was here is long gone," said the younger officer.

"Let's look around that dining-room window again," his partner said. "Maybe we missed something. That flower bed under the window is filled with pine bark mulch. We'll never get a footprint from that, but maybe there is something else."

"Only this long, crooked stick. It must have fallen from one of those trees. Maybe it scratched across the window when it fell. What do you think?" said the younger officer.

"I don't think we can find anything here tonight. Maybe I'll stop by in the morning and do a daylight check," the senior officer replied as he pulled a handkerchief from his pocket to blow his nose. He turned to leave the backyard without noticing his business card, which fell from his pocket and landed on the pine mulch directly beneath the window.

Louise was feeling a little less frightened as she watched the policemen walk up the steps to the front door. She opened the door and asked, "Did you find him?"

"No, there's no one in your backyard. We even checked the garage and your neighbors' yards. We couldn't find anything other than a stick that looks like it was blown from a tree. It may have scratched across your window as it fell. You did right to call us, but we are happy to report that, in our opinion, it was a false alarm caused by a falling limb. You can rest easy. You are safe."

"But I saw a bony finger scratching on my window," Louise protested.

"Ma'am, we think it was just a tree branch falling. Even if there was someone there, we can assure you that he won't be back tonight. That blue light on our car scares most would-be wrong-doers away," said the older policeman. "You have a good evening, and we'll put extra patrol on this street tonight."

When the policeman were gone, Louise went upstairs to bed. She didn't check on Frances. She lay in her bed shaking and crying until dawn.

\* \* \*

As they drove away, the younger of the two policemen turned to his partner and said, "You acted sort of funny back there. What's going on? Have you ever been to that house before tonight?"

Officer Leo Thompson replied, "Once. About a year and a half ago when the Mills family lived there. We had to inform the widow that her husband, Roger Mills, had died. God, I hate those death notifications!"

"Is that the guy who fell down the drugstore stairs and broke his neck?" asked Jimmy Kearns, the younger policeman.

"Maybe."

"What do you mean, maybe?"

"Roger Mills had a broken neck all right. The coroner ruled 'death by accident due to multiple cervical vertebrae fractures'. I just don't know how he got those fractures. The next day I went back to that drugstore and checked out the death scene. I saw some things that didn't add up, and yes, I kept quiet about it. I had no proof. The man was dead. His widow was planning to leave town, and she needed the life insurance. Stirring the pot would have curdled the soup. . . I've said too much. If you repeat any of this, I'll deny it, and who'll believe a rookie over a twenty-three-year veteran?"

"What did you put in your report?" asked Jimmy.

"I went with the coroner's findings, and I kept my mouth shut, just like you'll do."

"You mean to say you never told anyone what you suspected?"

"Only person I ever told before tonight was Father Michael, and he can't tell since he heard it in the confessional," Patrolman Thompson said.

"Think of me as Father Jimmy. You can count on me not to repeat stuff. I don't want the brass interrogating me. That's for sure. Besides, what you think you saw is just speculation. So, what made you have doubts? What do you think really happened in that basement?" asked Jimmy Kearns.

"Let's take a break and get some coffee at the all-night diner," Leo said.

\* \* \*

Over coffee, Patrolman Leo Thompson told his partner what he had seen and done on the morning of January 15, 1939.

"I stopped by the coroner's office before I went to the drugstore, but he wasn't there. His assistant said he was snowed in at home, and the death certificate wouldn't be available until after the autopsy was completed. So I went down to the morgue and asked about the autopsy on Roger Mills. I was told that the body was still in the cooler, waiting for the pathologist. The whole city was in the midst of digging out from the biggest blizzard in years. No one was concerned about a dead pharmacist that morning. I know my way around the morgue, and I decided to take a look for myself. I found the tray containing Mr. Mills's body and slid it out. There he was, with his toe neatly tagged, waiting for his autopsy.

"There was no visible blood that I could see. You'd think that falling down the stairs and breaking his neck would cause some bleeding, especially since there was a huge bump on the side of his head just above his ear. The really interesting part was his neck. There were marks that looked almost like rope burns. Right away I suspected some kind of strangulation, but strangulation marks are red, not white and bloodless like on that corpse. His eyes were open. They were clear to cloudy with none of those little red spots. Petechiae, I think it's called. Those red spots are always in the eyes when a body has been strangled or hanged. His hands and fingers looked normal, too, with no abrasions or broken fingernails like you see when someone has been struggling with a rope around his neck. I started to make some notes, but changed my mind. I decided to wait for the autopsy report.

"After the morgue, I went to the drugstore. It was cordoned off. No one was around, and I had the run of the place. Nothing seemed amiss on the main level. In the basement, I took a good look at the stairs. They were dangerous, for sure, with no handrail. I checked every step with my flashlight. Guess what I found? The old wooden stairs had more fibers in their crevices than you would think. It looked like a heavy sack of laundry had been dragged *up* those stairs. If Mr. Mills fell *down* those stairs, threads from his clothing wouldn't have been caught that way. I wondered if he had been dragged up and *helped* down. There was no blood anywhere in the basement. No body fluids either.

"There was a straight-backed wooden chair at the workbench, and I took a look at that. It was dusty except for some footprints in the center. Looked like small boot prints to me. I stood on the chair and checked the rafters. All were dusty except for one in the center of the room. When I took a closer look, I could see a few strands of rope fiber. I tell you, there had been a rope tied around that rafter. I searched and searched, but there was no rope anywhere in that drugstore."

"Could the deceased have committed suicide by hanging himself and someone else cut him down and faked an accident?" asked Jimmy, wide eyed.

"There's more to it than that," said Leo. "That body was dead before it was ever strung up."

"Are you sure about that?"

"Sure as water is wet, but I had no way to prove it."

"I'm starting to see what you were facing. No evidence, no facts, no witnesses, and only speculation that no one would ever believe," the younger man said. "You had to wait on the autopsy report."

"That was another problem," his partner continued. "While I was investigating on my own, and you know what trouble we get into when we do anything on our own, the widow and Father Michael were trying to figure out how to have a funeral with all that snow on the ground. At first, they thought the ground was too frozen to dig a grave and that maybe Mr. Mills should be cremated. Father Michael sent word to the coroner that Mrs. Mills had decided to have her husband cremated and didn't want an autopsy done. The body was transferred to the crematory. It seems the ground wasn't as hard as they had originally thought, and Roger Mills's ashes were buried the regular way, in consecrated ground. No autopsy. No body. No case."

"Well, who killed Roger Mills?" Jimmy Kearns asked.

"Damned if I know," replied Patrolman Leo Thompson.

# CHAPTER 21

At seven o'clock the next morning, Frances was up and dressed, ready for school. Her mother was still in bed, resting from a sleepless night. Frances made her own breakfast. She packed her own school lunch, as well. She felt sure the others kids would be showing off their Halloween candy at lunchtime, so she added two Tootsie Rolls to her lunch box.

"Bye," Frances called to a mother who never listened. She gathered her things, put on her coat, and exited through the kitchen door on her way to meet Dickey and Zina for the walk to school. As she crossed the backyard, something lying in the flower bed under the dining room window caught her attention. She went over to take a closer look. It was a small white card with printing on it. Frances picked it up and tried to read what it said. But, though she had made good progress in her reading endeavors, the words before her were too hard. Frances had no idea what this card was all about. *I'll get someone to read it for me.* She put the card in her pocket.

On the walk to school, Frances thought about whom she might ask to read the card she had found. *If I ask Zina, she'll tell Mom. I can't ask Daddy because he's out of town. If I ask Aunt Rose, she'll tell Daddy, and he'll tell Mom. If I ask Grandmother Mercer, she'll ask too many questions. I know. I'll ask Mrs. Adams. She is the best reader I know, and she said we could have secrets.*

The children were whispering about how much fun their trick-or-treating had been the previous evening when Mrs. Adams called the class to order. She said, "I'm glad everyone had a fine time celebrating Halloween. Did you know that Halloween means *hallowed eve*? The word *hallowed* means holy, and *eve* means the night before. The reason we celebrate Halloween is that it is the night before All Saints Day, which is a holy day. If your family doesn't celebrate All Saints Day, just enjoy knowing that you have candy and be happy." Everyone joined the teacher in clapping at that.

"If you brought candy to school today, please put it in your cubby space right now. You may get out one piece after you've eaten your lunch," Mrs. Adams continued. There was no clapping at this announcement. After each holiday, Mrs. Adams went into self-preservation mode. She didn't need twenty-five six-year-olds throwing up in the middle of her classroom. No, she did not.

Frances put her two Tootsie Rolls in her cubby space. She noticed that Mary Lynn didn't have any candy to store. At recess, Frances asked Mary Lynn, "Don't you have any candy from trick-or-treating?"

"I did, but my mean old brother took it all."

"How old is your mean old brother?"

"Nine. He always takes my stuff. I hate all boys."

"I hate Fred Mercer, and he is a boy. After lunch you can have one of my Tootsie Rolls," Frances said, and a friendship was sealed.

"I have to go to the bathroom," Mary Lynn said as she took off running in that direction.

Frances walked over to where Mrs. Adams stood, watching the children play. "Can you read something for me?" she asked, handing the card she had found to her teacher.

"Of course, Frances. This is a business card, and it says, 'Patrolman Leo Thompson, Allenburg, Ohio, Police Department.' There's a telephone number where you can call him. Where did you get this card?"

Frances didn't want Mrs. Adams to know that she had found the card just lying on the ground in her backyard. The teacher would want to know why the card was in her backyard, and Frances didn't know the answer to that. Mrs. Adams might ask her mother about the card, and her mother might say something strange. It was too complicated. Frances didn't want her teacher to think she had stolen the card because she hadn't. So, Frances told a lie—a little lie. "A man gave it to me."

"Frances, this is an important card. You should put it in a safe place and keep it. If you ever need help, call the number on this card," Mrs. Adams said, handing the card back to Frances.

"Okay. I will," said Frances, smiling up at her teacher. "I'll put it in my secret purse." She turned and ran toward the restroom where Mary Lynn waited.

Mrs. Adams watched Frances as she ran across the playground to meet her friend. *What is going on in the life of that poor child? She's been in my class two months, and I've never met either of her parents. Her aunt brought her to school the first two days. After that, the neighbor's housekeeper has been walking her to and from school. Frances is a puzzle with missing pieces.*

\* \* \*

Louise didn't get up until eleven o'clock that morning. She dressed, made her bed, and put on the teakettle. While she sipped her tea at the kitchen table, the darkness clouding her outlook began to lift. Things looked a lot less scary in the daylight. She spoke aloud to her teacup, "I don't believe those policemen. I'll do some investigating on my own."

In the backyard, under the dining-room window, Louise saw the downed branch that the patrolmen had accused of making the scratching sounds on her window. She went closer and stared at the branch for a few minutes, while she gathered the courage to pick it up. It felt like a frozen snake. She held it as far from her body as possible. It was a long, crooked piece of dead wood, bigger than a stick and smaller than a limb. Several small twigs protruded from the end of its *tail*. It appeared that other twigs had once been attached to the branch but had broken off some time ago. The two remaining twigs were thin and gnarled. She thought they resembled the crooked fingers of a skeleton. *Did someone hold this branch and scratch it deliberately against my window? Possibly.*

She considered the alternative—the police theory was right. The scraping sound had occurred without human intervention. Perhaps the wind had blown the branch against her window. But why? Whatever the cause, she resolved to tell no one about the scratching on the window. Louise remembered the policemen saying that the blue light atop their car would scare away anyone who was up to no good. Could others have seen the blue light, as well? She hoped not.

Actually, more than one person had seen the blue light the previous evening. Zina had watched the police come and go. She'd been concerned when the patrol car pulled up to the Hoags' house and two uniformed officers got out. From her window, she watched the patrolmen as they searched the Hoags' backyard and garage. They had even shined their flashlights over the fence into the Stevens's yard. Whatever they were looking for, they didn't appear to have found it. When they left without going inside the Hoags' house, Zina's concern turned to curiosity.

After lunch, she telephoned Louise. "Is it okay if I come over for a short visit?"

"That'll be fine. I'll put on the coffee pot."

As Zina crossed the backyards, she decided not to say anything about seeing the police car the night before, in case Louise was unaware of the incident. *I'll wait for her to say something.*

During their visit, Louise did not mention the police nor the scary sound at her window.

"I'm thinking about taking some classes so I can get another job," Zina said. "With Dickey in school all day, I have some free time. I'd like a change."

"What sort of classes?"

"Maybe something to do with nursing. I've had plenty of experience with Miss Jean and with Dickey, too."

"You'd be a good nurse, Zina, but getting a registered nursing degree takes a long time, and the classes can be expensive. Have you thought about a job as a practical nurse?"

"I don't really know the difference between *registered* and *practical*," Zina admitted.

"Well, my advice for you is to make an appointment at St. Mary's Hospital to talk to someone about the career options they offer in their nursing school. They have several programs, and one might be just right for you. They can explain all the details you'll need to know. After you make the appointment, I'll be glad to help you make a list of questions to ask."

"Thanks. That's good advice. I'll call St. Mary's tomorrow. I'd best not dally on this because I could be out of a job soon."

"Why do you say that?" asked Louise.

"It wouldn't surprise me one little bit if Dickey's father takes another wife, come spring. He's been seeing someone for a while. He'll wait a year just to be proper, but after that, who knows?"

"I didn't know he was seeing someone. Who is she?"

Without answering Louise's question, Zina said, "Speaking of job changes, I heard Rose will be starting a new job selling defense bonds on the first of December. Is that true?"

"Yes, she's already told her boss that she's leaving."

"Is Rose keeping her boss's name on her dance card?"

"No, that friendship is over."

"Guess Evelyn Fisher will be happy to hear about that. She's downright smitten with that jerk. Evelyn's been jealous of Rose since day one."

Louise was shocked. This was the first she had heard about the Evelyn-and-Boss friendship. "I don't think Rose knows about his friendship with Evelyn. What about his wife? They have five children still at home!"

"I don't know his wife, but I'll bet she doesn't care what he does as long as he pays the bills and leaves her alone. I've got to leave now and pick up the kids from school. Thanks for the coffee and the tip about the nursing school."

\* \* \*

Louise was sitting at the dining-room window looking out at the big white rosebush, now stripped of its summer leaves, when Frances came in from school.

"Hi," said Frances, taking the stairs two at a time on the way to her bedroom. Her mother didn't answer. Frances dumped her books on the bed, shed her coat, and dug into her dress pocket for Patrolman Leo Thompson's business card. She slipped the card into her secret purse and closed the snap.

Louise continued staring at the rosebush. It seemed to be trying to tell her something. The tall man who occasionally stood near the rosebush wasn't there today. Had he scratched on her window last night? Her mind was whirling—too much to process. Who had been in her yard? A trespasser? A Peeping

Tom? Or someone meaning to hurt or scare her? She dismissed the police theory. There had been someone out there. She knew it.

Her mind shifted gears to the prospect of Zina's moving away. Louise hated change. *What if Dickey's new stepmother doesn't like me? If Zina leaves, who will help with Frances?* Then there was the new twist in Rose's situation. Her sister-in-law's love life was always interesting, but a love triangle was even more interesting. *Should I tell Harry? Who else knows about this? Why did no one tell me? Why are they keeping secrets from me?*

# CHAPTER 22

The week before Christmas, Louise was in a holiday mood. She thought it would be a good idea to expand their Christmas-dinner guest list beyond the immediate family. Her first invitation went to Zina and Dickey.

"Sorry, but we can't make it. I'm going home to visit my folks, and Dickey's father is taking him to his lady friend's house. This is Dickey's first Christmas without his mom. His dad wants to get him away from the house and its sad memories. Thanks, anyway," Zina said.

Louise's next call was to Evelyn Fisher. "I'm calling to invite you and your mother to have Christmas dinner with us. I hope you can come."

"I wish we could, but we always go to my mother's cousin's house. I've already told her we'll be there again this year," Evelyn said. "These cousins have been getting together for Christmas dinner for over fifty years, and I can't disappoint them this year. It may be their last. I hope you have a Merry Christmas and Happy New Year."

As soon as she heard Evelyn's words, "Happy New Year," an idea sprouted in Louise's head. She would have a New Year's Eve party. That was a better choice. Everyone was too busy with family on Christmas Day.

"We do want to see you over the holidays, and we're having a News Year's Eve party, as well. Could you come for that?" asked Louise.

"I don't have any plans for New Year's Eve, and I'd be happy to come to your party. My mother can't stay up that late, but I'll be there."

Zina accepted the New Year's Eve party invitation on behalf of herself and Dickey. Ben Cole and George Mills both agreed to come. Rose, of course, would be there. Louise put down the telephone.

Then she started to panic. *What have I done? People are coming to our house, and they are expecting to have fun. I don't know how to have fun. I don't even know how to have a party. If it weren't for Frances, I could have been more socially active. I would have learned how to entertain,* she thought, adding yet another charge to Frances's ever-growing list of indictments. *Harry will have to help me.*

When he heard about the party, Harry said, "Don't worry about a thing, Louise. These are grown-up people. They can entertain themselves by talking to each other. I'll help keep the conversation moving. We'll put out a few snacks, some drinks, funny hats and horns. At midnight we'll turn on the radio and listen to the Times Square celebration. We can all sing *Auld Lang Syne* along with the radio. If anyone wants to dance, we can turn on the radio to either Guy Lombardo or Glenn Miller."

*How did Harry know these things?* Louise wondered. She was still nervous about the party.

* * *

The Hoags' Christmas was small, traditional, and uneventful. Rose gave Frances two pairs of white socks with lace trim. Harry gave his daughter a pair of roller skates with a tightening key on a shoestring that she could hang around her neck. Louise's gift to Frances was a surprise. It was a doll with a soft cloth body and hard composite arms, legs, and head. The doll was wearing a pink dress, a matching hat, and little shoes. She had authentic brown hair that could be combed.

"Her name is Madeline," said Louise.

"But the Madeline in my book has red hair," said Frances.

"That doesn't matter. If you don't want this doll, she can be mine."

With that, Louise took the doll from Frances and sat it next to her on the couch. Frances didn't say anything. She didn't much like dolls anyway. She wanted a bicycle. Rose and Harry looked at each other but didn't verbalize their thoughts.

Harry called Frances into his room just before she went to bed that night.

"Frances, I have something else for you," he said, holding out a house key. "This is a key to our house. Put it on your shoestring necklace with your skate key. You won't have to worry about getting locked out if you have your own key."

"When I'm locked out, I go to Dickey's or to Carol's," Frances said.

Harry had suspected that was the case.

That night Louise slept with Madeline. She liked the doll. Madeline reminded her of the doll she never had when she was a child. Unlike Frances, Madeline was totally compliant and would never cause trouble.

* * *

Between Christmas and New Year's, Louise vacillated between anxiety and depression. She convinced herself that the upcoming New Year's Eve party would be a disaster.

*Everyone will have a terrible time, and they'll blame me. What if Rose and Evelyn cause a scene? What unpredictable thing will Frances do? What if everyone gets bored and goes home early? Will any of them ever want to come to our house again?* These thoughts, along with a hundred others, ricocheted inside Louise's head like bumper cars crashing into outsized lumps of gloom.

She heard the gloom say, in an accusing voice, "It doesn't matter. No one likes you anyway. You'll never have any friends. You're useless. You don't even know how to have a party."

The morning before the party, Louise calmed her panic long enough to tell Harry, "I'm not up to fixing any refreshments. You'll have to take care of all that."

"Okay. It's not a big deal. People just want to get together to celebrate the New Year. The food doesn't matter. Don't worry. I'll take care of everything."

Louise listened as Harry called Jack Mercer and ordered a deli tray. "I'll pick up some beer and a couple of bottles of champagne later," he said.

Then he called his sister. "Rose, how about bringing some hats and horns and other stuff to make our celebration a real party?"

Louise's anxiety retreated slightly, but not entirely. She knew that George Mills and Ben Cole would bring their favorite beverages without being asked and that neither Zina nor Evelyn would show up empty handed. But what if they didn't bring anything? Would the deli tray be enough?

* * *

Zina arrived early, carrying a plate of homemade brownies. Dickey was with her, wearing his pajamas under his winter coat. Evelyn's contribution was a rather large bird's nest affair, constructed of celery spears stuffed with pimento cheese. Ripe olives, masquerading as eggs, filled the nest. The attention this curious arrangement drew caused everyone to focus on Evelyn's culinary skills rather than on her startling birthmark.

Louise stared at Evelyn. *She is so ugly. I don't know why everyone likes her. The way she combs her hair over her face looks just like a bird's nest, all right!*

The front door burst open and there was Rose, wearing a party hat and blowing a noise maker. She was carrying a box filled with hats, horns, noise makers, and rattles for everyone. "Happy New Year!" she shouted between blasts on her horn. The party went into full swing.

Louise watched as Harry played the perfect host and Rose assumed her role as life of the party. With interest, she saw George and Ben abandon their competition for Rose's attention and expand their circle to include Evelyn and Zina. *Why am I always the one who's left out?*

"It's nine o'clock, and the children need to go to bed," Louise announced.

"I don't want to go to bed. I want to see the New Year," said Frances. "I want to wear a hat and blow a horn."

*I knew it. I knew it. Frances is going to ruin my party.* Louise could feel hot tears threatening to breach the levee of her lower eyelids. *I will not cry.* She drew in a slow breath and retreated to a place where only she could go.

Ignoring Louise and turning her full attention to the children, Rose said, "Okay. Frances and Dickey, here are your hats. Now, choose a noise maker. We are going to do a New Year's Eve conga dance."

Under Rose's direction, everyone was up, wearing a hat and forming a line, one behind the other. They paraded through the living room, around the dining room table, and back again. Rose danced at the head of the line, chanting, "One, two, three . . . *Conga.* One, two, three . . . *Conga* . . ."

The laughter of the swaying dancers was seductive. *They are having so much fun. I want to have fun, too,* thought Louise as she left her seat and joined the others. From the end of the line, she could see Ben Cole was enjoying having his hands fixed on Evelyn's shapely waist. *That Ben Cole! He is always after the ladies. He is such a womanizer! I remember, not so long ago, when he made a pass at me.*

213

Dance over, drinks freshened, and the children put to bed, Louise spoke up, "I think we should all make a New Year's resolution. After all, it'll soon be 1941—a brand new year. You go first, Harry. Tell us your New Year's resolution."

"Okay. As you all know, I tried my hand at vegetable gardening this past summer. It didn't go as well as I'd hoped. Therefore, I resolve to be a better vegetable gardener this coming year. Your turn, Ben."

"I resolve to up the occupancy and turnaround rate of my clients' rental units," Ben said.

"What does that mean?" asked Louise.

"It means Ben will make more money," answered Rose, laughing.

"Okay, Rose, what is your resolution?" asked Ben.

"I resolve to sell more defense bonds than anyone else in the bond office. I won't make more money like Ben, but I might get a promotion."

Evelyn was next. She said, "I resolve to double my list of Fuller Brush customers and to triple my sales."

"Since most of you are talking about making more money, this is my resolution," Zina said. "I resolve to find a way to get into one of the nursing programs at St. Mary's Hospital."

Harry gave her an encouraging grin and a wink. "Good for you, Zina! I know you can do it."

Louise, along with the others, looked at George Mills as he began to speak. "Since I took over the drugstore, I've been putting off the chore of sorting through the old records left by my cousin, Roger. My resolution is to organize all the old store records this year, going back to my uncle's time."

"I don't envy you that job," Harry said.

*I would like to help with that chore,* Louise thought.

Rose said, "What about you, Louise? What is your resolution for the new year?" All heads turned in Louise's direction.

Louise was quiet. She sat very still, staring straight ahead, with her hands folded in her lap. She listened again to the recording in her head, replaying her thoughts of the past week.

*Something is not right. Something is very wrong. Something is making me sick. If it isn't sleeping with Harry, and if it isn't his drinking, then it must be something else. Maybe it's my diet. Maybe eating meat isn't good for me. All that animal flesh is hurting my brain and causing me to be nervous—to feel blue and discouraged all the time. That's it! It's the meat in my diet.*

When Louise spoke, it was in a clear voice, projected as though she were talking to someone in another room. She said, "My resolution may surprise you. It isn't about what I'm going to do. It's about what I'm going to become. I resolve to become a *vegetarian.*"

# CHAPTER 23

$\mathcal{A}$s the new year of 1941 began, the impending clouds of war moved closer and hurled their shadows across the Atlantic to darken the landscape of Allenburg, Ohio. The Hoags and their neighbors became resigned to the approaching conflict as news reports of the war in Europe became more ominous. They knew that America would soon declare war on Germany. They just didn't know when, and the uncertainty kept everyone on edge as they tried to prepare for war on the home front. Harry was making plans, too. He instructed the payroll department at his company to increase deductions for his monthly purchase of defense bonds.

"War, or no war, there are some things I don't plan to do without," Louise announced resolutely, banging her empty tea cup on the kitchen table.

Harry looked up from his newspaper. "What are you talking about?"

"There are rumors that soon we won't be able to get as much sugar as we want, and nylon hose may not be available. I need sugar for my tea, and I need nylons. I'm going to buy some extra nylons and put them aside for hard times."

"Louise, that's hoarding. We're constantly being warned against hoarding. It's un-American." Harry frowned at his wife.

Louise frowned back at him. *What does Harry know? He's only a man and he doesn't understand about needing nylons. I'll get all I can while I can, and I'll hide them where Harry would never think to look.* The following week, she bought six pairs of nylon hose and an extra ten pounds of sugar.

* * *

Louise was determined to stick with her New Year's resolution. The first week was easy. By the end of the second week, she began to miss the meat she had eliminated from her diet. She was headache free and less nervous, but she felt weak.

*I need more exercise. Walking is good exercise. I can go for a walk every morning after Frances goes to school. That will build up my strength.* The idea that she could walk Frances to school never occurred to her.

The following morning, Louise went for her first walk. She decided to walk around the block. After two blocks, in the four-block trek, her feet began to hurt. *I have the wrong shoes,* she lamented. *I need walking shoes.* She limped home and elevated her bare feet while she finished reading the morning paper. After a vegetarian lunch, she took the bus downtown to her favorite shoe store, where she bought a pair of sturdy saddle-oxford shoes and six pairs of nylon stockings.

The new shoes were perfect. Soon Louise was walking two miles every morning. Her legs were getting stronger, but the rest of her was getting weaker. *Too much sugar in my diet. No more sweets except for the sugar in my tea. That I must have.*

Louise's walks became longer and longer. Most mornings she could be seen, wearing her new saddle oxfords, not just in the neighborhood, but all the way up Boyd Boulevard. She began walking to town whenever she had shopping to do. It was only three miles from Collis Avenue to the downtown area. Three miles there and three miles back—six miles. *If I get tired, I can always take the bus.* She never did. On those shopping days, she skipped lunch. Before long she gave up lunch completely. She was losing weight at an alarming pace.

Harry was the first to comment on Louise's appearance. "Louise, you look so thin. Are you sure you're eating enough?"

"I'm fine. This new diet suits me. I haven't had a headache in months and my nerves are better. You don't want a fat wife, do you?"

"You've never been fat in your whole life, but now you're too thin. I'm worried about you. I think you should see the doctor for a checkup."

Louise erupted, "No. No. No. That doctor is a quack and I won't go back to see him."

By Easter, Louise had lost twenty-five pounds from her already slim frame. Her body was hard and lean, but weak and undernourished. Her weakness was disguised by the constant motion with which she surrounded herself. Her once pretty face was gaunt. She rattled in her clothes, which hung from her bones as though from a coat hanger. Many days she ate nothing except saltine crackers and hot tea. The neighbors began to whisper. Behind Louise's back, Grandmother Mercer said, "*Irgendetwas stimmt mit dieser Frau nicht.* (Something is wrong with that woman)."

Zina spoke directly to Louise. "You're as poor as a snake. You look like a bag of bones with a hank of hair sewed on top. You need to eat more. There's plenty that would be glad to have what you turn down. How about if I fix you a nice supper tonight?"

"No, thank you, Zina. I'm fine. There's nothing wrong with me. I'm stronger than I look." *When will people leave me alone?*

Louise was pleased with her diet and with her walking regime. It was working for her. She was convinced she had found the cure for her problems. She decided to reduce her exposure to germs by eating only white foods. She also gave up bread and all other bakery products. Her diet consisted of cottage cheese, canned pears, bananas, raw cauliflower, rice, and pasta.

"You can't see the germs on colored food," she told Harry. "White food is safer."

"You can drink milk," Harry said. "It's white, and it's good for babies. It'll be good for you, too. You need to gain some weight."

Louise considered her husband's suggestion, but decided against it. She didn't like milk, except in her tea. The pounds continued to melt away. By early May, she was down from her normal weight by thirty-seven pounds. Her daily energy allotment was spent entirely on walking. She had no strength for, or interest in, any other activity. Louise refused to believe that she was sick. She told herself, *I'm just a little tired, and no wonder, with that whirling dervish of a child, Frances, spinning all around the house. Just watching her is exhausting.*

\* \* \*

On the last day of school, Frances's teacher planned a playground picnic for her class. They would have Kool-Aid and cookies to go with their bag lunches. Frances was running late that morning and left her lunch sitting on the kitchen table. It was midmorning when she realized her mistake. *Maybe I can talk Mary Lynn into sharing. She always has enough for two or three, and she likes to share.*

Just before the lunch bell rang, Frances's first-grade class was surprised to see a thin woman standing in the doorway, holding a paper bag. Mrs. Adams was shocked at the sight of the emaciated form.

"Hello. I'm Frances's mother. She forgot her lunch," the skeleton said, extending a small bag.

"Hello. I'm Mrs. Adams, Frances's teacher. Please come in." She took the paper bag from the visitor and handed it to Frances. "You're welcome to join us for lunch. We're having a picnic on the playground. Maybe you can help me with the cookies."

Mrs. Adams's mind raced. *This is my chance to find out more about the home life of a very mysterious little girl who tries so hard to improve her reading skills, who is a budding artist, and who speaks German, but doesn't seem to know that it's a foreign language. What kind of a mother is this? Who teaches a child to count in Roman numerals? Frances is the only student I have ever had who never talks about her mother. And now, here's her mother, in person. What's wrong with this thin, frail woman? She must be ill.*

Out on the playground, Louise spoke to several of the children as she helped pass the cookies. The teacher watched as Frances's mother completely ignored her own daughter. Frances didn't seem to care. She and Mary Lynn were eating with two other girls near the big oak tree. Frances didn't even look in her mother's direction.

Mrs. Adams was shocked. *I don't believe this. What else is wrong with this picture?*

Her thoughts were interrupted. She watched in horror as the too thin figure before her fell to the ground like a broken doll.

# CHAPTER 24

*L*ouise lay motionless on the bare ground near the swings. Inside her head, the world spun out of control. She was awake, but for some reason, she couldn't manage to open her eyes, move, or speak. *Am I asleep?* Her eyes didn't work, and the only sound she could hear was the thumping of her heart. Her body felt numb. *Why am I stuck in this body? It won't move. Everything's so dark. I'm breathing, so I can't be dead.* Her world melted into black.

Sounds were all around her. Her head was still spinning. *What are those sounds? Are they voices? I hear a bird. He's so close . . .* Everything went dark again. *Oh, I smell something. What is it? Is it dirt? Does dirt have an odor of its own?*

The teacher's voice echoed in the distance. "Mrs. Hoag, Mrs. Hoag, can you open your eyes? Don't move. Just lie still and try to open your eyes. I'll get help."

The spinning in her head gave way to a tilting sensation. She moved back into a body that was no longer numb—a body screaming in pain. She lay with her foot twisted in an impossible position, pinned under her crumpled figure. She heard a moan. *Was that her?*

"Mom, Mom, get up." It was Frances. Louise opened one eye and saw her daughter leaning over her.

"Ohhhh . . . my foot, my foot. It's broken. Get away from me," Louise screamed.

"Here comes Zina," said Dickey, who was standing beside Frances and staring wide eyed at his neighbor. "She's is coming to eat lunch with us. She can help."

Louise saw a flood of relief sweep over Mrs. Adams's face as she recognized the housekeeper who shepherded Dickey and Frances to school each day and who was, at this very moment, hurrying in their direction.

*That stupid teacher! She's already forgotten about me. I don't trust her. I'm hurt. Zina will help me.*

"Oh, Zina, I'm glad to see you," Mrs. Adams said. "Frances's mother needs some help."

"What's going on?" asked Zina, instinctively taking Dickey's hand. "Louise, why are you on the ground? Did you fall?"

"Yes, she fell," answered Mrs. Adams. "It looks like she may have broken her ankle. I'm afraid to move her. Do you know how to get in touch with her husband?"

"He's away on a business trip, but I'll call his sister. Where's the school telephone?"

*Why are they talking about me as if I weren't here?* "Ohhhh . . . my foot hurts," Louise cried.

"I need to use your telephone. It's an emergency," Zina said, bursting into the principal's office unannounced.

223

"Hello, Rose, this is Zina. I'm calling from the principal's office at Frances's school. Louise fell down and broke her foot. We're afraid to move her. Can you come?"

"Is Frances okay?"

"She's fine, but I think Louise should go to the hospital."

"I'll call an ambulance from here and come to the school right now. Thanks, Zina."

At the hospital, the orthopedic doctor on call examined Louise's foot with care and ordered a series of X-rays. Two metatarsal bones in her right foot were broken, and her ankle had sustained a nasty break in two places.

"We can fix this," Dr. Brower told Louise. "However, we'll have to operate."

"I don't want to be operated on. What's the alternative? Will I die?"

"Not hardly. Broken ankles aren't known to be fatal. If we do nothing, your foot and ankle will eventually heal, but you'll never walk again. With surgery, we can have you up and about in a few weeks."

Louise signed the permission papers.

\* \* \*

"Where am I?" Louise asked as she roused from the fog clouding her mind. "Why is my leg tied to the ceiling? Why am I in this strange bed, and where are my clothes?"

"Hello, Mrs. Hoag. It's good to see you're waking up. You're in the hospital. Your surgery is over, and you're on your way to recovery," said the nurse standing beside her bed.

"My foot hurts," complained Louise with a loud moan.

"Your doctor has ordered medication for pain. You can have some now if you like."

The nurse handed Louise a small paper cup containing a codeine pill and held a glass of water near her lips.

Water had never tasted so good. Louise drank the whole glass and asked for another. Then another. Despite the pain in her foot, Louise realized she was hungry. *When was the last time I ate something?*

\* \* \*

After two weeks in traction, Louise began to feel better. The pain in her ankle bothered her only when she tried to move her foot. Her mind had cleared, and the hospital staff treated her as though she were special. Louise's appetite began to return slowly. She ate whatever arrived on the dining tray without comment or complaint.

*I am special. Harry comes to see me every day. He sent flowers, too. Rose stops by most days, and the neighbors have all been here to visit. I must have a dozen get-well cards and a nice letter from Helen. She's a good sister.*

When Dr. Brower made his daily rounds, Louise was waiting for him. "My main problem with the hospital is boredom. I do have visitors, but their visits don't last very long. They mostly want to talk about themselves and their uninteresting lives. Even with all the boredom, I like it here. I want to live here permanently."

"In a few more days, you'll change your mind and be looking forward to getting out of here," Dr. Brower promised. "I'm happy with the progress being made by your broken bones. They are healing nicely. I'm especially pleased to see that your appetite has returned. While you are here waiting for your bones to knit, I would like for you to see another doctor about your weight."

"Why are you transferring me to a new doctor? I'm doing fine with you," Louise pouted.

"Yes, you're doing fine, but I'm no longer the right doctor to help you. My specialty is orthopedics. Another doctor will be of more help with your other problems," Dr. Brower said.

"I don't have other problems," Louise stated in a defiant voice. "What are you talking about?"

"You were sick before you fell and injured yourself. I recommend that we find out why. There are other doctors, better trained than I, to help with that. Besides, I have bones to set, and your bones are well on the way to mending."

\* \* \*

Louise sat in her wheelchair, with her foot propped up, staring at the medium-sized man with lank hair and thick glasses sitting behind the desk in the comfortable room on the third floor. *His hair is too long, and it looks greasy. I'll bet he can't see very well, even from behind those glasses.* The man seemed harmless enough. So she relaxed a little. *He'll be easy to handle.*

The man rose from his chair and extended his hand to Louise across the desk. "I'm Dr. Couch—Dr. Robert Couch."

*What a lazy man! He didn't even come around his desk to shake my hand properly.*

"My name is Louise Hoag. Dr. Brower recommended that I talk to you."

"What would you like to talk about?" asked Dr. Couch, looking at his fingernails.

"I don't want to talk to you. This whole thing is Dr. Brower's idea. He just wants to shuffle me off to someone else. He can make more money setting bones than talking."

Not for the first time, the psychiatrist wondered just how much an orthopedic surgeon made.

"You aren't required to talk. Would you like some coffee? I'm going to have a cup."

"No, thank you," Louise responded, remembering her manners.

Louise looked around the room while Dr. Couch filled his coffee mug from a thermos bottle on the credenza behind his desk. The room resembled a living room more than a doctor's office. She approved of the decorations. The furnishings were tasteful and understated. The walls were painted a soft neutral tone. The few pictures hanging on the walls were serene landscapes, done in pastel watercolor. There were no obnoxious diplomas hanging about. All the chairs looked comfortable. Best of all, there was plenty of natural light coming from the two large windows.

"I could live in this room," she announced.

Dr. Couch looked up from his coffee, which he was stirring with a letter opener. "Why do you say that?"

"It's a nice room. I like it. No one would bother me here."

"Do people bother you?"

"Yes, lots of people bother me. You bother me. Don't you know its bad manners to stir your coffee with a letter opener?"

The doctor smiled for the first time. "I'll stop stirring if you want," he said and began cleaning his fingernails with the same letter opener.

Louise frowned at him. His personal habits were vulgar beyond her experience. He was worse than her initial impression had led her to believe. *He's just trying to ruffle my feathers and get me to cackle like a hen. He can't outsmart me.*

"I don't know why I have to talk to you. If I do talk to you, how do I know you'll even listen? What do you want me to talk about anyway?"

"Why don't you begin by telling me a little about your life before you broke your ankle?"

"Where do you want me to start?" Louise asked.

"Wherever you want."

"I did have a few problems before I broke my ankle. My main problem was sick headaches. They always came without warning. I tried everything . . ."

Out came the words, tripping over each other in their haste to find a listening ear. Louise talked and talked and talked. She had never talked so much and said so little in so short a time. Dr. Couch sat behind his desk and listened, wishing he could take a bathroom break.

Louise continued talking nonstop until they were interrupted by a knock on the door. It was a signal that their hour was over. The psychiatrist stood and said, "Our time is up. We'll have to continue our conversation tomorrow. I look forward to seeing you then, at the same time." Louise was ushered out by his secretary, and the doctor made a hasty retreat to the restroom.

Dr. Robert Couch was not nearly as lazy as Louise thought. Before the day was over, he had telephoned the Hoags' family doctor and explained his role in Louise's treatment. He requested and received by messenger a copy of her medical records, which he read with care. He asked his secretary to set up an appointment with her husband for early the following day, prior to his session with Louise. Then he saw two more patients.

As he was leaving for the day, his secretary said, "Dr. Couch, you look preoccupied. Is everything all right? Have I done something to upset you?"

"No. Everything is fine, and you did a super job today, as always. I was just thinking about what it would be like to practice orthopedics."

"I know they make a lot of money. Do you think their job is easier than yours?"

"Bones you can see and even fix. Brains are much harder."

* * *

The next morning, Harry settled himself in the same chair Louise had occupied less than twenty-four hours earlier. After introductions were made, he asked Dr. Couch, "How is my wife? When can she come home?"

"Your wife's foot and ankle are healing nicely, right on schedule. She has now been in the hospital almost a month, and we're pleased that she's gaining weight. Physically, she's doing fine. However, we do have some concerns about her mental stability. I saw her in this office yesterday, and we had a good session. I recommend that she be moved to this floor, which will be more convenient. I'd like to continue seeing her on a daily basis for the next two weeks. After that, we can reevaluate her situation."

"Are you saying she should be moved to the psychiatric floor?"

"Well, yes, I do think this floor is the best place for her while she's here. By the way, how have you and your daughter been doing?"

"We're fine. My sister has moved in temporarily, and the next door neighbor takes care of our daughter during the day. Frances is well cared for, and she's a happy kid."

"Does your daughter miss her mother?"

"Not really. They've never had the kind of mother-daughter closeness that some families have. If you think it's best to move Louise to another room, I'll trust your judgment."

For the next two weeks, Louise saw Dr. Couch at two o'clock every afternoon. She talked. He listened. She cried. He waited. After she left his office each day, Dr. Couch make copious notes. He reviewed case histories of patients with complaints similar to Louise's. She told him everything—almost everything. Sometimes he wanted to stop her when she told him too much. *Is detailing Zina's recipe for bread pudding just a way to burn the clock? What is Louise not telling me?*

Louise was not telling Dr. Couch about Roger Mills's mysterious death. Dr. Couch didn't even know that a pharmacist by that name had ever existed. After two weeks of therapy, Louise became convinced that it was Roger Mills who had been causing all her problems. He wouldn't leave her alone. He tormented her mind. He was trying to drive her crazy. She would find no peace until she uncovered the reason behind his death. Still, she saw no reason to tell Dr. Couch about Roger. *He can't help. He doesn't even know Roger. Never did.*

Dr. Couch sat behind his desk, toying with his letter opener. If only he could open Louise's mind. Tomorrow Louise would be released from St. Mary's Hospital. She would not be going home to the house on Collis Avenue. With Harry's consent, she would be transferred to the State Mental Hospital in Columbus for further treatment. Dr. Couch wrote his preliminary diagnosis on a sheet of paper and put it in Louise's file.

*Chronic, moderate to severe, anxiety syndrome, evidenced by panic attacks and hallucinations, and complicated by intermediate bouts of depression . . .*

Staring at Louise's folder, the psychiatrist's thoughts returned to his most recent conversation with her husband.

"I don't understand why my wife can't come home," Harry said in dismay. "Everyone says her broken bones are mending well. She has a sturdy cast on her leg for protection, and she is beginning to get the hang of using crutches. My sister and our

231

neighbor are on board, ready to help. You don't think Louise would hurt herself, do you?"

Dr. Couch gave his best professional opinion. "I think the only way your wife would hurt herself is by resuming her unhealthy lifestyle. When she was admitted to St. Mary's, she was dehydrated, undernourished, and on the verge of starvation. Now, she is beginning to understand how dangerous it can be to not have a balanced diet and to over exercise. Additional therapy can help her change her old habits. But, to answer your question, no, I don't think she's at risk of hurting herself in any other way. My main concern is for your daughter's welfare."

# CHAPTER 25

$\mathcal{L}$ ouise sat on the edge of the narrow bed in her room at the State Mental Hospital. Her leg, still in its plaster cast, was elevated on a pillow beside her. Harry sat in a chair near the window, facing his wife. The faithful big tin suitcase stood on the floor between them. It held all the possessions Louise would need for the next three months.

"I'll be glad to help you unpack and put your things away," Harry offered.

"No. I want to put my own things away. I don't need your help. Did you remember to pack my saddle oxfords and plenty of writing supplies?"

"Yes, your saddle shoes are in your suitcase. I bought some new shoelaces and polished the shoes myself. I also remembered to put in lots of stationery and some stamps, so you can write to Helen."

"What about the pens, pencils, and spiral notebooks I asked for? Did you remember the index cards?"

"I sure did. You have enough office supplies to start a business."

"Harry, you have to promise me one thing. Promise that you won't tell anyone where I am."

"Okay. If that's what you want, I promise not to tell anyone. I'll tell them you're staying with your sister, Helen, until your foot and ankle are completely healed."

A shadow crossed the floor. Louise turned her head to see a middle-aged, matronly woman standing in the open doorway. The woman was wearing a starched blue uniform, not unlike a housedress, and a look of utter indifference on her bland face. Ignoring Louise, she addressed Harry in a monotone voice. "Visiting hours are over." She motioned for him to follow her.

"I'll see you next week." Harry said, bending over to give his wife a goodbye kiss on her cheek.

Louise sat motionless until she was sure she was alone. With help from her crutches, she hopped to the center of the room where the big tin suitcase sat. She spoke to it. "We have come a long way together, you and I." She undid its clasp, opened the lid, and jerked back in surprise, almost losing her balance.

There, inside the suitcase, was the doll, Madeline, which she had given to Frances for Christmas and which she had repossessed the same day. A penciled note, written in the large print of a first grader, was pinned to the doll's dress. It said, "Get well" not "Love, Frances" not "I hope you get better." Just the words, "Get Well."

"I am well," Louise told the doll, picking it up and holding it close. "Where would you like to stay during the day?" She considered propping the doll on her bed but rejected that idea in favor of another. "I'll fix you a comfortable place in the closet where no one will find you. At night you can sleep with me."

After unpacking the suitcase and putting her things away, Louise sat in the chair near the window. *I like the view from this window. From here I can see the drive coming up from the main road. I'll be able to see who comes and goes before they see me.*

*They might have binoculars,* the Voice in her head warned.

"I'll put a big mirror over most of the window. Then when they look up with their binoculars, all they'll see is themselves," Louise countered. She and the Voice both thought this was very funny, and they laughed together. Madeline laughed, too.

\* \* \*

The first thing Louise learned about the State Mental Hospital was that it had a time and a place for everything—mostly a time. Everything revolved around an inescapable routine.

*What was that quotation? Oh, yes, " . . . A time to be born, and a time to die . . . a time to kill, and a time to heal . . . a time to weep . . . and a time to mourn . . . and a time to hate . . ." That was it. They needed to add, "A time to get up, and a time to eat, a time for consultation, and a time for group therapy."*

Louise had daily one-on-one consultations with Dr. Sloan, one of the staff psychiatrists. *He's okay, I guess. He doesn't annoy me nearly as much as that vulgar Dr. Couch. At least, Dr.*

*Sloan has some manners. He's just an old man ready for retirement, and he's a pretty good listener.*

During her sessions with Dr. Sloan, Louise babbled away, reiterating, almost verbatim, everything she had told Dr. Couch at St. Mary's. She suspected that Dr. Sloan wasn't really listening, but letting his mind float away on his retirement dreams. *He's probably heard it all before. I'll tell him enough— but not too much. He can't know about Roger.*

Louise's group-therapy sessions were a different matter. She hated every minute of every session. Six patients attended each meeting, along with one psychiatrist and one intern, who was there to observe. Louise noticed that the intern never said anything. He just sat there looking bored. She spoke only when the psychiatrist asked her a direct question. The other patients took turns discussing their hopes, fears, and complaints. Everyone sat in a circle, except one man who always moved his folding chair to the far side of the room, against the wall. One woman sat through each meeting crying into her hands, which covered her face.

"Everyone is competing for the whine title. This is just a bitch session," Louise muttered.

After a week, Louise decided to follow the example of the man who excluded himself from the circle. She moved her chair to the opposite wall. "I see our circle is getting larger," observed the psychiatrist. No one else seemed to notice. Louise felt better sitting away from the group. Their laments were of no interest to her. *I can use this time to plan.*

"If this group session is to be successful, everyone needs to join our circle," the doctor said.

Everyone ignored him, including Louise and the man on the opposite side of the room. The patient, who was in the middle of her recurring complaint, continued without missing a beat.

"I don't know what I could have done to make my mother-in-law hate me so much. She criticizes everything I do. I've tried being nice to her and to include her in our family activities, but she still hates me. If I answer the telephone when she calls, she doesn't even say hello. She demands to speak to her son. I love my husband, and I don't want to upset him. He gets so angry when I try to talk to him about his mother. I don't know what to do."

Turning to look at Louise, the doctor said, "Louise, you're married. How is your relationship with your mother-in-law?"

"Dead. Dead. She's dead," Louise answered.

"Good answer," yelled the man on the opposite side of the room. "Kill the bitch. Kill the bitch . . ."

The four remaining patients, sitting in the circle, took up the chant. "Kill the bitch. Kill the bitch . . ." Louise noticed that the intern seemed to be enjoying this impromptu chorus. He was tapping his foot and slapping his knee in time to the lively cadence.

The psychiatrist held up his hand for attention and said, "That is an alternative, but we need to think through what might happen as a result. What do you think would happen if we chose that alternative, Louise?"

"We'd need to make it look like an accident," Louise answered. Without warning, she began to shake uncontrollably. Her thoughts raced. Now she knew—someone had made Roger Mills's death look like an accident. "It was not an accident," she shouted across the room, as she continued shaking.

*I told you so . . . I told you so . . .* sang the Voice in her head.

\* \* \*

The group session was over for the day. Louise was escorted back to her room and given a sedative. She lay on her bed, pretending to sleep. When she was sure the nurse had left, Louise retrieved Madeline from the closet, and cuddling the doll, she hobbled back to the bed. Instead of sleeping, she lay still, staring at the ceiling.

"We've wasted enough time. We have work to do. Tomorrow we'll begin," she told the doll.

Louise awoke the following day with a rush of enthusiasm. She was eager to get started. She had *lists* to make. She had things *to do.* "I need a *to-do list.*" She laughed aloud.

*They run this place on a schedule. Well, I can have a schedule, too. I'll use my free time, one hour after breakfast, two hours after lunch, and the entire evening after dinner to write out the steps I'll need to take. One of my spiral notebooks can be used to outline my step-by-step plan. I'll treat this as a "project" with achievable goals, deliverables, and due dates. Where did I hear those words? Did I read them somewhere? Oh, never mind . . .*

During breakfast, Louise decided that she'd need time to get her plan in order. *I need to stay here until I'm ready for the implementation phase. When I go home, Harry and Frances will just get in the way. The first thing I need to do is to start watching what I say. Things will go smoother if I don't make waves. I can play their game better than they . . .*

That very afternoon, Louise began compiling a list of people she wanted to interview—people who might have known Roger Mills or members of his family. The list was longer than she expected. There were all the neighbors, all the drugstore customers, employees, and vendors, Father Michael, all the parishioners of St. Joseph's Church, and others that Roger's nephew, George, might suggest. *I'll have to prioritize this list before I start. I'll bet Rose's boss knew Roger. She said he knows everyone in town. I'll add him to the list, for sure.* Louise realized, with a start, that she didn't even know the boss's real name. *Oh, well . . . Rose will know.*

* * *

A month went by and then another. Louise's days were filled with individual consultations, group sessions, and the fine-tuning of her plans. Louise was determined to play nice. She worked hard to keep the random thoughts careening through her brain from catapulting over her tongue and crashing out between her lips. *My doctors think I'm making progress and I am—with my plans and my social skills. If Dr. Sloan thinks differently, at least he keeps it to himself.*

It was the middle of September. Frances's seventh birthday had come and gone without Louise even noticing. Frances was now in the second grade. That fact didn't register with her mother. Louise's thoughts stayed focused on herself and her plans. She was ready to go home and begin the task she had set for herself. When she arrived at the State Mental Hospital, Louise brought with her a big tin suitcase, a broken foot, a diagnosis of paranoia and depression, and a growing obsession to uncover the truth behind Roger Mills's death. When she left, she took with her everything except the broken foot, now healed.

On October 1, 1941, Dr. Sloan signed Louise's release papers and wished her well. "I have just one question, Louise, before you go. You've never mentioned your daughter. Why is that?"

"I have no daughter," Louise said, turning to follow Harry and the big tin suitcase down the hall and outside to the waiting car.

# PART III

# CHAPTER 26

*L* ouise was excited. It was wonderful to be out of the hospital and back in her own cocoon—the little house on Collis Avenue. Harry was at work, and Frances was at school. She had the entire house and most of the day all to herself. She was eager to get to work on her Roger Mills project. She was still undecided about where to start even though she had given the question an enormous amount of thought. *Should I start at the beginning by checking the Department of Vital Statistics for Roger's birth certificate? Or start at the end by researching the newspaper stacks for his obituary?*

The Voice said, *Look out the front window. If the first car to go by is going up the hill, start with the birth certificate. If it's going downhill, start with the obituary.*

Louise looked out of the window, waiting for a car to pass. The obituary won. She put on her saddle shoes, gathered her note-taking supplies, and took the bus downtown to the newspaper office. She explained her errand to the woman behind the front desk.

"Our stacks are not open to the public, but you might try the library."

The reference-room librarian was more helpful. She showed Louise to a study carrel near the stacks. After a few minutes, the librarian delivered a week's worth of newspapers beginning with January 15, 1939, the day of Roger's death. The headline read, "Lake Area Blanketed by Snow." The articles that followed were all about the record-breaking snowfall and the below-average temperatures. Not a single word about Roger Mills, not even in the obituary section. At first, this puzzled Louise. Then it made sense. *Of course, he must have died after the paper went to press.*

Grabbing the next day's paper, she turned immediately to the obituary page. There it was.

## ROGER WILSON MILLS

Allenburg, Ohio—Roger Wilson Mills died January 15, 1939. Mr. Mills was born September 1, 1899, in Allenburg, Ohio, son of Walter and Irene Mills. He graduated from the Ohio State School of Pharmacy in 1924. Mr. Mills was the owner and operator of the Mills Pharmacy on Boyd Boulevard. He is survived by his wife, Anna, and one daughter, Charlene Mills. A funeral mass will be said at 10:00 a.m. on January 18 at St. Joseph's Catholic Church.

For further details, contact Father Michael Galloway at St. Joseph's. Burial arrangements are pending.

Louise read and reread Roger's obituary. She moved her hand to let her fingers touch the newspaper. She covered the obituary with her palm. When she removed her hand, the article was still there. *It's real. I can see it and I can feel it. It's so short, but it says so much. "Burial arrangements are pending"— what does that mean? Oh my god, Roger is really dead!*

*Of course Roger is dead. You already knew that. Now, what are you going to do about it?* the Voice asked.

Louise looked at the newspaper. Her vision blurred. The print was a swarm of black ants, scurrying across the surface. The only writing she could decipher was Roger's obituary, which floated above the ants in perfect clarity. *I need to study this more closely. I need to copy it.* She took out her notebook and pen, but the pen would not hold still. It quivered and shook. She saw that her hand was trembling, too. Her thoughts raced. *I will tear out Roger's obituary and take it home.*

*The librarian will see the hole in the paper. You'll get in big trouble. Take the whole page,* the Voice advised.

The obituaries were confined to one side of one page. She folded the page and slipped it into her purse.

* * *

Louise didn't remember the trip back to the house on Collis Avenue, but there she was in her own kitchen, pouring a cup of hot tea. Her sweater was thrown over a chair and her purse sat on the table watching her. Louise picked up the purse and climbed the stairs to her room. She closed and locked the door. She removed the obituary page from her purse and spread it on the card table in the corner. The ants had vanished, and her hand had ceased to tremble.

*I'll cut out Roger's obituary and paste it in my notebook. But what if I lose the notebook? I'll make a copy first.*

After copying the obituary onto one of the large index cards, she retrieved her scissors and a bottle of glue from the desk caddy. As Louise picked up the newspaper, ready to snip, she turned the page over. She gasped when she saw the article on the reverse side.

## LOCAL PHARMACIST FOUND DEAD

Allenburg, Ohio – Roger Wilson Mills, owner of the Mills Pharmacy on Boyd Boulevard, was found dead in his store early on the morning of January 15. His unattended death has been ruled an accident by Allenburg Police. Sgt. Leo Thompson is quoted as saying, "Mr. Mills's death appears to be the result of a fall down a flight of stairs."

Roger Mills was a prominent and well-liked member of the community. He was the son of Walter Mills, also a pharmacist. Mr. Mills was active in civic affairs and a devoted member of St. Joseph's Catholic Church. He will be remembered for his work with youth groups and for his acts of kindness toward friends and neighbors. He was a loyal member of the Knights of Columbus and the St. Vincent de Paul Society.

Recovering from her shock, Louise read the article again, scribbling in her notebook a list of unanswered questions.

Who found Roger? How early in the morning? Why were the police there? Who was Sergeant Leo Thompson? Does he still work for the police? Who were these friends and neighbors? Who were the other members of the Knights of Columbus and St. Vincent DePaul Society? What did they know about Roger? Did he fall or did someone push him?

Downstairs a door slammed. Louise jumped to attention. "Who's there?"

"Just me, Frances."

"Why are you home? You're supposed to be at school."

"Its three thirty. School's out, and I'm hungry."

"Do your homework."

Louise heard the backdoor slam again. *Why won't that child leave me alone? I have work to do.*

Louise lay across her bed, trying to decide what to do next. *If I cut out the obituary, it will mess up the article on the reverse side. I need to save the whole page. I need to go back to the library and check the other newspapers in case there was a follow-up article. I can do that tomorrow.*

\* \* \*

Louise was awakened that night by the sound of someone gagging and crying. It was Frances, in the bathroom, vomiting. Harry was in the bathroom comforting his daughter.

"What's going on?" Louise demanded from the hallway outside the bathroom door.

245

"Frances is sick. I don't know if she ate something that didn't agree with her or if she has the stomach flu. Either way, she should stay home from school tomorrow."

"I guess you expect *me* to stay home with her," Louise groused. *There go my library plans.*

Frances did, indeed, have the stomach flu. She was out of school for five days. As the week wore on, Louise became more and more cross and agitated. *It's Frances again. She's getting in the way of my project. I wouldn't be surprised if she's doing it on purpose.*

\* \* \*

The following week, the fuel pump on Rose's car went out, and a new one had to be ordered. Harry offered to drive Rose to work while her car was waiting to be repaired if she moved in with them for the week.

"I don't want her here. She gets in the way," Louise told her husband in an angry voice.

"Calm down, Louise. Rose is at work all day. In the evenings she helps with dinner and the dishes, and she reads to Frances. Why don't you like Rose?"

"She's too cheerful, and she has too much energy," Louise said, fighting back her tears.

Later in her room, with the door locked, the tears came in earnest. She collapsed onto her bed and began sobbing. She felt as though she were falling into a big black hole from which there was no escape. Her head began to ache.

246

It took another week for Louise to regain her balance. Then it was fall break at school. Frances was home every day. Next came Thanksgiving and the first of December. The days hurried by. Louise stayed busy working around the house and revising her plans. They were important, but they, in themselves, didn't produce any results. Concentration was impossible.

"Shut up. Shut up. Just shut up," Louise yelled at the ever-present Voice. "What do you want me to do?"

*"Get to work."*

# CHAPTER 27

*L*ouise sat at the same study carrel she had used on her previous trip to the library. Spread before her were the local newspapers for January 17–21, 1939. She took her time as she perused each individual paper. The only mention of Roger Mills in the January 17 paper was a repeat of the obituary, which had appeared the previous day. On January 18, the day of Roger's funeral, the same obituary was printed, with one exception. Instead of saying, "Burial arrangements are pending," the last sentence of the obituary said, "Burial will be private."

"What do you mean *private*? You can't say *pending* one day and *private* the next. That's not right," Louise said to the newspaper she was holding.

"Shhhhhhh," came from the librarian.

*There must be a reason for that, and it's up to you to find out why,* said the Voice.

"I will. I will. Leave me alone."

"Shhhhhhh!"

Louise frowned at the librarian and then at the newspaper. She tried scowling at the Voice, but, try as she might, she only generated a series of grotesque faces. The Voice laughed at Louise. She knew she looked silly, and she laughed, too.

Louise resumed her reading. January 19—nothing to report. Nothing on January 20. Then in the January 21 newspaper, a small article appeared on the business page.

## MILLS PHARMACY SOLD

Allenburg, Ohio – The Mills Pharmacy on Boyd Boulevard has been purchased by George Mills, pharmacist, nephew of the previous owner, Roger Mills. Ownership will be transferred, pending the resolution of outstanding legal issues and financial arrangements. The new owner stated that he wants the pharmacy to be open and serving its customers without undue delay. Some limited cosmetic renovations are being planned.

*What legal issues? What financial arrangements? What cosmetic renovations? More questions. No answers. Do I need to do a property search at the Registrar of Deeds? Rose can tell me how to go about that. Are there liens on the property? Did Roger owe money to someone?*

Since the article was short, Louise copied it—word for word—onto one of her large index cards. As she left the library, Louise glared at the librarian and said, "Shhhhhh."

When Louise arrived home, she found Frances sitting at the kitchen table, holding a pair of scissors and that morning's newspaper.

"What are you doing?"

"I'm cutting out the new comic strip about Santa Claus."

"Why?"

"I like to paste them in my notebook. They're like a story with adventures. When Christmas comes, we'll know what happens and if all the presents get delivered."

"You're too old to believe in Santa Claus."

"Aunt Rose said Santa will come as long as I believe in him."

"Well, you can stop believing right now because Santa won't be coming to you this year."

Frances scowled at her mother and continued clipping the comic strip.

* * *

Two afternoons later, their paperboy, Fred Mercer, came flying down Collis Avenue on his bicycle, yelling at the top of his voice, "Extra! Extra! Read all about it! Japanese bomb Pearl Harbor!"

The houses emptied. The neighbors surrounded Fred. They bought newspapers as quickly as he could hand them out. The front page headline shouted, "America at War!"

It was December 7, 1941. Everyone's worse nightmare had come true. There was no waking up from this one. Louise shoved Roger Mills to the back burner of her mind while she devoured the terrible words in print. Frances grabbed the comic section and proceeded to cut out the Santa strip, originally intended for the next day's edition.

Talk of the war was like a fire, consuming every conversation. It raged across the country, turning citizens of every stripe into patriots. "We are Americans," they announced with one voice, waving their flags. Louise, Harry, and Rose could talk of nothing else. They moved the pins around on the wall map near the radio. Harry became a part-time air-raid warden.

"Do you really think the Germans will bomb Allenburg?" Louise asked Harry.

"I don't know, but we have to be prepared."

"I'm no longer selling defense bonds," Rose announced at the dinner table. "From now on, they'll be called war bonds. In Canada they're called victory bonds."

"Why is it so important to sell those bonds?" Louise asked.

"That's how the government plans to raise the money needed to finance the war. It's better than raising taxes. It'll take money out of circulation and keep inflation down," Harry said.

"I can buy savings stamps at school, and when my savings book is filled, I can get a bond," piped Frances.

"Well, now, aren't you the patriotic one? You can be my little Miss America any time," Harry said, giving his daughter a hug.

Louise looked up from her plate in time to see Harry and Rose exchange glances. *What do they know about bonds that I don't? Now that we are at war, and all this talk about bonds and*

*Germans bombing Allenburg, rationing is bound to come. I'd better get some more stockings and sugar, just in case.*

When Louise asked to buy stockings on her next visit to the department store, she was told that the store was out and would not be restocking until further notice. She stormed out in a huff. On her way home, she stopped by Jack's Deli for some cold cuts. Jack, his mother, and his wife were all in the front section of the deli. Louise told the Mercers about her thwarted attempt to buy stockings. A burning odor came from the kitchen, and the female Mercers headed in that direction. Louise and Jack were left alone near the cash register.

"How badly do you want those stockings, and how much are you willing to pay?" Jack asked.

"Do you know where I can buy stockings?"

"A friend of mine might know," Jack said levelly.

"How much?"

"Three dollars a pair."

"That's robbery. Everybody sells stockings for one dollar a pair."

"Everybody doesn't have stockings to sell. Do you want them or not?"

"I'll take six pairs."

Jack reached under the counter and handed Louise a wrapped package. She handed him a twenty-dollar bill.

"Jack, are you a black marketer?"

"Louise, are you a hoarder?"

They stared at each other. Neither smiled. Neither blinked. As Louise left the store, she could feel Jack's eyes on her back.

# CHAPTER 28

*L*ouise opened the cedar chest, which stood at the foot of her bed, and deposited the nylon hose she had just purchased from Jack Mercer. The new stockings joined the forty-seven other unopened pairs. She smiled. *Four dozen pairs of stockings should last a good while. I don't have to worry about stocking-rationing anymore. Jack can keep me supplied.* Her thoughts jumped ahead. *I'll buy some more sugar tomorrow.*

Since she had never learned to drive a car, Louise depended on Harry to take her grocery shopping on Saturdays. If he were unavailable or if she ran out of supplies during the week, she walked to the local grocery. If her purchases were heavy, like a ten-pound sack of sugar, Frances went along, pulling her red Radio Flyer wagon. Louise thought of it as *the sugar wagon.* By now, the kitchen pantry was well stocked with sugar, and the tin suitcase under her bed was almost filled with bags of sugar. Louise didn't think of herself as a hoarder. That applied to other people. She broke out laughing. A brilliant thought had just crossed her mind. *If Jack can get stockings, he can get sugar, too. After all, he runs a deli and needs sugar for all those coffee cakes, cheesecakes, and noodle puddings. The war won't bother me.*

\* \* \*

The second week of January 1942 brought a brief break in winter's icy grip on Allenburg. Though the nighttime temperatures sank well below freezing, the days were sunny with readings in the mid-fifties. Louise sat at the kitchen table, sipping her second cup of tea and reading the morning paper. It was all war news. *I don't want to hear any more about that war.* She turned to the obituary section, as had become her habit. Immediately, her eyes zeroed in on one particular entry. Sandra Evans, whom she didn't know, was being buried that afternoon at St. Joseph's Catholic Church. She looked at the paper's date. It was January 15, the anniversary of Roger's death.

"I'll go to that graveside service. It'll give me a chance to see the cemetery. After everyone leaves, I'll look for Roger's grave. What a perfect way to commemorate his passing!"

*It's about time you got back to serious work,* the Voice said.

"What should I wear?"

*It won't matter. The graveside service will be outside, and you'll be wearing a coat,* a squeaky voice answered. This was a new voice Louise hadn't heard before.

"Get out of my head," she screamed. "One of you is too many."

254

The graveside service at St. Joseph's cemetery had already begun when Louise arrived a few minutes late, as she had intended. She wanted to stand at the back of the crowd and remain unnoticed.

A priest was standing near the open grave, addressing the assembled mourners. He was short, almost bald, and had a perfectly round face, like a baby. His age was undeterminable. It was obvious that if he ever saw sixty again, it would be in an outdated church directory. *That must be Father Michael Galloway.* The small group stood in silence as Father Michael intoned the traditional prayers. Some dabbed at their eyes. Some looked at their watches. All crossed themselves and hurried to their cars when the service was over.

Louise turned to go, hoping Father Michael wouldn't notice her. Too late.

"Hello," said the priest in a friendly voice. "I don't think you and I have met. Sandra was a fine woman. She would be glad to know that you came to her funeral service. What was your connection to Sandra?"

"I'm not a relative," Louise said, turning to walk away.

*Now's your chance,* the Voice said.

Louise stopped and turned to face Father Michael. "Did you know Roger Mills?"

If the priest was surprised by this out-of-context question, he hid it well. His full-moon face was inscrutable. He continued smiling at Louise, but she saw the serious lines creep around the corners of his eyes as they narrowed ever so slightly. *He's watching me.*

"Yes, I knew Roger Mills. He was a parishioner here at St. Joseph's. He was a good man. Why do you ask?"

"I live in Roger's old house on Collis Avenue. I'm interested in writing a history of the house and its former occupants. Currently, I'm doing some research." Louise half lied.

"There's not much I can tell you about the house. I was only there on one occasion."

"But you knew Roger. Can you show me where he's buried? It would be helpful if I could see his grave."

Louise watched the narrowed eyes widen. She sensed that the priest was uncomfortable talking about Roger. This would not be their last conversation.

"I can show you Roger's grave. He's buried in the Mills family plot over this way. He's on this side of the fence. I'll walk you over. Everyone calls me Father Mike. What should I call you?"

"Mrs. Hoag will do."

As they walked the short distance across the brown grass, Louise and Father Mike discussed the welcome break in the weather.

*When people talk about the weather, they're really thinking about something else. Did you know that?* the Voice commented.

"Spring is my favorite season. I like to work outside in my flowers," Louise said.

"I like spring, too. It's the Easter season—the most glorious time of the year. Here we are. Roger Mills is buried right here, between the two graves with the big markers."

"Why is his marker so small?"

"His wife picked it out. That's what she wanted."

Louise moved closer in order to read the words on the headstone. Simple words—yet so final. "Roger Wilson Mills, b. 1899 d. 1939." That was all. Her face fell in disappointment.

Turning away from the grave, she said, "I was expecting more."

"Sorry. That's what his wife wanted—nothing ostentatious, as she phrased it."

Louise looked around. On the other side of the fence were a few more graves. They didn't appear to be as well tended as Roger's.

"Who is buried over there?" she asked, pointing across the fence.

"I take it you aren't a Catholic. In some cases it's more appropriate to bury a person outside of the fenced area. That's our custom. I'd be happy to explain it to you more fully if you'd like to meet with me sometime."

"That's not necessary. I'm just glad Roger made it to this side of the fence. Who decides these things anyway?"

"Like I said, it will take a little time to explain the circumstances. Are you sure you don't want to stop by my office one day soon?"

*Do it. Do it. Do it,* said the Voice.

"Okay. Okay. I'll do it," Louise yelled at the Voice.

"Excuse me. I'm not shouting at you," she said to the priest. "I'd like to talk to you further."

Louise turned away from Roger's grave and hurried out of the cemetery. Once outside the gate, she ran to the bus stop.

Father Mike was left standing alone. His round face wore a worried look.

* * *

The following Saturday, Rose parked her car in front of the house on Collis Avenue just as the other Hoags were returning from their weekly grocery shopping trip.

"Hi, Rose. Come on in, out of the cold, and have a cup of coffee with us. What are you doing out so early on a Saturday morning anyway?" Harry called.

"It's not so early. It's almost eleven o'clock, and I've been up for hours."

"Well, join us for coffee before you go home and get to bed," Harry teased.

Louise busied herself putting away the groceries while Harry and his sister sat at the kitchen table catching up on the week's events.

"How can you two find so much to talk about?"

"Come join us, Louise," Rose invited.

"I can't join your conversation because I don't know what you are talking about, but I do have a question."

"What's that?" Rose and Harry asked in unison.

"Why do Catholics have two cemeteries? Why are some people buried on the inside of the fence and some buried on the outside? That's what I want to know." Harry and Rose were startled into silence. "What's the matter with you? Don't you understand my question?"

"That's not it, Louise. You just caught us off guard. We weren't talking about cemeteries," Rose said. "Once, I asked my old boss the same question. He's Catholic, you know. Catholics believe committing suicide is the worst of all sins because you can't repent and that people who kill themselves don't belong in the same cemetery as the *good* folks."

"Do you know someone who committed suicide?" Harry asked.

"Of course not," Louise snapped. "I don't know people like that. Only cowards commit suicide, and I don't associate with cowards." She banged the cabinet shut and stormed out of the kitchen.

Harry slapped his forehead with his open palm. "Rose, what am I going to do about Louise? I'm really worried about her. She saw a psychiatrist while she was in St. Mary's, and she just finished spending three months in the state hospital. Still, she's no better. She's getting worse by the day."

"If you think Louise will kill herself, forget it. She is too self-centered. You know that."

Harry continued to sit with his head bowed. Rose walked to his side of the table and put her arm around his shoulders. "We'll figure something out. Do you think she would agree to see that doctor at St. Mary's again—what was his name? Dr. Couch? Give him a call and see if he accepts private patients. I'll help you work on persuading Louise to see him."

Harry patted his sister's hand, giving her a weak but grateful smile.

# CHAPTER 29

*L* ouise woke up to a bright light shining in her eyes. The morning sun was streaming through her bedroom window, and the clock on the dresser showed a few minutes past nine.

*It's about time you woke up. I thought we were going to have to stay in bed all day*, the Voice said.

*I don't mind staying in bed all day*, Squeaky responded.

"Shut up, both of you. This is a special day, and I have special plans."

Neither voice responded, but Louise knew they were watching her.

"Today is February 2—Groundhog Day. That's bad because the groundhog will see his shadow, go back into his burrow, and we'll have six more weeks of miserable weather. It's a good day, too. Nice and sunny. I don't care if it is cold. It'll be a good time to visit Father Mike," Louise told the voices.

Two hours later, Louise stood, unannounced, before St. Joseph's rectory. She looked at the house. It was old—like the church—and built with identical bricks. The yard was tidy and the windows sparkled as though they had been recently cleaned. There was a brass knocker attached to the front door. Louise banged it up and down with vigor. No one answered. She banged the knocker again. No answer.

"Where is everybody?" she asked aloud. "A priest should stay home except when he is in the church or visiting sick people in the hospital. I wonder if he is in the church now."

She decided to take a shortcut through the rectory's back yard on her way to the church next door. As she rounded the corner of the house, Louise heard a banging and someone cussing or fussing—which was it?

"Oh, the natural perversity of inanimate objects!" shouted Father Mike angrily as he struggled to free himself. He was standing near a toolshed with a long metal measuring tape coiled around his ankles. The tape was refusing to return to its case. Louise watched Father Mike with amusement. Every time he tried to untangle the tape from one ankle, it wound around the other. He hopped from one foot to the next.

"Pretty soon that snake is going to bite you," Louise said.

Father Mike jerked around at the sound of her voice. The tape didn't follow. They fought. Father lost—lost his balance—and down he went. His bottom side hit the ground with an audible *splat*. Louise broke into a gale of laughter.

With Louise's help, the tape was domesticated and returned to its case. Father Mike was righted again. He invited Louise to wait in the rectory's parlor while he changed from his yard outfit to proper attire. Louise surveyed the room. It was dull and boring, but cozy. Most of the furniture looked like hand-me-downs, or castoffs, from parishioners. *Fitting, I suppose. He isn't expected to be worldly.*

"I'm glad you came for a visit. Would you like to know more about our final rites and burial customs?" the priest asked.

"No. I want to ask you about Roger Mills. Did he commit suicide?"

"Why do you ask?"

"Because of all those graves on the other side of the fence. My sister-in-law said that was for people who took their own lives."

"I showed you Roger's grave. It's inside the fence."

"It's so small, and my neighbor said Roger was a big man."

"It's a rather long and confusing story, but I can share a few details if you are interested.

"Oh yes. Please."

"Allenburg was buried by blizzard conditions when Roger Mills died. In some places the snow had drifted above four feet, and the ground was frozen. We weren't sure we could dig a grave under those conditions. Anna Mills, Roger's wife, asked the undertaker to dress the body in his Sunday suit and a special pair of socks, knit by their daughter. When I told her we weren't sure about digging a grave, she decided to have her husband cremated.

"Now, the story gets a little confusing. One of our parishioners, Ronald Lay, whom you may know, does yard work for the church and fills in as a gravedigger when needed. He came to me and said the ground wasn't as frozen as we had originally thought and that digging a small grave would be possible.

"It was too late. Roger Mills's remains had already been sent to the crematory, and his wife couldn't arrange the transfer back to the undertaker in time. So we buried his ashes in the small grave you saw. Charlene, the daughter, was upset that her father had been cremated. Thus, the private burial."

"You didn't answer my question. Did he kill himself?"

"I told you all I know about the circumstances of his burial. I wasn't there when he died."

*This guy knows how to keep secrets. He'll never answer your question*, the Voice said.

"Did many people go to Roger Mills's funeral?" Louise asked.

"Oh yes. The church was packed. Roger was very popular. He had a lot friends. Many of his neighbors and drugstore customers showed up, too."

"Sounds like everyone was there except poor Roger. Guess he was busy deciding between a coffin and an urn," Louise giggled, inappropriately. "Who went to the graveside service?"

"The funeral was on January 18, and his ashes were buried two days later. Roger's wife was the only one to attend the interment service."

"What about the daughter?"

"She was still upset by the cremation and decided not to go."

"What else do you know about Roger Mills?"

"Roger Mills was a good man. He was baptized at St. Joseph's and remained a faithful member throughout his entire life. He was an altar boy when I was transferred to this parish. He and his wife, Anna, were married in this church and their daughter was baptized here. They were a good family."

Louise rose to leave. "Thanks, I guess. I still don't know how Roger Mills died, but I will keep looking."

"The truth shall make you free," the priest responded, opening the front door for his guest.

Father Michael stood at the window, watching Louise as she left the rectory and turned toward the church. He saw her bypass the church in favor of the adjacent cemetery. From his window, he could see her standing near the Mills's family plot. She stood still for a long time, just staring at the grave. She took a large white handkerchief from her pocket and blew her nose. Giving the grave one last look, she turned and hurried in the direction of the bus stop.

Father Michael made a fist and rubbed it against the side of his face. He sighed and turned from the window.

*That poor woman is troubled. Her apparent obsession with Roger Mills's death is likely only one symptom of a serious illness. Despite her challenges, she'll probably keep digging. She's onto something, and I suspect she knows it. She's wading into dangerous waters. I doubt she knows how dangerous. I wish her well and I will pray for her.*

# CHAPTER 30

The groundhog's shadow had, indeed, fallen across Allenburg, Ohio. Winter hung on for another six weeks. Then at last, April burst upon the landscape, bringing with it the promise of warm days to come. When Harry was in town, he and Louise spent their evenings poring over seed catalogs. Louise looked at the pictures of beautiful flowers. She could imagine them blooming in her garden. Harry looked at the packets of vegetable seeds. He was excited about having a victory garden.

"Look here, Louise," Harry said, holding up the Saturday morning newspaper. "The government is setting up a special victory garden branch right here in Allenburg down at the County Agent's office. They'll give free advice on growing vegetables and pass out yard signs to everyone who registers. They plan to have a contest and award a prize for the best victory garden. I'm going to register, and I'm going to win that prize."

"Let me see," said Louise, taking the paper from her husband. "I don't understand about the yard sign. What are we supposed to do with that?"

"Put it in the front yard so everyone will know we have a victory garden."

"I don't want a sign in front of our house. It'll look tacky."

"The sign will be something we'll be proud of. Everyone will know that we are patriotic and doing our best to help the war effort. I'm going to drive down to the victory-garden office now. Do you want to come with me?"

"No. If you do bring home a sign, it had better not be tacky."

When Harry returned home two hours later, he found Louise in the backyard showing Rose and Zina where she wanted to plant the new annuals she had ordered from the seed catalog.

"Hi, Harry. Where have you been?" asked Rose.

"Down at the County Agent's office getting officially registered with the victory-garden people. I'm going to have a great victory garden this year. I entered the contest they are having, and they gave me a sign to put in the front yard."

"It had better not be a tacky sign. I want to see it before you put it up," Louise said.

"I can do better than that. They let me have three signs. You ladies can choose which one you like best."

The first sign showed a handsome man dressed in a white dress shirt and tie, his foot pushing a shovel into the ground. The caption read, "Dig for Victory."

The second sign featured the Statue of Liberty, raising a hoe instead of a torch. It said, "Plant a Victory Garden. Our Food Is Fighting."

The third was Lady Liberty, draped in a flag, walking through a plowed field. It said, "Sow the Seeds of Victory. Ensure the Fruits of Peace."

Harry voted for the first sign. Rose and Zina both wanted the third. Louise grunted in disgust and walked into the house.

\* \* \*

When Harry was away on business, Louise spent her evenings organizing and reorganizing her growing collection of data concerning Roger Mills. She laid out a timeline, filling in the pertinent dates and major events in Roger's life.

*There are too many blank spaces on your chart,* the Voice said.

*Better get back to work,* chimed in Squeaky.

Louise spoke to the voices. "Memorial Day weekend is coming up soon. Harry and Rose will want to go to the cemetery to clean and visit their parents' graves. Well, I want to go to the cemetery, too—just not that one. Poor Roger has no one to clean his grave. I'll do it, and I'll take him some flowers, too."

*Harry won't like that,* warned the Voice.

"I'll go on the Saturday before Memorial Day. He'll never know the difference."

Louise got up early. It was a lovely Saturday—warm and sunny. The apple trees were in full bloom, and the big white rosebush was covered with blossoms. The backyard flowers filled the air with fragrance and joy. Louise could smell and see the beautiful flowers and feel the warmth of their unselfish bounty.

*Should I stop by the florist shop and get some flowers for Roger? No. I think he would prefer some of the white roses from his own backyard.*

"Harry, I am going downtown to the public library. I'll take the bus so you can work in your victory garden," Louise called up the stairs to Harry as she left carrying a bouquet of white roses wrapped in an old newspaper.

The cemetery gate was open. Louise walked through and looked around. She could see only a few people wandering between graves on the far side of the property. No one was near the Mills's family plot.

Standing beside Roger's grave, she spoke to the small headstone. "I brought you some flowers. They are white roses from your backyard. I hope you like them. I've come to clean the weeds away from your marker and to let you know you aren't forgotten."

She began pulling the wayward weeds and grass crowding the tombstone. A smile spread over her face as she began to see the results of her work. She squatted near the grave and stroked the marker. With her right index finger, she traced the indentations in the granite stone that spelled Roger's name.

"Hey, Mrs. Hoag. You trying to take my job?" she heard Ronald Lay ask as he walked toward her, grinning.

"Hello, Ronald. What are you doing here?"

"I work here part time. Question is, why are you here?"

"I brought some flowers for Mr. Mills's grave."

"He'd like that," Ronald said, looking at the white roses.

"Did you help bury Roger Mills?"

"Maybe and maybe not. I dug the grave, and I covered it up."

"I don't understand. What do you mean by *maybe not?*"

Ronald gave Louise a curious look as he stood chewing on his bottom lip.

"I don't know why you're interested, but I guess I can tell you what I know. Mr. Mills died the time we had that bad snowstorm. I tell you, it was cold! Father Mike asked me if I would dig the grave, and I told him the ground was probably too frozen. I was relieved when his wife had him cremated. Usually, the box, urn, or whatever with the ashes is delivered to Father Mike. That time it was different. Father asked me to go to the crematory and pick up the ashes. When I got there, the man in charge asked me whose urn I wanted. I told him I came for Roger Mills. He said, 'Well, he is in two different urns.' That made no sense to me, but I didn't figure it was my business. I told him to just give me one urn. He said he couldn't do that because the wife was picking up both urns herself."

"What did you do?" Louise asked.

"I drove back to the church and told Father Mike it was a wasted trip because Mrs. Mills was picking up the ashes herself. Father said he was sorry I had to drive across town for nothing. He said Mrs. Mills had just called him and said she would bring the urn over and that I was to meet her near the gravesite at ten the next morning."

"Did you meet her?"

"I sure did. Right at ten o'clock, there she was standing near the Mills's plot holding an urn. I dug a hole the right size, and she handed me the pot. It was as light as a feather. Now, I have buried plenty of ashes in my day, and that container didn't feel heavy enough. I didn't say nothing. I just buried it anyway."

"Did you stay for the graveside service?"

"Yep, I did. Funny thing, Mrs. Mills was the only one who showed up. Just her and Father Mike and me."

"Do you think the urn was empty?"

"I didn't say that. I said it was light. I don't go around looking in burying pots. I got to go now," the handyman said as he turned and walked away.

*You're putting flowers on an empty urn,* the Voice laughed. Squeaky giggled.

"Roger, if you're not in that urn, where are you?" Louise shouted aloud in the deserted cemetery.

No one answered.

# CHAPTER 31

School was out for the summer. The neighborhood children were home all day—every day—including Frances. It would be another three weeks before Zina's nursing classes took a break. Louise was *it*.

"These children are crowding me. They're in and out of the house all day long. I don't have a minute to myself. Now, I have to watch Dickey, too! It's not fair," Louise complained to Rose.

"After all the time Zina has spent taking care of Frances, you owe her," Rose said. "Cheer up, Louise. I talked to Evelyn yesterday, and she said she'll be teaching Bible School at the Presbyterian Church again this summer. It starts next week. You could send Frances and Dickey there and have your mornings free."

"I'll do it," Louise said with enthusiasm.

\* \* \*

Louise took advantage of her free time. Frances and Dickey were now old enough to cross the street and walk unattended to and from the Presbyterian Church.

*How did they get to be eight years old? Am I getting older, too?*

As soon as the children were out of the house, on the first day of Bible School, Louise went to her room. She sat at her card-table desk and turned to a new page in her notebook. At the top of the page, she wrote the date of her last visit to St. Joseph's cemetery. Then she wrote three column headings: Facts, Questions, and Actions.

*What facts did I learn?* She could think of only three: 1) Roger's ashes might not be in the urn buried at his designated grave site. 2) Two urns had been involved. 3) Ronald Lay knew more than he claimed. She listed each fact under the first heading.

*What questions do I have?* She wrote the word, "Why?" under the second heading beside each fact.

*What action should I take?* The Actions list was much longer: 1) Talk to the manager of the crematory. 2) Talk to the undertaker at the mortuary. 3) Talk to Father Mike and Ronald Lay about the burial, again. 4) Talk to Grandmother Mercer about the Mills family. 5) Ask Roger's cousin, George, for the address of Roger's widow and daughter. 6) Search the garage for any signs of a burial urn.

Pleased with herself and her plan, Louise went to the window and looked out onto the backyard. Her gaze was drawn, not to the flowers, but to a tall man standing beside the white rosebush. He was the same man she had seen several times before. This time he was looking at her with a broad smile covering his face.

*I don't have enough time today to interview anyone on my list. But I do have time to check the garage.* A shiver of excitement ran up her spine.

On her way to the garage, Louise tripped and almost fell over something long and thin lying curled in the grass. At first she thought it was a snake, but it was only Frances's jump rope. She snatched it up and yelled, "You tried to kill me."

Inside the garage, she hung the jump rope on one of the hooks holding the rope collection and looked around. *Where do I start?*

*Start at the top and work your way down,* answered the Voice.

Louise climbed the ladder and inspected the top shelves. They were deep in dust and filled with things no one wanted or would ever need. The disturbed dust blew around, sending Louise into a sneezing spasm. Between sneezes, she continued her search. Nothing of interest was discovered on the top shelves.

*If you fall off the ladder, I'm going to laugh,* said Squeaky.

"Shut up," said Louise as she climbed back down the ladder. The three remaining shelves contained only the usual assortment of garage items—nothing that resembled an urn or a box suitable for storing cremated remains. She put the ladder back in its place and started to leave.

*Wait a minute. You didn't check the garage floor. There is stuff piled against the walls and in the corners under the bottom shelves,* a Raspy voice said. It wasn't the Voice or Squeaky. This was a new voice—one that Louise had never heard.

"Go away. There are too many of you. I hate you all," Louise snarled, as she began searching the inside perimeter. *Junk, junk, junk—just junk!*

On the floor near the door leading to the alley was a pile of old rags. Harry often tore these rags into strips, which he used to tie up his tomato plants. The rags looked filthy. Louise didn't want to touch them. She poked at the pile with Harry's turning fork. She pretended she was pitching hay. Nothing there—just dirty old rags used to wipe up paint and oil spills. Near the bottom of the pile, a bright object caught Louise's eye. She fished it out for further inspection. It appeared to be a sock—an argyle sock.

Louise carried the sock outside, still impaled on the tines of the turning fork, and dumped it in the grass near the outdoor spigot. She turned on the garden hose and gave the sock a thorough hosing down. She then hung it on the fence to dry. Under close scrutiny, Louise realized that this wasn't just any sock. It was a woolen sock with a well-executed design of red-and-green diamonds, intersected with narrow white lines. It appeared to be hand-knit. It looked special.

*What are you going to do with just one sock? You need a pair,* the Voice said.

\* \* \*

Zina and Dickey joined the Hoags for dinner that evening. During the meal, Harry asked the children how their morning at Bible School had gone.

"It was pretty much fun. Miss Evelyn read us a story, and we sang songs, and we got to play in the side yard next to the church, where all the cars park on Sunday. We ran races, and I won," Dickey bragged. "I liked the cookies and lemonade, too."

"The very best part was the craft hour. We made sheep," Frances said.

"Why sheep?"

"Because our Bible story was about a boy named David who had a lot of sheep and who used to go around playing a harp and singing palms."

"Psalms—not palms," Louise corrected.

"After the story, Miss Evelyn got out the crayons, colored pencils, construction paper, glue, and a big wad of cotton. She told us to draw a picture about the story. Carol and I drew sheep," Frances said.

"What on Earth was Carol Mercer doing there? They're Jewish. She shouldn't be going to a Presbyterian Bible School," Louise said.

"It's okay because we're studying the old part of the Bible this week. Next week we'll study the new part. Carol can't go then," Dickey explained.

"Tell us about your sheep," Zina said, looking at Frances.

"My sheep was very pretty. He was white, and I glued cotton all over him to make him fluffy. Carol's sheep was little, and he looked dead. She said he was a lamb and she was going to eat him," Frances said.

"What does Carol Mercer know about eating lamb?" Louise asked.

"She said they ate lamb for dinner at their house all the time and that her daddy can get all they want, even if lambs cost a lot of ration stamps."

Louise put down her fork and said, "I'll bet he can."

Zina gave Louise a quizzical look. Harry looked at his plate.

When dinner was over and the dishes were done, Louise walked Zina and Dickey to the backyard gate. The now-dry argyle sock was still hanging on the fence. She put it in her pocket and returned to the house. After going to her room and closing the door, she opened the cedar chest and nestled the red-and-green sock among the packages of hoarded nylons.

*I like that sock. It's very well made and the colors are pretty,* Louise thought. *Where is its mate?*

*Stockings go on feet and socks go on feet. Now both are at the foot of the bed! I love it!* Squeaky said, laughing.

*You're silly,* croaked Raspy.

"Should I look for the other sock?" Louise asked.

*You know the answer to that question,* the Voice said.

# CHAPTER 32

*L* ouise was jolted awake by a loud crash of thunder just before dawn. Her eyes flew open and she gasped as a blaze of lightning lit up the room. A storm was raging outside. She heard the howling wind lash the rain against the window pane. All of the old terrors returned. She pulled the covers over her head, burrowed her face deep into her pillow, and began to sob.

*Why is this happening to me? I don't think I can survive another thunderstorm.*

Her body began shaking, and she couldn't make it stop. Extending one arm from under the covers, she reached to the far side of the bed and pulled the doll, Madeline, into her bunker. Clutching the doll like a life preserver, she said, "Help me." No response.

It had been a long time since Madeline had spoken. "You're just a dumb doll." No response. Even the voices had deserted Louise. She was truly alone.

It was still raining when Louise gathered enough courage to get up and dress. The worst of the storm was over, but the rain continued. Harry and Frances were at the kitchen table when Louise joined them.

"That was really some storm we had early this morning," Harry said. "Did it wake you?"

"I hate storms—they frighten me."

"It looks as if we are in for a rainy day. I'll drop Frances and Dickey off at Bible School on my way to work. Evelyn can drive them home."

Louise looked at her daughter, who was eating a bowl of cereal and drawing a picture on her paper napkin with a broken crayon.

*That is a very strange child. She isn't even afraid of thunderstorms. Something bad will happen to her someday.*

Something bad did happen that day—not to Frances, but to Evelyn Fisher.

* * *

Louise heard the mailman dropping letters into the mailbox on the front porch. She waited until he left before going out to get the mail. Looking up the street, she saw four figures walking in the rain, three short and one tall. Each was carrying a black umbrella. The three small figures were laughing and splashing as they jumped from rain puddle to rain puddle in their bare feet. The tall figure was marching steadily toward the Hoags' house. This strange parade consisted of Grandmother Mercer, Carol, Dickey and Frances.

"Why have you brought them back from Bible School so early?" Louise asked as the group sloshed onto the porch, shaking their umbrellas.

"Evelyn Fisher tripped over the curb on her way to get something from her car and broke her arm. She's at the hospital now getting it set. The other teacher telephoned and asked me to come for Carol. I knew no one would go for Dickey and Frances. So I took extra umbrellas and brought them all back," Grandmother said.

"Well, now that you are here, you might as well come in and have a cup of coffee," Louise said without thanking Grandmother Mercer.

Over coffee, Louise asked, "Do you knit?"

"Of course. I knit hats, scarves, sweaters, and all the socks for the men in my family. Why do you want to know about knitting? Are you working on something? I can give you all the advice about knitting you'll ever need."

"No. I'm just curious about the kind of socks you knit. What do they look like?"

"I'm sensible. I only knit black socks. They're all alike and don't have to be matched up. Everyone can just reach in the sock drawer and get two socks without any fuss."

"What about colored socks with a diamond pattern?"

"No. Those are argyles for the Scots. We are German, and we wear black socks."

Changing the subject, Louise asked, "How well did you know Roger Mills?

"Louise, you ask strange questions. First socks, now Mr. Mills. I don't know why you're interested in him. I can tell you he was little bit odd, pretty much kept to himself in the neighborhood, but as friendly as a pup at the drugstore. Jack knew him better than I did. They used to play poker on Wednesday nights."

Louise continued to question her guest about Roger, but gleaned nothing new. After Carol and her grandmother left, Louise made lunch for Frances and Dickey. After lunch she told them to listen to the radio while she made a pound cake.

*I'll cut the cake in two and take half to Evelyn when she comes home. Evelyn isn't the brightest one on the block, but she might know something else about Roger. I'll ask her.*

Evelyn was sitting in her living room, looking forlorn, when Louise arrived with the cake. At the last minute, Louise had decided to take the Fishers only two slices—not half the cake, as she had originally planned. No need to waste perfectly good cake on Evelyn.

"I was sorry to hear about your accident. Will you be able to continue with the Bible School?"

Evelyn looked at Louise with tears in her eyes. "No. I'm out of Bible School for this year. I won't be able to do much of anything for weeks. I can't drive my car with this cast. How am I going to deliver my Fuller Brush products? I'll lose my customers."

"Your legs aren't broken, and you can walk to every house in the neighborhood and take their orders for brushes and such."

"I'm not much of a walker."

"You can learn to be a walker. I used to walk for miles and miles. You just need some saddle oxfords. In the meantime, I guess your broken arm will slow down your knitting."

"I don't knit. I never learned how. What made you think I was a knitter?"

"Just a guess—a bad guess. Do you know any knitters around here? I need some knitting advice," Louise said.

"Grandmother Mercer knits, but it was Charlene Mills who was the knitting expert."

\* \* \*

Louise opened her notebook and turned to a new page. Under the Facts heading, she wrote, 1) Argyle sock found in the garage. 2) Charlene Mills was an expert knitter. Under the *Questions* heading, she listed two queries: 1) Did Charlene knit the argyle sock? 2) Where is the other sock? She stared at the Actions heading. It was harder.

*I don't know where to start on this argyle-sock hunt. Who else can help me with this?*

*We can help,* the Voice said.

"Okay, what should we do?" asked Louise. No answer.

\* \* \*

"Miss Evelyn fell down and broke her arm, and we can't go to Bible School anymore," Carol announced at the Mercer dinner table that evening.

"Good and bad," said Carol's father. "*Good* because you won't be going to that school, and *bad* because of the broken arm."

"Louise Hoag isn't happy about having the children home all day. She was counting on the Bible School to do some babysitting for her," Grandmother Mercer said.

"How do you know she isn't happy?" asked her son-in-law.

"Oh, Jack, you know how she is always trying to get out of caring for her child. She invited me in for coffee this morning when I walked the children home, and she didn't even seem to notice her own daughter. She just started asking questions about knitting and about Roger Mills."

"What kind of questions about Roger Mills?"

"She wanted to know how well I knew him. I told her I hardly knew the man outside of the drugstore."

Jack Mercer's face took on a hard edge, and his muscles tensed. His antenna was up. He said, "Pass the rolls."

# CHAPTER 33

With Bible School no longer an option, Louise was stuck at home with the children every day. Zina was in class at the hospital, and there was no one to talk to—no one except Evelyn, still nursing her broken arm. Evelyn began coming over to see Louise every morning after she finished getting her mother's breakfast. She always had some excuse.

"Can you help me button my sweater? Can you help me write a note for the milkman? Can you help me do this? Do that? How's Rose? Is she seeing anyone?"

*Evelyn is more than ugly. She is boring. She just wants to find out about Rose's old boss. He must be neglecting her. She is becoming a pest. I need to get rid of her.*

*Not yet. Ugly people can babysit, too,* the Voice said.

Turning to her neighbor, Louise said, "Evelyn, I need your help. I have some errands to do tomorrow. Could you possibly stay with Frances and Dickey? They can fix their own lunch, and I won't be gone long. If you have a problem, you can always telephone Grandmother Mercer."

* * *

Before going to bed, Louise made an entry in her notebook. Under Actions she wrote, "Find the other sock. Call the mortuary. Call the crematory."

*This is like a scavenger hunt,* said Squeaky, with childlike enthusiasm.

Early the following morning, Louise telephoned the Kingsley Funeral Home. "Hello. This is Mrs. Hoag, and I have a question for you."

"We are here to serve you. How can we help?"

"In January 1939, you served the Mills family when Roger Mills died. Do your records show what clothes he was wearing when he was in your care?"

"We don't keep records of the deceased's personal possessions that far back. However, I do remember the circumstances concerning Roger Mills. His wife brought us a lovely suit and tie in which to dress him. But, due to inclement weather, she changed her mind and decided to have her husband transferred to the crematory. When we made the transfer, we sent the suit and tie along. That's all I know. You'll have to check with the crematory for further details."

"Thank you," Louise said as she hung up the telephone.

*One down. More to go. You can cross the funeral home off your list,* said the Voice.

"I don't know whether to call the crematory or to go there in person," Louise told the Voice.

*You're at a dead end on a cold trail. If you go to the crematory, you might get warmer*, said Squeaky, sputtering with laughter.

Before Louise could make another telephone call, she heard a knock at the front door. It was Evelyn, ready to babysit. In her good hand she carried several movie magazines.

"I'll be back in a couple of hours," Louise said, waving goodbye.

\* \* \*

Louise stared out of the window as the bus passed St. Joseph's Cemetery and headed downtown. At Third Avenue she transferred to a west-end bus, which the driver assured her would pass the crematory. He gave Louise a nod as she got off the bus in front of a low cinder block building, painted green. She walked to the front door and rang the buzzer. The door was answered by an elderly man, who looked as though he might be his own next customer.

"Please come in," he said, holding the door wide.

Louise followed him into a dimly lit parlor. She felt claustrophobic. The whole place was too quiet. She wanted out—out into the sunshine. She clasped her hands together in her lap as she sat perched on the edge of a small leather-covered chair.

*That chair is covered with dead animal skin*, Raspy warned.

"My name is Mrs. Hoag. Who are you?"

"I'm Mr. Lewis, and I'm the owner of this establishment. How can I help you?"

ELIZABETH T. MILLER

"I would like to ask you a few questions. What do you do with your customers' clothing?"

Louise hesitated. She wondered if *customers* was the right word.

*One thing, for sure, they aren't repeat customers,* giggled Squeaky.

"How long have you worked here?"

"I'm the original owner. I started this business over thirty years ago. As to the clothes, that depends—depends on the wishes of the family."

"I'm interested in a man who died in January 1939. His name was Roger Mills. I understand that he was transferred to you from the Kingsley Funeral Home. Can you tell me what happened to his clothes?"

Mr. Lewis cocked his head to one side and looked at Louise. He was still standing. "I do remember that situation. It sticks out in my mind because of the terrible snowstorm we had that week. Because of my business, I rarely get a day off. People keep needing our services whether it snows or not."

"What happened to Mr. Mills's clothes?" Louise repeated.

"I telephoned Mrs. Mills and asked her if we should dress her husband in the suit and tie sent over by the funeral home. She said not to bother with the clothes and that she would pick up the ashes herself."

"Did she pick up the ashes?"

"Yes, she did. She was here within a few hours after I notified her that the remains were ready. When I handed her the urn, she asked if we had another one exactly like it. She said that she and her daughter were going to divide the ashes so

286

each of them could keep a part of Mr. Mills close by. I asked her if she wanted the suit. She said no. Then she paid me in cash and left. I never saw her again."

"What about the suit? Do you still have it?"

"I knew from the newspaper that Mr. Mills was a member of St. Joseph's Church. I always read the obituary column. It's my favorite part of the paper. I called Father Michael and told him about the suit. He said I should send it to the church and that he would put it in the clothes closet for the needy, so that's what I did."

"Thank you," Louise said, rising and walking toward the door.

"Please visit us again," Mr. Lewis said, smiling.

*The next time you come here, you won't get warm. You'll get hot,* Squeaky said.

*Two down. More to go,* commented the Voice.

* * *

Louise got off the bus in front of St. Joseph's. She crossed the lawn to the rectory and rang the bell. When the housekeeper answered the door, Louise announced, "I've come to see Father Michael."

"He's on the telephone just now. Would you like to wait in the parlor?"

"No. It's a pretty day. I'll sit on a bench in the garden and wait for him."

"Hello, Mrs. Hoag. It's good to see you. Would you like to come inside?' the priest said as he joined her.

"I would rather sit out here. This is a nice garden," Louise said, admiring the flowers.

*After that creepy old man at that creepy old crematory, I need some fresh air and sunshine.*

The two sat, like old friends, enjoying the sunshine and a summer breeze. Across the lawn, they could see Ronald Lay mowing the grass near the cemetery.

"How much do you pay Ronald?" Louise asked.

"Nothing really. He's just mowing his way to heaven."

*That's an odd thing to say. I'll ask Ronald about that later when he comes to mow our grass.*

"Father Mike, after Roger Mills was cremated, what happened to his clothes?"

The priest gave Louise a surprised look but answered in a calm voice. "The crematory sent over a suit and tie, and I put them in the clothing closet where we keep things to donate to the poor. Later, I decided to give the suit to Ronald Lay."

"Why did you do that?"

"I wanted him to feel better about himself. He needed something to be proud of."

"What other things do you keep in the clothing closet?"

"Actually, *clothing closet* isn't a very accurate name, but I couldn't think of anything else to call it. We often get household items and other donations. Right now our cupboard is just about bare. We put everything worth having in our last rummage sale. We're down to a few knickknacks and a few odd socks."

Jumping to her feet, Louise asked, "May I have a look?"

"Sure. If you want to, but you won't find much. If you have some things you no longer need, you can always donate them here. I guarantee they'll go to a deserving cause."

Louise and Father Mike walked to the back of the church and entered through a rear door. Halfway down the hall, Father Mike opened a large walk-in closet. He was right. It was almost empty. In one corner stood a bushel basket containing odd bits of unwanted clothing.

"I want a closer look," Louise said.

"Help yourself."

Louise reached into the bushel basket and sorted through a mishmash of lost gloves, worn hats, old ties, what looked like a dresser scarf, and one sock—a red-and-green argyle sock.

In her excitement, Louise could barely speak. "I want that sock," she said, snatching her prize from the basket.

"Why would you want one sock?" asked the bewildered priest.

Louise stuffed the sock in her purse and pulled out a five-dollar bill. She thrust the bill at Father Mike, turned, and ran from the room. Father Mike followed her outside and watched as she ran down the drive, away from the church.

Once on the sidewalk, Louise began to hyperventilate. She was too agitated and excited to take the bus. Her energy level was too high to ride. She needed to walk. Besides, it would give her time to think.

*I need the exercise. I need to get stronger. I can't help Roger if I'm not strong.*

*We are getting stronger every day,* said a chorus in her head.

# CHAPTER 34

*T*he house on Collis Avenue was deserted when Louise returned from her visit with Father Michael. She went from room to room, calling, "Frances. Evelyn. Dickey." She looked in the backyard and in the garage. No one was there—neither inside nor outside. She called again, louder this time, "Frances. Evelyn. Dickey." No answer.

*Good. I'm glad everyone is gone. I need to work with the socks. But first I need to eat lunch.*

Louise fixed a sandwich and a cup of tea. She ate only half of the sandwich. Abandoning the remaining half, she went up to her room, clutching her purse. She closed the door and opened the cedar chest. She dug through the unopened packages of nylon stockings until she found the first argyle sock—*the garage sock*, as she called it. She retrieved the *clothes-closet* sock from her purse and laid them, side by side, on her bed. They were an identical match—a perfect pair. Both socks were dirty but still in good shape.

Louise spoke to the socks, "I'm going to give you two a bath."

She was in the bathroom squishing the socks up and down in the sink, which was filled with warm water and her mildest face soap, when the door burst open.

"I need to go," said Frances rushing to the toilet. "What are you doing?"

"I'm washing socks," her mother said.

Frances completed her mission and stood beside her mother at the sink. She looked at the socks. "I never saw socks like that. Whose socks are they?"

"They're new. I bought them when I went shopping today."

"Why are you washing new socks?"

"You never know. They might have germs on them."

"Who are they for?"

"I'm going to give them to your father for his birthday. It's a surprise. You must not tell him about the socks, or you'll spoil the surprise."

"Okay," yelled Frances as she ran down the stairs to join Dickey, who was in the kitchen finishing Louise's sandwich.

Louise rinsed the last of the soap from the socks, rolled them in a bath towel, and took them to her room. She blocked the socks to their original shape and laid them on the towel near the open window to dry. Then she telephoned Evelyn.

"Hi, Evelyn. This is Louise. I'm back now. I want to thank you for watching the children this morning. Have they had lunch?"

291

"Hi, Louise. I was glad to help out. They were no trouble at all. Since I had to come home to get my mom's lunch, I brought them along, and they ate over here. I can't talk now. I need to call some of my regular customers and try to make some sales. We may have figured out a way for me to deliver the orders. Frances can tell you all about it. Bye, now."

Louise replaced the telephone on its cradle.

*I don't care how she makes her deliveries. I need her to stay home and help watch the children.*

\* \* \*

All the Hoags were in a good mood at dinner that evening. Everyone had something to share.

"I have a job," announced Frances. "Dickey and I are going to help Miss Evelyn deliver her Fuller brushes. We'll put the brushes in a big bucket, and Dickey and I will take turns carrying the bucket from house to house. Miss Evelyn will come along and show us where to stop. She'll collect the money, and she'll pay us."

Harry beamed with pride. "That sounds like a fine solution to Miss Evelyn's delivery problem. I'm surprised that she thought of such a good plan."

"It was my idea," said Frances. "Miss Evelyn said she would pay us ten cents for each trip."

Louise beamed, too—with relief. It was a fine solution to her problem of getting time to herself without Frances. She said, "I don't think Evelyn has any walking shoes. I'll give her a pair of my old saddle shoes. You can take them over to her tomorrow, Frances."

"How generous of you, Louise," Harry said, giving his wife a grateful smile.

"I have a job announcement, too," Harry began. "We're bringing in more orders than the rolling mill can fill. It's because of the war. Sheet metal is needed for jeeps, tanks, guns, ammo boxes, steel hats, and everything else you can think of. We are opening a new plant right here in Allenburg, and I'll be coordinating all sales efforts for both plants."

"So you won't have to travel so much?" Louise asked, trying to keep the disappointment out of her voice.

"It'll take about six months to get the new plant up and rolling. While it's under construction, I'll be busier than ever, making sure we secure enough back orders to keep the new plant busy. Actually, I'll be on the road more than usual for the next six months. After that, I'll probably have fewer out-of-town trips, but I'll be traveling farther afield when I do go away. My ultimate goal is to get a contract with one of the big car makers in Detroit."

"Are you getting a raise?" Louise asked.

"Oh yes. The company offered me a generous raise, but I might settle for a smaller raise and a larger commission percentage. We're in negotiations on this now. The great part is that my boss is backing me in these talks."

"I'm very happy for you, Harry. You deserve more money. You work so hard," Louise said.

*I'm happy for me, too. More money and more free time. Less Harry, Frances, and Evelyn.*

Louise looked around the table. "I have a good idea. I think we should hire Ronald Lay to do more than mow the grass. He could do your gardening work, too, Harry. Your victory garden can't go unattended while you're away. Ronald would be perfect for the job. Ben Cole and Father Michael from St. Joseph's both recommend him. How much should I offer to pay him?"

"Sixty cents per hour seems about right. First, you need to check and see how much time he has available."

* * *

The following morning, Louise reviewed her list of people to question concerning Roger's death. *I'll start with the police. No need to wait. I'll do it today.* She rode the bus to the central police station. As she climbed the building's front steps from the sidewalk, it occurred to her that she didn't know the name of any of the policemen.

*Ask to see one of the policemen who came to the house when you heard that scratchy noise,* said the Voice. *The older one might know something.*

*The younger one was cuter,* laughed Squeaky.

Louise took the Voice's suggestion. She explained the circumstances to the officer on duty and asked to see the older of the two policemen. "I want to thank him personally. He was so nice and polite. I appreciate all he did," she said, smiling sweetly. "Do you have a calendar of who answered my call that night? I don't even know their names."

Louise followed the desk clerk down a long hallway, painted an anonymous, dull beige. She was ushered into a small office near the end of the hall. It, too, was painted the same boring color and was shared by two policemen. They were the same two who had investigated her prowler episode. Introductions were made. Louise thanked them both profusely.

"How can we help you today?" asked Officer Leo Thompson, offering Louise a chair.

Louise took a deep breath and began. "I'm working on a history of Collis Avenue and all the people who have lived there through the years. I'm not having any luck when it comes to the house where I currently live. I understand that the previous owner, Roger Mills, died suddenly in 1939. Can you tell me anything about him or his death? I would ask his family, but I understand that they no longer live in Allenburg. The neighbors don't have any information. I'm sorry to bother you, but you are my last hope. What can you tell me?"

"I remember Mr. Mills. The poor man fell down the stairs and broke his neck. It was ruled an accident by the coroner. That's all I know, except that he died during the worst snowstorm we have had around here in years," the older policeman replied.

"That all happened before I joined the force," Patrolman Jimmy Kearns said.

Louise tried to hide her disappointment. It was obvious that if these policemen had any further information about Roger, they weren't going to share it. She thanked them and left.

Turning to his younger partner, Leo Thompson said, "That woman is asking too many questions. Let's keep an eye on her for her own protection. We can do it off the books."

"Okay. That's probably a good idea. By the way, doesn't Jack Mercer live on Collis Avenue? I think we should keep an eye on him, too."

"Don't worry about Jack Mercer. The Feds are watching him," said the older man without further explanation.

\* \* \*

Before going home, Louise had two more stops to make—the drugstore and the deli.

At the drugstore, she bought a bottle of over-the-counter cough medicine, which she didn't need, and a birthday card for her sister, Helen. Then she walked over to the pharmacy counter.

"Hi, George. I stopped by to see if you needed any help organizing the old records in the basement. I remember the New Year's resolution you made. I have some extra time, and I'd be glad to help."

"Thanks, Louise, but no. I did what I could with the old records. Then I threw the rest in the trash months ago. See, I did keep my resolution, after all."

Louise went next door to the delicatessen. Jack was alone at the front of the store. He stood at the cash register, counting the morning's receipts. It looked like an awful lot of money to Louise.

"What do you have today in the way of coffeecakes?" she asked.

"We have cinnamon, blueberry, and our special—brown sugar and raisin."

"I'll take the raisin and a small platter of your mixed cold cuts."

"What about a blueberry coffeecake, too? The last time you came in, you said that your daughter didn't like raisins. She would enjoy the blueberry cake. All kids like blueberries."

"Well, Frances isn't doing the shopping. I am, and I want only raisin."

"Instead of cold cuts, why don't you get a nice roast beef?" Jack suggested.

"Don't be ridiculous! A roast would cost a month's worth of meat-rationing coupons."

Jack looked directly at Louise and said, "Or ten dollars."

Louise returned his look. She handed him a ten-dollar bill and no coupons.

# CHAPTER 35

$\mathcal{F}$rustration accompanied Louise on her walk home from Jack's Deli. Nothing was going right. The police were of no help. Her one chance to study the drugstore records was gone. Jack had taken the last of her grocery money. Her carefully thought-out plans to uncover the facts behind Roger's death were at a dead end. She was angry at the world.

Before her anger could give way to depression, Louise saw the mailman coming down the front steps of her house on Collis Avenue. Sticking out of her mailbox was a square white envelope. At first, she thought it might be a wedding invitation—but no—it was a wedding announcement.

*Mr. and Mrs. Robert Rice*
*Are pleased to announce the marriage*
*of their daughter, Shirley,*
*To William Stevens*
*On Friday, July 31, 1942*

*So Dickey's father did get married, as Zina had predicted. I'm glad we got an announcement instead of an invitation. I don't want to go to a wedding. What if the new Mrs. Stevens doesn't like me? Grandmother Mercer said she was a floozy anyway. Maybe I won't like her! Since it's only an announcement, not an invitation, I don't need to send a gift.*

*We agree,* said the voices.

Later that afternoon, Louise invited Zina over for coffee. "Zina, what's the story about Dickey's father getting married? We received an announcement in the mail, but no invitation."

"You didn't get an invitation because they didn't have a real wedding. They eloped and were married down at the courthouse by a justice of the peace. No one was invited. They were planning to keep it a secret until her mother said they had to mail out announcements."

"Now what? I assume she'll move into the Stevens's house? Does Dickey know? What about your job?" asked Louise, trying not to show the anxiety she was feeling.

"The new wife is moving in tomorrow. Last night Mr. Stevens told me that they wanted me to stay on as their housekeeper because *she* won't be doing any of the housework. He said she doesn't know much about children and that Dickey still needs me."

"How does Dickey feel about having a new stepmother?" asked Louise, hoping Zina would mistake her curiosity for caring.

"I don't think Dickey cares much. I told him things wouldn't change. He rarely sees his father, and he thinks of me as his mother since Miss Jean died."

Louise noticed that Zina didn't refer to the new wife as "Mrs. Stevens" or as "Miss Shirley." She had always spoken, with affection, of the first wife as "Miss Jean."

"Have you met her?"

"Once. She was in the car when Mr. Stevens stopped by the house to pick up something he had forgotten. He was taking her to get her fingernails done. Who ever heard of such a thing?"

"What's the matter with her? Why can't she take care of her own fingernails?"

"I don't want to talk about her anymore. I've got some news of my own. You will never believe who I saw at the hospital last week. I was walking through the emergency-room lobby and there was Clyde Arthur. He's from down in the country, where I grew up. We went to high school together. Now he's working at the hospital as an orderly. His bad knee is keeping him out of the draft, but he can still do orderly things at the hospital. He's classified as what they call 4-F. Most girls don't want to date 4-Fers. Anyway, we had lunch together, and he asked me to go to a movie Saturday night. That's my night off, and I said yes. We went out a couple of times way back when. Clyde is awfully nice, but he wasn't too popular with the girls, even then, because of his limp."

"What caused his limp?" Louise asked.

"When he was just a kid, he fell out of a barn loft and landed on his knee. The knee bone was crushed so badly it couldn't be fixed. When it did heal, he couldn't bend his knee and ended up with a limp for life."

"I had surgery on my broken ankle and foot. Now, I can walk as well as before," Louise said.

"Clyde doesn't want surgery. Even if he did, he can't afford an operation. He says his knee doesn't bother him, and it doesn't bother me. I like him anyways," Zina said, blushing.

\* \* \*

It was almost Labor Day before Louise met her new neighbor. As August came to a close, Allenburg was besieged by a late summer heat wave. The relentless sun bore down, wilting the people and Louise's flowers. There had been no rain for weeks. Louise spent her mornings in the backyard with the garden hose aimed at her flower beds. The yardman, Ronald Lay, stopped by daily to water Harry's vegetable garden. Home air-conditioning wasn't an option for the residents of Collis Avenue. The movie theaters had the only air-conditioning in town.

While the adults and the plants suffered, the new Mrs. Stevens seemed oblivious to the dry, scorching heat. There *she* was, stretched out in that lounge chair, cooking herself again. Her skin glistened through its glaze of baby-oil-and-iodine ointment. Dickey was also in the Stevens's backyard, dutifully performing his assigned chore of watering the shrubs behind his house.

Louise moved closer to the fence to get a better look. Her new neighbor was only a few feet away.

*That skimpy bathing suit doesn't leave much to the imagination*, said the Voice.

*Hubba-hubba. I like it,* said Squeaky.

*I hope she gets a bad sunburn,* said Raspy.

Louise's attention was drawn immediately to her neighbor's hands. Every finger wore a gaudy ring, proclaiming, loud and clear, that it was not attached to a working hand. Both fingernails and toenails were painted a shocking pink. A sparkling bracelet encircled one thin ankle. Long, shoulder-length, blond hair flowed from under a floppy hat, adorned with artificial flowers. A crackling noise was coming from under the hat, as its owner snapped her chewing gum. Sunglasses covered her eyes, and she was drinking an orange soda. A movie magazine lay nearby.

Louise had seen enough. Before she could control the impulse, *Squeaky* grabbed her by the wrist and pointed the hose squarely at the figure reclining in the lounge chair. Louise watched in horror as the water rose and arched over the fence, making a direct hit on its intended target. She didn't know what to do. Instinctively, she handed the hose to Frances, who was standing nearby, and ran into the house.

From the dining room window, Louise watched in amazement as the new neighbor leapt from her chair, grabbed the hose from Dickey, and doused Frances. Dickey snatched the hose back from his stepmother, and a water fight ensued, with squeals and laughter everywhere. The new Mrs. Stevens was bent double with laughter. Louise couldn't believe what she was seeing. Dickey's father had married a child!

\* \* \*

After lunch, Louise decided to make a proper call on her neighbor. She would apologize for Frances's behavior with the hose. *I can say Frances was trying to hit Dickey with the water. That sounds believable.*

Dickey opened the door at Louise's knock. "She's resting," he said in answer to Louise's inquiry.

"Is she ill? Does she have a headache?"

"No, she always rests after lunch. That's when she listens to the radio. She likes mushy soap operas. I like *Terry and the Pirates.* She's on the couch in the living room listening to the radio now. You can go in if you want."

Louise did want. She put on her friendliest face and walked in the direction Dickey indicated. She paused under the arch between the entrance hall and the living room and said, "Hello. I'm Louise Hoag from next door. I hope this isn't an inconvenient time for a visit."

"Hi. I'm Shirley. You won't believe what Stella Dallas is up to now. Do you listen to the soaps? Come on in and have a chair. We can listen together."

Louise smiled secretly to herself. She would never admit to anyone that she enjoyed such lowbrow entertainment. Her hostess had invited her to listen to *Stella Dallas.* That was her favorite. Louise wanted to be a polite guest, so she sat and listened. Oh, that Stella!

When the radio program was over, the two women faced each other. Louise began by saying, "I'm delighted to meet you, Shirley. I want to offer you two apologies. First, I'm sorry I took so long in welcoming you to Collis Avenue. Second, I'm sorry about my daughter's part in the water fight this morning."

"The water fight was fun. Lord knows it's hot enough! Zina just made a big pitcher of lemonade. It's in the ice box. Feel free to help yourself."

*Shirley certainly isn't burdened by an overload of manners and formality. I can put mine down for a while, too. I'll jump right in.*

"Shirley, how did you and your husband meet?" Louise asked.

"We met at the restaurant where I was working as a waitress. He ate there often—sometimes with business people and sometimes alone. I was always extra nice to him because he was such a good tipper. One night he asked me out and that was it. We've been together ever since. I couldn't believe it when he told me he lived on Collis Avenue, right next door to the Mills's house."

Louise almost choked. She felt a wave of shock crash into her, nearly knocking her off her chair. Had she found another source of information about Roger? She sputtered, "Did you know the Mills family?"

"Oh, sure. Charlene and I were best friends. I was at her house a lot. I really missed her when she and her mom moved away after her dad died. I still miss her. For a while we wrote letters, but it's been a long time since I've heard from her. She's probably busy with college and stuff like that."

"Did you know her father?" Louise asked.

"Not very well. He wasn't around much—always working at that drugstore. I knew her mom really well. She was nice.

You know, Charlene looks exactly like her mom. Just as nice, too."

"Why did they move away from Allenburg?"

"I guess they both wanted to get out of town and start over. There were a lot of bad memories here, and after the funeral, there was all that gossip."

"What kind of gossip?"

"Later. It's time for *Ma Perkins* now," Shirley said, glancing at the radio.

"You're right. It is getting late. I need to leave now. Please come over and visit with me soon," Louise said to a girl whose attention span had shifted to radio land.

# CHAPTER 36

*A*llenburg's late summer heat wave was nudged off stage by the Labor Day weekend. As the cooler weather moved across the Buckeye State, its residents welcomed the dewy mornings and cool evenings. The summer-weary residents were ready for fall. Both Louise and her daughter were ready for the new school year to begin. Frances was now in the third grade. She and Dickey were old enough to walk to and from school alone.

It was a glorious fall. The summer storms, scooping up cloud loads of water as they rolled over Lake Erie, and the heat of July and August had suited the hardwoods just fine. To celebrate fall, the trees put on a spectacular display of reds, golds, and oranges. The cloudless sky was bluer than blue. Frances called it *an October sky*.

She and Dickey walked to school together in the mornings. In the afternoons, Frances and her friend, Mary Lynn, paired up for the walk back to Collis Avenue. On the way home, they walked past vacant lots with unkempt weeds. They picked goldenrod and the little purple asters growing among the grasses, gone to seed. They caught grasshoppers and held the hard-shelled bodies tight, as the insects spat tobacco juice into their hands. They scavenged for ripe beechnuts under the big beech tree in front of the Presbyterian Church. Frances often spent the rest of the afternoon at Mary Lynn's house. Her mother didn't mind. She didn't even seem to notice.

* * *

Louise was too busy to think about her daughter. She was working on a new plan for investigating Roger's death. The old plan had uncovered some interesting facts, but it didn't go far enough to discover what she was looking for—the real cause of Roger's untimely death that cold, snowy January night. *Should I go back and interview everyone on the list again? Should I add some new names to the list? What about Shirley Stevens? I'll invite her over for coffee now. I'll tell her that I want to learn more about the Mills family and to bring any old pictures she might still have of the time when she and Charlene were close friends.*

Louise was in her kitchen, awaiting Shirley's arrival. The coffeepot was busy hiccupping percolator gurgle gulps when the phone rang. It was Shirley.

"Hi. I did find some old pictures, and I'll bring them over for you to see. I forgot to tell you that I don't like coffee. I only drink healthy fruit drinks, like lemonade with lots of sugar, Kool-Aid, and orange soda. I'll bring my own soda. See you in a sec. Bye."

*Healthy? I don't think so! What a waste of coffee-ration coupons! Harry will just have to drink leftover coffee for breakfast tomorrow.*

Louise looked out of the living-room window and saw someone she was not expecting coming up the front walk. It was Evelyn Fisher, carrying two buckets—one in each hand.

*Evelyn is the last person I want to see right now. What can I do?*

*You can invite her in. You might learn more than you think,* said the Voice.

*I want to see what she has in those buckets,* said Squeaky.

Evelyn came inside and set her buckets down. With one quick motion, she pulled her long hair over the disfigured side of her face, hiding the big red blotch. Louise pretended not to notice.

"Evelyn, I'm glad to see you. I just put on a pot of coffee, hoping you'd stop by," Louise lied. "Why are you carrying those buckets?"

"It's all because of my broken arm. It didn't mend right. After the cast came off, I couldn't bend my elbow. The doctor said I should carry a bucket of sand around to encourage my arm to bend. I still can't drive my car. Since the kids are in school, I am delivering my orders in the bucket they used to carry. Two buckets—one for sand and one for deliveries."

There was a knock at the back door. It was Shirley. She, too, had her hands full. One hand held a bottle of orange soda. In the other hand, she carried a scrapbook.

The three neighbors sat at the Hoags' kitchen table with Shirley's scrapbook open before them. Louise suffered through page after page of pictures showing various silly poses of Shirley and her teenaged friends. When Shirley turned a page near the end of the album and pointed to a picture of herself with another girl, Evelyn exclaimed, "Oh, there you are with Charlene!"

Louise pulled the scrapbook closer to get a better look. "Charlene was attractive."

"Still is, as far as I know," Shirley replied. "Looks just like her mother." Turning the page and pointing again, Shirley said, "This is a picture of her father. He wanted me to take a picture of his prize rosebush, with him standing in front, so he could show everyone how big it was. See, it's the tall one. He's the short one—and he was over six feet tall."

Louise gripped the edge of the table to keep from falling. She stared down at the photograph, immediately recognizing the familiar face. It was the rosebush man she had seen so often in the backyard and even sitting on the end of her bed as she worked with her files. She could not speak. She could only stare. The man in the picture was indeed tall, with long, gangly arms and legs. He had a gaunt look about him, as though he had recently lost weight. His pleasant face—not exactly handsome—radiated a proud look. His head was turned slightly to one side as though he were admiring his rosebush. The picture must have been taken in summer. The bush was covered with white roses, and the man was wearing a white dress shirt and a necktie. No coat. No hat. Louise could not stop staring at the image in the photograph.

"If you're so interested in that rosebush picture, you can have it," said Shirley, removing the picture from the scrapbook and handing it to Louise. "I've got to go now. It's time for *Ma Perkins*. See you later," she called as she picked up her photograph album and hurried home.

Evelyn helped herself to another cup of coffee and said, "I remember Mr. Mills. Strange as he was, he loved that rosebush. He wouldn't let anyone touch it. He'd go out every day and prune away the faded blossoms. Only he could pick the roses. Mrs. Mills and Charlene had better leave that bush alone."

"What else do you remember about him?" Louise asked, struggling to keep her voice steady.

"Not much. I do remember the terrible snowstorm we had the night he died. It had been snowing all day, and I was worried about getting snowed in if it didn't stop. I looked out of my window just before getting into bed. You know my bedroom window faces our backyard. From it I can see all the way to the back alley. It was almost eleven o'clock, and there were two men in the alley. I wondered, at the time, what they were doing out in the snow at that time of night. They stood out there like they were waiting for someone. Pretty soon I saw another man join them. The three of them talked for a while. Then the first two walked off in one direction and the other man walked back the way he had come—toward the Mercers' house."

"Did you recognize any of the men?" asked Louise, daring to hope.

"No, it was snowing too hard. I don't think they were the kind of men I would want to know anyway. Something didn't seem right about them. I've got to go now. Thanks for the coffee."

Louise clasped Roger's picture to her chest with both hands as she hurried up the stairs to her room. She propped the picture against the lamp on her desk. She sat down and stared at it. She stared and stared. She didn't know what else to do. Maybe Roger would tell her what to do. He didn't say anything. He just stared back at her, smiling.

*If you want to keep that picture, you'd better hide it,* said the Voice.

Louise looked around the room. *Where can I hide Roger's picture? It should be out of sight but accessible when I want to look at it. I know! No one ever looks in my purse. I'll put it in there. Then Roger will be near me everywhere I go.*

It was a great comfort to have Roger's picture safely in her possession, but it wasn't enough. Having his picture didn't get her any closer to solving the mystery of his death. She needed to add two more questions to her plan. *Why was the rosebush so special? And who were the men in the alley the night Roger died?*

With Roger's picture as an inspiration, Louise renewed her obsessive pursuit. She was oblivious to anything outside of her own private world, where she and Roger were the costars in the only drama she cared about.

# PART IV

# CHAPTER 37

*M*s. Sally Ambrose was Frances's third grade teacher. She loved to play the piano and sing. Her favorite songs were either patriotic ones or tunes on the current *Your Hit Parade* lineup. She used her students as an excuse to indulge her musical hobby. As she sat at the classroom piano, banging away, the students were expected to sing along to such melodies as "The White Cliffs of Dover," "Coming Home on a Wing and a Prayer," "Glory, Glory, What a Hell of a Way to Die," and her all-time favorite, "Praise the Lord and Pass the Ammunition." Louise was horrified.

"That woman has absolutely no taste in music," Louise announced at dinner.

"Maybe she's just being patriotic, singing all those war songs. Can't blame her for that," Harry said.

"Everything is about the war," Louise groused.

"Miss Ambrose said we should save all our newspapers and tie them in bundles and bring them to school every Friday. We are going to save string and tin foil, too. We can mash the tin foil together and wind the string into balls. We should save our money and buy savings stamps, which we can stick in a book. When I get enough books, I'll get a bond," Frances said.

"I'm impressed with how enthusiastic you are about being a home-front soldier. Frances, you make me proud," her father beamed.

Louise was proud, too, but she didn't say anything. *Maybe I really am a good mother. Frances should be glad to have me as her mother.*

"I'm going to save empty tin cans. We can cut off the ends and mash them flat. They can go for the war effort," Louise said, offering the only contribution she planned to make.

\* \* \*

October was coming to an end. It would soon be Halloween. Frances was determined to go trick-or-treating this year, costume and all. She wanted to go from door to door and get her own candy—not stay at home, handing out candy to the other kids.

"Well, who is supposed to give out the candy at our house?" asked Louise. "You are beyond selfish, Frances! You know I don't like to stay home alone on Halloween."

Frances was not to be dissuaded. She went trick-or-treating, wearing the witch hat Aunt Rose had given her the previous Halloween. Louise locked the door and turned off the lights. She stayed in her bedroom, hiding under the covers, until the last of the trick-or-treaters had gone. Then she heard a sound. She lay very still. It was only Frances coming up the stairs.

"I locked the door. How did you get in?" Louise asked.

"I have my own key. Daddy gave it to me."

Louise was surprised. No one had told her that Frances had a key. *What else haven't they told me? Why do they always leave me out?*

\* \* \*

The day before the Thanksgiving holiday break, Miss Ambrose did an inspection. She spread a newspaper over each student's desk. She walked up and down each aisle, from desk to desk, carrying a long, thick knitting needle. When she stopped beside a desk, the student was to put his hands in his lap and lean over the newspaper covered desk. Miss Ambrose then poked and prodded her way through the student's hair, with her knitting needle, looking for lice. Everyone had to be very quiet and help listen for any wayward louse hitting the newspaper as he fell from his former home in an eight-year-old head of hair. The boys had it easy. They hair was too short for lice to take up residence. The girls were more problematic. Frances passed the test—no lice in her hair. Miss Ambrose moved on to Mary Lynn's desk. As the teacher combed through Mary Lynn's gigantic bush of yellow hair, a *ping* sound reverberated around the classroom. Then another *ping* and another. *Ping, ping, ping.* The golden mop was home to a colony of lice. Mary Lynn was sent home that day carrying a note to her parents.

Frances didn't see her friend over the holidays. When school resumed after Thanksgiving, Mary Lynn appeared at the classroom door for the last time. The children gasped when they saw her blond hair—cut shorter than any boy's in the class. Mary Lynn stood still, looking down at the floor. She didn't even glance in Frances's direction. She was accompanied by Henry, the Hall's gardener/butler/chauffeur, wearing his funny black hat. He handed the teacher a note.

After reading the note, Miss Ambrose said, "Mary Lynn, you can go ahead and get your books and other supplies from your desk and clean out your cubby space now. Do you need help?"

"Show me where her things are and I'll get them," Henry said. "Miss Mary Lynn can wait in the hall while I gather up her things."

After Mary Lynn and Henry had gone, Miss Ambrose addressed the class, "Mary Lynn won't be in our class anymore. Her parents have decided to have a tutor work with her for the rest of the year. Next year she will be going to private school. I know you will miss your friend. Let's get out our paper and pencils and all write Mary Lynn a letter. After our letters are done, we'll sing a song to remember her by."

No one seemed to mind that "Little Bo Peep Has Lost Her Jeep" wasn't a traditional farewell song. At least it was cheerful and all the children knew the words.

Frances felt like Little Bo Peep. She hadn't lost her Jeep, but she had lost her best friend. She missed Mary Lynn. They always had fun together. Frances loved being at her friend's house. Her bedroom was like a toy shop. She had a bicycle of her own, which she let Frances ride. Mary Lynn actually enjoyed sharing. They told and kept secrets. They giggled about how stupid the boys in their class were and about how Stanley, the janitor, was creepy enough to trick-or-treat without a costume. Now, Mary Lynn wasn't allowed to play with her or with the other public-school children.

With Mary Lynn gone, Frances found another walking-home friend. Carol Mercer was in the grade ahead of Frances, but they were both going to Collis Avenue at the same time and soon began walking together.

Dickey walked home with Bobby each afternoon. They would run ahead, hide in the bushes, and jump out to scare the girls. "No one is afraid of you, Dickey Stevens." Frances yelled in her outdoor voice. "If you and Bobby don't leave us alone, I'm going to tell Zina."

"I'm going to tell my grandmother," threatened Carol. That got the boys' attention, and they found other games to play.

When Frances and Carol walked home together, they counted the service stars in the windows. A silver star meant a family member had been wounded in service or was missing in action. A gold star meant someone the in family had been killed in the war. The girls had a running contest to see which side of the street had the most stars. One house on the corner had three gold stars in its front window and a black wreath on its door.

Sometimes Frances would spend the after-school hours at the Mercers' house. She didn't enjoy being there as much as she had liked being at Mary Lynn's. Grandmother Mercer was nice about giving them milk and cookies, but as soon as the cookies were gone, Carol had to do her homework—no time to play. Grandmother Mercer told Frances that she could stay and do her homework, too. Frances didn't like that idea because Grandmother Mercer was always in the living room making Kurt practice his walking. It was hard to watch, but Kurt was improving.

One afternoon when the girls got to Carol's house, a great uproar was in progress. Carol's other brother, Fred, had joined the military. Grandmother Mercer was yelling, first in German, then in English. As Frances left, she heard Carol's grandmother yell one final command, "You can shoot at Herr Hitler, but you better not shoot at any German people."

* * *

News of the war continued. Harry listened to the evening broadcasts after dinner on the nights he was home. After the news was over, he and Frances moved the pins around on the wall map. Everyone was doing their bit to help the war effort as the country beat its shovels and plows into tanks and guns. The government's propaganda mills continued to grind out their ceaseless slogans. Patriotic posters, produced by the Office of War Information, were everywhere. They screamed at the citizens proclaiming, "Uncle Sam Wants You," "Build Your Navy – Enlist Now," "Loose Lips Sink Ships," "You Give

Us the Fire. We'll Give 'Em Hell," and Frances's favorite—Rosie the Riveter saying, "We Can Do It."

Rationing escalated. Everything seemed to be rationed. Gasoline and tires were added to the ever-growing list. Harry took the tires off the Terraplane, turned them in for recycling, and put cinder blocks under the car's wheels. He would drive the company car assigned to him until the war was over. The Terraplane's immobility didn't bother either Frances or Louise. They couldn't drive anyway.

Harry's job was considered critical to the war effort since he worked for a rolling mill—rolling out a steady stream of steel for the military. He was working harder and harder. He was away more often and for longer times. His stash of war bonds continued to grow.

Along with the rationing of consumer goods came price controls. Louise Hoag and Jack Mercer didn't let that technicality bother them. They continued as before.

With Miss Ambrose's help, Frances marched and sang her way through the third grade.

# CHAPTER 38

*T*he last day of the school year was always special. It was impossible to tell who was more excited about the coming summer—the children or the teachers. This year there were no lunchtime picnics on the playground. Instead, a special award ceremony was held in the gymnasium. Prizes were given for outstanding results in a variety of efforts. Some children were recognized for their scholastic achievements, others for perfect attendance. Frances was sitting with her class, watching the proceedings, when her name was called by the principal.

Frances had won the paper-drive award, not only for the third grade, but for the entire school. She couldn't believe it. Although no one had been more diligent than she in collecting newspapers for the weekly paper drives, she hadn't expected to win the award. As soon as the paper drive was announced, she had asked Aunt Rose to save newspapers for her. She asked Evelyn Fisher, too, and the people living on the other side of the Fishers. She even asked George Mills at the drugstore to save the papers that didn't sell. She had a regular list of suppliers. Each Saturday, Frances made her rounds, pulling her Radio Flyer wagon, collecting newspapers. On Fridays, Aunt Rose drove her niece to school with the neatly tied stacks of papers piled in the rumble seat of her little two-seater car. Some of the children teased Frances and called her "the paper girl." She didn't care. She was proud of her contribution. Her award was a red, white, and blue ribbon, which she showed to her father that evening.

"Oh, Frances, I'm so very, very proud of you," Harry said, snapping to attention and saluting before giving her a big hug. "You're doing your part to help us win the war. With good Americans like you, we can't lose."

Frances's mother continued reading her book without looking up.

* * *

Along with summer, came Vacation Bible School, taught again this year by Miss Evelyn. Frances and Dickey attended daily. The Mercers had other plans for Carol, who had just turned ten. Carol was enrolled in the Hebrew school taught by the rabbi at their temple. While Frances and Dickey walked to the Presbyterian Church each morning, Carol rode the crosstown bus to the synagogue.

On Tuesday, after Bible School was over for the day, Frances went home for a quick lunch, hoping to spend the afternoon playing at Carol's house. This was not to be. Halfway through lunch, Louise placed her glass of iced tea firmly on the kitchen table and said, "Frances, I don't want you to play with Carol anymore. I don't want you to go to the Mercers' house again."

"Why? Carol is my friend."

"You'll just have to find other friends. I want you to stay away from Carol. Playing with her is a bad idea."

Frances burst into tears. "I want to play with Carol. I like Carol. Why don't you like Carol?"

That evening at dinner, Frances appealed to her father. "Mom said I can't play with Carol anymore. That's mean. Carol is nice. Please . . . why can't I play with Carol?"

Harry turned to his wife and asked, "What's this all about? Why don't you want Frances to play with Carol? Louise, you had better have a good reason."

"They're Jewish. That's reason enough. And they're German, too."

"Carol is not a German. She and her brothers were born in this country. They're as much American as you are. Their being Jewish is nothing new. We've always known that."

"They are *too* Jewish. Carol is even going to Hebrew school. Everyone knows that they speak German around their house."

"I don't know how a person can be *too* Jewish. At least Carol will be fluent in three languages. She'll be the best educated kid on the block. I think you're letting your prejudices get in the way of what common sense you have left," Harry said, letting his exasperation show.

Louise was shocked. Harry had never spoken to her like this—and in that tone of voice. She stood up and glared at her husband. Throwing her napkin on the table, she said, "There's a war going on, and it's not good to be seen in the company of Germans, especially German Jews. This conversation is over. I'm going to my room. Tomorrow, I hope to see that *you* have regained whatever common sense *you* have left."

Harry sighed and shook his head. He gave his daughter a resigned look and said, "It's okay by me if you play with Carol, but it might be a good idea not to invite Carol to our house. That will just upset your mother even more. You know, Frances, you probably have more common sense than either your mother or me."

Despite the disagreement over the propriety of associating with the Mercers, Frances continued to play with Carol, out of her mother's sight and without her mother's permission. Harry continued to attend Jack Mercer's weekly poker games, and Louise continued to shop at Jack's Deli.

* * *

The long dormant seeds of open hostility between Frances's parents had sprouted, and the arguments began. Louise and Harry disagreed about everything. When they weren't arguing, a cloud of discontent hung in the air. Harry tried to reason with Louise, but she took issue with everything he suggested. Harry's frustration neared the boiling point. Louise froze him out, as she moved further from reality. Rose's visits became less frequent. His poker-playing friends were busy with their own lives. The Hoags' house was no longer a place for coffee and hospitality. The only bright spots in Harry's personal life were spending time with his daughter and chatting with Zina. Thoughts of Zina began to occupy the space in his fantasy life vacated by Louise.

Harry telephoned his sister from his office. "Rose, what have you been up to? We haven't seen much of you lately."

"I know, Harry. I've been busy. I've missed seeing you and Frances, too. What about if I come over Saturday morning? We need to have a talk. I have some really exciting news to share."

"What news?"

"Oh, you'll find out on Saturday. Is nine o'clock too early? . . . Okay. Bye"

\* \* \*

At exactly nine o'clock the following Saturday morning, Rose bounced up the walk to the Hoags' house. Harry and Frances were on the porch waiting for her. Louise was in the kitchen slicing herself a piece of the raisin coffeecake she had purchased the previous day. She ate the pastry over the sink and then hid the remainder where her husband and daughter weren't likely to look. Brushing the crumbs away, she joined the others on the porch.

Zina and Dickey's new stepmother soon joined the Hoags. Frances moved to the front steps, and Shirley sat down beside her. She had two bottles of orange soda, one of which she gave to Frances. Opening her secret purse, Frances took out a pack of chewing gum Carol Mercer had given her. She offered Shirley a stick.

"Where did you get the gum?" Shirley whispered. "It's not even on the rationed items list. It's totally unavailable. The stores haven't sold gum in months. They send all the gum to the soldiers."

"I have a source, but I can't tell. It's a secret," Frances whispered back, closing her purse.

Rose asked, "Zina, how's your love life going? Are you still dating Clyde?"

Zina blushed at Rose's questions. She blushed even more when Shirley said, "They are getting serious, too. Tell them about your plans, Zina."

"Clyde and I have been dating for over a year now. We've known each other all our lives, and we've decided to get married. Clyde asked me to set the date, the sooner the better."

"Congratulations," Harry managed to say through a forced smile, hiding his disappointment.

"I'm so happy for you. I want to hear all the details about your wedding plans," said Rose.

Louise didn't say anything. The idea of Zina's not living next door was frightening. *Who will be my friend now? Who would help keep an eye on Frances? I need Zina next door.*

Frances was quiet, too. She didn't want Zina to move away. She loved Zina. "Will we still see you after you get married?" she asked in an uncertain voice.

Zina got up from her chair and sat beside Frances on the steps. She put her arm around the little girl and said, "Of course. I'll still be working for the Stevens part time. I'll be here on Wednesdays and on Saturday mornings. Clyde and I will have our own apartment near the hospital. You and I will see each other every week. We will always be good and true friends."

Louise felt a lump of jealousy in her throat. No one had ever said they wanted to be *her* "good and true friend." Harry had loved her once, she knew that. Now, she wasn't so sure. *Who cares? I never loved him!*

"I have news, too," said Rose. "I've been dating someone special since the first of the year. We aren't planning to get married, or even thinking about it, but I do enjoy his company. He's assigned to the Washington, DC bond office. He travels all over Pennsylvania and Ohio, selling bonds to the Amish and the Quakers. They are exactly like the bonds I sell except they are called peace bonds, instead of war bonds."

"Why do the bonds have different names?" asked Frances.

"Well, honey, the Amish don't believe in war, but they do believe in saving their money. They are more than willing to buy bonds if the word *peace* is printed on them. What's even more interesting is that in Canada the same bonds are called *victory bonds*."

"Who is he? What's his name? Is he married?" asked Louise, jerking the conversation back to where *her* interest lay.

"His name is Jim, and he's never been married. He's very nice. I'd like for you to meet him the next time he's in town."

Before Louise could ask another nosy question, the porch-sitters saw Evelyn coming up the walk. She was crying.

"Evelyn, come and join us," Rose invited. "What's wrong? Why are you crying?"

Evelyn sat down heavily on the step below Shirley, Zina, and Frances. She bent her head, put her face in her hands, and sobbed loudly. "It's all my fault. It's all my fault. Now he's gone and it's my fault."

"What's all your fault? Who's gone?" asked Rose.

"The man I was seeing has left me and joined the navy. He's gone, all because of me. He joined the navy to get away from me."

"Why do you think that? Did you say something to upset him?" asked Harry.

"Yes, I told him I was in *a family way*."

The porch-sitters were speechless. They leaned forward in unison. Their mouths hung open. Their eyes widened. Shirley was the first to find her voice. "You can't be *in a family way*. You're not married." Evelyn responded by crying even harder.

"Shirley, you know better than that," said Zina. "Remember the birds and the bees?"

"What are you talking about?" asked Frances.

Harry and Rose rolled their eyes. Louise, who had more curious bones than sympathetic ones, tried to change the direction of the conversation, without turning it off completely. She said, "Frances, you should go play in the backyard. This is grown-up talk."

Ignoring her mother, Frances turned to Evelyn. "Who joined the navy? Who? Who? Who? What's his name?"

"Al."

"Al? Al? Al who? I don't know any Als," Louise said.

"I once knew an Al," Rose said. "Al White was my old boss."

Frances jumped back into the conversation, "I know an owl, too. A white owl. He's in my picture book, *The Owl and the Pussycat*."

Everyone, except Evelyn and Frances, broke into laughter. Harry, Rose, Zina, and Shirley shook with merriment. They hooted with hilarity. Louise ran into the house to keep the others from seeing her laugh. The child in Shirley couldn't resist the urge to play. She stopped laughing long enough to ask Frances, "What did the owl in your book do?"

"He went to sea in a boat, like the navy does."

"Between laughing and gasping for air, Shirley asked, "Where did he go?"

"To the land where the Bong Tree grows."

Harry coughed, sputtered, and snorted. A geyser of iced coffee erupted from his nose as he threw his head back and roared. Tears of mirth ran down Rose's cheeks. Zina held her sides. Shirley succumbed to a fit of giggles. Seeing Harry, even Evelyn started laughing hysterically. Each struggled, without success, to regain some degree of composure. Just as she got her laughs under control, Zina looked at Harry and started laughing again. Then Harry looked at Zina and burst into uncontrollable howls.

Louise, who had been listening from just inside the front door, returned to the porch. Fighting desperately to keep a straight face, she asked Evelyn, "What are you going to do?"

"I don't know what to do. I thought maybe you could tell me what to do. Should I write him a letter of apology?"

"Certainly not!" Louise said. "This is not your fault alone. He has a responsibility, too."

"Oh, but it is my fault. I was mistaken. I'm not in *a family way*. I just thought I was. By the time I realized I was wrong, it was too late. He had already enlisted."

"Serves him right," Louise said.

# CHAPTER 39

$\mathcal{R}$ight on schedule, September came, once again, to Allenburg. The children were back in school. Harry was busy getting the new mill into production. Louise looked forward to time alone, but first, she had a party to give—a going-away party for Rose, whose application for a transfer to Washington, DC, had been approved. She would be moving at the end of the month.

Louise was aware that Harry was both sad and happy—sad because Rose was moving away—happy because his sister was getting what she wanted. She knew Frances was crushed by the thought of losing her beloved aunt. Louise, herself, didn't care what Rose did. She rather liked the idea of a going-away party and was pleased when Rose supplied the guest list. She had always been curious about Rose's friends—none of whom she had ever met.

The party was a success. Rose's friends were nice. Louise noticed that Harry knew most of them.

Rose sold her car and furniture to Clyde, Zina's fiancé, who had just rented an unfurnished apartment near the hospital. She packed her clothes and a few favorite belongings and took the train to Washington, where a new life and her friend, Jim, waited to embrace her.

\* \* \*

Finally, Louise had time enough to breathe. She renewed her efforts to uncover the identity of the three men Evelyn had seen lurking in the back alley that fateful night in January 1939. She prowled the neighborhood and the shops on Boyd Boulevard, asking questions of everyone she met, whether she knew them or not.

"Were you living around here back in 1939? Have you ever seen three strange men hanging around this block, this store, this area? What about two?"

Those she questioned shook their heads and gave her puzzled looks. People began to eye her with suspicion. "Is she just some nutty neighborhood woman? Is she a government undercover agent? After all, there is a war going on and you know about *loose lips*," they whispered.

Louise's favorite stalking ground was Jack's Deli. A seemingly endless parade of assorted people came and went, in and out, at all times of the day. Louise filled her notebook with pages of useless information.

*Talked to middle-aged woman today, wearing a very ugly hat. New to the neighborhood.*

*Watched a short, stocky man at lunchtime eating a sandwich and drinking a Dr. Brown's cream soda. Ignored my questions.*

*After lunch Jack went upstairs with two suspicious-looking men.*

*Conclusions: Most of the women buy food items. Some leave with packages wrapped like my weekly roast-beef purchase. Many of the male customers buy food, too. However, some have other business with Jack. They huddle in the back of the store, where they talk in low voices and sometimes exchange envelopes. No one will answer my questions. They all have something to hide.*

It didn't take long for Jack to get fed up with Louise's snooping around and annoying his customers. It was time to take action. He faced the two men who had followed him upstairs. "Guys, I've got a job for you. It's different from some of the other jobs you've done for me. Here's the story. There's a woman who's been making a pest of herself in the deli. I don't want her around here anymore."

"What do you want us to do?" asked the taller of the two.

"I want you to give her a good scare and keep her away from my place."

"You want her roughed up?"

"No. Not now. I just want her scared away."

"How much is it worth to you? We've got to make an honest living," said the shorter man.

"Who is this dame? You got a picture? Where does she live?" his friend asked.

Details of the arrangement were agreed upon. The three shook hands and returned to the deli. Louise was still there, talking to Carol's mother. Jack jerked his head in her direction for the men's benefit. They nodded solemnly and left the store.

* * *

The last week of September hosted an early cold snap. Out of Canada, a frigid front rolled over Lake Erie, bringing with it a killing frost. It wilted the remaining annuals in Louise's flower garden. It blackened Harry's vegetable garden overnight. The summer season was over, or so the residents of Allenburg believed. However, mid-October had a lovely surprise in store for them. The temperature rose, and a dry, warm, sunny Indian summer came to visit.

It was Saturday morning, and Frances was bored. She had made her newspaper-collecting rounds the previous afternoon. Carol was at the synagogue with her family. There was nothing to do, so she decided to take a walk. She walked up Collis Avenue to the end of the block and stopped in front of the house with the three gold stars in the window. If she turned left, she could walk another block and be on Boyd Boulevard near the bus stop. If she turned right, she could go over to First Avenue, where she rarely walked. Frances turned right.

As she walked up First Avenue, Frances saw the figure of a woman in the next block. It was her mother, walking in the same direction as she was going. She watched as Louise crossed the street and continued walking. She decided to follow. As Frances was getting ready to cross the street, a slow-moving car crept past where she was standing beside the curb. The car was keeping pace with the walker ahead. Inside were two men Frances had never seen.

"There she is—up ahead. What should we do?" the driver asked his partner.

"Let's just follow her for a while and see where she goes. Go slow. Stay behind her. I want her to know she's being tailed. That'll scare her."

"Sure is weird she lives on the same street as Jack. Even weirder that she lives in the same house as that drugstore guy. What's his name?"

"I told you not to talk about him," was the cross reply. "Let's pull up beside her and see if we can get her in the car."

"Then what?"

"We'll take her for a ride to the other side of town and give her the message to stay away from Jack's store, or else. Then we'll shove her out of the car and make her walk home. That should do it for now."

The car picked up speed and headed for the curb on Louise's side of the street. She stopped abruptly. Before she could turn around, she saw someone walking toward her from the opposite direction. He was wearing a suit and tie and had a familiar walk. It was Ronald Lay.

"Ronald, where are you going all dressed up? You look like you're going to a funeral."

"I am. One of our elderly parishioners died, and I'm going to be a pall bearer."

"That's a lovely suit you're wearing and a nice tie, too. You look downright dashing."

"Father Mike give me this outfit. The suit's a little big, but it's the only one I've got that's good enough for funerals. It's the best suit I ever had. Sorry, got to run. Can't be late for a funeral," Ronald said, continuing his brisk walk toward the bus stop.

"What the *crap*! It's Ronald Lay, of all people—what a *fag*!" said the car's driver. "And he's wearing that drugstore guy's suit. If that don't beat all. I'll never forget that suit—looked too good to wear in a drugstore."

"I told you not to talk about that drugstore man. Now, pull over beside the bitch."

"Hey, lady. We want to talk to you," said the man behind the wheel.

Louise turned and stared directly at the two men in the car, idling beside the curb. She remembered them from Jack's Deli. They were the same two who had gone upstairs with Jack just a few days ago. Why were they following her? She froze, speechless.

"Mom, Mom, wait up," called Frances, running across the street.

The man in the passenger seat turned to see Frances hurrying toward them. "Come on. Let's get out of here. First that loser, Ronald Lay, now a kid. We don't mess with no kids."

The car drove away at a normal speed. Frances ran to her mother's side. She took the frozen statue that her mother had become by the elbow and guided it down the street. "We need to go home now."

Louise followed her daughter, docile as a lamb, too panicked to object.

\* \* \*

Frances had just finished brushing her teeth and was going toward her bedroom when she heard her parents arguing downstairs. She sat on the top step of the staircase and listened.

"Harry, I tell you, some men were following me today. They were in a car, and they followed me on my walk. You have to do something. I'm afraid of those men."

"No one is following you, Louise. You're just imagining things. Sometimes you see things that aren't there. It's just a trick of your mind—like a mirage."

"If you don't believe me, you can ask Frances. She saw them, too."

"Stop right there. We're not bringing Frances into this. You're the one seeing things. I'm sorry, but I don't believe you. Your wild ideas are laughable."

"Are you laughing at my beliefs?" Louise shouted.

"That's just it. Your beliefs are *beliefs*. They are not facts. There's a difference, and you had better stick with the facts from now on," Harry shouted back.

Frances heard banging and slamming sounds coming from downstairs. Her mother banged the kitchen cabinets closed. Her father slammed the front door as he left.

"If he doesn't believe her, he won't believe me either," Frances whispered to herself.

\* \* \*

Harry made three personal phone calls from his office on Monday morning. The first was to his sister, Rose. He told her about Louise's worsening condition and his growing concern for Frances. Rose reassured him and said that she would be home for Thanksgiving, when they could talk more. She also told him about her new job and her gentleman friend, Jim. The second call was to Helen, Louise's sister in Roanoke. Harry gave her an update on Louise and told her about the safety deposit box at the bank, where the bonds he had been saving for Frances's future education were kept. Helen told him that Frances could come and stay with her if Louise's situation became untenable. The third call was to the Hoags' family doctor.

"...I'm not surprised that your wife is having hallucinations. That's a common symptom of paranoia. She needs more help than I can offer. She needs to be under the care of a psychiatrist. I suggest you take her to see Dr. Couch. She got along well with him when he saw her during her hospital stay several years ago."

That evening, Harry suggested to his wife, as gently as he could, that this might be a good time for her to talk to Dr. Couch again. Louise flew into a fuming fury. Another argument followed. The quiet truce they had shared for so long erupted into a full-blown battle. The World War, raging abroad, continued its global invasion as it spread into the little house on Collis Avenue.

\* \* \*

Frances spent more and more time next door at the Stevens's house playing with Dickey. When Zina was at nursing school, Shirley sat on the floor and played card games with the children. Her favorite was Rook. Dickey's favorite was War. Frances liked Rummy.

This afternoon's card game was interrupted by a knock at the door. Shirley opened the door to see a Western Union delivery boy standing on the porch.

"I have a telegram for Miss Zina Atkins," he said, handing Shirley an envelope.

"Miss Atkins lives here, but she's not home right now."

"If this is her house, you can sign for her."

Shirley closed the door and stood looking down at the envelope in her hand. "Should I open it? It might be important."

"You shouldn't open other people's mail," said Dickey.

"That's not mail. It's a telegram," Frances said.

Shirley opened the envelope and read aloud, "Going home (stop). Dad had stroke (stop). Must cancel Saturday (stop). Love, Clyde (stop).

"What does that mean?" asked Dickey.

"I'm not sure. It's only ten words, but they could mean a lot," Shirley answered.

# CHAPTER 40

$\mathcal{Z}$ina laid the telegram on the kitchen table and looked at Shirley. "We'll just have to wait and see what happens. I would call Clyde, but his family doesn't have a telephone. I do hope his dad isn't too bad off."

"No telephone? Everyone has a telephone," Dickey said.

"Not everyone, Dickey. Some people don't have a telephone or an electric refrigerator or even an indoor bathroom," Zina said, looking out of the window into the backyard. "Collis Avenue is a long way from where Clyde's family lives."

"Didn't you used to live in the same county as Clyde's family?" Shirley asked.

"That was a long time ago. I don't live there anymore."

* * *

Two weeks after his father's stroke, Clyde returned to Allenburg, driving his father's pickup truck. The truck was old and had seen better days, but it was good for hauling things, and Clyde had things to haul. Remembering that it was Zina's day off from the hospital, he drove straight to the Stevens's house on Collis Avenue.

"Clyde, it's so good to see you. I've missed you. How's your dad doing? Tell me all about it," Zina said, throwing her arms around her fiancé. "Come in the kitchen, and we can have coffee while we talk."

"I've missed you, too. Dad is much better. He's out of the hospital and back at home. His mind is fine, but the stroke left him paralyzed on the left side. He can't walk. He sure can't do any farm work. With both of my brothers in the service, there's no one to run the farm. My family needs help in the worst way."

"What will they do?"

"We talked it over and decided the best plan was for me to move back home. Zina, it's what I want, and I want to take you with me as my wife. We can get married right away. We can live in the old farmhouse with my family. I can do the farm work, and you can keep the house going. That way my mother can spend her time taking care of Dad."

"What about your job at the hospital? What about your apartment and your furniture?"

"Oh, I'll quit the job. I was getting tired of it anyway. Hospital work doesn't suit me. I miss the land. The lease on the apartment is up at the end of the month. I brought the truck to haul the furniture to the farm. It's a sight better than any my folks ever owned. They'll welcome the furniture. They'll welcome you, too. It's where we belong, Zina."

"Clyde, it's not where I belong. I belong at the hospital. I belong in the city. My farm life is in the past. Your dream is not my dream."

The discussion continued, with each pleading their case, until both Clyde and Zina came to the realization that a marriage between them was not to be. Their visions for the future faced in opposite directions. Clyde stood up and put his arms around Zina. They embraced one last time and wished each other well. Clyde kissed Zina on the top of her head and left in the old pickup truck. Zina felt an empty space somewhere inside her chest. She brushed her tears away and turned her face toward a future without Clyde.

* * *

Zina spent the following week thinking about Clyde and their broken engagement. She would miss Clyde. He was a good man. However, a life with him came at a cost—the cost of her dream. She had spent the first twenty years of her life trying to escape from a poor family farm filled with never-ending work and no future, all the while dreaming of a career in nursing. The idea of going back to a farm filled her with dread. As Clyde's wife, her dream could not come true. She knew her resentment would build as the years went by. She cared too much about Clyde to tether him to an unhappy wife, filled with bitterness. She longed for a sympathetic ear in which to pour this sudden, distressing reversal of her engagement plans. She wanted to talk to Harry.

"Come in, Zina. Always good to see you," Harry said, answering the knock at his back door. "Louise is upstairs, locked in her room, as usual. You need to help me finish this coffeecake."

"Where's Frances?"

"She sneaked off to the Mercers' house to play with Carol. She does that when her mother isn't looking. Frances knows I look the other way when it comes to her playing with Carol. Is there something special you wanted to talk to Louise about?"

"Harry, I don't want to talk to Louise. I want to talk to you. I have a problem, and I don't know what to do. I thought maybe you could give me some advice. Men have a different way of seeing things."

Harry listened while Zina detailed the circumstances of her and Clyde's broken engagement. Her disappointment and her distress were obvious, even without the tears welling in her eyes. Harry could see that Zina was hurting. He reached across the kitchen table and squeezed her hand. She smiled up at him. He continued to hold her hand.

"What should I do, Harry?"

"I'm not the best person to ask. I've made my own mistakes. You see, Zina, I married the wrong woman. I fell head over heels for Louise the first time we met. I thought the reason she often felt blue and depressed was because she was working so hard at a full-time job and trying to get through college at the same time. I pushed my doubts away because I loved her. I thought she loved me, too. I know now that Louise isn't capable of loving anyone. She is a very sick person. I've tried and tried, but Louise is broken and I can't fix her."

"I've watched you for a long time, Harry. You're like someone trying to swim upstream, wearing heavy boots."

"Well, what should I do?

"First, you need to take off those boots. Then you need to listen to your head instead of your heart. I came close to making the same mistake. From now on we should both listen to our heads."

Harry smiled at Zina as he gave her hand a squeeze. She smiled back. Frances, who was standing in the doorway, smiled, too.

"What are you doing there, Frances?" her father asked.

"I live here. And I'm good at keeping secrets."

* * *

Two days before Thanksgiving, Rose telephoned Harry at his office. "Hi, Harry. It's me, and I have sad news. I won't be able to come for Thanksgiving this year. Things are crazy here. The bond department thought sales would be down because people would be spending money on the holidays, instead of saving. Then they had a great idea. There's going to be a special campaign—advertising war bonds as the perfect Christmas gift. The new campaign will kick off the Monday after Thanksgiving. We only get the one day off. We have to work on getting ready for the new bond drive all day Friday and the weekend, too. I'm so sorry. I was looking forward to seeing you and Frances. Sorry, sorry, sorry."

"That is sad news. You don't need to apologize. I understand about rush jobs at work. They always seem to come at inconvenient times. What will you do on Thanksgiving Day?"

"Jim and I'll have Thanksgiving dinner with his family. They live in Baltimore. That's just two hops and a skip away. His mom is a great cook, almost as good as Zina. How is Zina, anyway?"

"Zina has called off her engagement to Clyde. He is moving back to the country to take over his family's farm, and Zina doesn't want to spend the rest of her life on a farm. She wants to continue with her nursing. I can't blame her for following her dream."

"Too bad it didn't work out for Zina. She'll be okay though. She's a survivor. What about Louise? How's she doing?"

"I'm sorry to say, Louise is getting sicker. She is having hallucinations and wants to argue all the time. Life around her is unbearable. If it weren't for Frances, I'd leave. I honestly don't know how Frances gets by when I'm out of town."

"Frances is a survivor, like Zina. She'll make it in spite of her mother. Harry, you need someone to spend the night with Frances when you're away. What about asking Zina?"

"Why didn't I think of that? It's the perfect solution. I'll talk to Zina tonight. Frances will love having Zina stay at our house. Louise will be more than glad to hand over what little responsibility she has for Frances. Thank you, little sister. You're still the smartest one in this family."

"I've got to go now. I'll do my best to get some time off at Christmas. Happy Thanksgiving. "

"Happy Thanksgiving to you, too."

"Love you. Bye, now."

# CHAPTER 41

When Harry arrived home, Zina and Louise were sitting in the dining room, watching Frances put the finishing touches on a large turkey she had drawn in her sketch book.

"Hi, ladies," Harry said, joining them.

"Hi, Daddy," said Frances. "What color are turkey feathers? I've never seen a turkey with his feathers on."

"Turkey feathers are any color you want them to be. Are we having turkey this year? What with meat rationed, do we have enough coupons, Louise?"

"Yes, I ordered a turkey hen from Jack's Deli today. He said he would deliver it on his way home. As you well know, I'm not fond of turkey. Someone else will have to cook it this year. I suppose Rose will want turkey."

"I got a phone call from Rose today. She can't get time off from her job and won't be coming home for Thanksgiving. She did promise to try to make it for Christmas, though."

"I want Aunt Rose to be here for Thanksgiving," Frances said emphatically, trying not to cry.

"Me, too," said Harry. "I'll tell you what. Next summer, when you turn ten, you can take the train all the way to Washington to visit Rose."

"On the train? All by myself?"

"Why not? You'll be a big girl then. You're growing so fast everyone will think you are a grown-up."

"I'm taller than Dickey. When we had the class picture made, I stood on the back row because I'm so tall."

"I can cook the turkey for you, Louise," Zina offered.

"I thought you always went home to be with your family on Thanksgiving."

"Not this year. I want to keep a distance between Clyde and myself. Besides, Dickey's father is taking Shirley to Niagara Falls for a delayed honeymoon. He asked me to stay and look after Dickey."

"Why don't you and Dickey have Thanksgiving dinner with us?" Harry asked.

"Thanks, Harry. We'll take you up on that. Dickey and I would love to share Thanksgiving with you," Zina said, smiling directly at Harry. "Don't you worry, Louise, I'll fix everything—turkey, dressing, cranberry sauce, pumpkin pie—the works."

Harry walked Zina to the door. While she was putting on her coat, He gently squeezed her shoulder. "I'm the one who should thank you, Zina. I don't know what we would do without you," he said. "There's something else I want to talk to you about. I'll walk you home."

On the way to the Stevens's house, Harry told Zina about Rose's suggestion that she sleep over when he was out of town.

"Was that your idea or was it Rose's?"

"Rose was just voicing an idea that's been in my head for a long while. Frances and I both want you to live with us, even if it's only part time."

Zina didn't answer. Instead, she stood on tiptoe and kissed Harry on the cheek. "Now, don't let that go to your head."

\* \* \*

The Monday after Thanksgiving, Harry's boss was waiting for him when he arrived at work.

"Hi, Harry. Hope you had a good Thanksgiving. I have some important things to discuss with you. Let's go in the conference room," said the vice president. When they were seated at the table with their morning coffee mugs before them, he continued, "Harry, there are going to be big changes in the company, and those changes are coming soon. Allenburg Rolling Mills has been bought by an automobile manufacturer out of Detroit. I know how hard you've worked trying to get the auto people to sign on as customers. It seems you helped them to see the wisdom of having access to a dependable source of sheet metal. They just took it a step further and bought us out. They want exclusive control, as well as access."

"When will this change in ownership happen? What about the people working in the mills?"

"The buyout will go into effect the first of January. Very little should change with the mill workers. They will keep their jobs. The mills will keep on rolling out the same sheet metal. The employees' paychecks will just be signed by a different owner. Their benefits will increase, since they'll all be members of the United Automakers Union. The only personnel changes will be on the management level. There may be some moves to Detroit."

"Will you be moving to Detroit?" Harry asked. "What about my job? Where do I fit in?"

"The answer to your first question is no. I won't be moving anywhere. I'm going to retire at the end of the year. I'm sixty-seven years old and should have retired two years ago. I stayed on because of the need to gear up production to satisfy the war demands for sheet metal. I'll do what I can to ease the transition for the remainder of the year. Then I'd like you to step in and smooth out the wrinkles that always come with acquisitions. I can't offer you a promotion or a raise. Only the automobile company can do that. Harry, you're more than a great salesman—you are a leader. You know how to motivate people and keep them productive. I'm counting on you. You know, I've always thought of you as the son I never had."

"Congratulations on your retirement. Your doctor will be happy to hear the news."

"Thanks. I'm not so sure about my wife. She is busy looking for a hobby to keep me out from under her feet all day."

The vice president took a sip of his coffee and looked at Harry. "The answer to your second question is a lot harder. I don't know how you'll fit into the new management structure. There's no need for salesmen in the auto business right now. They have full-time government contracts making tanks, jeeps, and trucks for the military. If they own the rolling mills, no one needs to sell them sheet metal."

"If I can sell sheet metal, I can sell automobiles or government contracts," Harry said. "Sales is all about convincing people they have a need and offering to fill it. I'd like to meet with the new management right after the first of the year. Can you arrange a meeting?

"Good idea. I'll do it. I'll introduce you as an opportunity they can't afford to miss."

Harry spent the rest of the day attending to routine matters. Before leaving the office, he made a decision—he called Zina to tell her that he had changed his mind about having her sleep over part time. Instead, he wanted her to move in full time.

"That's a fine plan, Harry. I already told the Stevens I was moving out and working for them only part time when I got married, so they're ready for the change."

Driving home, he made the second of many decisions to come. He resolved to keep the changes in his work situation to himself until he had a chance to discuss them in person with Rose at Christmas.

\* \* \*

Between Thanksgiving and Christmas, Louise spent most of the daytime hours sleeping in her bedroom with the door locked. She told Zina that she had a headache and needed time to herself with no interruptions from either Harry or Frances. Everyone assumed that she was lying prone in her bed, with the room darkened, suffering through another of her migraines. Not so.

At night, she prowled. When she was not prowling aimlessly around the house, she was busy at her desk, consolidating her notes on Roger Mills. She read and reread everything she had written, crossed out many entries in her notebooks, condensed and combined the most important bits of information until she had reduced Roger's life to seven large index cards. She secured the cards with a wide rubber band and put the packet in her traveling purse. In the back of her closet, she found an old canvas tote bag, which she no longer used, and stuffed it with the remaining documentation from her Roger Mills project.

During this time, Louise refused to eat, or at least she pretended not to eat. After everyone was asleep, she crept out of her room and negotiated the stairs in the dark. She slid silently into the kitchen, where she helped herself to whatever food was available. Thanks to Zina's cooking, there were always plenty of leftovers. Each night she took a spoon from the silverware drawer, opened the refrigerator and ate right out of the first container she found. After she had eaten all she wanted, she filled her pockets with nonperishable items— apples, bananas, cookies. Before leaving the kitchen, Louise wiped the spoon clean with a dishcloth and returned it to the drawer.

The night before Rose was scheduled to arrive, Louise stole silently down the stairs to the kitchen, as had become her nocturnal habit. This time she had a very different errand in mind. She was carrying the old canvas tote bag, filled with the leftovers of her Roger research notes. She looked out of the kitchen window. It was cold, but not that cold. The only snow was lying in little, dirty patches, waiting for reinforcements. The full moon shared its reflected light with the backyard. Louise put on her coat and buttoned it over her robe. She stuffed her feet into her boots. She opened the back door and went into the backyard, carrying the tote bag.

In the garage, she found a shovel, hanging from a hook. Leaving the garage by its back door, she looked for a place to dig. Thanks to Ronald Lay, the soil behind the garage was easy to turn. When the hole was about two feet deep, she dropped the tote bag into it. She refilled the hole with dirt. To disguise the freshly turned earth, she sprinkled a few shovelfuls of mulch over the newly dug grave. Louise smiled as she looked down at the final resting place of the proof of Roger Mills's existence. She returned the shovel to the garage and walked back toward the house.

Louise wasn't the only one awake that night. Frances looked out her bedroom window as she was returning from a bathroom visit. She watched her mother walk to the garage and back again. Hearing sounds in the bathroom, Zina got out of bed to check on Frances. Now, she stood beside the little girl, holding her small hand, and gazing down at the figure of a woman, alone in the backyard in the middle of the night.

# CHAPTER 42

At nine thirty the next morning, Rose bounced out of a taxi cab in front of the little house on Collis Avenue. Harry, Frances, and Zina all rushed to give their dear, dear Rose welcoming hugs. Struggling to return their hugs, she dropped half of the gaily wrapped gifts she was carrying. Everyone scrambled to recover a package and to help Rose with her luggage. The happy group, all babbling at once, tumbled unceremoniously into the house.

"I'm so glad to see all of you," Rose said. "I've been traveling all night. I left yesterday right after work and took the express train from DC to Philadelphia. Out of Philly, I had to take a local to Cleveland because that's the only train that stops in Allenburg. Long trip, but it is so worth it—getting to be with my favorite people again."

"You must be exhausted after traveling all night. Did you get any sleep at all?" Zina asked.

"I slept on the train. Don't worry about me. I can sleep anywhere."

"Some things don't change," Harry teased, winking at his sister.

Laughing, Rose blew her brother a kiss and said, "I love you, too."

The next two days were a whirlwind of Christmas activity. Frances wouldn't let Rose out of her sight. She and her aunt were inseparable. In one of her many packages, Rose had brought an assortment of Christmas tree decorations from around the world, which she had purchased at an international shop in Washington. These ornaments were the hit of their tree-trimming party. As the special decorations were unwrapped, Frances marveled at each shining object. Their colors and shapes fascinated her.

Louise joined the family for Christmas dinner. She was cool but polite and in control. She returned to her room shortly after dinner.

When Frances's bedtime rolled around, Zina tactfully excused herself so that brother and sister could spend some uninterrupted time alone.

"Okay, Harry, I know you have been waiting to talk to me, but let me talk first. I've missed you, and I've missed Frances. You need to know that I like my job. I like living in Washington. I love Jim. We have talked about getting married someday. Just not now. Maybe after the war is over. That's my news. What's up with you?"

Harry began by explaining the changes in his company's ownership and the uncertainty about his job situation. "I'm going to Detroit to meet with the new owners the first week in

January. If they offer me a good deal, I plan to take it, even though it might mean a move to Detroit."

"Have you told Louise? I'll be surprised if she wants to move."

"No. I'm not planning to tell her now. I don't have an offer yet. If I do move to Detroit, I'm not taking Louise with me. It's time to make other arrangements for her. "

"What about Frances? You can't leave Frances!"

"I won't leave Frances. She goes with me. It'll be just me, Frances, and Zina."

"Zina? Harry, have I missed something? You and Zina? Wow! Tell me more."

"I guess I've been in love with Zina ever since she helped me out of the mess I got myself into, stuck in the apple tree, trying to put up a swing for Frances."

"I have to ask—does she feel the same way about you? Does she know about the possibility of a move to Detroit?"

"I haven't talked to Zina yet. I want to wait until my job situation is clear. She deserves to know what she is committing to before making a decision. I know people, and I don't think I'll be disappointed in her reaction."

"What will happen to Louise if you leave her? Where will she go?"

"As for Louise, she is getting sicker and sicker. She has hallucinations, talks to dead people, hears voices, and thinks people are following her. Much of the time she is not in touch with reality. Recently, she has started to do what is called nocturnal prowling. Our doctor says that it isn't unusual for people suffering from her condition. Nocturnal prowling is dangerous. She could hurt herself or injure someone else. Finally, I've come to my senses and accepted the fact that she won't get better. Last week I met with her psychiatrist at the hospital. Dr. Couch agrees that Louise should be hospitalized. He gave me the paperwork to start the process of having her committed to the State Mental Hospital. He is not hopeful that she will ever recover to the point of being released."

"Oh, Harry, Harry. I'm so sorry for all you've had to deal with these past years. My heart bleeds for you and for our dear little girl. You're both so brave. I love you, Harry. I want good things for you and Frances. Do what you must do. Then do what makes Harry happy."

"Thanks, Rose. Having your support means a lot to me. Now, we had better turn in. You have a long day of travel tomorrow."

When it was time for Rose to leave for the railway station, Frances clung to her aunt and cried. "I want to go with you. I want to move to Washington and live with you forever."

"Don't cry, Frances. You can come for a visit next summer," Rose said, giving her niece a special hug. As her taxi pulled away from the curb, Rose leaned from the window, waving goodbye and blowing kisses.

"Frances, your aunt is like a ray of sunshine," Zina said, putting her arms around the little girl.

\* \* \*

Harry began preparing for his trip to Detroit by buying a new suit—the most expensive suit he had ever owned. For the past year, he had been saving ration coupons for a new pair of shoes, but he decided on a new leather suitcase instead. Frances could have his old suitcase. He finished packing, making sure to include the new shirt Zina had given him for Christmas. He completed as much of the commitment paperwork as he could and took the papers to his lawyer's office. The lawyer and Louise's doctors would complete the rest. Harry asked that no action involving Louise take place until he returned from Michigan.

The day before his scheduled interview, Harry boarded the train to Detroit. As the train sped along, he made a list of the questions he wanted to ask and the points he felt were negotiable. He knew there would be bargaining over compensation. The trick was to get them to make an offer first. Then he could propose a counteroffer. Satisfied, he turned his attention to plausible answers for the questions his prospective employers were likely to ask. This was the biggest sales job of his life, and he was the product. He had to sell himself to the *Big Boys.*

\* \* \*

An efficient, professionally dressed woman, who introduced herself as the personal secretary to the vice president in charge of sales, ushered Harry into a palatial conference room. He was early for the meeting, but others were already sitting around the conference table. Introductions were made, and Harry took his seat.

One of the junior executives looked at Harry as though he were the defendant in a trial. He began firing a staccato of questions concerning the auto industry. Harry smiled inwardly to himself. *This guy wants to sit at the head of the table. He doesn't care about my answers. He wants to impress his boss.* Harry could feel himself relaxing.

"I'll be happy to answer all of your questions. Where would you like for me to begin?" Harry said, smiling broadly.

The vice president interrupted. "I have another meeting in ten minutes. I only have one question for you, Mr. Hoag. Why do you think this company exists?"

Choosing his pronouns carefully, Harry responded, "Currently, *we* are helping America win the war. After the war, *our* mission will be to make a profit for *our* shareholders by selling cars and trucks."

Everyone, except Harry, was surprised to hear a hearty laugh come from the head of the table. "I need to get back to doing exactly that right now," said the vice president, rising from his chair. He shook Harry's hand and headed for the door.

The other men seated around the table weren't dumb. They were impressed that Harry seemed totally unintimidated by the Big Boss. The meeting continued until lunchtime, with each person asking questions. Harry caught the queries they hurled his way with grace and good humor. When he didn't know what they were talking about, he responded with a question of his own. The meeting went from an interrogation to a discussion.

After lunch, Harry met with another group in a different conference room. The serious negotiations over compensation, perks, and responsibilities began. Harry was both flexible and firm as he maneuvered the man from personnel into making a salary offer first. He had learned at Jack Mercer's poker table that once a wager is placed, it can always go up, but never come down. Before the day was over, Harry had signed an employment contract with terms beyond his most optimistic fantasies. The only catch was that he had to agree to be available on the first day of February.

As Harry was leaving the office building, he heard a voice call, "Hey, Hoag. Harry Hoag. Wait up." It was one of the managers from the afternoon session. "If you're staying over, I'd like to treat you to dinner. I'm meeting my daughter, Linda, at an Italian restaurant, and we'd like for you to join us. You don't need to eat alone when there're friendly folks like us around."

At seven o'clock that evening, Harry and his new friend were seated in an Italian restaurant not far from Harry's hotel. Soon they were joined by two young women. The manager introduced one as his daughter and the other as the daughter's roommate. Harry focused on remembering the daughter's name, but he didn't catch the roommate's name. While the manager and his daughter were exchanging family news, Harry made polite conversation with the roommate.

"Are you from Detroit?" he asked.

"Not really. I moved here from Chicago about a year ago. Before that I lived in Ohio. After my papa died, Mom and I moved to Chicago and lived with her sister while I went to college. Aunt Grace developed a serious heart condition and went to live in a nursing home. Then Mom got married again and moved to Kansas City. I was all alone in Chicago. I got a job offer here in Detroit and Linda, my old college friend, suggested we share an apartment. That's my story. What's yours?"

Harry, who had been only half listening, said, "I live in Ohio, but I'll be moving to Detroit the first of February. I have a little girl who is going on ten. She and her nanny will be moving here with me—just the three of us."

"Ladies, would you like some wine?" asked their host. "How about you, Harry?"

"None for me. Wine gives me a headache. I'll stick with water and lots of spaghetti. This restaurant's a great choice. I love Italian food. While we're waiting for our orders, I'll make a quick trip to wash my hands. Please excuse me."

"I need to powder my nose," said the roommate. "Be right back."

The roommate waited in the ladies' room long enough for Harry to finish in the men's room and return to the table. Instead of joining the others, she walked to the coat-check desk and spoke to the attendant on duty.

"I have a note for the man seated at the table with the young woman and the middle-aged man wearing a red tie. I don't want to interrupt their dinner. Can you put this note in the younger man's overcoat pocket? I sure would appreciate it," she said, handing the attendant a folded note and a five-dollar bill.

"Sure. It's all in the job. Thanks for the tip."

Before slipping the note into Harry's overcoat pocket, the nosy attendant took a peek. Written on the note were a single name and a single telephone number,

*Charlene Mills, Detroit 6040.*

When Harry checked out of his hotel the following morning, he was carrying a signed employment contract, his new suitcase, and his overcoat, thrown over his arm. He didn't look in the overcoat's pockets. He used his time on the return trip to lay out a schedule of things he would need to get done. There was a lot to do and only three weeks to move mountains.

# CHAPTER 43

*H*arry arrived home to an empty house. Frances was still at school, and Louise was nowhere in sight. Zina was working a seven-to-three hospital rotation. Harry was bursting with excitement. He couldn't wait to share his news with Zina. Throwing his overcoat onto the couch, he headed for the kitchen with a spring in his step.

Hearing the front door open, Harry hurried to greet Zina. He gave her a hug and said, "Come in the kitchen. I have some news. I hope you'll think its good news. I've accepted a job working for an automobile manufacturer in Detroit. Frances and I will be moving there the first of February, and we want you to come with us."

"Slow down, Harry. That's a lot to digest. Now, start over again and tell me all the details."

They sat at the kitchen table, holding hands, while Harry explained his company's acquisition and his meeting in Detroit. He confided in Zina about Louise's impending commitment to the State Mental Hospital. He finished by telling her of his hopes for their future relationship.

"Zina, I'm in love with you. I've loved you for years and just didn't admit it to myself. Frances loves you, too. I want to marry you. Together, we can make a happy and stable home for ourselves and for Frances. It will take some time to untangle myself from Louise, but I'm determined to start divorce proceedings as soon as it's legally possible. Will you think about marrying me when I'm free?"

Zina reached across the kitchen table and grabbed Harry by the ears. She pulled his face close to hers and gave him a kiss—a kiss that let him know her answer was an unequivocal yes.

"I love you, too, Harry. I guess I've loved you ever since you got stuck in the apple tree."

They were interrupted by the sound of the front door closing. "Hi, Daddy, did you bring me a surprise?" called Frances from the living room as she began rummaging through her father's overcoat pockets, looking for a treat.

A single slip of folded paper was all she found. She read it quickly. It contained only a name and a telephone number. Frowning, she hid the note in her secret purse. She didn't want her mother to find that note. It could start another argument, and Frances was tired of arguments.

"Hi, to you, too. Zina and I are in the kitchen. Come in here and let me give you a hug."

* * *

Harry's lawyer had the commitment papers ready when Harry stopped by his office the following day. "Everything is signed and ready for the hearing. We've already sent a copy to the judge's office. The hearing will be on January 20. Don't worry, the hearing is just a formality. The real work is done. Immediately after the hearing, the sheriff will serve the papers. Louise will be taken to the local hospital where she'll be under Dr. Couch's supervision until she can be transferred to the State Mental Hospital. Here's your copy. You'll need to be at the hearing to answer a few simple questions. Again, it's just a formality. Don't worry. I'll go with you."

That afternoon, Harry got a telephone call from his new boss asking him to attend an orientation session at the Detroit office on January 15. Harry assured him that he would be there.

"I may come up a day early to do some house hunting," Harry said.

"If you can get here by the fourteenth, I'll have a real estate agent lined up to work with you. And Harry, take the train. When you go back to Allenburg, you'll be driving a brand new car. It will definitely be an upgrade from the model the rolling mill has you driving."

\* \* \*

On the morning of January 15, Louise was awake early. She was excited. Today was the fifth anniversary of Roger's death. Actually, it was the day after his death, but Louise always celebrated January 15 because that was the day her poor, dear Roger's body had been found. She lay quietly in bed until the house was still. Harry was out of town. Zina was at the hospital, and Frances was at school. She put on her nicest house dress and a new pair of nylon stockings. She took extra care with her hair and her makeup. Admiring her image in the bathroom mirror, she smiled—pleased with herself.

After a light breakfast and a cup of tea, Louise began the ritual of making Roger's memorial pound cake. She put the cake in the oven and checked the mantelpiece clock in the living room. The cake would need an hour to bake. That would give her time to check on other things. She went upstairs and put fresh sheets on her bed and clean towels in the bathroom. She looked in Frances's room. Everything seemed to be in order. Then she went to Harry's room. His bed was neatly made. There were no stray clothes or other items out of place, but something didn't feel quite right. She walked to the dresser and opened the top drawer. There lay a large brown envelope.

Curious as always, Louise opened the envelope. She looked at its contents and screamed. She looked again and shrieked in horror.

*Now you know,* the Voice said.

"These are commitment papers! Harry's planning to have me committed! I've got to get away!"

*Run, Louise! Run! Run! Run!* yelled Squeaky.

Louise ran down the stairs and into the kitchen. She took the cake out of the oven and stood in the middle of the room shaking. This was not her imagination. This was real, and she needed help.

*Frances can help,* said Raspy.

It took all of her strength and determination, but somehow, Louise managed to pull herself together long enough to telephone the elementary school and ask that Frances be sent home right away. She told the first lie that popped into her head. "I forgot to tell Frances that she has a dental appointment."

\* \* \*

Frances was not surprised when her teacher relayed the message. Her mother was always full of surprises—mostly unpleasant. As Frances crossed the schoolyard, she saw two men sitting on the bench at the bus stop, just on the other side of the fence from the old toolshed. She recognized them as the same two who had followed her mother with their car, the day she took a walk on First Avenue. Frances didn't like these men. They scared her.

The old toolshed was where Creepy Stanley, the janitor, kept his snow shovels, lawnmowers, and other yard tools. It was never locked. The children had been warned many times to stay away from the shed. Today, Frances ran toward it. The door was ajar, and she slipped inside. There were no windows in the shed. A couple of loose boards across the back let in a faint stream of light. Frances crept to the back and hid behind an overturned wheelbarrow. She could see out, but no one could see in. She could hear the men talking.

"I'm getting sick and tired of following that stupid broad. It takes too much time and the pay stinks. We need to talk to Jack about a better paying job," said one of the men.

"Well, I'm fed up, too. I say we ditch Jack and split this town. I've got a cousin in Miami and he can get us better paying gigs. My cousin, he's connected."

"How're we supposed to get to Miami? That car won't make it, and we'd never get enough gas with all the rationing, anyway."

"I say we tell Jack that we need an advance, a big advance, to keep following the bitch. Then we take the money and buy train tickets to Miami. Leave him holding the bag for once."

"What if we tell Jack we'll bump her off for a few extra bucks?"

"You know what we said from the start. We don't do no kids and we don't do no killing."

"You should've thought about that before you killed that drugstore guy five years ago."

"I never killed him. He fell and hit his head on the corner of that marble lunch counter when *you* pushed him."

"It was just part of the job. Jack said to push him into paying up. I don't even know how much he owed Jack."

"At least I had the sense to string him up so it'd look like he done himself."

"That was pretty funny. The word on the street is that the guy had an accident—fell down the stairs and broke his neck. Wonder who cut the loser down?"

"Probably his old lady. That way she'd collect the insurance. I heard she split right after the funeral."

"Enough about killing. We don't need to bump the dame. We'll just let Jack think that's our plan. He'll give us what we want. We know enough to put him away for a long stretch."

"I'm in. I like the way you think. If we go straight to the deli now, we'll have time to catch the next train to Philly. From there, Miami will be a piece of cake."

Frances watched through the crack between the boards until the men had walked out of sight in the direction of Jack's Delicatessen. When she was sure they were gone, she eased the shed door open and ran all the way home. This was something she had to tell someone. Her mother would have to listen. Maybe her mother had been right all along.

\* \* \*

Frances burst through the front door, out of breath. "Mom, Mom, where are you?"

"Frances, come up here right now and get your things packed. We're leaving. We're taking the train to Roanoke."

"I need to tell you something important. You need to listen."

"Get up here right now. I have no time to listen to your foolishness. You need to pack. Hurry! You can put your things in your father's old suitcase. I'm ready to leave as soon as I can get this tin suitcase closed. It's being difficult. Where's your jump rope? I need to tie it around my suitcase. Come on. Move!"

"Please . . . listen to me. It's important," Frances begged.

"No. Not now. There's no time, and I'm not interested in anything you have to say. Now get busy, young lady."

"I don't want to go!"

"You don't have a choice. Do what I tell you. Hurry up!" Louise shouted at her daughter.

Frances was frightened. She began packing. She put her *Madeline* book on the bottom of her suitcase. Next, she packed the envelope containing the nasturtium seed, carefully gathered from the bright, happy flowers that past summer. Finally, she put in her clothes and closed the lid on the little brown suitcase.

Louise tied the jump rope around the bulging tin suitcase. When she was sure the lid was secure, she looked around her room to make sure she hadn't forgotten anything. Madeline, the doll, sat on the bed watching her.

"Frances, you'll have to carry Madeline. There's not room for her in my suitcase, and I can't manage carrying both her and this big tin thing."

"I don't want to carry that stupid doll. Leave it here."

"No. Madeline's going with us, and you're carrying her."

With Madeline between them, Louise and Frances sat huddled in the back seat of the taxi as it pulled away from the curb.

"Hurry!" Louise shouted to the driver.

# CHAPTER 44

$\mathcal{F}$rances and Louise pushed their way into the Allenburg Railway Station, joining the horde of luggage-laden people scurrying about. In addition to the regular passengers, the station was crowded to overflowing with service men in uniform. Soldiers, sailors, and marines were everywhere. Some carried duffle bags on their shoulders. Others sat on the hard wooden benches with their bags between their feet. Since seating was in short supply, several uniformed men improvised by using their duffle bags as portable chairs. One tired sailor was stretched out on a bench, taking a nap, using his bag as a pillow. Their bodies were young and fit. They looked so strong and brave. However, their eyes told a different story. They were the eyes of boys who had been forced to grow up too fast and who had seen, or who would soon see, too much horror.

Most of the men not in uniform wore nice suits, ties, and hats. They seemed to be in a hurry, pacing around, continually looking at their watches or at the clock near the ceiling. Two men stood out from the crowd. Their suits were of cheap-quality gabardine, and they carried mismatched suitcases. Neither wore a tie. Both wore hats, shading their faces. From her perch atop the big tin suitcase, Frances watched these men out of the corner of her eye, just as she had watched them from the schoolyard toolshed. She knew who they were, but this time she wasn't afraid. Lots of brave soldiers were around. Besides, she had heard the men say they didn't hurt kids.

Louise was standing in line, waiting to buy one-way tickets to Roanoke. In the line next to hers, the two men in gabardine suits stood, waiting to buy one-way tickets to Philadelphia. They saw her, but she didn't see them. One man elbowed his partner and nodded toward Louise. They both grinned.

"Wow! Don't that beat all? The stupid broad is tailing us now! Wonder where she's going? Let's give her a little scare to send her on her way."

Louise counted out the fare, took the tickets, and put them in her traveling purse. She walked back to where Frances was still sitting astride the tin suitcase. A polite older gentleman stood up and offered Louise his seat. She sat down, without thanking him, and motioned for a passing porter to handle their luggage. Frances was left standing, holding Madeline in one hand and her secret purse in the other.

Louise glanced up. From across the waiting room, she saw the men in the gabardine suits walking slowly toward her. She recognized them immediately. *They are coming to kill me!* Blind with terror, she jumped from her seat, leaving her purse on the bench behind her, and ran through the door to the platform. The station master called in his loud voice, "Track Ten. Arriving from . . . Departing for . . . and Philadelphia."

The men stopped, turned, and walked briskly toward Track Ten.

Voices were coming at her from all directions. The station master was announcing the arrival of the Roanoke train on Track Four. She had to catch that train. She had to get away. She could not miss that train. She could not ... could not ... miss that train.

*They are coming. They are coming. They are coming after you,* shouted the Voice.

*Run! Run! Run!* yelled Squeaky.

"Mom! Mom! Mom!" called Frances.

The train's whistle shrieked in her ears, announcing its arrival. The brakes screamed as they locked, pressing the wheels against the steel tracks.

"Stop! Stop! Stop!" Louise shouted. "Wait for me! Wait for me! Don't leave me!"

*Jump! Jump! Jump!* roared the Voice, Squeaky, and Raspy in unison.

Frances stuck her arm through the handle of her mother's pocketbook, and grasping her secret purse, she ran across the waiting room and through the swinging doors to where her mother was rushing back and forth on the empty platform, waving her arms and screaming for the train to stop.

Louise's panic went into overdrive. She became a whirling dervish as she reached for the train with outstretched arms, in a hopeless attempt to slow it down. As Frances stood watching, her mother leaped from the platform, flying toward the moving train. She spun in the air, almost touching the train with her grasping hands as she hurled up, then down, onto the unforgiving tracks. The train ground to a halt, but it was too late. Louise Hoag was dead.

A crowd rushed to the edge of the platform, where they stood gawking in horror at what was left of Louise Hoag. Frances stood perfectly still, staring down at her mother's legs, protruding from under the train's iron wheels.

"Get back, little girl," someone ordered. "There has been a terrible accident. You don't need to see. You could get hurt."

A hand came out of the crowd and pulled Frances back into its midst, away from the edge of the platform. She could no longer see her mother. She turned and squeezed between the people as she wriggled her way to the back of the crowd and into the waiting room. She sat on one of the now-vacant hard wooden benches, far from the platform, with Madeline propped beside her, not moving and not saying anything, not even to Madeline. No one paid any attention to the little girl sitting alone with her doll.

Other waiting room doors flew open. Firemen, policemen, and some men carrying a stretcher rushed toward the platform. Frances sat very still as everyone continued to ignore her. After what seemed like a long time, the door from the platform swung open, and the men reentered the waiting room. On their stretcher was a large bag with its zipper closed. They made their way to the exit door, more slowly this time, carrying their bundle with care. Two policemen stayed behind, talking to everyone who had been near the platform. Finally, they, too, started to leave. As they passed near where the silent Frances sat, she overheard them talking.

"I guess we can write it up as an accident. No one actually saw what happened, but most think she probably slipped and fell. We'll never know for sure."

"Someone knows, and they're not telling," said his older partner, Leo Thompson.

* * *

Frances opened her mother's purse and looked inside. The first thing she saw were two train tickets to Roanoke. She held the tickets in her hand. *I wonder how much it costs to go to Washington, where Aunt Rose lives. Could I trade in two tickets to Roanoke for one ticket to Washington?*

She crossed the waiting room floor and stood in the ticket line. When it was her turn, she asked the ticket agent, "How much does it cost to go to Washington, DC?"

"One way or round-trip?"

"One way. Can I trade two tickets to Roanoke for one to ticket to Washington?"

"We're not supposed to do that, but sometimes there are exceptions. Do you need to make a trade?" the agent asked.

"Keep the line moving," said the station master, looking directly at Frances and frowning.

"I'll think about it," said Frances as she turned and walked back to the hard bench.

The station master announced in a loud voice, "Due to an accident, there has been a scheduling change. The train leaving for . . . and Roanoke will now be leaving from Track Six instead of Track Four. All baggage now waiting on Track Four will be transferred to Track Six." He repeated this announcement then added, "Track Six. Departing for . . . and Roanoke. Track Six departing for . . . and Roanoke."

Frances sat and thought. She looked at the tickets and thought some more. She thought about the policeman's card in her secret purse, but she didn't know how to call him. She had never used a pay phone. Finally, she put the tickets back into her mother's purse and walked out onto the platform. Still carrying both purses, she stood near a family with two small children. When the conductor called "All Aboard", she followed the family to Track Six, where the train to Roanoke waited. She boarded the train behind them, leaving Madeline sitting alone on the hard station bench. Frances found a vacant seat beside a window and settled herself into it. From the window she watched the baggage handlers load the big tin suitcase and the small brown one into the baggage car.

When at last they were underway, Frances opened her mother's purse and peered inside. The center section contained the two tickets to Roanoke, two linen handkerchiefs, and a pack of index cards, secured with a rubber band. Stuffed into a corner at the bottom of the purse was a pair of argyle socks, rolled into a tight ball. A compact and a tube of pink lipstick nestled in a small zippered section. In a larger zippered section was her mother's billfold, holding a lot of money—seventy-eight dollars, according to Frances's count. The billfold also held a somewhat faded photograph. It was the picture of a nice-looking man standing beside a huge white rosebush. Frances didn't recognize the man, but she did know that rosebush. It grew in the backyard of the house on Collis

Avenue. She turned the photograph over. Written on the back were the words, *Roger Mills, 1938.*

Frances transferred the photograph and the money to her secret purse. Then she examined the index cards. Written on the cards, in her mother's handwriting, was a condensation of Roger Mills's life. The last two cards were a summary of Louise's speculations concerning his death. None of this was news to Frances. As she returned the index cards to mother's purse, she wondered, *How can all of a person's life be written on seven index cards?*

When the conductor came down the aisle with his hole-punch, Frances handed him her ticket. She then turned and looked out of the window. She played Cow Polka, counting silently to herself in German. When they crossed the Ohio River, she counted the barges in German. When they passed through West Virginia, she counted the coal tipples and tunnels in English.

Shortly before they crossed the Virginia state line, the conductor came down the aisle one more time. In a tired voice, he announced, "Mason-Dixon Line. Jim Crow car in the rear. Mason-Dixon Line. Jim Crow car in the rear." The hot-chocolate people formed a parade and trudged toward the rear of the car. Frances followed them, carrying both purses.

When the parade continued into the next car, Frances stopped and went into the small restroom on the right. She locked the door and removed the index cards from her mother's purse. Carefully, she tore each index card into small pieces and dropped them into the toilet. When all the cards had been shredded, she flushed the toilet. Then she took the photograph from her secret purse. She looked at the picture and at the writing on the back, one last time. Methodically, she ripped the photograph into tiny bits. She dropped the scraps into the toilet bowl and watched as they floated in the water. Flushing the toilet for the second time, she stared as the water swirled around and around. The trap door under the toilet bowl opened, and she saw Roger's shredded picture drop onto the railroad tracks below. Frances wondered on which side of the Mason-Dixon Line Roger Mills had fallen. She was glad he was gone.

She left the restroom and glanced up the aisle toward her seat. After checking to make sure no one was watching, she bent down and slid her mother's purse beneath a vacant seat near the restroom. She returned to her own seat and gazed out of the window until she began to feel sleepy. Using her rolled-up coat as a pillow, Frances curled up to take a nap, with her head resting on the windowsill and her secret purse clasped tightly with both hands.

# CHAPTER 45

Frances was peering from the train's window as it pulled into the Roanoke station. She recognized her aunt, who was standing on the platform, waving.

"Frances. Frances. Over here. I'm over here," called Aunt Helen as the passengers began disembarking from a train, still hissing steam. Wrapping her arms tightly around her niece, Helen said, "Oh, you poor, darling girl. I'm so glad you got here safely. I've been so concerned about you. Don't worry. I'll take care of everything. Do you have a suitcase? Which one is it?"

"It's the little brown one sitting over there," said Frances, pointing toward the baggage car. "It's next to the big tin suitcase tied up with a rope. My mom's clothes are in the tin one."

"Good. You wait here, and I'll get your suitcase. I'll make arrangements for the big tin suitcase to be shipped back to Allenburg. We can talk on the drive to my house. Are you hungry?"

"No. I ate in the dining car on the train. For dessert, I had Jell-O with whipped cream."

Seated on the uncomfortable sofa bed in her small living room, Helen held her niece's hand and said, "I have some sad news, Frances. The reason your mother wasn't on the train with you is that there was a terrible accident at the station in Allenburg. I guess you had already gotten on the train when the accident happened. You must have been very frightened traveling alone without your mother. Frances, you are a brave little girl, and I'm proud of you. Sadly, your mother was killed in the accident. I'm so, so very sorry."

Helen had gotten the facts muddled, but Frances was too tired to care. She just wanted to forget about everything that had happened. She hung her head and tried to look sad. She didn't say anything for a long while. Finally, she looked up and said, "How did you know about the accident? Who called you?"

"Zina called me. She called your father and your Aunt Rose, too. They will be in Allenburg waiting for you when we get there. We'll spend the night here and leave in the morning."

\* \* \*

Allenburg, Ohio, was a magnet, pulling Hoags from all directions. Rose took the train, west from Washington, DC. Harry drove his shiny new car, south from Detroit. Frances and Helen took the train, north from Roanoke. Zina took charge on the home front, informing the neighbors of Louise's accident and beginning some of the preliminary arrangements she and Harry had discussed over the phone.

Harry was the first to arrive. He and Zina exchanged brief hugs at the curbside. Inside, they embraced each other in earnest. Harry wrapped his arms around Zina and laid his head on her shoulder. When he looked up, he was wearing his serious face.

"It's time to make plans. Louise always said she wanted to be cremated, and I'd like to go with that. Since we aren't members of any church, I think a small private memorial service would be best. Did you check with the crematory? Do they have accommodations for holding such a service?"

"Yes. I talked to Mr. Lewis, the owner. He said they have a special parlor and that he could lead the service if we wanted. He asked about the disposal of the remains. Have you thought about that, Harry?"

"We can go to the crematory tomorrow morning and choose an appropriate urn and set a date for the service. I want to talk to Rose before I make a definite decision about what to do with the ashes. She'll be here around noon tomorrow."

"Your sister-in-law called from Roanoke. She and Frances will be here tomorrow, too. They will get in late. She said Frances is being very brave."

\* \* \*

The next day, Harry and Zina met Rose's train, which arrived right on schedule. Rose greeted Zina, then turned to her brother. "Harry, I'm really sorry things turned out this way. Such a shame! How is Frances doing?"

"I think Frances will be fine. Apparently, she was unaware of her mother's death until Helen broke the news to her. Poor Helen. I wish I had been there for Frances. She and Helen are on their way from Roanoke now. Their train gets in late this evening. Rose, if you're not too tired, I'd like to talk to you before they get here."

While Rose was freshening up, Zina said, "Harry, I went ahead and made some sleeping arrangements. Helen can sleep in Louise's room. Rose can sleep on my cot in Frances's room, and I can stay next door with the Stevens. I hope that's okay. Oh, one more thing—there's an envelope addressed to you upstairs on Louise's bed. You may want to look at it before Frances gets home."

Zina led the way upstairs to Louise's room. She and Rose stood in the hall while Harry walked over to the bed and picked up the envelope with his name scrawled on the outside. He opened the envelope and withdrew a single sheet of notebook paper. He read the words silently to himself.

*Harry, I am leaving you. You will never have me committed. Never! Never! Never! I am going to Roanoke. If anything happens to me, I want to be cremated. Give my things to Father Michael at St. Joseph's Church . . . P.S. Taking Frances.*

Harry read the note again. Louise's words puzzled him. Was this a suicide note? What was her connection with St. Joseph's Church? Why was Frances just a two-word footnote?

Did Louise take Frances with her just to hurt him? Harry tore the note in half and put both halves in his pocket.

"Was the note from Louise? What did she say?" asked Rose.

"She said she wanted to be cremated. She must have had a premonition about her death."

Harry spent most of the afternoon on the telephone. He called various people at the rolling mill and his new boss in Detroit. He called Ben Cole, the rental agent, to tell him about Louise's unexpected death and to say that they would be moving away by the end of the month. He called the newspaper office and dictated Louise's obituary. He telephoned the Mercer household and talked to Grandmother Mercer, who voiced her condolences and announced that she would attend the memorial service. When Harry told her the service was to be private, she pretended not to hear him. Harry's last call was to Father Michael. He told the priest of Louise's wish to donate her personal effects to the church and asked that someone stop by to pick them up. On an impulse, Harry invited Father Mike to the memorial service

While Harry was busy with his calls, Zina and Rose boxed up Louise's personal items, ready to go to the church. At five o'clock, Zina made a pot of coffee, and they took a break. They sat at the kitchen table drinking the hot brew, each thinking their own thoughts.

Harry was the first to speak. "We still have two hours before it's time to collect Frances and Helen from the station. I'd like to discuss some things with both of you. First, Rose, you should know I've asked Zina to marry me. We thought that couldn't happen until I was able to get a divorce from Louise. Now, things have changed. Usually, people wait a year before remarrying after the death of a spouse, but I don't want to wait. I want Zina to go with me to Detroit now. We can get married there."

Rose showed her delight by trying to hug both Harry and Zina at once. "Oh, Harry, Harry, if you're asking for my approval, you've got it. It's time you had some real love. When will you tell Frances?"

"Not until after the memorial service," Zina said. "Children don't know much about the custom of waiting to get married. They do know about love. You have a very generous brother, Rose. Harry has offered to pay my way to college, once we get settled in Detroit. I can get a four-year degree in nursing and be a real registered nurse."

"Yes, I do have a generous brother, and soon you'll have a generous husband."

Harry smiled at the women. "I appreciate the two of you packing the things for the church. Father Michael said Ronald Lay would pick them up tomorrow. I've decided to give Ronald my car, the faithful Terraplane, and all of my gardening tools. I didn't turn out to be much of a gardener."

"That's a great idea, Harry," said Zina, smiling broadly. "You are generous."

"Rose, I have been thinking about what to do with Louise's ashes. I don't want to take them to Detroit with us. What should I do?"

"I thought about the same question while I was on the train. You're right about Detroit. Louise never even visited

Detroit, and I don't think she would want to be taken there now. The one thing Louise really loved was her flower garden. Why don't you bury her here, right among her flowers?"

"I like that idea. Louise would want to be close to her beloved flowers. The logistics might be a problem though. We can't be digging up the backyard with Frances watching."

"You could ask Ronald Lay to bury the ashes while we are at the memorial service," said Zina. "He might even go to the crematory and pick up the urn."

* * *

Early the next morning, Ronald Lay stopped by the house on Collis Avenue. He loaded the boxes containing Louise's personal effects into his pickup truck. He shook Harry's hand with delight upon learning of the offer of the Terraplane and the gardening tools.

"I never had a real car of my own. This pickup truck and the one before it are the only transportation I ever had. And all those gardening tools—rakes, hoes, everything I need. I can sure use those ropes in my work. Thanks, Mr. Hoag."

"There's another rope around here that you might want. My daughter used it as a jump rope when she was younger. It's tied around my wife's suitcase. Actually, you can take the suitcase to the church, too. Maybe someone can use her clothes.

'Father Michael told me that you often worked in the cemetery, digging graves and burying funeral urns. We want to bury the urn containing my wife's ashes among her flowers in the backyard. Would you be willing to help?'"

"Glad to help. I bury people all the time. It's part of my job. I can pick up the urn from the crematory, too. They know me there. When do you want me to do the burying?"

* * *

Ronald Lay tucked the urn containing Louise's ashes into a cardboard box. He put the box on the floor of the passenger side of his truck and stuffed a pillow beside it. One of his greatest fears was of spilling final remains and having to explain what happened to either a grieving family or to Father Mike, or to both.

After the family left for the memorial service, Ronald carried the box containing the urn to the backyard. Holding a shovel, he looked around for a suitable site. He considered the flower bed where the nasturtiums bloomed each summer. However, he knew that wasn't the right resting place for Mrs. Hoag.

Instead, he walked over to the big white rosebush and began digging, removing the soil with great care. Ronald knew exactly where to dig. When the hole was the right size, he lifted the urn and lowered it gently into the ground, snuggling it beside another urn—the one containing the ashes of Roger Mills, which he had buried there exactly five years ago. Ronald covered the urns with dirt, stood up, and removed his hat. Crossing himself, he said, "Ashes to ashes."

# CHAPTER 46

$\mathcal{F}$ather Michael picked up the morning newspaper and turned to the obituary section. One short article caught his eye.

## LOUISE MARTIN HOAG

Allenburg, Ohio—Louise Martin Hoag died January 15, 1944, as the result of an accident. Mrs. Hoag is survived by her husband, Harry Hoag, and one daughter, Frances Louise Hoag, both of Allenburg. She is also survived by her sister, Helen Burns of Roanoke, Virginia, and her sister-in-law, Rose Hoag of Washington, DC. Final services will be private. Memorial gifts may be sent to St. Joseph's Catholic Church, in care of Father Michael Galloway.

\* \* \*

Louise's memorial service was not only private. It was small. The only attendees were the Hoags, Zina, Father Michael, and Grandmother Mercer, who arrived carrying a square white box tied with a string. They were ushered into a small parlor by Mr. Lewis, the owner of the crematory. A single row of chairs was arranged in a semicircle. Rose took the chair on the far left side. Frances sat beside her. Harry occupied the next chair, between Frances and Zina. Helen sat beside Zina. Seated in the last two chairs were Father Michael and Grandmother Mercer, still holding her white box.

Mr. Lewis began the memorial service by welcoming everyone and smiling at each in turn. He had, long ago, perfected the habit of smiling with his mouth firmly closed and his eyes sending sympathetic signals. He always spoke in a hushed voice, barely above a whisper. His hands were positioned at his waist, his right hand holding the fingers of his left hand. Harry thought that Mr. Lewis would make a terrible salesman, unable to shake hands or pat prospective customers on the back. However, all of Mr. Lewis's customers were beyond thinking about his hands.

Looking at Harry, Mr. Lewis said, "When we talked, you told me that Mrs. Hoag was not a religious person, and since your family doesn't attend any of Allenburg's houses of worship, I'll begin by reading a poem. Afterwards, we can sing an appropriate song if you would like." Harry and Rose both shook their heads at the singing idea. "Very well. We'll use that time to remember the deceased."

Mr. Lewis reached for a book on the table behind him and began to read the longest, most obtuse, and most convoluted poem any of the attendees had ever heard. The poem was totally incomprehensible but pleasant to the ear as read by the much practiced Mr. Lewis. The poem's anonymous author and Mr. Lewis droned on and on. Frances began to tap her foot and look around. Other than the people and the furniture, the only other item in the room was a vase containing an arrangement of white roses. There was no card attached to the arrangement.

At long last, the poem came to an abrupt end. Mr. Lewis smiled and looked pleased with himself. "Would anyone like to say a few words concerning the deceased?"

When no one volunteered, he said, "Well, I'll begin. Then we'll go around the room." He cleared his throat. "I met Mrs. Hoag on only one occasion. She was an interesting person. I'm sorry I didn't get to know her better."

He turned his frozen smile toward Rose and nodded.

Rose said, "Louise loved flowers. She had a beautiful flower garden."

Mr. Lewis looked at Frances and asked, "What would you like to say?"

Frances hung her head and squirmed in her chair. "She was my mother. I knew her all my life."

Next it was Harry's turn. "I loved Louise for a long time."

Zina squeezed his hand. "Louise was a good listener."

Helen was quiet for a minute, then said, "She was my sister. I cared about her."

Father Michael was next. He spoke directly to Louise. "May God be with you, my child. I pray that you have found *peace* at last." He bowed his head and crossed himself.

All eyes turned to Grandmother Mercer. She rose from her seat, still holding her white box by its string, and stood at attention. She looked straight ahead and intoned in a loud, clear voice, *"Shalom."*

Glancing around the room, she settled her gaze on Father Mike and smiled. "I have a cheesecake in this box. Would anyone like a *piece*?"

Father Mike answered for the group, "We all want a *peace*."

"Amen," said Harry and Rose in unison.

Mr. Lewis walked them to the door. Harry handed him a check and thanked him for his services.

Mr. Lewis gave them one last smile and said, "I hope to see you again."

"You will," Father Mike replied.

Rose and Helen spent the afternoon packing their things, ready for the long train trip each faced the following day. Zina helped Frances sort through her clothes, books, and toys as she chose which items would go to Detroit and which would be donated to the clothing closet at Father Mike's church. Harry called a moving company and made arrangements to have their furniture moved to a storage facility until it could be forwarded to its new home in Michigan. He called his Detroit hotel and asked that they upgrade his accommodations to a two-bedroom suite, where his family could stay until they found permanent housing.

At the train station, Frances hugged Rose as though she would never let go. "I'll miss you, too, honey. Your dad said you could visit me next summer. We'll have fun then."

The next morning, Harry locked the front door of the house on Collis Avenue for the last time. He put the key under the doormat, as Ben Cole had asked. The shiny new car was packed and ready to return to its place of origin. Zina sat in the front seat beside Harry. Frances sat in the back seat with her coloring book and her secret purse.

At one o'clock, they stopped for gas and a lunch break. As they left the restaurant, it began to snow. Frances stopped walking. She looked at her secret purse, contemplated its contents, and deliberately tossed it into a trash container.

Her father and Zina were already in the car, waiting. She took her place in the back seat and settled into the soft leather cushions. As Harry pulled the car onto the highway, Zina turned and looked at Frances. "I saw you throw your purse in the trash. Why did you do that?"

"I'm tired of other people's secrets."

THE END

# ACKNOWLEDGMENTS

Writing **On Collis Avenue** was fun. Editing, recasting and rewriting was hard work. This book could not have happened without the help of many people along the way. To each of them, I say, "Thank you, thank you. I am forever grateful for your efforts and your expertise."

First and foremost, I want to thank my beta readers, Beth Stewart-Ozark, Eleanor Hammond and Barbara Rivers. They struggled through every word of my initial draft, pushing and kicking my manuscript toward the finish line, all the while encouraging me with their insightful comments and suggestions. My daughter, Mary Ann Gordon, also deserves my gratitude. As she read the first draft, her interest and enthusiasm kept me searching for the next plot twist to hold her attention.

Many members of my novel critique group, sponsored by the Charlotte Writers' Club, provided invaluable suggestions. I especially appreciate the comments made by Dorothy Morrison, who never let me get away without a reasonable explanation.

My editor, Nicole Ayers of *Ayers Edits*, did an excellent job of tidying up the manuscript. Her suggestions were concise and right on target. I admire and appreciate her professionalism.

Finally, I want to thank everyone who reads *On Collis Avenue*. I hope you enjoy it because I wrote it for you.

*Elizabeth T. Miller, 2018*

# ABOUT THE AUTHOR

ELIZABETH T. MILLER grew up on the Ohio River during WWII. She attended public schools in West Virginia. She is a graduate of the University of North Carolina. Elizabeth worked in accounting and information technology before retiring from her day job to become a professional quilt artist. She is the mother of four children and currently lives in North Carolina. *On Collis Avenue* is Elizabeth's first novel.

Made in the USA
Columbia, SC
12 November 2020